COURT OF NIGHTFALL

COURT OF NIGHTFALL

Karpov Kinrade

DARING
BOOKS

KarpovKinrade.com

Published by Daring Books
Edited by Anne Chaconas

Second Edition

ISBN-10: 1939559324
ISBN-13: 9781939559326

License Notes

Disclaimer

This is a work of fiction. Names, characters, places and incidents are products of the author's imagination, or the author has used them fictitiously.

For Patti Larsen
To all of our epic adventures

And a huge thanks to all our betas: Rebecca, Cindyk, Amy, Patti, Nicole, Gemma, Michele, Beth Ann, Amanda, Tracy. You are our Super Secret Agents of EPICNESS!

And to the Marketing Ninja herself, Anne Chaconas, for her marketing, editing, moral support and overall epicness.

TABLE OF CONTENTS

PREFACE

Some say my story began when my parents were murdered. It did not.

Others say it began when I died. They are wrong.

I remember the pain.

The bullet of fire entered my body and moved through me, leaving a trail of burning agony in its wake.

I slumped over the crystal box that held the weapon we'd all fought to protect, my blood seeping out of me, staining the opaque quartz.

Red. Scarlet. Evie whispered the color of my own name into my ear as I slowly died.

My last vision was of that blood—still just grey to me—spreading into the cracks, into the intricate carvings that decorated the encasement. It almost seemed to glow, and I smiled and closed my eyes as the crystal shattered and darkness took me.

My story begins long before that—and if the historians take issue, I care not and neither should you. It's my story. I begin at the start.

With the test.

With the twins.

And what happened to them.

SHADES OF GREY

"Negative."

"Test me again."

The nurse shakes her head. "Sorry, Scarlett."

I slide off the table, rubbing under my shoulder where she took my blood. "The test is wrong."

She frowns. "Most kids would be grateful."

I walk to the door. "I'm not most kids."

The nurse escorts me to the waiting room, informs my parents of the results, and leaves. My parents sigh and exchange a look. My mom drops down to one knee and hugs me. "I know this isn't what you wanted, but—"

"The test is wrong," I say.

My dad stares at me for a moment. His voice is soft. "Why would you think that, Star?"

"I heal quick. I'm stronger than other girls my age." And I can just tell. It's my body. I can tell.

He bows his head.

My mom squeezes me tighter. "You're healthy. That doesn't make you Zenith."

They look tired, so I don't say any more. This day has been hard for everyone.

My mom sighs. "Why don't you go play outside while we fill out paperwork?"

I shrug and walk out the doors, passing posters of Zeniths stolen from their homes. A little girl with big eyes and a sad smile stares back at me from the eScreen in front of the office. She's out there somewhere. They all are. And it's no mystery who took them. It was Apex. He who runs the self-named group, The Apex, that traffics Zeniths for profit. But no one cares. So it will just keep happening. I understand why my parents are relieved. I just wish they understood why I'm not.

Kids squint at me from the playground, checking if I was tagged. When they don't see anything new on my ear they turn back to their play. One boy dives head first down the slide. It's red, with cracks in the thick plastic. I asked my dad the color once. I don't know what red looks like, but it's my favorite color. I turn away and run the dirt track around the school. Dust flies up around me. I build speed and jump, glancing at the gray sky, imagining I can fly. Not with an airplane, but with wings. I wish for them. But I don't tell anyone.

You don't dream of flying.

Not if you want to live.

...

There is war. You can hear it in the sobs of a mother weeping for her daughter. You can taste it in the rationed food and smell it on your tattered clothes. You can see it in the empty houses and roads and faces. You can feel it inside.

I'm a child, so people assume I know little of such things. But when you are young and free and happy, pain stands out all the more. I'm too little to fight, so I spend my days playing and planning. I plan to end the suffering.

"Why don't the Nephilim give up?" I ask, sitting on the swing, making patterns in the gravel with my foot. "They'll never conquer the world. It's a stupid plan."

"It's not about that," says Jax. He sits on the swing next to mine, his shirt dark and his pants darker. I can't see colors. I never have. But I imagine Jax is wearing blue. I hear it's a calm color. And I find Jax calming.

The sky is dark and cloudy. The rusty carousel we used to play on creaks in the wind. Two boys sit by a nearby anthill, poking at it with sticks as they laugh. So many of the children are gone.

Jax leans closer and lowers his voice. "One night, I heard my dad yelling at the eScreen. He said the Nephilim were fighting for their rights. He said all the news was a sham. I think he'd been drinking."

I cringe. My parents let me try wine last New Year's. The taste still disgusts me. But I noticed something about my parents that night. They answered all of my questions. "Sometimes, drunk people are more honest. Maybe your father's right. Maybe we should give the Nephilim rights."

He shakes his head, his hair falling in his eyes. "It's not so simple."

"No. But it can be." I finish a circle in the gravel. "One day, I'll leave the kingdom of Sky, and I'll train to be a Knight."

Jax sighs. "If we had the right families."

"I'll join a Domus first and work my way up the ranks, gain patronage, gain a patrician family. Then, I'll apply to be an Initiate. It's been done before."

Jax grins. "Then I'll join you. We'll be Jax the Courageous and Scarlett the Clever."

I giggle at my title. I only wish I understood my name better. Scarlett. I've tried to imagine the color, only to learn imagining a new color is impossible.

People tell me it's fiery and fierce.

I like that.

Jax looks over to the sand pit where a girl builds a castle. I've seen her around the playground and the park. We've spoken twice, both times about how to build proper fortifications. Her name's Brooke.

"Poor girl," says Jax, his eyes distant.

"What do you mean?" I ask. And then I see it.

The tag in her ear.

She tested Zenith.

The two boys notice the tag, too. The big one frowns and spits on the anthill. He nudges the small one, and they approach Brooke.

She doesn't notice them.

They kick her castle down.

"Hey!" she yells, standing, her hands balled in fists.

The big one shoves her back. "Get lost, Zenith scum," he says.

"Get lost, biter," says the small one.

They pick on her because she is different.

I've been different all my life. When people speak of colors, I speak of shades. It makes me no worse. They think this girl is weak and alone.

They are wrong.

I jump off my swing. I walk up behind them.

My parents tell me to approach things peacefully, but bullies aren't peaceful. They understand one thing. So I pick up a rock.

And throw it at the big one's head.

The collision with his skull is nearly silent. But the boy is not. He yells and collapses, grabbing at his bloody hair. His eyes are foggy.

The small one backs away.

The big one climbs to his knees. "Stupid Zenith lover. My big brother knows how to deal with you. He'll find you."

Jax walks up beside me. He's three years older and almost as big as the bully.

I palm another stone.

We say nothing.

The bullies exchange looks. Then the small one helps the big one up, and they walk away. "My brother will hear about you biters," yells the big one.

Fine. Let him tell others what I've done.

This world likes violence and winning.

And I'm good at both.

...

"Are you okay?" I ask.

The girl in front of us is tiny. My age, but shorter, more petite. She brushes a strand of hair off her face and shrugs. "Yeah. Thanks."

"Brooke! What happened?" Another girl runs up to us.

"Nothing. It's fine, Ella." Brooke turns to us. "I'm Brooke, this is my twin, Ella. Who are you?"

They look a lot alike, both dark haired with almond-shaped eyes and skin a few shades darker than my paleness, but where Brooke is unremarkable, someone who would blend into the crowd if not for how small she is, Ella would never blend in. She's got the face of a pixie, with big eyes and full lips and a dimple in her cheek. She's beautiful.

"I'm Scarlett. This is Jax."

We all awkwardly shake hands. They are both tagged. We aren't. If any of the teachers saw us they would separate us, but I don't care. I don't go to this school. I'm only here for the testing. They can take their segregation and discrimination and eat it.

"Do you want to play together?" I ask.

Brooke raises an eyebrow. "Really?"

Jax smiles. "Why not?"

We sit in the sand with them and begin building a castle. Brooke and Ella exchange a glance, then sit with us. Our hands dip into the cool sand and we pack it into shapes as our creation comes to life.

"Do you go to school here?" I ask, to break the silence.

Brooke nods. "Yes."

I smile. "We're homeschooled."

Brooke looks at up at us. "Are you brother and sister?"

I blush, but I don't know why. "No. But we might as well be."

"We've grown up together," Jax says with a grin. "I was there when Star was born."

We fall into silence after that, building our castle bigger and bigger. The twins occasionally exchange glances, and I wonder if they have a secret language like me and Jax. A way to communicate so others don't know.

I'm trying to add a tower to the castle when my sand collapses. "Again?"

Jax chuckles, tracing out a detailed window with a stick. "That's what happens when you don't plan out the foundation." We once competed in a wood carving competition. He built a palace with miniature knights. I built a house, though a lot of people mistook it for a rock.

Brooke grins and looks at Ella.

"Be careful," says Ella.

Brooke nods, then looks back at me. "Let me help."

She holds her hand over the castle, and the air buzzes. The sand comes together and floats. With care she moves her hand until the sand is packed into a tower.

"You're a Gravir," I say. "That's awesome."

Brooke smiles, but it slips from her face a moment later. "No one else would think so."

"They would, and they would be envious, and they would never admit it."

"Are you envious?" she asks.

I pause. "I try not to be."

Brooke bows her head, her eyes glistening.

I reach over and pat her hand. "There's nothing wrong with you. The problem is with them."

"How old are you?" Brooke asks me.

"I'm nine."

Brooke squints her eyes at me. "You don't sound like a normal nine-year-old."

Jax laughs. "She's not. I keep trying to figure out how she got so smart. I can only assume it's the great company she keeps." He nudges me playfully and I laugh with him, but inside I, too, wonder why I'm so different. I don't think like others, or respond like others my age, or even older. It's why I don't really have any friends other than Jax. The twins look at us strangely.

I don't know what more to say on the subject of my oddity, so I turn to Ella. "What can you do?" I ask, wanting to compliment her on her abilities as well.

Ella blinks a few times. "Notice my eyes?"

I squint. "What about them?"

Jax sighs. "Star's colorblind. She can't tell the difference."

"Oh," says Ella, playing with her hands sheepishly. "I can change the color of my eyes. I'm a dud."

I shake my head. "You may be listed as a dud in the system," I say, pointing to the building we came out of, "but that doesn't mean your abilities are useless. My mom is always trying to match her outfits to her eye color. You'll never have to worry about that."

After a moment, Ella smiles.

My parents emerge from the school, ready to go, but I ask if Jax and I can walk Brooke and Ella home instead. My mother glances at the tags on the girls' ears. "Where are your parents?" she asks.

"Home," says Brooke. "They knew we'd test positive."

My mom sighs, her lips in a tight line. My dad puts a hand on her shoulder. He looks at Jax and me. "Walk them home," he says.

We pass two people on the way. One sneers. The other takes one glance and imagines we don't exist. It takes five minutes to get to their house. On the porch, I ask if we can visit.

Ella turns stiff, but only for a second.

"Maybe," says Brooke. "I'll ask our mom. Thank you, for—"

There's a thud, like someone walking into a table, and a man in a loose tank top opens the door. His grey beard is uneven, and he smells like alcohol. He points at me with a beer bottle. "Who are you?"

"Scarlett. This is Jax."

"You bothering my kids?"

"No. We're friends."

He smirks like he doesn't believe me. "Brooke, Ella, come inside. You have chores to catch up on."

"Yes, Dad," says Brooke. The twins enter the house, and, with a swig of his beer, their dad slams the door shut in front of me. I sigh, hoping he treats his daughters with more manners than he treated me.

We walk down the porch, and I notice a mark below one of their windows. They must not have seen it yet, for they would have removed it. I clench my fists, wondering who painted the black A. Someone knows Zeniths live here.

Someone wants them gone.

...

On the way home, we pass a gated community, a Zenith-Free sign on the door. Old posters of a Knight in silver armor cover the light posts. The text underneath reads: *Zenith? Then we want you. Fight for the Orders.* A figure cloaked in black with a mask of white is spray painted on a wall. The words *Nox Aeterna* are written next to him in thick spiky text. The graffiti is of Nyx, leader of the Nephilim, the one they consider a saint, maybe even a god. The boy who painted it was captured and executed two days ago. I saw it on the news.

I stop and stare at the painting, surprised no one has removed it yet.

Jax looks at me. "I know what you're thinking," he says with a frown.

"What am I thinking?" I ask with a challenge in my voice.

"Dangerous thoughts."

"It's not dangerous to dream," I tell him.

"When those dreams involve flying with Nephilim it is."

I've never told Jax about my secret dreams to fly with the Nephilim, but he knows me too well. He always has. I scowl at him. "You don't know anything about it, Jaxton Lux."

He grins and nudges me. "You can't hide yourself from me, Scarlett Night. I see you."

I ignore him and keep walking. He just chuckles and catches up with me in long strides.

We pass the small church. The grass around it is dead. I attend, but only when it's mandatory. I respect the religion, the values, but the priest preaches more. He speaks of Fallen Angels and how they had children with man. How those children, Nephilim, are our enemy. And how if you are Zenith, then your ancestors bred with Nephilim, and your bloodline has sinned, and you are sinful, and you must repent every day of your life.

I do not believe people should be held accountable for the mistakes of others. Even if the Angels who fell were cruel and deadly, why does it make all their children so?

Every year, the priest reminds us that we used to be three estates: plebeian, patrician, and clergy. It was only plebeians, like me, who chose to mate with Angels. They created the sinful Zeniths. And now, we are four estates. It is why patricians rule, he says. Because they remained pure.

I focus back on the present as Jax and I turn the corner. A Streetbot, which looks like a large ball on wheels, hums and beeps irregularly. The robot strikes the curb over and over, stuck until its battery dies. Years ago, a maintenance crew would have fixed the issue in a few hours. Now, no one will come. I grab the Streetbot and turn it around, and it rolls down the road, on track once again.

Jax stands beside me, staring ahead. "It won't get any cleaning done. Its dusters are jammed."

"I know. It just seemed wrong to leave it that way."

"What way?"

"Stuck in a life it wasn't meant for," I say softly.

He nods, and we watch the robot disappear into the sunset.

...

We arrive at a sprawling farmhouse with a chipped roof. Faded paint peels in the corners and the front porch creaks, but it's home, it's where I was born, and it fills me with a kind of peace.

A small tree grows in our front yard, shifting in the wind. I pat the dirt— freshly watered—and check the strength of its branches. They're strong.

My dad and I planted the tree a few months ago. He let me pick, and I picked a weeping willow. They remind me of the maidens in old tales.

It grows darker, and Jax and I walk inside. My mom and dad sit together on the couch, watching the eScreen. There is an image of a man in shackles. There is a crowd around him, throwing stones and food. They scream for blood. The man—

The eScreen turns black.

My dad holds the remote. He smiles. "How was the walk?"

"Long," I say. "What are you watching?"

"Boring grown-up stuff. You know how we are." He chuckles and stands. "Hey, how about you and I go flying?"

I know this a distraction, but it's a good one. I nod.

Jax faces my mom. "Anything I can help with?" he asks.

"There are some dishes left."

Without hesitation, he marches into the kitchen. I hear the tap water start. Jax always helps around the house, and he stays here most nights. His father doesn't seem to mind. He and Jax don't get along.

I follow my dad outside, to the small runway behind our house. He hands me a clipboard with the preflight checklist. "Want to help me out?"

I take it from him and focus on checking the engines and gas. My palm flattens against the cool steel of the plane and I close my eyes, imagining the flight, the feeling of weightlessness as the air currents propel me into the endless sky.

I work in a daze, and when I'm done, a large hand lands on my shoulder—strong, warm, comforting. I look up at my dad.

"Ready?"

I climb in next to him, my heart beating harder in my chest as my body prepares to surrender to the shift in gravity. My dad turns on the engine, and the seat rumbles beneath me. We drive down the strip.

And become airborne.

My stomach drops and my heart stammers. But as we drift higher, amongst the clouds, my breathing slows. Here, up in the sky, I am at ease.

I grin out the window and try to imagine what a blue horizon would look like. Though the sun is setting now. There would be reds and oranges then. Not blue. It's hard to remember how things change in colors. For me it's only shifting shades of grey.

I watch our house fade into the distance. "When I grow up," I say. "I'm going to be the best pilot the world has ever seen."

My dad glances over at me, his smile briefly wilting. "You have lots of time to figure that stuff out, Star. No need to rush."

He doesn't understand, but he will someday. I know the course of my life. And nothing will change me.

...

That night, while Jax watches movies in the basement, my parents sit me down, and my mom hands me a cup of hot chocolate. It's her way of asking forgiveness for what's about to happen.

"What's wrong?" I ask.

My parents share a look and a frown.

"Nothing," my dad says. "Everything is fine. But we wanted to talk to you about your future."

I relax into the kitchen chair and smile. We've had similar talks before. They said I shouldn't go into a Teutonic Domus with my heart set on being a pilot. I said I'd consider their opinion.

They exchange that parental glance that's endearing and annoying at the same time. Their wordless communications that I envy.

My mom presses her lips together in a line. "So you want to be a pilot?"

I nod and sip the hot drink. "That's the plan."

"Star, there are requirements for getting into that program. For even getting a pilot's license. Physical requirements."

I look between them, confused. "I'm healthy. Strong. And when I'm older—"

"There's a vision test," my dad says.

My heart flutters in my chest. "I can see just fine."

"Star—"

"My vision is 20/20. Better, even."

"Star—"

"It doesn't matter that I can't see color."

My mom sighs and takes my hand. I know what she wants to say, and I don't want to hear it. She must know it, too, because she smiles. "Maybe they'll change the rules by the time you're older. But... " she raise a finger before I can interrupt, "But... you should have another plan."

I swallow the rock in my throat. I don't show emotion in my voice. "I'll consider your opinion."

They nod.

I leave my half-finished hot chocolate on the table. Then I stand and run upstairs and slam my door. I fall into my bed and weep.

...

My parents think they can control my path. They are wrong.

I grab my laptop. The airplane sticker on the cover is half torn. I tear off what remains. Then I search for the video my parents wouldn't let me see. It's not available publicly online yet, but that's not a problem. My mom got me hooked on computers as a kid. When I could barely walk, I was already learning to type. A year ago Jax declared me the world's best hacker.

I find the video and play it. A man, handcuffed, is escorted down a street by another man dressed in long robes. People gather around, gawking.

I hear someone twist the handle on my door, and I click the power button to shut down the video before they come in.

"What were you just watching?" my mom asks.

I shrug, playing it cool. "Just something I found online. It's—"

She sits down next to me on my bed. "Scarlett? Are you lying right now?"

I debate whether to keep lying, but my mom would know. She always knows. "Yes," I say, shoulders slumping.

She smiles gently. "Then let's try again. What were you just watching?"

"The news reel you wouldn't let me see. I hacked the news network."

I glance up at her to gauge her level of mad, but she's suppressing a grin. "Why?"

"Because you wouldn't let me watch it. Zeniths are being mistreated, and people need to do something. *I* need to do something."

"What do you intend to do?" she asks, still curious more than anything.

I think about it, glad I'm not in trouble—yet. "Well, I haven't settled on a plan. With some time, I could hack the Inquisition security system."

She shifts on the bed to look at me better. "If you do, they will find you."

"I could cover my tracks."

She tilts her head, a long curl coming undone from her clip and falling over her shoulder. "Some of them. But, Star, understand that other people have been at this for far longer than you. Whatever you can do right now, no matter how amazing, Inquisition security can do much better."

I fold my arms across my chest, knowing I probably look like a pouty kid but not caring. "But I have to do something."

She smiles again, her eyes crinkling. "You can keep practicing."

"Practicing doesn't change anything," I say, dropping my chin to my chest as feelings of impotence and frustration build in me.

My mom is still for a moment, her eyes distant, reflective, before she focuses on me again. "Come with me," she says. "I want to show you something." She stands and leaves the room, walking downstairs.

I hurry to follow. "What?"

"The video I didn't let you watch," she says over her shoulder.

The eScreen in our living room covers nearly the entire wall in a grey reflective material. With it we can access networks or play videos sent via satellite signal from an eGlass. My parents both own one. I have one on my Christmas list.

My mom clicks her eGlass and a video appears. A man is tied to a beam on a wooden platform surrounded by hay. People circle him, throwing food, stones, rotten vegetables, calling him names and sneering.

Another man dressed in a cloak walks forward holding a torch, speaking to the crowd, but the people are too loud to hear the Inquisitor's words.

"That man on trial was a hacker," my mom says. "He wiped multiple Inquisition bank accounts. They found him a day later."

I feel a small surge of pride for what he did. "He must have really messed them up."

My mom sits on the couch, and I join her as she asks, "Do you think those accounts mattered?"

"I imagine they would. Money's important, right? But... " I think about it more and realize... "The Inquisition isn't hurting for money, are they? They can always get more."

My mom nods.

"Well," I say, "at least he showed people they could fight back."

"Did he?" my mom asks. "Or did he simply become another example of the Inquisition's power?"

I look back up at the video just as the Inquisitor sets the torch to the haystack. As the hacker begins to burn, his cries mixing with the cheers of the crowd, my mom shuts off the video and sets the display to a serene mountain scene.

She turns to me and reaches for my hand, squeezing. "My Star, one day, when you're older, you'll make a difference. A *real* difference. But you need to be ready. Hone your skills. And..." she ruffles my hair, "try to avoid stupid mistakes." She stands and walks toward the kitchen, and I slump in the couch, depressed.

All of my practicing was for nothing. I don't want to end up like that guy in the video. "I guess I'll stop hacking then," I announce to the world in all my despondent pre-teen angst.

My mom turns back, a mischievous grin forming on her face. "I didn't say to stop," she says, winking. "I just said to be careful."

MYRDDIN

I have always been a creature of knowledge. When the other children drew flowers in the sand, I drew plans for war. When they stared at clouds and gave them names, I studied the wind and predicted the weather. When they did as their parents asked because their parents said they knew best, I asked my parents why and how, and they did their best to explain—though even they said there were things a child should not hear. I did not understand why they said it.

To me, knowledge was power, and I wondered, if that was why adults kept it from children, why patricians kept it from plebeians. Those with knowledge controlled those without, and I would not be controlled. If you were to ask me what I think now, I would tell you this: I still think knowledge is power, but I no longer think that power is always good.

When I was a child, I snatched up information wherever I could. From Jax, I learned building and carving. From Ella, I learned how to knit and mend cloth.

I learned to fly from my father, and from my mother I learned the workings of computers and code, but it is Myrddin who taught me how to wage war. In the end, I suppose, many will wish he had not taught me at all.

...

It's a weekend, and I have no schooling, so I ask Jax if he'd like to go downtown. He would, he says, but he needs to help his dad fix the lawnmower, so I go alone. It's market day, and I'm sure to find something more interesting than watching grass grow in my backyard.

Crisp, cool air mingles with the scent of ripe apples, and turned leaves dust a vibrant pattern over walkways and stone paths. It's the kind of day a girl like me could get lost in. Even in grey the world comes alive, awash with the smell and nip on my cheeks, filled with anticipation.

I'm crunching an apple, licking the sweet juice off my fingers, as I walk through the market. Farmers and crafters gather here to sell their wares. A juggler throws flaming sticks into the air while blindfolded. Children play Four Orders in nearby fields, or sometimes right through the crowd of annoyed adults.

It's a mostly plebeian crowd. The pats have their own events, though it's not completely uncommon to see a few here and there even still. They often pop over to handle business or pick up something they can't find in their private world. Typically items requiring a skilled Zenith. Those are usually sold on the Black Market, my dad once explained. I found it instantly fascinating, of course, this dichotomy of humans who in one breath demonize and dehumanize an entire segment of the population who are not as they, while in the other breath coveting them and what they can do. Is it truly so difficult for people to live in honor of themselves and their own truths?

I toss the core of my apple into a compost bin, when I catch the eye of an old storyteller spinning a tale of war. He sits on the back of his carriage, pulled out into a small stage. At the front stands a glorious white buck with long white antlers. His carriage is draped in leather tied with rope and painted in shades of dark and light, like a night sky.

"Come closer," the old man says, with large gestures of his arms. He's a white-haired man who has lived a long life, a hard life. He wears the proof on his skin, in deep grooves and fading scars. But his eyes, they are bright and sharp, and he knows how to wag his tongue. "Come and hear the tale of the great Juliana and the Templars. Come and hear the rise of the Four Orders. Listen now, for our tale begins before Juliana, before the Knights. It begins at the start of all things."

This is a story we've all heard, a tale we all know, and the crowd responds to its part. "The Cataclysm!"

The old man smiles, pleased with his star pupils. "Yes. The Cataclysm. It was then that the world was torn asunder. It was then that history was erased and mankind broken. A few of us remained, and we began to rebuild, but we were not alone."

"The Nephilim," the voices say as one.

"Yes. The Nephilim, too, survived. And they enslaved what remained of our people. They clad us in chains and forced us to build temples. They beat us and used our blood to feed. They made us less than men, but..."

The crowd's voice is louder now, as fists are raised into the air. "They did not break us!"

The storyteller stands, opening his arms to pull us all in to his tale. "One hundred years passed. Then, in the deep shadow of night, at the base of the silver mountain, a child was born. And her name was Juliana."

Children in the crowd whisper in excited tones.

"She grew up a slave, doing as the Nephilim told her to do. She married the man she loved, a blacksmith, and she lived a simple life. Then, one day, her husband displeased his Nephilim master, and so the monster killed his slave. It was then that Juliana picked up her husband's hammer and, with it, struck down the one who killed her love. It was the first time in one hundred years that a human killed a Nephilim. It was the first time we won."

"It would not be the last," the crowd calls.

The old man continues, leaning heavily on a thick wooden walking stick. "Juliana gathered supporters and, together, they began a rebellion. They took one city after another, liberating all those within. Juliana resurrected the Four Orders. Templar, Teutonic, Hospitaller, and Inquisition. She freed the people and created a truce between man and Nephilim. But the truce didn't last..."

One man cries out, "Because of Nyx!"

"Yes. Long after Juliana passed away, a Nephilim called Nyx decided to overthrow the Twilight Queen and wage war on humanity. It is him we fight now! And we shall be victorious!"

The crowd whistles and shouts, and people file by the storyteller, dropping coins and flowers in his basket.

I stand to the side, in the shadows, watching.

As the last of the crowd disappears around the bend, the old man pulls in the stage, grabs a bag from the back and hops out, locking up the carriage and turning to walk towards an alley. He glances around, as if to make sure no one is watching him.

I want to know what he knows of the war, but I also want to know where he's going, so I follow him in the shadows, hiding behind houses, staying out of sight, as he takes a bit of food out of his pack and lays it out. No fewer than twenty cats appear, frantic for their share. He stands there a moment, petting them, letting them rub up against his legs, when two Inquisition Officers flank him, holding their batons.

"What have we here?" the tall one to his right says.

"Looks like a pleb breaking the law," the short one replies.

I can hear my heart in my head, thumping like a ball on the ground.

The tall one takes his baton and rams it into the old man's gut. A cat throws itself at the officer's legs, only to be kicked away.

I have to bite my knuckles to keep from screaming. I can't have the Officers see me.

"Regulation 442.3 specifically states that plebeian citizens are forbidden from distributing foods of any kind to animals or humans in a public manner," the short one says, holding his baton in the air.

My eyes are glued to the old man, in dread anticipation of seeing his skull cracked open. The Officer strikes.

And the old man blocks with his walking stick.

In a flash, he spins around, his long white robes swirling as he wields his stick like a Knight on the eScreens. He strikes the Officer in the shoulder, then arm, then gut, then foot. My eyes can barely keep up. One more hit to the head, and the Officer falls unconscious. The old man turns and growls. "Get out, keep your mouth shut, and I will forget this happened. Take this pile of biter rot with you." He kicks the tall man's body.

The Officer grabs his buddy with shaking hands and pulls him away. "You're one of them, aren't you?" He doesn't wait for a response as he leaves the alley.

The old man checks on the injured cat. She's whimpering and not walking on her leg, so he picks her up and bundles her in his jacket, then limps back to his cart.

I wait until he climbs in and settles the cat into a comfortable bed, and then sets her leg. She meows, but he gives her an herb of some kind wrapped in cheese, and she settles down, half sleeping as he wraps her leg in a tiny brace.

Once he has put away his supplies, I knock boldly, feigning more confidence than I feel.

He turns his head and sees me standing outside the back of his carriage. "What do you want?" he asks gruffly.

"First, I want you to invite me in. Then, I want to know how you learned to fight like that."

"I don't know what you're talking about, girl. Go away now."

I take a deep breath and climb into the back of his carriage. It's now or never, I tell myself over and over again. I pause for a moment, looking around. It's a tall carriage, large enough to stand, and it's lined with bookshelves that house hundreds and hundreds of books. I can't help myself as my hand reaches out to them. So many ideas. So much knowledge. Then, I remember why I'm there and turn to him. "Before you send me away, hear me out."

He stares at me a long time before sighing. "What are you doing here?"

"Teach me to fight like that. Please. It's important."

He guffaws. "Why? You want to be a Knight like in legends? A hero for the ages? The next Juliana?"

"Yes," I say honestly.

"You're like all the rest. Stupid and ignorant as biter bait. Young girl wanting to be something she's not. Thinking Knights are so amazing. So lovely."

"No, I don't think they are amazing or lovely or heroes," I say. "I think the system is wrong, it's corrupt. And if I were a Knight, I'd change it. Fix it from within to be what it was meant to be, not what it's become."

He tilts his head, staring at me for too many breaths to count, though I was hardly breathing at all.

"Get out of here, I'm tired."

My shoulders slump forward. It was worth a try. I crawl out of the back of his carriage and walk away.

"Girl!"

I turn back.

"Come back tomorrow at sunrise. Then we will train."

...

It's an hour before dawn when I wake from the sound of the rain. I dress quietly, and pull on my raincoat and rain boots. I leave my parents a note that I went to town, then I grab a biscuit to eat on my walk to the storyteller's carriage.

I'm ready for sword training, combat maneuvers, hand-to-hand grappling. I get… sitting.

I've been in this position, legs crossed over each other, spine straight, for the last three hours. My stomach has long since used up that one biscuit, and it makes its protest known loudly in the silence. "This isn't working," I say, opening my eyes.

"Because you're not focusing," the storyteller says. When I arrived, he told me to sit. I asked him what we would be doing. He said learning to think. I asked his name. He said it didn't matter what his name was. I introduced myself and he finally confessed his name to be Myrddin, "not that it matters a bit." And then I sat and now still I sit as he talks.

"The Method of Loci will give you the greatest gift anyone could have, the ability to remember, to think critically, to plan and strategize with all the information you need accessible in your mind. Now, let's try it again. Close your eyes and imagine your house. In each room, place one of the Latin phrases I wrote down, visualizing it not just as a word, but as a real thing."

I work another hour at this visualization. I'm not allowed a break until I can recite from memory the ten phrases he gave me.

"About time," he says when I finish.

I cross my arms over my chest. "That was hard. Not many people can remember ten obscure Latin phrases in one day."

"Before I'm through with you, you'll be able to recite one hundred without stress."

I laugh. That's impossible.

But now I want it. I want a mind that could do that.

He tears off bread from his loaf and hands it to me, then sets out cheese, fruit and meat for us. As I eat, he asks me how exactly I plan to become a Knight.

"I'm going to be a pilot. Get the attention of a wealthy pat family. Get adopted."

He wipes his mouth with his sleeve. "That's a pretty ambitious plan. For a color-blind girl, especially."

I look up in surprise. "How did you know I was colorblind?"

"When I mentioned the red curtains, your eyes didn't flick to them. There are three sets of curtains in here, each different colors, and you didn't know which ones were red. And when I asked you to bring me the blue book, but pointed to the green, you brought the green."

I shrug, impressed despite myself but determined not to show it. "Doesn't matter. They have surgeries to fix it. I can save up, go to one of those places." The Black Market. They have everything there.

"Careful girl, those aren't people you want to mess with, unless you fancy having your eyes plucked out and sold to collectors."

I shiver. "That happens?"

"That and more."

I've lost my appetite, and I place the slab of meat I was about to bite into back on my plate. "Well, there will be other options. I'll find a way."

He tilts his head. "I actually think you might, girl. You just might surprise us all. So best not waste your potential. Back to your spot, I've got fifteen new Latin phrases just for you."

...

The sun is high in the sky, a big burning ball of fire that stands between us and an ice age that would destroy life on our planet. It's a delicate balance, this business of staying alive. So many tiny adjustments, unseen and unknown, keep us on the brink of extinction without tossing us over.

We almost fell over that edge during the time of the Cataclysm and the Age of Juliana. Now we know we can survive anything.

Well, almost anything.

Boring almost-summer days are sometimes hard to endure.

I pump my legs, kicking the porch swing forward as Jax walks up to my house. "So, what have you been up to?" he asks.

I sigh and stare at my shoes. They used to be white but too much running around playing has left them a dirty grey. "Nothing. I'm—"

"Sorry, I should have said, where have you been sneaking to in the mornings?"

"You noticed, huh?"

He chuckles. "Come on. Tell me."

I smile, a very not boring idea entering my mind. "Let's get Brooke and Ella."

We shout to my mom that we're going to the neighbors' and then run off, kicking up dust as we do. It becomes a race, but Jax is too fast and always wins.

I try to be a gracious loser as we approach their property. There's a broken down car collecting dust, and spider webs by the side of the small house. The paint that used to be bright is now so faded and cracked it looks like vomit. Jax knocks three times with sharp knuckles, and we wait.

Brooke comes to the door first, her small face peeking out. When she sees us she smiles. "Jax! Scarlett! What are you doing here?"

"You want to do something fun?" I ask. I suddenly feel a bit shy and I look back down at my sneakers.

Brooke hollers for Ella, and their mother comes to the door, opening it wider. The smell of liquor and cigarettes assaults me and I try not to cough. Their mother doesn't look anything like my mother, who is young and pretty with big eyes and a wide smile. Their mother looks much older, though she probably isn't. Her skin looks stretched too tightly over her cheekbones, like a skeleton that tried on someone else's skin and found it didn't fit right. Her eyes are big, but in a haunted, empty way. Her face looks... lost. Forgotten. A fading memory of a life once lived.

"You came to invite my girls to play?" she asks, a hint of incredulity in her voice.

Jax nods. "Yes, Mrs..."

"Conray," finishes Brooke.

Mrs. Conray smiles, her stained broken teeth showing through her parted lips. "Of course. But, are you sure? They're... " She pauses.

"Zeniths. We know. We still want them to come play," I say. There's no point in feigning ignorance. We all know it's uncommon and frowned upon for pure-bloods to associate with Zeniths. I don't care.

"And your parents don't mind?" she asks, still blocking the door from Ella and Brooke, who are behind her bouncing up and down in their excitement to leave.

"No, they don't," I say, wanting this conversation over.

Their mom steps aside, half a cigarette dangling from her right hand, the ash hanging precariously from the end. I watch it, fascinated, to see if it falls to their carpet, but it hangs on with admirable tenacity. I find myself rooting for that bit of ash, that it can hang on against the odds.

Ella and Brooke walk with us back to my house. Ella is quiet, trailing a step or two behind. Brooke keeps up a steady stream of words, talking about how they will be changing schools this fall since they tested positive. "They send a special bus that carts all us pleb zens to a whole different city for school," she says, her nose crinkling in disgust. "They could at least have zen schools in every city if they're going to segregate us like we're biters."

"I've never even been to a plebeian school," I say. "Do you think the Zenith schools will be terribly different?"

Ella is still silent, letting Brooke speak for them both. "'Course it will be. The only thing worse than a pleb is a zen. Seems so unfair that pats get everything—pure blood, money, power—while we get what? A slight chance at hopefully getting into a Domus and becoming a slave to the Orders? And only *if* you don't test as zen. Once you're zen, it's over. We will never amount to anything now."

I suck in my breath, struck by her bleak words. But she's right. Unless you're born royal into the patrician class, you can't become a Knight. But plebeians can apply to join a Domus and rise in the ranks slowly that way—unless they test positive as a Zenith. There are no options for Zeniths but menial labor and poverty.

As we near my secret destination, the conversation shifts to the Fortuna Festival in a few months. It's the highlight of summer. Ella finally speaks. "I've heard it's amazing."

I smile. "It is. The Queen and other royals will be there, and everyone is dressed so fancy. There's lots of yummy treats and they even share with the lower classes. You should go this year."

Brooke frowns. "Our parents never go."

"Come with us," I say, hoping my parents won't mind. "It'll be fun."

They smile, and we arrive at the wagon. I knock on the door.

Myrddin pokes his head out, his bushy grey hair a mess. "What! Who is... Oh... it's you. We already had a lesson today, girl."

I gesture at my company. "These are my friends. They'd like to train too."

Myrddin rolls his eyes. "So you're all going to be Knights, is that the plan?"

Jax nods, his eyes filling with excitement.

The old man sighs. "Oh, by the Orders. You, boy, help fetch a ball and two nets."

"I have some at my house." Jax runs off.

Ella pulls on my sleeve. "Who is he?"

"A friend," I whisper. "You can trust him."

She nods, and after a few minutes, Jax returns with the supplies. He hands me a net, and we set them up on opposite sides of my yard, facing each other. They're big enough to catch a ball the size of a half loaf of bread, but small enough to be guarded by one player if needed.

"So, what are we doing?" I ask.

Myrddin pulls out the feed for his buck and walks around to the front of the wagon, his robes dragging on the grass. "You ever play Orders?"

"Of course." Every kid has played Orders.

"That's what you're doing."

I groan. "That's not training."

Myrddin pauses, then pulls something from his robes. He holds up a golden pin carved to look like a leaf. "Got this from a stuck-up Knight, I did. Winner gets the bloody pin."

Jax grabs the ball. "I call Teutonic."

"I'm Inquisition," Brooke says, yanking the ball from him.

I look to Ella. "What would you like to be?" I ask.

She smiles shyly. "Hospitaller."

I nod. "Ella and I will be a team, and Jax, you and Brooke can be one. I want to be Teutonic as well."

Myrddin chuckles. "Sorry girl. You have to be Templar. You need one of each Order."

While that's technically true, I've seen it played without a Templar. But I sigh and go along.

Ella and I meet near our net. "Okay, we need a plan. Jax is really good at this game," I say.

Ella shrugs. "So is Brooke."

"Jax will be able to freeze us with a touch, and Brooke can throw us in jail. That makes them dangerous. We don't have active talents, but you're at least immune to freezing and can unfreeze me if I get tagged. And if one of us gets thrown in jail, I can break us out. We have to play offensively and protect our net until we have a good shot at getting the ball in theirs. Sound good?"

Ella nods meekly, and I worry our chances are not strong. And I don't like losing.

Despite our best efforts, we are not able to keep up with Jax and Brooke. They are fast and coordinated, moving through us, freezing and jailing us faster than we can unfreeze and free each other. They score three points before we even score one. The game will be over when the first team reaches ten.

I attempt a score, but the ball rolls past their net and stops at Myrddin's feet. He picks it up and smiles at me, waving me over.

I jog to stand by him, my face reflecting my grumpy disposition.

"Why the long face, girl?"

"This game sucks blood," I say, hoping to shock him with my vulgarity. He just laughs.

"Why's that?"

"The Templars never do anything. I can help, but I don't get to fight like Teutonics or even like Inquisitors. Templars are weak."

He kneels down to face me eye to eye. "That's a strange idea of what strength is. A Templar isn't going to be the brute force like Inquisitors or Teutonics. Their strength comes from their mind. They are experts in strategy and subterfuge, and use their skills to hide and sneak and deceive until they can strike. The key is to stay out of sight until you're needed most. Stay behind enemy lines and think things through. Don't play like Jax and Brooke. Play like Scarlett."

I think about his words and nod. I'm almost ten and I know how to be sneaky. I smile, ready to try playing the way he suggests.

I run away with the ball. Jax chases me, but I lose him between two trees and rush into a maze of bushes. I hear Brooke calling for him, but he ignores her and tracks me. I don't let him find me.

Brooke looks for him, leaving their net free.

I could take the shot, but it's risky.

Ella is there, standing quietly, waiting.

If I throw it to her and she misses, we will lose another point.

But she's my teammate.

I throw it to her. Her eyes widen in surprise, then she smiles and sinks the ball into the net.

Score!

We manage four more points until Brooke and Jax win. Brooke has the most points, so Myrddin presents her with the pin. I'm not sure I've ever seen her happier.

...

Our Order games become a regular event over the next few months, and my training with Myrddin continues.

I play each Order many times, but I come to prefer the Templars after all my fussing. Myrddin was right. Templars are powerful when you play the game right.

We're in another cutthroat game, tied nine to nine, when horns blare throughout the city. It's so loud I would swear my parents could hear it all the way at our house. Above us, in a clear sky, a hologram of the Queen of Sky appears. She is dazzling in an Eden Fashionables outfit of white and bright shades. Tiny white birds are perched on her shoulders, their miniature cloth wings flapping as if they were real. Baby flowers blossom and close in her light hair, and a crown of jewels sits on her head. She smiles, her tan face youthful, light eyes sparkling like the jewels in her crown. "Citizens of the Kingdom of Sky, today is a great day of celebration. Nyx, war leader of the Nephilim, has been captured. The reign of terror that has plagued humanity since the fallen ones mated with puremen is now over. Soon, the rest of the Nephilim will be hunted down, and they will be gone from our lands forever."

Myrddin places a hand on my shoulder, a frown marring his face as he watches the sky.

"In celebration, all food and fuel rations will be doubled for a month, and each family will receive a special treat to commemorate the day humanity was freed from tyranny. Long live His Holiness and the Four Orders."

"Long live His Holiness and the Four Orders," we all say out of habit. Ending with, "Long live the Queen." Her image fades from the sky.

Myrddin sighs, his eyes dark. "Go home. There will be no more training today."

"But—"

"Go home," he murmurs under his breath as he disappears into his carriage, slamming the door shut behind him.

The four of us run back to my house. My dad and mom already have the eScreen on when we come barreling through the door, out of breath and covered in dust from the roads. A vision of Italy covers our living room wall. A reporter speaks in front of the Vatican. "Pope Icarus has retreated in private to pray for our world, but today is a day to celebrate His Holiness. Newly elected to his title, and the youngest our history has known, Pope Icarus has proven himself a man of his word. He chose his name after the legend of a man who reached too high and paid the price. Pope Icarus vowed to never reach too high, that he would stay humble even as he was elevated to the highest position in world government. Today, in light of the greatest victory in history, he has proven just such a pope, retreating into his private quarters to humbly celebrate the fate of humanity as others bask in the public accolades due to him."

We watch with bated breath as the camera pans to a stadium set up with a cutting block. Ella gasps and I cover my mouth. "They're cutting his head off?"

Jax holds my hand and I squeeze his, gripping it tightly as we watch Nyx brought out by two armed Inquisitors. He is dressed in black, his mask still on. His wings are hidden, but he has the build of a man who knows war.

"Why is his face covered?" I ask.

My dad raises an eyebrow, but it's my mom who answers. "No one knows what he looks like, but everyone knows his mask. This is how people see him."

There's something in her voice that makes me wonder, but I don't have time to think on it.

Because a moment later, an axe strikes through Nyx's neck, and his head rolls off the stage, landing with a splat on the floor, a trail of blood dripping from his now headless, lifeless body.

Nyx, the Lord of Night, the Prince of Darkness, is no more.

The crowd cheers, chanting the name of the new Pope, as the reporter tries to speak through the chaos.

Something about Nephilim groups already surrendering and disbanding, but how the war isn't over yet, how it will be years before we are truly safe. But no one is listening.

To the world, the death of Nyx is the beginning of a new era. He was the hope of all Nephilim, their Juliana, and without him, they are lost, their battle over.

We have lived in a war-racked age for so long, I don't know how to feel. I slump on the couch, my mind spinning. We have fought the Nephilim for over seven hundred years. And now, we have won.

PLEB

For several months now, Ella and Brooke have spent a lot of time with me and Jax, training under Myrddin, pretending to be Knights. But today, it's only me and Ella. Brooke is sick and Jax is gone with his dad. We don't have enough people to play Orders, so I teach her how to play chess instead.

She sits across from me, quiet, still, studying the board as I explain how the game is played. She moves first, and I counter, talking her through her plays just like my dad did for me when I first learned.

When she takes one of my pawns I cheer for her. "You're a quick study," I say.

She smiles. "Thanks." She looks around our small house, and stares with wide eyes at the wall full of books across from us. "You have so many," she says as I make my move.

"My parents love books. They are a rarity, especially amongst our class, but somehow they manage to get their hands on them."

"Have you read any?" she asks.

"Yes, most of them."

"I can't read well," she confesses. "My parents can't read, and my school doesn't do a good job teaching stuff like that."

This surprises me. I can't imagine not knowing how to read. "Do you want me to teach you?" I ask.

She smiles and nods. "Yes, please."

We leave our game of chess and I pull out a book for little kids, figuring it would be easier to start there. We go through the alphabet and I cover a few basic Latin rules before we begin.

"You're so smart," she says. "You should have been a patrician. You seem like one. You even look like one."

I don't know what to say to that. It's true patricians often have more finely chiseled features, but I've been a pleb my whole life, just like them.

"My mom says I look like my grandfather, but he died before I was born. Both her parents did. He was a historian. I think I would have liked him. My dad's parents liked to fly. He said I get my love of flying and planes from them. But they're dead, too."

"The war?"

"Yeah. Seems everyone's got someone who died in it."

She nods.

As I go through books, looking for something she would like, I stumble upon a book full of old symbols. One catches my eyes. It's the infinity symbol with a cross coming off it with two lines through it. The text calls it the Leviathan Cross. I stick the book on the end of the shelf and finish my afternoon with Ella, picking a selection of stories for her to look through on her own.

That night, after Ella leaves, I bring the book I found to my mom. "What's this?" I point to the old symbol that caught my eye.

She studies it. "That's a very old Templar Symbol. It symbolizes the balance of masculine and feminine. It's been used by other organizations throughout ancient history, but it always came back to the Templars."

My mom's eGlass blinks and she leaves the room, speaking quietly and quickly. Normally a family in our class is issued one government eGlass to share, but my parents, though not merchant class, have somehow acquired two. One for each of them. I admit to some jealousy about this. I would give a limb for an eGlass of my own.

I'm getting ready for bed, my teeth brushed and long pale hair pulled into a braid, when my parents both come into my room.

They have their serious faces on.

My mom sits on the edge of my bed and pats the spot next to her.

I sit and wait, my belly turning to nervous bees.

"Your dad and I have to take a trip, and we'll be gone a few days."

I'm so surprised I don't know what to say. They've never left me before. Ever. "Where are you going?"

They exchange a look, the one that says they are keeping things from me because they still think I'm a kid.

"We have some business to handle," my dad says. "But you'll be staying with Jax and Mr. Lux while we're gone, so we expect you to be well-behaved and helpful."

I wrinkle my nose. "Can't I stay here? I'm old enough."

My mom laughs. "You *are* growing up fast, but you're not old enough to stay here alone overnight. Sorry, kid."

"When are you leaving?" I ask.

They look at each other again, an uneasy edge to their smiles. "Right now."

...

A few days have turned into over a week, with no word about when they will return. I try not to worry as Jax and

I play house, cooking, cleaning, and managing the day-to-day life of staying alive as his father does his best to stay soaked in a haze of alcohol.

Mr. Lux stares at the eScreen, watching with unblinking, unseeing eyes, the stories playing out in front of him, beer clutched firmly in hand. He seems to have a never-ending supply of the bitter brew.

It's dark out as Jax and I lay on our backs staring up at the stars. "What kind of business would an accountant and school teacher need to do that takes them away for this long?" I ask.

"I don't know, Star," he says. "But I'm sure they'll be home soon. Want to borrow my dad's eGlass to call them?"

"No," I sigh.

A shooting star streaks across the sky and I grab Jax's hand and squeeze. "Make a wish," I whisper.

I wish for truth. To know the truth of things.

A part of me wishes I had not.

"Let's go to my house," I say, sitting up, my heart beating faster.

"Why?" Jax asks.

"My parents are gone. And the bunker..."

I let him guess the rest.

He grins, mischief dancing in his eyes.

...

"Seriously, what do you think is in it?" I tap my foot on the steel door forged into the dirt and rock. Jax leans against one of the many ponderosa pines on our property. The trees tower over us like sentinels guarding a secret. Pine needles scatter over the bunker's entrance as a breeze blows the gentle scent of vanilla off the sun-warmed bark cooling in the chill of evening.

He shrugs, his shoulders still those of a boy though he's a teenager now. I'm still just a kid in his eyes, but I feel older. Like him. "Don't know," he says. "Maybe your family is really rich and this is where they keep all their money?"

A laugh croaks out of me like a frog. "Right. That's why we're living off rations and my mom waters down our vegetable soup to make it last longer."

His mouth turns up in a wry grin. "They're frugal? I read about wealthy people way back before the Cataclysm who had millions but lived like us."

I can feel my face scrunch up. "Why? And where did you read this?"

"That's just how they lived. I read about them in old newspaper scans, back when the news was printed on paper."

"Can you imagine people wasting all those trees just to print news and transient information on paper? It's so weird. Books are one thing. They last. But the other stuff? That's just wasteful." I often think about what life must have been like for people before. Before the Nephilim and Zeniths. Before the Angel Technology. Before the Great War. Before the Cataclysm. Before the Orders. Before. They led such odd lives.

"If not treasures, then what?" he asks, going back to the contents of the bunker.

The bunker is the great mystery of my life. It predates my own existence and is the one place on all the acres of our property I've never been allowed to go. And no one will tell me why. "I think it's something magical. Some epic secret that will save the world."

He rolls his eyes and I want to punch him in the arm. "Why would your parents have something like that?" he asks.

I glare at him. "I don't know. But why would they have a secret bunker we're never allowed in anyways?"

"Maybe your dad is telling the truth and it's just survival gear they don't want you messing with."

I cross my arms over my chest and flinch. My breasts have started to swell and they always hurt. I don't know how I feel about this. I want to be older, but I don't want to have *breasts*. "Maybe. Let's break in and see what's in there."

"How?" he asks.

I look around and grab a branch from the forest floor. "Maybe we can pry it open?"

He nods and finds a rock. "Maybe we can use this, too."

We set to working on the door, using our body weight as leverage to pop it open. It doesn't work. We drop to the ground, panting from our failed exertions.

"Where's the key?" Jax asks.

"My dad keeps it on him at all times," I say. I've tried to sneak it from him, but he's like a Templar with that key. So secretive, so sneaky.

Jax leans back on his hands and looks up into the sky, a moonbeam falling on his face. My heart leaps a bit as I look at him, and I blush and glance away, irritated at myself for acting so flustered.

"I guess we'll never know," he says, oblivious to my strange feelings, which is definitely a good thing.

I sigh. "I'll never give up. Someday I'll find out what my parents are hiding."

...

For the first time, Myrddin and I train at night. We forage in the forest as moonlight glints off grass and the hum of crickets fills the air.

"Moon Flowers only blossom under a full moon's rays," says Myrddin. "We must only pluck them then to seduce their powers. Do you remember the three things Moon Flowers aid in?"

I tick them off one by one as I search for the tiny glowing white petals in the thick underbrush. "They aid in a woman's monthly cycle. You can use them as a tonic to induce sleepiness. And… "

I know this, but I can't quite—

"Find it in your mind," he says.

Oh yes, in the basement! "They soothe a colicky babe."

"Very good, Scarlett," he says.

I beam. He only ever calls me by my name when he is particularly pleased with me. We've been training for months and my ability to map ideas in my mind is growing. "Myrddin, how do you know all of this? Who trained you?" I ask this each time we train. And each time we train, his answer is always the same.

"A little fairy taught me." I'd like to meet this little fairy someday.

He blinks, looking up at the full moon and sighs. He seems sad tonight, quieter. Nicer. I'm worried. "What's wrong? You're not yourself."

He sits on a rock and looks up again. "It is a sad night. On this day, twenty years ago, I lost my daughter to war."

I never imagine the old man with a family. I put a hand on his knee. "I'm sorry, I didn't know."

He looks down at me. "You remind me of her sometimes. Both of you stubborn as a biter. I should have trained her better. If I had… "

His voice trails off, but I know what he's thinking. "That won't be me," I say.

Sitting there, gnarled hands clutching his walking stick, he looks his age or more. You would never imagine he could move as fast as he does. Think the way he does. He pats me on the head. "Let's hope not, girl. Now, back to work. What can you tell me about the poison Red Fairy?"

I easily find the room with the answer. "It will cause someone to burn with fever and become weak-muscled until it kills them. The antidote is Dark Leaf."

He keeps asking the questions, and I keep answering as we hunt for the elusive Moon Flower.

…

My parents don't tell me when they finally return home. I would be more upset, but instead I'm locked in place behind a tall pine tree as I watch them stand over the open bunker door. I almost imagine it glowing from within as they stare down into the depths of its underground belly. It's dark out and I'm technically supposed to be helping Jax make dinner, but I told him I needed some time alone.

I didn't tell him it was because I missed my own house and needed to see it.

I wasn't expecting my parents to be here.

They talk in soft voices that carry quietly in the night. I don't hear words, only the cadence of their speech. My mom gestures to the ground—to the bunker—her face set tightly and her shoulders held too close to her ears. My father is calm, always the rock to my mother's dynamic wind, but even he is holding his body too rigidly.

This is not how an accountant and school teacher are meant to behave—shrouded in secrets and mystery trips and phone calls.

What are you hiding from me?

I weigh my options. I could sneak back to Jax's house and pretend I never saw anything. In other words, I could do what I've always done.

Or I could step out of the shadows and ask them outright what's going on.

My heart thumps in my chest and my palms slicken with sweat as I consider both options.

I realize in that moment there's a part of me that's scared to know the truth.

I step around the tree and walk toward them.

I am ready.

My dad sees me first and his face shuts down. All the fear and stress I saw there turns into a mask of pleasantry even as he closes the bunker door. It clicks into place, locking with at least three different mechanisms I can hear.

"Scarlett, honey, what are you doing out so late?" he asks with that too pleasant singsong voice usually reserved for door-to-door salesman.

"What are you doing home?" I ask. I try not to sound upset, but it slips through. I've been waiting two weeks for them to come back and they don't even tell me when they do?

My mom turns to me and smiles, but it doesn't reach her eyes, which are still filled with some unnamed worry. "We were about to go get you. We picked up some new supplies while we were gone and we wanted to load them into the bunker before we picked you up. Did you have a good time with Jax?" she asks, walking away from the bunker.

She's trying to distract me.

It's not working.

"What supplies did you get? Can I see?"

They share a look, and I square my shoulders and make eye contact with them. My dad taught me people don't like to make eye contact when they lie.

But they both look me straight in the eyes.

And they lie.

And if I didn't know them so well, I wouldn't even know I was being lied to. They are good.

"Not tonight, honey," my dad says. "We're already locked up, and you know we don't like you playing in there."

"Why do we need new supplies? The war is over. We're safe now, aren't we?"

My mom puts an arm around my shoulders and guides me to our front door. "It is over, but there's a lot more to do before any of us are truly safe."

She looks over my head at my dad, frowning.

And it hits me. They don't agree about something. Something involving me. They always agree on everything. They have been a united front since I can remember, but this, whatever this is, is something they are arguing about.

Unfortunately, I don't get any answers that night. They drive me to pick up my stuff from Jax's house, and we settle into an evening of dinner, reading and a game of chess with my dad.

I'm getting better at playing him, and tonight I even beat him. I'm sure it's because he's distracted, but it reminds me of something important. Something I hold on to.

I won't always be a kid. Someday I will be an adult, and they won't be able to lie to me then. I'll have a right to know the truth. And if they don't tell me, I'll find the answers myself.

LEAVE-TAKING

I've never had a birthday party with friends other than Jax. But I'm turning ten and this is a big deal. At least it feels like it is. I don't like that Jax is already a teenager and I'm not even in the double digits yet. He doesn't treat me like a baby, but I feel the distance between us growing as he develops interests outside of our friendship and family.

So I work really hard on my handmade invitations, one each for Ella and Brooke. Ella's has flowers on it, because I noticed she loves the flowers we have in our backyard. I read the colors on the crayons carefully, making sure to draw the flowers in colors that are fitting. It's strange to create something that I can't see, that only others will be able to enjoy in its fullness.

For Brooke, I drew stars because she loves looking at the sky like I do. Fortunately, stars are easy to color.

I can't help but run most of the way to their house, my sneakers pounding the packed dirt roads. I feel fast. Strong. Free. I spin in the sun-dappled shade of the trees, loving the feel of the beautiful weather. I've read that there are amazing black and white photographs of nature that people like to print and hang in their houses. How funny that someone would deliberately strip the world of color. Does it add something to the way a thing is seen? Someday I will find a way to get a genetic modification so I can see in color. Even if I have to save every penny I ever make and use the black market to get the surgery. And then I will know if these trees look better in black and white or in color. I imagine that when I can finally see in color I will never want to see black or white or gray again. I will fill my life with reds and blues and greens and yellows, whatever they look like. I've heard good things about purple and am excited to make its acquaintance. It's the color of nobility. Of the patrician. I don't know why, but I will wear purple and smile.

When I arrive at the twins' house, I stop short, my sneakers digging into the dirt. I drop the invites I worked so hard on as I hear the screaming coming from upstairs.

Their father's voice carries far and wide. "What did you say to me? What did you say to me, biter?" One of the girls cries out, and I hear a smack and a small body fall to the floor. I don't think. I just run inside, throwing the door open as I look around.

Their mother is sitting on the couch in the living room staring at a blank eScreen with a crack down the middle.

"Mrs. Conray?" She doesn't respond. Her eyes are glassy with heavy lids covering half her pupils. Her body is limp. She is drugged or drunk, I can't tell.

I hear more screaming upstairs and I run up, taking the stairs two at a time. I don't know what I'm going to do, but I have to do something.

The girls share a bedroom upstairs and they are in there now, their father looming over them with a leather belt in his hand. "I'll call The Apex on you biters," he says, spittle flying from his mouth and hitting Brooke in the face.

"I didn't mean to, Daddy. I'm sorry." Brooke is crying and there's a long red welt down her right cheek.

"You know how much that eScreen cost, you little biter?" He raises his hand and smacks her with the belt, hitting the side of her head. She falls to the floor, blood trickling from a cut on her head. Ella screams and scurries to her from across the room.

I look around for something to fight him with, and my eyes land on a lamp by the side of their bed. I pick it up. It's heavy and will work enough.

His back is to me. He raises his belt again, but before he can land another blow on my friend I scream and hit him as hard as I can in the head with the lamp.

"Run!" I tell the girls. They do, hiding in the hallway bathroom.

Their father is on the ground moaning, his head bleeding.

My hand is shaking as I walk up to him still holding the makeshift weapon. It has his blood and hair on it.

I lean over his body and he looks shocked when he sees me. His mouth curls into a sneer. "You little blood lover. I'll destroy you."

I take a deep breath and smile. I'm deliberately nonchalant, like my dad taught me. *The person who stays calm always maintains the upper hand.*

"You can't destroy me," I say to him. "But I can destroy you. I did some digging. It's amazing what you can find through the Net. It's also amazing how much gambling debt you've racked up with someone called Black Jack? He seems very unforgiving given the list of people who have gone missing after failing to pay their debts. I hear he's looking for you. You've managed to hide from him, good for you. But what do you think he'd do if a little bird handed him your address?"

I dug up dirt on this man as soon as I realized the kind of home life Ella and Brooke had. You never know when information can be valuable. My mother taught me that.

Mr. Conray doesn't move, and I know I have him by the fear in his eyes. "You're going to go downstairs,"

I tell him. "You're going watch the eScreen with your wife, and Ella and Brooke are going to stay with me for a while. Do you understand?"

He nods.

"You will not hurt them again. If you do, I'll make sure Black Jack knows about it."

He nods again, then stands, leaning on the dresser. His walk is unstable, but he makes it downstairs, and I hear the cracked eScreen turn on.

I take a deep breath, finally letting my fear show in the shaking of my hands. I knock on the bathroom door. "It's safe to come out now."

They emerge with wide eyes and shivering lips. I hug them both. "Pack up your bags. You're coming home with me."

...

My parents don't hesitate to take Ella and Brooke in. We make up extra beds for them in my room, and for the first time ever I have roommates. It's an interesting dynamic. Brooke's head heals well, with gentle ministrations from my father. It's her heart I'm more worried about. She's been moody, withdrawn, angry. I don't blame her. I just worry for her.

The safe space seems to help Ella come out of her shell, though. She's become more talkative, more inclined to say what she wants and offer something new to a conversation. I find myself drawn to her especially. She's quiet, shy, uncertain, but under all of that she's smart, savvy and interesting. I find we are kindred spirits in ways I hadn't expected.

I continue teaching her to read and she picks it up with real talent.

We picked up the birthday invites left in the dirt as we made our way back to my house, and Ella has hers propped up by her bed. "You did a great job with the colors," she says with a shy smile.

On the day of my party I'm all giggles and silliness. My parents decorate the house with ribbons and candles and my dad bakes a chocolate cake. He wanted to add marshmallows, but there weren't any in the rations. Brooke gapes at the cake. "Your dad cooks?"

I nod. "Of course."

The cake has perfect stars drawn in frosting all over it. There are ten candles on the top and everyone present sings to me as I blow the candles out and make a wish. My wish, as it is every year, is that I will someday catch the attention of a high ranking patrician family who will formally acknowledge me and give me their house name so I can join the Four Orders and become a Knight.

After cake, it's time for presents. Jax gives me his first. It's a medium-sized box, and I peel the paper and bows off to reveal a model airplane.

He grins at me. "Thought you'd enjoy putting it together. It actually flies once it's made," he says.

I squeal and throw my arms around his neck. "Thank you, thank you, thank you! I love it!" I kiss his cheek and he blushes and smiles some more.

"You're welcome, Star."

I can't wait to build the airplane, but I have other presents waiting.

I don't expect anything from the twins, but Ella surprises me with a rectangular box wrapped in light paper. "It's not much, but..." her voice trails off self-consciously.

Brooke scowls at her and juts her lower lip out, but after a moment, she smiles. "I'm sorry, Scarlett. I didn't know she was getting you something. I..."

"It's fine," I say.

I open the gift and find a hand made wooden box with a lid. I open the lid and inside there are three compartments, each containing a single item. I look up, confused but intrigued.

Ella explains the gift. "I know you can't see colors, so I wanted to give you something that might at least help you *feel* colors."

Brooke scoffs. "You can't feel colors, dummy."

Ella shrugs, shutting down, but I smile. "That's amazing, Ella. Thank you."

She points to the first compartment. "That's blue," she says. I pick up the rock, which is cold to the touch, like ice. "Blue is a cool color," she says. "It's calm and deep, like the ocean or the sky."

I hold the rock in my hand and close my eyes, imaging the feel of blue. It pours over me, this sense of blue, and I open my eyes, smiling. "Yes, I can feel it."

She claps excitedly and points to the second compartment. "That's red. It's hot, fiery, fierce."

"Like your mother," my dad says with a nudge of my mother's shoulders. She laughs.

I pick up the second rock, which is hot. It almost burns my hand and I drop it. But with that one touch I could feel red. It gets into your soul, that color.

"Yellow is the last primary color," she says. "All other colors are found by combining these three."

There's a sprig of moss in the compartment and I pick it up, holding the mushy moistness in my hand.

"Yellow is the color of the sun. It gives life to everything. It's warmth and new things and lushness," she says.

I put the moss back into the box and close it, my heart too full to speak. I lean over and hug Ella, whispering into her ear so her sister can't hear. "This is the most amazing gift anyone's ever given me," I say.

She hugs me harder, a hitch in her breathing revealing how much my words meant.

When I pull back, Brooke is glaring at us both, so I smile at her, hoping she doesn't stay grumpy all day.

My parents give me their gift last, and when I open it I sit there with my jaw hanging open, gaping.

"What is it?" Brooke asks.

I still can't speak.

I just pull it out of the box and everyone gasps. Even Jax.

"But... how?" Brooke asks. She looks over at my parents like they just sprouted Nephilim wings.

I look up at them, the same question written on my face. How could my parents have afforded this?

"An eGlass?" I say, still staring at the small device in my hands. It's sleek and perfect and fits over my ear as if it was made for me.

I open the manual and figure out quickly how to turn it on.

The AI built into it greets me with a British accent. "Hello, Scarlett. Happy birthday. I'm Evie."

"Hi, Evie," I say, my face hurting from the aggressive smiling I can't seem to stop.

My mom grins. "We have our ways. I took the liberty of tweaking her programming so she's more customized. I can teach you how to do it, too, so you can make her one-of-a-kind."

"What can she do?" I ask.

I soon find out. When I see something new, Evie's beautiful accented voice chimes in, telling me the colors of things.

"Colors? She can see colors?"

Evie answers. "Yes, of course. I can see everything. What would you like me to do for you?"

So much, I think. So very much.

...

The party ends, and I go outside to fiddle with Evie and learn her ins and outs. The sun is setting, and everything around me turns iridescent with the fading light (*Gold and orange*, says Evie, and I giggle). It's been a long day. A great day, but a long one. And having Ella and Brooke staying in my room has made alone time more challenging. I need space, but then Jax walks out onto the porch with me, and I realize I never need space from him.

I put my eGlass on, marveling at the feel of it on my ear, and ask him if he wants to play Orders. "I can get Ella and Brooke."

"No," he says, looking too serious for my liking.

My stomach sinks. "What's going on?"

He looks over at me with his beautiful eyes (*blue*, says Evie, *with brown hair*).

"I'm going to be leaving for a while," he says.

I feel sick. "Where are you going?"

"I've been accepted to a Castra Domus," he says softly. Then he is silent, and I think he wants me to respond, but I am frozen. The closest Castra Domus, a private school that prepares children for a full Domus, is in Vancouver. I've always wanted to go, but my parents don't want me to live so far away. I finally understand. When I think of Jax that far away, my eyes turn watery.

"It's a chance to learn what I need," he says. "And when I turn seventeen, I will apply to a Domus, I will make a difference. The dream you spoke of, I will make real."

My words are slow and tender. "But in my dream we are together."

"And we will be again," he says, taking my hand. "But this is my way out of this life, Star. My dad's too drunk to help me accomplish anything, and I can't stay stuck in this town forever. I'll make a name for myself, and you'll join me when you're ready, and together we'll change things for the better." His smile is warm and full of hope.

I will not ruin it with selfish words, so I hold back the tears and grin. "One day, you will be a Knight, Jaxton Lux." And I hope on that day, a pat and a pleb can be friends.

...

When I arrive for training the next day, Myrddin is packing up to leave.

I felt something in the air for a few days, but ignored it, hoping it would go away. Now I know what I felt. It was the feeling of things ending. First with Jax. Now with Myrddin.

"Don't go," I say.

He turns to me as if he didn't know I was there. He of course did. He always does. "I have to, girl. I've told all the stories I know to tell here. Without gold coming in, Myrddin's heading out."

"Maybe I could pay you," I offer. "For training and stuff. To stay."

"You couldn't afford me," he says, fidgeting with the leather straps on his buck.

"But, who will train me to be a Knight if not you? To fight with a sword, to pick the right herbs, to think the right thoughts."

He turns to me now, a frown on his face. "Don't let anyone tell you which thoughts to have, Scarlett Night. I taught you to think so you could choose your own thoughts and not be a puppet of others."

"See? This proves I still need you. I'm not ready."

He kneels in front of me on one knee and looks me in the eyes. "Scarlett, you do not need me. You already are who you are meant to be, you just don't know it yet. And worry not, girl, we will meet again someday, of that I am sure. By the Orders, I am sure."

FESTIVAL

Myrddin is gone, but Jax won't be leaving for a few weeks. He'll still come to the Fortuna Festival with us. It'll be our last time together for a while, and it's a bittersweet experience. Like biting into a fairy fruit to find it's rotten inside.

But I try not to dwell on the sad. This is the summer solstice and it's a time for luck and laughter. My mom has brought out her jewelry-making kit for us all to use as we make our good luck charms to wear to the festival.

I make a charm for Ella out of small beaded flowers. When I give it to her she beams and Brooke scowls. "I want one, too," she demands.

So I make her one, but with a lot less joy. Brooke is great when she forgets she has to be the center of attention. I wonder if it is because of her parents. If they pay her less attention than they do Ella.

The last one I make is for Jax. It's made of stars. "For luck," I say. "But you won't need luck."

He hugs me and accepts the charm. "I'll keep this always."

My dad pulls out a huge chest he keeps in the closet and it's filled with costumes and outfits. We dig through it, trying on ridiculous costumes and masks until we have all settled on what we're wearing.

It takes a few hours to drive to the festival, and another eternity to find parking. But it's worth it. We spend all afternoon exploring the booths, playing games (Jax beats me in a race, but I beat him at a puzzle), eating more sugar than is good for us and watching the parade of royalty go by as the Queen waves. I'm most enamored by her dress and extravagant hair, which Evie informs me is purple. People with money to burn have hair that changes color on command, and they wear clothes that change shape and style on some kind of schedule. Our costumes pale in comparison, but I don't mind. I'm happy, I'm with my family and friends, and I'm having the best day of my life.

Until we get home.

We are still chattering about the day, our fingers still sticky from honey bread and candied apples, when our doorbell rings.

My father answers it and speaks in low firm tones, finally turning to us with a frown. "Ella, Brooke, your father is here."

I jump up and run to the door. I never told my parents what I did to Mr. Conray and I don't intend to. I'm about to yell at him when my dad puts a hand on my shoulder. "Star, they are his children. He has a right to see them."

Their father stands at the door, a meek and contrite expression on his downturned face. He's dressed in an old suit and holds a top hat in his hand. His thin hair is combed and his eyes are clear. He doesn't smell like alcohol, just cigarettes.

"I'm here to get my daughters. I realize I've made a terrible mistake," he says, tears in his eyes.

"You beat them," I accuse. My dad squeezes my shoulder gently, but doesn't say anything.

"I did. I know. And I will live with that pain for the rest of my life. But I'm on a new path and I want to make it right to them."

Ella is standing next to me, shaking. But when he holds a flower out to her she runs to him, crying and hugging him. Brooke is slower to be won over, but even she eventually cracks, joining the hugs and tears.

They leave our house with their bags and smiles and I slump against the door in a heap of confusion. I don't trust him.

I'm mopey and restless, and when I find a slice of honey bread the twins left behind, I use it as a chance to see them.

"They need some space," my dad says.

"I'm just dropping off their treat. I won't stay."

He sighs. "Okay, but be back before it's dark."

I'm out of the house before he finishes his sentence. I just need to make sure my friends are okay.

When I arrive at their house, my heart skips a beat and I drop the honey bread in the dirt, my hands shaking.

There's an unmarked Bruiser outside their house. I've seen Inquisition Officers use white ones before. But this one's different. It's black and big as a tank. Through the window I see two men talking with Mr. Conray. One wears a long black coat, his face covered under a hood. The other is huge, with large muscles that bulge from his body like they were grown in a lab. They probably were.

I tap my eGlass. "Evie, what can you tell me about this Bruiser?" She scans the license plate. "I'm sorry, but there is no information."

"Can you hack the Motor Vehicle database and look?"

"Hacking is illegal and wrong," she says.

I'll have to change her mind, but not now.

I sneak around the back of the house and see Brooke and Ella sitting, tied to chairs in the kitchen.

Brooke looks up and sees me. Her eyes are red and swollen. I point to my eGlass and point to her dad's sitting on the kitchen table. She nods in understanding and focuses all her power on moving the eGlass.

It bumps against the wooden table, shuffling, but not moving enough. She squints her eyes and tries again. This time it hovers and starts to move closer to her until it lands on her ear.

"Evie, call Brooke's eGlass."

Evie puts the call through and Brooke answers. "Scarlett... Scarlett..." Her words are shaky, and I can see in her eyes, she is lost in fear. I too am trembling, but it is not the same. Some people are frozen by terror. I am spurred to action.

"What's going on?" I ask.

"I don't know. Men are here talking to my dad. They tied us up," she whispers. "I'm scared."

"You'll be fine," I say in a soothing voice as I scan the area. There's no back door, but the windows are large. "Listen, you need to—"

The tall thin man with the hood walks into the kitchen. His black cloak is an Eden Fashionable. Snake designs coil around him and move over the fabric. A black "A" tattoo peeks out from under his sleeve.

"Get out of there!" I yell. "They're Zenith traffickers. The Apex. Your dad is selling you to them." Probably to pay off his gambling debts.

Brooke shakes her head, scared. She can't get out. She's tied up.

I use Evie to zoom in on the kitchen, looking for a knife but not finding one. Maybe something heavy... "Use your powers. Throw the microwave at him."

While she focuses her abilities, I tell Evie to call emergency dispatch and get ahold of my parents. My hands are covered in sweat, and I wipe them on my pants.

"I have alerted emergency dispatch, Scarlett, but I cannot reach your parents. Shall I keep trying?"

"Yes," I say, my heart hammering so hard against my ribs they feel bruised.

The microwave slides over the counter as Brooke manipulates the object's gravity. She lifts it into the air and throws it at the man's head. He tries to dart out of the way, but he's too slow. It hits him with a dull *thunk* and he falls to the ground, unconscious. Evie's microphones pick up the metallic clang as the microwave hits the tiled floor. Others would have heard it as well.

"What do I do now?" Brooke asks.

"Can you use your powers to cut the rope?" I ask.

She shakes her head. "I can't be that precise."

A shadow enters the hallway behind her.

I think for a second. "Okay, break the chair."

She nods and focuses until the chair cracks and she falls free. She quickly unbinds Ella. "Now what?"

I scan the house. The door outside is blocked by their father, and the other man is heading to the kitchen. Maybe the downstairs windows… Not enough time. "Head upstairs and lock yourselves in a room. Hurry!"

They race upstairs to their bedroom, and the tall man, the one with the tattoo, maybe Apex himself, follows, speeding up into a sprint. The black snakes on his coat flash past the downstairs window, hissing at me, and I hope they can't communicate with their master.

The big man Brooke knocked out starts to regain consciousness.

I hear a thud and slam. "We're in our room," screams Brooke. "He's breaking down the door." There's muffled crying in the background. Ella. And then more slams.

I give them the next set of instructions. "Open the window and climb out. You'll have to jump to the tree and climb down. Can you do that?"

Brooke says yes, but I can hear Ella breathing heavily. She's scared. They both are. I feel impotent. Stuck outside hiding behind bushes.

I can see them crawling out. Ella doesn't follow quickly and I bite my tongue, resisting the urge to yell at her to hurry. They don't have much time.

Another slam, and the man with vipers emerges at the window.

Ella screams, and she slips, falling the last bit of the way and twisting her ankle. Brooke grabs her and helps her stumble toward me.

"Hurry," I say. "Hurry!"

The man sees them running toward me and jumps out of the window with the reflexes of a cat. He runs after them, mud splashing under his boots, and they stumble to me. They have the lead. If they can move faster...

But they can't. They're slowing down.

"Brooke, what's happening? You have to run!"

"I can't... move." Her words slur and I see them both slump to the ground, as if drugged.

I'm frozen, unsure what to do.

The tall man approaches them, the snakes on his coat hissing in the cool air.

He shakes his head and speaks into his eGlass. The big beast of a man comes out of the house and joins him, picking up both girls, one in each hand.

I can't help it. I run out of the bushes to confront them. I can't let them take my friends.

"Stop!" I scream, staring straight into the dark eyes of the man with snakes. His coat, his tattoo, are permanently imprinted on my brain. I make a special room just for them.

He walks toward me, a smile on his thin lips. "Be glad we are not here for you," he says, holding his hand out to me. He wears a ring with the Apex crest upon it, and from the ring emerges a small blade. He cuts my hand with it.

It doesn't hurt right away. But it bleeds. And my head gets fuzzy. He seems far away now. He sounds like he's talking through water.

"Go to sleep, girl."

I feel the poison infecting me. Killing me slowly as I fall to the ground.

"I'll find you," I whisper with my last breath.

His laughter is the last thing I hear before darkness takes me.

ASHES

The deer stretches its lean neck to the fresh grass, grazing on lunch as the sun warms its (*taupe*, says Evie) coat streaked with white.

The scar on my right hand itches, but I ignore it, as I pull my bow and aim my arrow at the deer's heart. I take a deep breath, steady my arm, hold my gaze, and release on the exhale.

The arrow shoots twenty meters through the field, striking the ground next to the deer's leg. It startles, its large eyes darting around as it leaps into the air and runs off, its lunch forgotten with the impending death threat from an unseen assailant.

I curse under my breath and sprint to retrieve my arrow. My dad waits in the brush for me to return, his face gentle and steady. "You're not focused," he says.

"I don't like killing."

"I don't either, Star." He preps his own bow and stands, his body motionless. Another deer appears, oblivious to the short breath of life it has left.

His aim is true and the arrow impales the creature's heart, killing it instantly.

I cringe. That poor animal didn't have a choice in this. It woke up this morning believing the day would end with another sunset. Instead, its life ended with an arrow to the heart.

I've learned to track, I've learned some basic wilderness survival, how to use a bow and arrow, and my hacking skills are already at an expert level. I have not learned to kill yet.

I scratch at the scar on my hand. My parents insist the poison that nearly killed me is no longer in my system, but I can feel it, just under the surface, aggravating my skin. My dad stitched me up. It only took three to bind the wound, but recovering from the poison—that took months. I nearly died a few times, according to my parents. When I finally broke free of the fevers and nightmares, Jax was there, pale, frightened, too skinny, as if he'd been the one sick. He had postponed his training to stay with me. My mom later told me he was there by my side every day and every night, holding my hand, reading to me from my favorite books, talking to me in whispers throughout the long nights. They had to force him to eat and sleep. A month later, he finally left for training, only returning for summers. From time to time, he'd show me the martial arts and tactics he was learning, and we'd laugh like we used to.

It's been three years. I'm finally a teenager. But I still feel the evil that Apex infected me with.

My dad pulls the deer into the bushes with us. We would normally go home now and skin it, but I know he wants me to make a kill.

"Star, this is necessary. The future is uncertain in the best of times, and we do not live in the best of times. The greatest gift I can give you is the ability to survive and feed yourself and others. Just clear you mind and focus."

We wait, and it doesn't take long for another deer to cross our path. This time I'm ready. I don't clear my mind, like he suggests. Instead, I paint a new target over the innocent deer. He wears a snake skin coat and a black hood, and has a tattoo on his hand. He has a ring that kills. He is Apex, leader of those who traffic Zeniths. The man who kidnapped my friends. I've spent the last three years trying to find them. I haven't succeeded. Yet.

But I will.

I loose my arrow and the man falls to the ground, dying.

I walk over to examine my kill. It's no longer a man. Just a deer. But this deer will help feed the poor in our town for weeks.

A hunting license is a rarity in our kingdom. I still don't know how my parents got one. Using any kind of weapon is strictly forbidden if you aren't with a Domus or an Order. We aren't allowed guns to hunt, even with a license. But you can do a lot with a bow and arrow.

Especially if you can hit a moving target.

And so I will build my skills. I will become lethal.

And someday that arrow will pierce the heart of evil.

...

This is my first kill, and my first time gutting and skinning an animal.

It's a messy business that leaves me feeling slightly nauseous and tempted by a vegetarian diet.

My dad pulls out his tools. A four inch blade. Gloves for each of us. String to secure the bladder, urethra and intestines. Towels and baggies for the heart and liver plus game bags to store the meat.

We do my deer first, dragging it into a clearing and laying it on its back.

"First, cut along the anus and free the anal track from the hide and membranes that hold it to the pelvic bone," my dad says, handing me the knife.

"Evie," I say into my eGlass.

"Yes, Scarlett?"

"Is there any chance you could do this part somehow?"

"I'm sorry, Scarlett, but I am not equipped with a physical form. You'll have to suck it up and do it yourself."

My dad guffaws at Evie's response. "When did she learn that?"

"Last week I tweaked her humor and emotion calibration. I might have to lower it a bit. She's getting too snarky for my liking."

"She sounds like you," he says.

"Exactly. Too snarky."

He laughs as he guides my hands and I cut into the body. The knife is sharp, but it's not easy to cut through flesh. My hand aches as I push harder.

"Careful," he says as I pull out the freed anal track and tie a string around it. "You don't want to spill any of that and contaminate the meat."

"Yeah, that's not the only reason I don't want to spill deer crap all over myself," I tell him.

He laughs.

I'm not laughing.

We then turn the deer on its side downhill and let the guts fall out. It's as glamorous as it sounds. When my dad guides my hands into the cavity near its spine to cut off the fat holding the intestines in place, I swallow bile and feel beads of cold sweat break out all over my body. I almost cut too hard and nearly pierce the bladder when my dad's hand pulls mine back.

Next we cut off the diaphragm to remove the entire intestine and then remove the heart and lungs.

I am dripping in deer blood, but the horror isn't over. We now have to string the deer upside down from a tree and skin it.

We repeat this process with my dad's kill, and it's dark when we finally head home with our meat. Another family my parents work with will butcher it for our community. It's a small way we try to give back and help those who are starving.

There was a time we thought we wouldn't have to help, because the war was over. We thought things would get better. And, in a way, they did—but not for the plebs, only for the pats. To them, we are still those who serve, and we deserve no more than scraps.

I'm ready for a long shower, then a longer bath, then another long shower, by the time we get home. I strip out of the top layer of blood-soaked clothing before entering the house. My mom is pacing, her eGlass on as she speaks rapidly to someone on the other line. Her face is pale and her movements are jerky, nervous.

When she looks over at us her eyes are filled with tears.

My mother never cries.

My throat goes dry as my dad takes three long steps to reach her, putting a hand on each of her arms as if to steady her. "What's happened?" he asks.

She looks at me and then at him. "Jax is badly injured, and his father... his father is dead."

And my insides feel as if they tumble out of me, like that deer on the hill. My guts spilling onto the floor as I run upstairs.

...

My hands shake as we drive to the hospital where Jax is being treated. "Is he going to be okay? What happened?"

My dad is driving as my mom waits on hold with the hospital trying to get more information. "You know everything I know right now, sweetie."

I don't believe her. They always know more than they say. How can Mr. Lux be dead? And what's going to happen to Jax? He's only sixteen. He can't be alone. He's been gone for months on Castra Domus training. He was supposed to come home in a few days for winter break. We were supposed to go flying together.

This wasn't supposed to happen.

The moment my dad parks I sprint out of the car and into the hospital. "I need to see Jaxton Lux," I tell the nurse at the front desk.

She purses her lips at me. "And who might you be?"

My mom steps up behind me. "Family. We are his legal guardians," she says, tapping her eGlass. The nurse's computer beeps and she looks down in surprise, then looks back up with a softened expression.

"Of course Ms. Night, Mr. Night. Follow me."

I pretend I'm included and follow along with my parents to a private wing of the hospital. My heart pounds erratically, fluctuating dangerously between beats. As we walk, I hear the nurse answering my mom's questions.

"They were in a car accident," she says. "Mr. Lux died at the scene. His son was seriously injured and flown in for treatment."

When we arrive at his hospital room, I pause and rest a clammy hand on the door frame. This is Jax. My Jax. I take a deep breath and step in.

The room is too bright, with fluorescent lights casting the off white room in a garish frame. The room smells like antiseptic and infection. The eScreen is muted but displays clips of news reports showing the efforts to eradicate the last of the Nephilim. Three years since the war ended, but we are still at war.

We will always be at war.

Humans were not bred for peace.

I finally pull my eyes to the bed. Jax is laying there, his eyes closed, his face all hard lines and pale skin. His arm is in a sling and he is hooked up to IVs. One side of his face is littered with cuts and bruises.

I rush to his side and take his good hand. "Jax?"

The nurse is about to scold me, but my mom lays a hand on her arm. "She's his best friend," my mom says.

Jax slowly opens his eyes (*blue*, Evie reminds me, as if I'd ever forget). When he sees my face, he gives me the shadow of a smile. "Star," he says.

His voice is thick and filled with the effects of his medicine.

"Jax," I say again, relief pouring through me. "I'm so sorry."

He squeezes my hand. "Me, too."

There's another layer to his words that I don't understand. But he's just lost his father. I don't expect him to return to normal right away.

But he would never return to normal.

And neither would I.

...

A few days later, Jax comes to live with us.

The same day as his father's funeral pyre.

My father clears out his office to give Jax his own room, even though I offered to share.

"That wouldn't be appropriate," he tells me as I help him move a bed in to the room.

"Why not? He's like a brother."

"But he's not your brother. And you are both teenagers."

I roll my eyes at him. Nothing would ever happen between me and Jax. We're family. But we set up his room and pick him up from the hospital. I put up some of my Order posters in his room, and I hang the model airplane he gave me at my tenth birthday over his desk. I also insist on being the one to pack up his belongings and bring them to our house. It's a more painful process than I imagined, seeing remnants of his life with his father.

"What will happen to their house?" I ask.

"He will probably sell it," my dad says.

We pick Jax up that afternoon and he is quiet on the drive home. I've never seen him this serious. This... distant. I try to give him space, knowing he must be going through more than I can imagine.

It's hard.

Every part of me wants to make him better. But I can't. Instead, I let him hold my hand when he reaches for it, and we sit in the back seat during the two-hour drive, sharing the silence together.

It's winter and the roads are tricky. The drive feels dangerous. An ice-covered death trap waiting to kill us like it did his father.

I still don't know the details of the accident. Where were they? Were they heading home? How did it happen?

These questions stay locked in me. I wouldn't put Jax through the pain of reliving his trauma to satisfy my own curiosities.

We are in his new room, sitting side by side on his bed, when he finally speaks.

He reaches for my hand and rubs his thumb over the scar left by the Apex. "Everything changed that day," he says.

I nod. "We never talk about them."

He looks into my eyes. "I thought I would lose you then. You shouldn't have lived. They sent you home to die. No one believed you would make it. But I did. I knew you would. You're strong. Stronger than anyone knows. Strong enough for what's ahead."

His eyes get a faraway look and I drop my eyes to the jagged scar I will always carry with me. What does he know about life that I don't? What have the last few years or days taught him that I have yet to learn?

I rest my head on his shoulder, and he sighs. "We are both harder. Older than we should have to be," he says.

"We live in a world that hardens people," I remind him. "We are like callused feet. If we walked through life with smooth skin, we'd tear apart our flesh. We need the hardness to survive."

"Since when did thirteen-year-olds get this wise?" he asks, smiling. The smile fades quickly. He kisses the top of my head and stands. "You're right. It's necessary. I just hope it's worth it."

I stand and hold out my hand. "It's time."

He shakes his head. "I'll meet you down there in a bit. I need a minute alone."

I nod and walk out, the door clicking closed behind me.

Mr. Lux's body is outside and my parents have set up the funeral pyre far enough away from the house to be safe. I stand a distance away, looking at the body of the man I knew as he rests on top of wood and cloth.

I cross my arms over my chest and shiver in the cold. Icicles are forming on the wood. Soon fire will burn through it all, leaving nothing but dust.

After half an hour of waiting in the cold, I creep back into the house to find out where everyone is. I hear arguing upstairs. Jax is yelling at my parents! He's never raised his voice to them.

They both sound patient but earnest. I can't hear everything they're saying, but Jax is angry. He doesn't want to attend the pyre.

I can't say this shocks me. He's grieving. He's hurt. This can't be easy. I want to tell my parents to leave him alone. To let him have his space. But maybe they know more than me in this. Maybe he needs to say his goodbyes and have closure even if he doesn't want it.

I go back outside, convinced I'm still the outsider in my own life, living in the shadows of secrets others have created.

The three of them eventually join me outside. Jax stands to the side, at a distance, clearly unhappy to be there. My father says a few words about the man we've known my whole life, and then he sets the fire. It will burn through the night until nothing remains.

It is customary for the immediate family to stand witness until the burning is done, and so we do. I stay for Jax, but also for Mr. Lux, who treated me like his own child—as badly as he treated Jax, but also as well. He's never been the same since his wife died, I was told. That might tug at my heart strings more if he hadn't been such a biter to his son.

The moment the last ember is extinguished, Jax turns and leaves, slamming the door on the way to his room.

I look over at my parents who are frowning and holding each other. My face feels like ice and I can't move my fingers. But I don't rush back in the house. Instead I watch the dust swirl in the early morning breeze. From ashes we are made, to ashes we return.

THE TEST

Five years of training and I am still the girl who stood by Jax as we watched his father burn.

But now I am also the near-woman who is ready to make her own mark.

Five years.

I will turn eighteen soon. I will test for my pilot's license. I will embark on a new chapter of my life.

Five years of flying, of hacking, of hunting and tracking, of chess and strategy, of learning Latin and reading everything I can about the Orders, our history, the ancient history before the Cataclysm—back when the times were divided by BC and AD. Back when my kingdom of Sky was actually divided into states in a government known as a democracy. Though from what I've been able to find out about this time, it doesn't sound like it was very democratic towards the end. It seemed even then the strong and rich wanted to control the minds and hearts of the rest and control their religion, their freedoms, their choices.

At least we do it in the open, not slyly under the guise of freedom.

Though I wish we had more benevolent monarchs.

Jax and I haven't seen a lot of each other in the last few years. Not since he was accepted into the Teutonic Domus. Of course I'm not surprised. The only thing surprising is that he is not allowed in the Orders as a Knight. If he were a pat he would be. Why has no one adopted him and made him a Knight? It makes no sense to me. I asked him once if he was doing what he could to find a patrician family to sponsor him, but he shrugged it off and said he was happy where he was.

I don't accept that. I'm applying to the Teutonic Domus air force division. I am going to become a pilot and find a way into the Orders, where I can make a real difference.

For five years I have honed myself into the best weapon I can.

Soon, I will aim this weapon at the one man I have been hunting since I was ten years old.

Soon, I will find a way to take down Apex and his organization. Soon, I will be the arrow to pierce his heart.

...

The day before my eighteenth birthday, I listen to the news, and I hear how the Shadow of Rome killed an Inquisitor.

"Volume level six," I tell our eScreen. The volume increases and a well-dressed newscaster gives a half smile, the kind that says "I'm sympathetic but also beautiful," as she describes the failed attack on Vatican City. "The Shadow of Rome, a leader of Zenith rebels, struck a blow against the Orders when she used her pyromatics to kill an Inquisitor. But fear not, for she has now been captured."

Her execution is scheduled for the coming week at the Fortuna Festival. Looks like she's not lucky this year.

I turn the eScreen off, shaking my head. The Nephilim were eradicated years ago, but still there is fighting. Will the world ever change?

I am just about to leave when I hear my parents coming in the front door. They are arguing.

They've been arguing more than usual lately and it saddens me. Something happened when Mr. Lux died. Something changed in all of us, and I still haven't figured out what.

This argument is about me.

I duck around the corner and lean against the wall, stilling my breath so they don't hear me.

"She needs to know the truth," my mom says.

"She needs to be protected," my dad counters.

My mom sighs. "We have protected her, Marcus. But we've also taught and trained her. Now we have to give her the choice. She needs to know her heritage."

"And what if they find out? What if they find out the whole truth? Then what?" he asks.

"Then we protect her with our lives."

Her words have finality to them, and I shiver.

My dad is silent for a moment. When he speaks, it's so softly I almost can't hear the words. "We will tell her. But let's wait until after her birthday. This time of year is hard enough for her as it is, and she has her vision test soon. Let's wait until after that. Deal?"

"Deal. But we will tell her everything. No more secrets."

"No more secrets."

They enter the room and smile at me. I want to ask them about their secrets, but I fear an argument. I wish I had been braver.

Maybe it would have saved us all.

...

On the day of my birth I walk into the backyard and pick the freshest flowers I can find, slipping them into a vase.

My dad watches from our porch as I walk down the old road, heading toward the house of old friends.

When Mrs. Conray opens the door, her eyes are clear. She stopped drinking and using the day her husband sold their daughters to Apex.

A few weeks later, her husband died of mysterious circumstances. The news reported it was likely the result of gambling debts. Looks like he didn't pay Black Jack in time. Pity.

Mrs. Conray opens the door to me and I step in. It smells clean and is tidy, if old. This is the home Ella and Brooke should have had.

"Can I offer you tea, Scarlett?"

I shake my head. "I have to get home soon, but I wanted to bring you these."

She accepts the flowers and places them on a fireplace between pictures of the two girls. My throat thickens at the sight of their young faces. There's a picture there of the four of us, as well. Ella, Brooke, me and Jax. We were their only friends. They were our only friends.

"You don't have to keep bringing me flowers, dear girl," she says kindly.

She felt guilty for many years. I could see it in her eyes each time I came. I know she still blames herself, but she's also trying to live. I admire that.

"I know I don't, but I want to. Someday, we will find them." I've been vowing that to her for eight years, and I still mean every word.

She reaches for my hand. "I know you will. If anyone can, it's you."

She doesn't know what I can do, but maybe she sees it in my eyes. I will find The Apex and destroy them, and if Ella and Brooke are still alive, I will bring them home.

...

It happens at nightfall. My mom sleeps on the couch where she spent all day recovering from fever. Dad and I play chess by the fireplace. I'm a few moves from winning, though I've thought so before, only to be proven wrong.

My Dad takes my bishop, and the eGlass around his ear beeps. He flips it over his eye and studies the display. "I'm sorry, Scarlett," he says, "but we'll have to finish later." He walks upstairs.

He's had calls like this before. My mother is usually awake and able to keep me from overhearing, but not today. I sneak up the stairs and stand outside my parents' room. The door is slightly open, cutting the dark hallway with a streak of light.

I'm drawn closer, wondering why he didn't close the door as he always does.

I peek inside.

My dad paces his room, speaking. When he receives calls alone, he is often quiet. He is not quiet this time. His voice is full or urgency. "We don't have more time."

"You believe someone has found you?" responds a deeper, older voice.

My father steps toward his desk and outside my view. "They left a message."

"A threat?"

Papers shuffle. He must be searching for something. "We need to move," he says.

"You've been safe for years. You are still safe."

"Sir, I won't—"

"You will do what is necessary."

The shuffling stops. My father sighs. "What if they return?" he asks softly.

The voice doesn't respond.

My father chuckles. There's no joy in it. "You're willing to take the chance."

"Do your duty," says the voice. There is no more talking. The call has ended.

Footsteps.

Toward the door.

I rush for the staircase and start walking down.

"Scarlett?" My father stands in the doorway, his dark hair a mess. His eyes tired. "Did you... " He points inside his room, then shakes his head. "Never mind. You should get some rest. Your test is..." He looks around, distracted.

"Tomorrow," I say.

He focuses back on me. "I know. Have you considered what I said?"

I nod. "When I pass, I'm joining the Teutonic Domus."

He bites his lip. "You know why I don't want you to—"

"I know, Dad."

He smiles, but he doesn't look happy. "Get some sleep."

"I will." I walk downstairs and put out the fire. Then I go to bed, trying to block out the questions spinning in my mind. Tomorrow I will test to become a pilot. Tomorrow is the day my future is decided.

After an hour, sleep claims me with dreams of flying. It doesn't last.

I wake in the middle of the night from my father's screams. He has nightmares from his time in the War. The terrors come and go. Tonight, they plague him for hours. I can only make out two words through the sounds of pain.

Forgive me.

...

I've spent my life in shades of grey. And my future, my dream of becoming a pilot, rests on my ability to see past my two-toned world and into the nuances of shades that will help me pass this test.

I stand in the middle of Sky Airfield, surrounded by airplanes, some taxying, some grounded, all of them beautiful. I long to be in the cockpit of one of them, to feel the power and thrill of controlling a 300,000-pound metal tube with wings amongst the clouds.

Dr. Crayton stands beside me, his glasses perched on the end of his nose, clipboard in hand, as we wait for the controller in the air traffic control tower to flash the first light from the light guns.

I will have to identify which lights are green and which are red. If I pass, I'll get an exemption for my color-blindness and will be allowed to start flight training.

If I fail, my dreams will end.

I will not fail.

I've been dreaming of flying since I was a child, since the first time I went up in a plane with my dad.

When my parents realized I was color blind, they tried to dissuade me from this career path, but I refused to budge. When my parents told my doctor the severity, and rarity, of my condition, he insisted it would be a waste of time. I insisted we try.

Somehow, someway, I would fly.

Dr. Crayton, the FA Medical Examiner responsible for issuing me a Second Class Medical Certificate—something I need before I can train for my pilot's license—texts someone with his eGlass and then looks up at me. "Miss Night, are you ready to begin?"

I take a deep breath, reining in my nerves, and nod. I can do this. I tried to make a case that these restrictions were outdated rules from a bygone era that lacked the technology of today. I have my eGlass, and Evie—the most advanced artificial intelligence. She guides me through this colored world I live in grey by telling me what I see. I'll never be a danger or risk when I fly. But they persist, convinced that I have to navigate the sky without the aid of AI, just in case we ever lose it. But we are as likely to lose the ability to fly, so I fail to see the sense in this. Still, I've been training without Evie for weeks to pass this one test. I'm ready. I nod and focus my sight on the horizon.

"Very well," he sighs, a resigned look of smug knowing on his face.

I want to kick his kneecaps but that won't help me get his stamp of approval. Instead, I close my eyes, control my breathing, and let my body relax. I imagine a world of color, a world denied to me since birth, and I will the lights in the sky to tell me their secrets, to give to me their truth so that I can see beyond the grey.

When the first light flashes from the tower, I hesitate. Red or green? Red or green?

Dr. Crayton clears his throat. "Red or green, Scarlett?"

"Red," I say, sure that the shades I see hint at what I've learned to be red.

The next light gun flashes. Red. Then green. This one's different. I'm sure of it. Red again. Three more greens. We continue this way for an eternity that's likely no more than twenty minutes. The heat from our warm summer beats down on me. Sweat pools under my arms. I ignore it and stay focused.

Finally, he texts someone again, then clasps his pen to the clipboard. "Very well. We're finished. I'll message you with your results, once I've spoken to the Controller."

"Can you give me any hint as to whether I did okay?" I'm not above begging to stop this pain in my gut. My future hangs in the balance of his decision.

"I'm afraid not." For the first time, his brown eyes soften and he almost smiles. "I'll let you know soon, though."

...

The Airport of Sky is huge, like a city of silver with tall buildings and long roads, people rushing to their destinations, lost in their eGlass displays. A Streetbot hums past me, and I'm not surprised they have those too. This place is bigger than my town, with security everywhere. Teutonic guards patrol the area, their white armor bulky and gleaming, and Inquisition Officers randomly inspect civilians for drugs, weapons, or contraband. A group of them starts searching a dark-haired man with a tag in his ear on the sidewalk. No surprise. Zeniths are always searched first. I keep my head down, hoping I'm not singled out next as I walk to terminal three.

I pull my eGlass from my pocket and slip the small device around my ear. It turns on and Evie's voice speaks in her clipped British accent. "Hello, Scarlett. How did your test go?"

"No idea. Any chance you can hack into their system and get my results for me?"

"The hacking skills you've programmed me with are likely sufficient. I can try if you would like."

Tempting. So very tempting. But if they found out, I'd jeopardize everything. I'll just have to wait. I don't have the most current eGlass—haven't upgraded since my parents first gave me the eGlass Three—so I can't give Evie the upgrade to do untraceable hacking. But I've made some of my own modifications. To the point that it can do more than any on the market today—well, the legal market, anyway.

I don't see my parents anywhere, but Jax comes out of the terminal carrying two cups of coffee. He smiles big, his eyes (*They are blue*, says Evie) locked on mine as he walks toward me. I accept the drink he hands me, relieved to finally see a friendly face.

"How'd it go?" he asks.

"I don't know," I say between sips.

He tousles my hair. "I'm sure you aced it. I've never seen you fail at anything you set your mind to."

"Have you seen my parents?" I ask, trying to steer the conversation elsewhere.

"They're inside."

We enter the terminal, and I see my mom finishing up a call on her eGlass. She flips it back over her ear as my dad pulls her onto his lap. "Do you have a moment, Mrs. Night?"

She grins at him, in that private way they have. "A moment for what, good sir? My time is valuable."

He pulls her closer and caresses her face with his hand. "A moment for me to look upon the most beautiful woman I've ever seen."

She runs her hand through his dark hair, smiling. "For that, I suppose I can indulge you." She leans in and kisses him as I approach.

When she sees me, she laughs and pulls away. "Promise me, Scarlett, you will find a man as loving as your father."

I don't often admit this, but I secretly enjoy how crazy in love my parents are. And it makes me happy seeing them cozy with each other, given their recent arguments.

My dad comes up to me, arms outstretched for a hug. "How'd it go, Star?"

"Hard to tell," I say, stepping away so my mom can get her hug, too.

His smile doesn't waver at my own uncertainty. "Well, no matter what," he says, "you'll find a way to fly."

My mom hugs me next, her face still soft and glowy from flirting with my dad. "I'm proud of you no matter what. I know you think I don't support you in this, but I do, honey. I just want you to be happy doing something you love. That's all I've ever wanted."

"I know, mom," I say.

She and my dad make a handsome couple standing together. Him tall, dark and rugged, her petite and pale like me.

Jax pulls something out of his pocket and hands it to me. "I got you this gift. As a good luck charm."

I take the small silver bag from him and open it. Inside is a silver pin of wings with an 'N' in the middle. My initial! I look up into his handsome face, my heart full of unexpressed emotion. "These are pilot wings," I say.

"Whatever happens today, you're a pilot, Scarlett, born and bred. You deserve your wings."

He takes the pin from me and attaches it to my tank top.

I hug him hard and whisper into his ear. "Thank you." He understands more than anyone what this means to me.

...

My parents leave the airport because they have work to do, but Jax and I stay and eat at a restaurant, sharing things we did while we've been apart. Jax beat one of his mentors in a sparring contest. I won a chess tournament. Two hours later, he drives me home, and we say goodbye. "I'll come over tonight," he says, smiling.

"We can watch something." He still lives in the house he inherited from his father. I know he hates it, but it's hard to get a different place. It took him years to save up for even a car.

"See you," I say, entering my home as he drives away. Harsh voices carry through the kitchen and into the living room, and I drop my purse on the couch, my gift from Jax tucked inside. My parents are arguing again, and I shamelessly eavesdrop.

My mom sounds frustrated, like she's repeated herself too many times already and doesn't want to say it again. "We've been ordered to stay."

"They've found us, Violet." My dad sounds equally frustrated, though he does his best to hide it. Of the three of us, he has the most patience.

His words send a chill up my spine. Who's found us? And why would anyone be looking for us to begin with?

"We don't know that for sure," my mom says, walking out of the kitchen, my dad following. When her blue eyes land on me she smiles, but it doesn't soften the anxiety on her face. "Hi, honey. We didn't realize you were home."

"I just got in," I tell her. And I decide that it's time I knew exactly what was happening. "What's going on? Who's found us?"

My dad, running his hands through his hair, looks at my mom, and she nods, her lips pressed into a thin line. Turning his attention back to me, he takes a breath. "Come with me. I'll show you."

I remember the conversation I overheard earlier. "Why now?" I ask.

"Because... "His eyes are sad. "Perhaps we were wrong. Perhaps we've been wrong about everything."

THE BUNKER

My dad walks toward the front door and I follow, expecting my mom to come, but she reaches for the call button on her eGlass instead as she brushes aside a lock of blond hair. "If you're sure about this... I've got to tell the Council we're leaving. I'll be right out."

My dad nods sharply once, then leads me outside and behind our house. Toward the bunker.

I'm about to find out the truth, and that knowledge sends pinpricks of nerves over my skin. I rub my hands together, forcing warmth back into them despite the heat of the early evening. "Dad, what's going on?"

"I wish I had time to tell you everything in a more... gentle way. But, the time for training is done. Now, we can only hope you learned everything you needed to." With those cryptic words my dad brushes aside leaves and branches and dirt that hide the door. He keeps his left hand clenched, and I realize he's holding something small and dark, but I can't tell what it is. Using his thumbprint, he unlocks the door and pulls it open, triggering an emergency light.

Shadows dance beneath me as I follow my dad down the ladder. Once inside, I prepare myself for something extraordinary, but am disappointed to find that it's fairly typical looking. Canned foods, extra water, guns and ammo, three cots, blankets... all the survival basics. "Why didn't you want me in here?" I ask.

"Because of what you might find," he says.

I pick up a can of beef stew and raise an eyebrow. "Really?"

He chuckles, almost sounding like my normal dad. "Not that." He opens an electrical panel and flips some of the switches. "Stand back," he says.

I take two steps back, and then my breath catches in my throat. The wall in front of us begins to open, revealing a secret room.

There are weapons laid on tables to either side of us. More guns, but also swords, knives, a javelin. Weapons I recognize from books but have never seen in real life. Weapons that are polished, sharpened and well-cared for.

Between the tables, to our right and left, are two large steel cases, each embossed with an intricate tree with the carving of a hand in the center.

I tap my eGlass, setting it to record. I want to document whatever it is I'm about to discover. I watch, a stillness taking over my body, as my father walks to the case on the right and places his hand in the carving. It fits perfectly, and streams of light begin to form around his hand, filling the crevices of the carving like liquid, pooling out until it fills the whole tree. Once each leaf glows with the light, the case begins to unlock, clicking and moving through a series of internal gears until my father can pull the front panel open.

Inside, silver (according to Evie) armor polished to a high sheen adorns a mannequin roughly my father's size and shape. The armor is covered with a design of elegant, stylized branches.

"My old armor," my father says, almost to himself. He slides his free hand over it with care, the other still clutching something hidden, then begins taking the armor off the mannequin.

I stand there, dumbfounded, trying to fit this new information with what I know of my mild-mannered father who crunches numbers for a living. "Dad, who are you *really*? What are you *really*? Because clearly you're not just an accountant." I stare at his armor as he releases another clasp on it. "Unless the definition of business-wear has changed."

He chuckles again, and the familiarity of that sound helps me to breathe easier, if only just a little.

"I *am* an accountant, Scarlett. But I wasn't always one. There's more to me than that."

His palm opens, revealing what he's been holding. A black ring, ancient-looking, with small spikes lining the inside. He sets it down on the table next to me and begins putting on the armor. I focus on the ring, fascinated by the piece of jewelry that looks more like a torture device. I touch it and cut myself, a pool of blood forming on my finger. "Ouch! What on earth?"

My dad looks down at the ring. "A Token of Strife," he says.

"What's that?" I ask as I watch my dad transform into an armored warrior. He looks like a Knight.

"It means an old argument is to be settled, one way or another," he says as he finishes putting on his armor. He picks up the ring again and looks at it, his eyes distant and sad. Then he slips it onto his finger and grimaces in pain as the spikes bite into his flesh. A small trickle of blood runs down his hand.

I watch in shock. "Why did you do that?"

He looks up, surprised, as if he forgot I was here. "Sometimes pain can serve as a reminder to finish what we start."

Thanks, Dad, that explains everything.

He hooks the last piece of his armor, his helmet, to his side. "I'll explain more later, but right now, I need your help."

He walks to the very end of the room where one more case stands, this time with two handprints on it. He puts his hand in one, then looks at me. "Place your hand on it," he says.

I do as instructed and once again everything begins to glow, spreading over the design until all the crevices and carvings fill with light. The locks shift and move with the sound of old metal being woken up.

I pull my hand away and stare at it. "This was made for me?"

"No, for your mother," he says. "But you're close enough genetically for it to work."

The case opens, revealing a solid piece of... glass? I run a hand over it, marveling at the beauty, even in black and white. This isn't glass; it feels like crystal. A huge rectangular crystal box, taller than my dad, and several feet deep. It's carved with more intricate designs, and I can almost make out something within the crystal. "What's in there?"

"A weapon," my dad says. "One we must protect at all costs." From under one of the tables he pulls out a furniture dolly and places it at the base of the case, then switches a lever that lowers the crystal box out and onto the dolly.

"Neat trick," I say, and I realize my parents must have built all of this themselves.

"We need to get this to the truck." He puts his helmet on top of the weapon.

I picture the entrance to our bunker, and imagine us trying to push this huge mass of crystal up to the surface. I'm surprised, not because it seems impossible, but because I don't doubt we'll succeed. I've always known I was different. I've always been stronger than others my age. I've always healed faster.

I push and he pulls until we stand under the open door. "Climb out and wait for your mother," he says.

When I reach the top, she's already there.

My dad has already pushed the crystal the rest of the way so that the top reaches the opening. "Ready?" He calls from below.

"Ready," my mom says, gripping it on the right side. "Get the other side, Scarlett. There's a carved handle."

I move to the other side and find the groove in the crystal where my hand fits.

"On three," my dad says from below. "One, two, three!"

I pull with everything in me.

And, by the Orders, the thing moves. A bit shocked that we actually moved it, I let go of my side, and the weapon slides back a few inches.

My dad grunts and my mom centers herself to grab both sides, her body draped over the top of the weapon as her muscles flex and she pulls the box out by herself.

I scramble to help, belatedly, and assist in getting the tail end safely on the ground as my dad climbs the stairs with the dolly.

I knew we would succeed, but I'm still amazed at what we just accomplished.

She doesn't even look at me, just helps my dad get it on the dolly again. Like all of this is totally normal. She looks at my dad with a serious expression. "Are you sure?"

He nods. "They will come."

She holds his gaze for a long moment, then nods as well. "Okay, then. Let's hurry."

As we get the crystal to the truck, my mom looks at me, a frown on her face. "I'm sorry, honey. You weren't supposed to find out this way."

What have I actually found out? "Was I ever supposed to find out?"

She bites her lip. "I have to go back to the bunker for my armor. Let's get this in the truck quickly."

I throw open the back of our truck, which resembles a small moving van.

My parents make short work of getting the weapon into the truck while I watch and wonder. "Who are we protecting this from?" I ask.

My dad looks down at his horrible ring, the Token of Strife. "An old friend."

I'm about to ask more when the crack of thunder fills the sky. All three of us look up. The clouds catch the rays of the setting sun, bursting with the colors of the retreating day. But then they change, shifting, spinning like a whirlpool in the air, forming a funnel.

"They're here," my dad says, his voice too calm, too quiet. Too controlled. Because I can sense that whoever 'they' are, it's bad. Really bad. And my heart skips a beat, shifting and bumping erratically in my chest.

But I can't pull my eyes away from the sky as the center of the whirlpool lights up and a beam of golden light blasts down into the field beside our house.

Even without Evie whispering the colors in my ear, I know. The golden light of it burns into my soul.

And then a figure emerges from the light, clad in shining golden armor, holding a sword in the sky like an avenging hero.

No, not a hero. As the golden wings unfurl, as the light brightens and radiates around the figure, I see the truth.

Not a hero.

A Nephilim.

CHECKMATE

The Nephilim emerges from the beam of light, and others follow. They wear similar armor, but they don't have wings or a sword. Instead, they march toward us with long silver guns in their hands, guns that weren't made by humans, guns I've never seen before. I stand in shock. Nephilim don't exist anymore. They were exterminated during the War. And this one, I've never seen anything like it, not even in news clips and videos. The wings are bigger, brighter, more glorious than anything I've ever seen or imagined.

My dad moves to stand in front of me and my mother. "Go. Now! I'll hold them off."

My mother looks at my dad, her face filled with such sorrow it chokes my heart. It's the look of someone saying goodbye.

Forever.

I turn back to my dad. "If you're staying, I'm staying."

The Nephilim and soldiers are still a distance away, trudging through the overgrown grass that surrounds our house. But they'll be here soon enough.

My dad grips my shoulders as he faces me. His torture ring digs into my skin. "We can't win this, my little Star."

I want to argue, but with a tear trying to escape his dark eyes, I can't.

"It's too late for that," he continues. "Get the weapon to safety. Don't let this be for nothing."

He makes eye contact with my mother one more time, then reaches for her hand. She runs into his arms with a sharp cry. He kisses her once, whispers something in her ear, and then turns away. "Go!"

He moves quickly, inhumanly fast, as his armor begins to glow blue, the carvings lighting up. He dashes around the soldiers, avoiding the gunfire that comes out of their weapons like streams of flame, cutting them down one by one with his sword. He fights the way I saw Myrddin fight, but even faster, more precise. He fights like a Knight of legend.

The Nephilim hovers over our field, watching the carnage.

"Scarlett, get in and close the door!" My mother is in the front seat of the truck. I move as if fire runs in my veins, jumping into the back of the truck, next to the weapon.

Don't let this be for nothing, he'd said. My stomach clenches. By 'this' he meant his death.

I watch as he continues to fight soldier after soldier. As he kills each one, a new one pours from the portal. Hope plants itself in my heart. My dad can win this. He can.

Finally, he faces the Nephilim, who moves away from the bright (*golden*—thanks Evie, I get it, everything's golden) light. The portal shimmers and fades the closer the Nephilim comes to my father.

"Let us end this," my father says, holding his sword forward.

I thought my father moved fast. But the Nephilim turns into a blur, moving at speeds the human eye can't even hold on to. Before my dad can react, the Nephilim slams a giant fist into the side of his face, knocking off his helmet.

I feel the blow in my own body, or at least that's what it seems like. My dad flies backward, toward me, smashing into the ground below me. Half his face is torn to shreds, broken, blood pouring out of flesh and bone.

I swallow my own bile, tears sliding down my cheeks. The truck lurches forward, and I grip the crystal box to keep from falling out.

My mom is leaving.

Without my dad.

I look down at him again and see his chest rise and fall, slowly, painfully. He is still alive.

"Scarlett, close the door!" My mother sounds desperate with fear.

But I can't be the good girl right now, doing what I'm told, following the commands of others. I can't blindly obey. Not when my father is dying and needs my help.

It seems hopeless, that much is true. A memory, unbidden, comes to me. Of playing chess with my dad. His dark hair falling in his eyes as he moved the chess pieces around the board. I'd lost everything but my king. He still had an army. "I give up," I told him. "You win."

My dad smiled. "It's not over. If you persist, you can still tie the game. If you're left with no moves, then it's a stalemate. One can triumph over many, as long as she's too stubborn to lose." His grin was infectious, and I smiled back at him.

And I didn't give up. I used my one last piece on the board to tie the game.

As the truck moves again, I know I have to make a choice.

Leave with my mother.

Or stay and help my dad.

I jump off the truck. Maybe I can't win against the angel of death, but I can at least tie the game. One piece can still stop this.

I run to my father and fall to my knees over his body just as the Nephilim arrives in a flurry of movement and rushing air.

The Nephilim raises a glowing sword and lets it fall over my father's throat.

One cut and he will die.

I play the only move I have left to play.

I hold out my hands.

And grab the blade in midair.

GREY BLOOD

Pain.

Agonizing pain.

My attention flickers for a moment as I wait for the sword to slice through my body like warm butter.

But the Nephilim freezes, as if in shock.

I hold the blade as it cuts through flesh, hitting bone. As blood covers me. As pain tears a new hole in me. I hold the blade. This monster will not take my father from me.

I know I can't last long, that I have to do something before my hands give way to the bitterly sharp steel.

Everything happens in a breath.

I let go with one hand and try to grab my father's sword, but the Nephilim lifts a powerful, armored leg and kicks me in the gut. All the air in my body rushes out in one near-fatal *whoosh*. My lungs crack, and I fly into the night like a broken doll, limp and useless.

My body crashes to the hard dirt ground, and I tumble across the field. I struggle to catch my breath, to regain my vision, to stay alive. Through a haze I see the Nephilim ten meters away, soaring toward me with wings ablaze, sword smeared with my blood.

I can't move, can't think.

I have no pieces left to play.

I choke on my own blood as I prepare for death, knowing I've failed my father.

But before the Nephilim can reach me, our truck crashes into it. The sound of metal crunching fills my head.

My vision blurs again, reality fading in and out. My mother. She came back. She could have left, could have saved herself, protected the weapon, but she came back.

I want to scream at her to leave, that dad was right, we can't win this one. It's too late. But she exits the truck, her small body coiled and ready to strike. She looks at me, her eyes moist. "Run. Scarlett, you have to find a way to run. I'll distract them. I love you."

I try to sit up, to stop her, to tell her we can leave together, but a wave of dizziness and pain sends my mind tumbling into the past.

Another time. Another place. A hot pipe falling toward me. I was little, just a girl. My mother pushed me out of the way and the pipe hit her instead. She carries the scar to this day. She calls it the scar of a mother's love.

And now my mother will sacrifice her life to save mine.

Just as my father had.

My mother runs toward the Nephilim. I wait in horror to see her cut down by that bloody sword, her petite frame impaled upon it.

But she surprises me, fighting with a speed and ferocity I didn't know she possessed.

Still, she won't last long against the Nephilim. I have to find a way to help.

My eyes fall on a dead solider clutching his otherworldly gun. I stand, legs shaky, everything on my body hurting so much the pain almost takes on a new form, as if I'm a ball of pain and nothing more. I embrace it, let it fuel me as I take a step, then two, faster, until I'm stumble-running toward the gun.

I grab it with my torn and shredded hands. It slips from them, the blood giving me no grip. Using my shirt, I wipe my hands, flinching as tissue pushes out of the cuts in my flesh, as my bones poke out. I pick up the gun again, trying to determine if it has a safety. When I discover nothing, I aim the muzzle at the Nephilim, ready to fire. I pull the trigger.

Nothing. I flip my eGlass over my eye. "Evie, can you identify this gun?"

She scans it, and the image of a red X appears. "I'm sorry, Scarlett, but nothing like this exists."

Well, obviously that's not true, since I'm holding the thing in my hands.

The Nephilim roars with a sound that shakes the heavens and grabs my mother, smashing her against the truck. A loud crack rings through the air, and her body falls limply to the ground.

She doesn't move.

There's no rise and fall to her chest.

I shake the gun, my rage consuming me as I will it to work. I aim again and pull the trigger. It spits out fire and something else, a bullet that blazes into the Nephilim, knocking it to the ground.

The creature looks into the sky, and another whirl-pool forms, bringing down a new wave of soldiers.

Will this never end? "Evie, search all databases for Nephilim weaknesses."

"As you wish," she says.

I know Nephilim are born of human and Angel blood, though no Angel had been seen on earth in many hundreds of years. Since biblical times, really. They're almost myth. If not for the Nephilim, and the Angel technology we've acquired through them, I'm not sure anyone would still believe in Angels.

A stream of information flickers in my eGlass, none of it helpful.

Gun in broken hands, I limp to the truck, knowing I only have one chance of living through this night and killing these monsters.

My mom's body lays on the ground, so still, so pale. I can't look at her, can't process the loss of her just yet. I have to act. Have to keep my head.

Because I was wrong. I'm not out of moves. Not out of pieces to play. I have one last move, and I have to use it now.

The crystalized weapon is still in the truck. I run my hand over it, trying to find some way of opening it, using it. I find nothing.

The soldiers move closer to me. They'll be here in moments, and I'll be dead.

Out of all ideas, I hold my gun up and aim it at the crystal case.

I fire once.

The crystal cracks, one small line that runs its blemish through the beautiful carvings.

I wait.

Nothing else happens.

The soldiers reach me. They aim their guns and fire before I can even turn around.

I thought I couldn't feel more pain. That I'd maxed out the human capacity to endure.

I was wrong.

The bullet of fire enters my body and moves through me, leaving a trail of burning agony in its wake.

I slump over the crystal box, my blood seeping out of me, staining the opaque quartz.

Red. Scarlet. Evie whispers the color of my own name into my ear as I slowly die.

My last vision is of scarlet blood—still just grey to me—spreading into the cracks, into the intricate carvings that decorate the encasement. It almost seems to glow, and I smile and close my eyes as the crystal shatters and darkness takes me.

TOKEN OF STRIFE

I should be dead.

That's my first thought as consciousness forces itself onto me.

I know I'm not dead because of the smell. I smell like blood and sweat and fear. Surely the afterlife doesn't smell so very human.

I peel my eyes open and am relieved to find that my head doesn't explode in pain. Relieved and confused. I look at my hands. Though not completely healed, I can no longer see bone. My body is healing itself at an alarming rate, unusual even for me, and I've always healed fast.

I feel for the hole in my chest and find only the remnants of a wound, still open, still bleeding, but not piercing through my body. On top of my chest I find the bullet that had once been inside me. Somehow it was pushed out. I brush it off me as fuzzy memories dance in my mind.

Of my blood filling the crevices of the crystal.

Of it cracking.

Of… something else. Something inside.

My blood! I look at my shirt and gasp. My blood. My red blood. Scarlet blood. I'm covered in it. Covered in red.

"Evie, you there?"

Nothing. While I've survived, my eGlass hasn't.

But I don't need her voice to tell me the colors. I can see them.

I can see in color.

The white interior of the truck. The clear brilliance of the now broken and empty crystal box. The lines of crimson that fill the design. My blue sneakers with dark red blood drying on them.

The pale cream color of my skin.

It's dizzying, the nuances of color all around me. Everything also smells stronger, sharper, *more*.

I shake my head and stand, grateful I have balance and can walk. I need time to catch up to whatever my body is doing, but not now. Blinking, adjusting to so many new spectrums of sensory overload, I grab the gun lying next to me and then pause to examine the crystal box that now stands open. A crack runs through it, an empty hollow where the weapon had once been.

Mist rises from within and smells like something wet that's been burned.

I crawl out of the truck, gun in hand, and press my eGlass again. Still nothing. I take it off my ear, slip the memory chip out of it, and leave the eGlass in the truck. It's beyond repair, but I can hopefully retrieve something from the chip later, so I stick it in my shoe. Whatever happens tonight, I want to keep this with me. It's my only evidence. My only clue.

Another memory slides back into my mind, unclear and full of shadows. A man in black leaning over me. And... someone fighting.

Around the truck lay all the soldiers who attacked me. Dead.

I didn't do this. Someone's been here.

I don't know how long I've been unconscious, but the sun has fully set, and to my right a weeping willow blazes with fire. I remember planting the seed with my father. He told me we'd have our whole lives to watch it grow.

But his life has been cut short.

Grief grips my heart, and I don't see the soldier still alive until it's too late. He grabs me, knocking the gun out of my hand and throwing me to the ground next to the bodies of my parents. Someone moved them. Someone laid them together. I stare at their lifeless forms, but it doesn't seem real. None of it could possibly be real. They look fake, like Halloween props gruesomely arranged for the most fright.

But I know. In my heart I know this is not a dream. This is not fake. I grip my father's hand, a sob breaking free from my throat. His ring, the Token of Strife, digs into my still wounded flesh. I pull it off his finger and clutch it to my chest.

The soldier holds a gun to me while he speaks to someone through an eGlass in a language I don't understand. I know I will die and, despite what my father taught me, I can't see another move in this horrible, bloody game.

I just want to lay there with them. Die with them. The grief is too much, the pain of their loss too big to feel fully. My heart hurts more than any injury I've ever sustained.

So I lay there, and I wait for the soldier to kill me.

But as I look at my mother, I remember her sacrifice. How she wanted me to live. She gave her life so I would live.

And I remember stories my father used to tell me about Knights. As a little girl, I didn't dress in princess costumes and play with dolls, I dressed as a Knight and saved worlds. My father talked to me about how they could be dangerous when they abused their power, but they could also be great.

He never told me he was a Knight himself. He and my mother. Why hadn't he told me?

In the end, they were both heroes who died for me, and I will not let their sacrifice be in vain.

With a renewed will to live, I raise my head, sit up, and face the soldier who is poised to kill me.

I have no plan.

No Knight to save me.

He holds his gun to my head and prepares to squeeze the trigger.

I leap up and grab him, pushing his gun away as I hold onto his arms.

A wave of heat pulses through me. My head swims with double images. Power swells in me like a hungry fire. The soldier freezes, staring at me.

And I'm in his mind, seeing myself through his eyes. This bruised, bloody, beaten girl with torn clothes and dead parents. I feel his loathing for not just me, but all of humanity, in our weakness and lowliness.

And I see him again, in my eyes. It's as if I exist within us both, seeing us each through the eyes and heart of the other. Soldiers I hadn't noticed approach from behind him, likely to see what's going on with the captive.

Everything in my mind jumbles together in that moment. Him, me, them, all of it. In fear, in a last ditch effort to save myself, I raise the gun—his gun—and fire at the soldiers moving toward us.

They drop to the ground, dead, and I fall back into my own body, hitting the ground with a thud, hands shaking, reality still fragmented by whatever I just did.

The solider before me, the one I controlled, turns and aims his gun at me.

Then a sword impales him in the chest.

I look up and into the eyes of the last person I expect to see tonight. "Jax?"

Jax falls to his knees in front of me, the sword still clutched in his right hand, his jaw hard, face determined. He doesn't look shocked. He should look shocked.

"Are you okay, Scarlett?"

I don't know how to answer that. No. I'll never be okay again. But I'm alive. I'm not going to die from my injuries. That's probably what he wants to know. I give a brief nod.

He glances at my parents' bodies, but keeps his face emotionless. "Do you know where the weapon is?"

"You know about that?" I ask.

"Yes, I know about everything. There's no time to explain. We have to get out of here, but first we've got to secure the weapon."

"It's not there," I tell him. "It's gone."

"Show me," he says.

He helps me stand, and I lead him to the truck, where the crystal remains are still swimming in pools of my blood.

"We have to go," he says after a quick examination. "Now."

"I can't leave them." I pull him back toward my house. "We have to get my parents."

His eyes aren't unkind, but they hold no room for sentiment either. "We don't have time. You're in danger. If we don't leave now, they will come back, and we'll both be dead."

As if cued by his words, lights once again appear in the sky. I can't be responsible for another death. For another life.

We run toward my father's plane, and I try not to spare a glance at my parents' fallen forms, but I can't stop myself.

As Jax preps the plane, I look at them one last time, lying together on the cold earth, their hearts forever stopped.

I've never seen them in color while they were alive. They were always shades of grey to me. Now, in their death, I see the rich oak of my father's hair. The golden beauty of my mother's long braid. I just wish I could see their eyes. Just one last time, I wish I could look them in the eyes and tell them how much I love them.

Jax nudges me toward the plane, and I clutch the Token of Strife in my hand, relishing the pain it causes.

Their death will not be in vain.

...

The inside of the plane smells like my dad. His cologne. A musky, minty scent that makes my eyes burn with unshed tears. I run my hand over the control panels. I know this plane better than I know my own bedroom. I've spent countless hours flying in it with my dad, learning what every light and button means.

I can fly it myself, but everything inside me has gone numb, so I let Jax take the controls. I still have so many questions, so many things that don't make sense about this night, but I only have the voice for one.

"Where are we going?"

He doesn't take his eyes off the controls as we taxi down our short runway. "Castle Vianney."

So we're going to New York. The place where Knights are trained. "What's going on?"

Jax doesn't show any emotion. "Everything will be explained when we get there."

The plane leaves the ground, and my stomach drops. I've always loved this feeling. Relished it. But tonight, there is no joy, not even in flight. I hug myself, trying to keep warm.

Jax finally looks at me, his eyes softening. "I'm sorry, Scarlett. I'm so sorry. I can't tell you anything more. I'm not allowed. But, I promise, you'll understand soon. Can you trust me? Just for a little while longer?"

His dark eyes plead with me, but my heart remains unmoved. I am too torn by fear and anger, by sadness and grief, by the whirlwind of events that has swept me away. My parents betrayed me. Lied to me. I trust no one.

But...

I can give him time. He's my link to discovering the truth. And if he doesn't give me what I want—I reach down and feel the bulge in my shoe, making sure the chip is still there—I have one other place to look for answers.

I close my eyes and the weight of the day smothers me in darkness.

...

His back is to me, the tall man with broad shoulders, a black cloak billowing around him. Woods surround us, dark, foreboding, the trees towering over us with long shadows born of the night. He walks forward, and I run to him, but the woods stretch before me, putting him forever out of reach.

The air around me is thick, heavy, coating my lungs, making it hard to breathe. Dead leaves fall from the trees as I run past them, catching the moonlight on their frail brown skin.

The man before me stops. I run faster, knowing I must reach him, knowing he is important, but again the woods trick me.

I trip and look down, expecting to find a root has caught my foot.

It is not a root, but a hand. A skeletal hand attached to a decaying body. I scream, stumble forward, only to land on more dead things. I realize that what I thought were piles of leaves are piles of corpses, eyes forever open, staring at me with accusations unspoken but heard nonetheless.

I keep running, trying to escape the death around me. I arrive in a clearing where the corpses form a hill of dead bodies. The man in black stands at the base. On top is a throne, a giant gleaming thing made of midnight, with a blood red banner over it.

Sitting on the throne is a little girl in a white lace dress, her long blond hair parted into braids with white ribbon. She's playing with a giant glowing ball. Our eyes meet. She smiles, but something isn't right with that smile. Her teeth. Two of them protrude, too long, too sharp. She holds the white glowing ball out to me.

The man, his back still turned to me, speaks, his voice filling the clearing. "Choose!"

The girl's voice repeats. "Choose."

Together, they chant, "Choose."

I don't understand. "Who are you?" I ask, but my voice is carried on the wind and dies before it reaches him.

I run to the man, grip his shoulders, turn him to me...

...

I wake with a start, my head still filled with the voices of that man and that girl. The plane hits the pavement of a runway. That's what woke me. We've landed.

I look out the window at my first glimpse of Castle Vianney.

CASTLE VIANNEY

To understand me, you must understand the castle. It sits upon the eastern shore, a wall of faded white stone, and behind them, a city conjured in the dreams of children. The streets are wide and open as winter's fields, the buildings old and varied as autumn's leaves, the people bright and eager, always a smile upon them. They are merchants, workers, performers, for the castle holds all kinds of men, but above all, it holds Knights. They are bigger than most men, not in weight or height, though of course some are, but in the way they carry themselves. They walk with a dancer's grace, and their eyes never look down. They move for no one, but when two Knights come together, and then always one yields. In their eyes, you see it is not an easy thing. These are not creatures made for bending. These are creatures for war.

These are creatures like me.

But they are also more, as if they are gods, and I made in their image. I want to be one of them, not because I crave power, but because I fear weakness. It is the way I have always been; I cannot be weak. The price is too high.

...

When I first see the castle, I do not imagine it would ever be my home. For it is so old and grand, and I am so young and small. For I am a pleb, and this is a place of old lords and high ladies, of puremen and rich men, of Knights and Princes: of patricians.

When I dreamt I would study there, I had dreamt too big. For what do I know of politics? What do I know or ruling? After a moment, I realize, it is my doubt speaking. I tell it to be quiet.

I climb out of my father's plane, out of the last familiar piece of my life—and walk into a world that blends the past and the future into something new. There is a tower, draped in red banners, with a balcony amongst the clouds, looming over me. I see a glass elevator ride up to the top, the people inside gawking at the people below.

Jax sees me staring as we walk down the airstrip, the ground beneath us gleaming silver under a silver moon.

"This castle was built in France," he says, answering the questions I have yet to ask. "It was transported here piece by piece."

"Why not just build something new?"

"They say the building itself holds ancient magic. Strange things have been known to happen in the castle, though I suspect it is not magic behind them, but A-Tech."

I can't pull my focus from the world around me. I marvel at the colors, at how much I've missed with just Evie translating my black and white existence. I wish she were here to help me identify the different shades mixing before me. Reds. Blues. Oranges and greens. They're dizzying, turning my stomach, but the feeling is worth the view.

I wish more fiercely than anything I could share this with my parents, but I shove the painful thought away. I'll pull it out when I'm finally alone and have a moment to break down. Because once I start crying, I fear I'll never stop.

And there are still answers to uncover.

"Where are we going?" I ask. My clothing has stuck to me with blood and sweat and dirt. My hair hangs in clumps around my sore, bruised head, the normal pale blonde stained red. But I hold my chest high, ignoring the glances of those around us.

"We're going straight to the Council. I tried to argue you needed rest first, but they want to talk to you. With the weapon missing, it's a matter of global security."

I stare at Jax, the boy I grew up with, the boy I mowed lawns with as a child. His jaw is set in a hard line and he walks with purpose. He walks like a soldier. And he looks like a stranger.

"Why am I here?"

He stops and looks at me, and for a moment a flicker of the boy I knew flashes in his eyes. "Because this is the only place you'll be safe, Scarlett." He reaches for my hand and holds it. "I failed your parents. I can't fail you too. I can't lose the last person I love."

Earlier today, those words would have brought me comfort. Now, they fall at my feet like a dead thing. I say nothing and follow him through the parking structure to a black car with Order plates.

"You work for the Orders?" I ask, not even surprised anymore.

"I'm a Teutonic Knight. A Guardian. Like my father was, once. I work for the Four Orders under the authority of the Pope."

Everything, all of it, my whole life has been a lie. "Your father didn't die in a car crash, did he?"

I get into the dark car and slam the door shut. Jax starts the engine and pulls out. "No, he didn't." His face looks haunted, and I can tell he won't elaborate.

So I don't ask for more. In this moment, as calloused as it sounds, I don't care about his father while my own father's body was left to rot on our lawn.

"My parents were patricians," I say. It's not a question.

"Yes."

"And I'm..." The words don't come, for tonight, I only wish to be Scarlett Night. I only wish to be the homeschooled pleb who lives with her parents in the Kingdom of Sky. I only wish...

That girl still lived.

I say nothing more, and we begin to drive. The sights of the town blur past me. Storefronts and small homes with big yards, a downtown area with street vendors set up on cobblestone streets. Ever-Glow lights line the walking paths, and a steel sculpture of a cross hovers over an intersection. We flew for three hours, and most shops are closed at this time of night. I reach up to tap on my eGlass, but remember it's not there.

Jax catches my movement. "I'll pick you up a new one. I know you need it to help with colors."

That's not true anymore, but I know I can't tell him, though I don't know why. "Thanks." I'll need it for other reasons, though. I'll need it to review the chip I have, and to keep tabs on the outside world. The people Jax works for would of course bug whatever device I get, but I can override that easily enough and make it my own—bring my Evie back. I've spent too much time custom-coding her to lose all that now.

We drive onto Vianney Bridge, a drawbridge, currently open. It's the only path I see to the castle fortress, which is cut off from the walled city by a moat. It is much like a smaller version of the island, which is separated from the mainland by rivers. We pass through the giant open gates, covered in engravings of Knights. The grey stone façade of the Castle gleams in the moonlight with chips of obsidian.

At the end of the moat, two guards stand to either side of the gate dressed in light armor with a "V" crest on the right side of their chest and a Celtic cross on the left. Jax holds out his hand and shows them his ring, something I didn't notice him slip on. It has the crest of Teutonic Knights, wings in red and black. They nod and he ushers me into the Castle courtyard.

A gentle breeze blows the hair off my face, cooling my fevered skin as we walk down a path surrounded by trees and gardens. "This is where many students come to walk, hang out, read or study," he says. We only see two students this late at night. Both have on black cloaks with the V crest embossed in gold and silver thread on their chests and their back. "Those are Initiates," he says. "They'll receive their final uniforms when they're accepted by an Order."

The Four Orders... Teutonic, Inquisition, Hospitaller and Templar. "What Order were my parents?"

He looks at me, his eyes holding deep sadness. "Your parents were Templars."

Of course. Templars are the protectors and keepers of secrets, the inner circle that knows things no one else does.

It's these secrets that killed my family. It's these secrets I have to unravel.

Jax leads me into the castle, with high ceilings and walls covered in ancient paintings and tapestries depicting great battles. Torches light the hallways, but rather than fire, they contain a different kind of light, smokeless and blue rather than red—Angel light. Old and new. Ancient and modern. The past and the future.

My body aches. I am tired and hungry, though when I think of food nothing sounds remotely appetizing. A deep thirst digs a hole in my gut, but I ignore it. I study my hands, still cut, still bloody, but nowhere near as destroyed as they had been. I remember seeing my own bone protrude through the gashes. Now, though the wounds are deep enough to show flesh, they will heal. They *are* healing.

We wind through passages in the Castle and stop in front of a great wooden door. Jax holds out his hand, his eyes digging into mine. "I know I lied to you, Scarlett. I know you don't trust me right now, and that's okay. But please know that our relationship has never been a lie.

My feelings for you, even the ones I... I haven't been able to express, they have never been a lie. I won't let anything happen to you. I swear it on my life."

I take his hand. What choice do I have? I have to believe the boy I grew up with is somewhere inside the soldier before me. I have to believe that something in my life has been real. I can't deal with the alternative.

It hurts to hold his hand, but I don't pull away and neither does he as we enter a large hall. Five great stone seats form a semi-circle above us.

In the middle sits an old man with a long grey beard and grey hair. He wears silver glasses and carries a carved walking stick with a crystal globe on the top. His black robes hang from sharp shoulders, and he has the V symbol on one side of his chest and a red cross, the Templar symbol, on the other.

Jax points to the woman to his right. "She's the Head of Hospitaller."

The woman looks to be in her early forties, Spanish, with cold, calculating dark eyes. Her A-line dark, straight hair frames her face sharply.

Next to her sits a man with a hawk nose, dark, squinty eyes, and a smile that makes my skin crawl. "That's the Head of the Inquisition," Jax whispers. "Stay away from him if you can."

He doesn't need to tell me twice.

To the left sits the Head of the Teutonic Knights, a young-looking blond woman who holds a sword and wears armor similar to the men at the drawbridge.

"Next to her is the Second Templar. The Chancellor in the middle is the Head of Templar, but there must be five council members always, so his second acts as the fifth."

The Chancellor turns to look at me, and the Council quiets down. To our left and right stands an unmoving line of Teutonic guards. They don't make me feel any safer.

"We bring this gathering to order," says the Chancellor with a commanding British accent. "We have come to hear witness the testimony of Scarlett Night on the death of Marcus and Violet Night and the theft of the weapon the Nights were tasked to protect."

Jax steps forward. "I have brought her as instructed," he says in a formal tone.

The Head of his order nods. "What's become of the weapon?" she asks, sitting forward on her chair.

The Inquisition Head gives her an irritated look. "It is the Chancellor's job to inquire, Gabriella. Can you not go through one meeting without speaking out of turn?"

The Chancellor pounds his walking stick on the ground. "Silence." He turns to the man. "And it is *also* my job to correct anyone on this council who speaks out of turn, Ragathon."

Ragathon bows his head, but his eyes do not look contrite.

The Chancellor turns his eyes to mine, and then they are all staring at me, each looking as if they will devour me with their questions. "Tell us everything that happened tonight."

With the fewest words possible, I recount everything I can remember of the evening, editing out details I don't feel entirely comfortable sharing. The chip I took. Shooting at the weapon. The man I vaguely remember seeing. The way I controlled that soldier and got him to kill the others.

"And what happened to the weapon?" the Chancellor asks.

"I don't know. I was injured and lost consciousness, as I said. When I woke, the crystal box was empty."

Ragathon's head shoots up. "The weapon was removed?"

"Yes."

"Where did it go?" Gabriella asks.

"I have no idea," I say truthfully.

The Head of Hospitaller, who has so far been silent, speaks. "Can you describe the exact details of the casing? What it looked like when you woke up? Anything you can remember, no matter how small or inconsequential it may seem?"

I've already said everything I'm willing to. I didn't tell them about the blood, because I couldn't have lost that much blood and survived. And my current wounds won't account for the amount of bloodshed I saw. But, they'll know if they have a team there. I decide on the partial truth. "There was blood everywhere. My blood. My parents' blood. Probably some blood from the soldiers my parents killed before dying. It was dark, so it was hard to tell."

Ragathon scoffs. "It's not that hard to see blood. Even in the dark."

"With all due respect," Jax says. "Scarlett is color blind. For her it would be hard to tell. She can't see any colors at all."

Ragathon ignores him and turns to the Chancellor. "With all due respect, Chancellor," though with the way his voice sneers, I don't hear any respect, "this does not add up. There's no way anyone could have penetrated the... box. Nor could the Nephilim have returned. I do not think the girl is telling the full truth."

Up until this point I've been mostly numb. I wanted to find out what happened to my parents, and I hoped that answering all their questions would accomplish that. It's becoming clear that's not the case, and I've had enough. Rage builds in me, boiling up from the new holes in my heart. Before anyone can ask me another inane question, I speak, my voice strong, firm, commanding. "I am not a 'girl', Ragathon, I am a woman with full agency and legal rights, and I do not appreciate being spoken to, or about, in this condescending manner."

I make eye contact with each of the council members. "As for the rest of you, I'm done answering your questions. I've told you everything I know. This morning, I thought I had a normal life and normal parents. Now, my parents are dead. I am standing here covered *in their blood.*" I see the Chancellor flinch.

"I've been attacked, injured, beaten, and I've lost everything that mattered. I'm hungry and tired. I need a shower and time to mourn my parents and figure out what I'm going to do next. I don't owe you anything. I don't know any of you, and you don't know me. Whatever arrangement you had with my parents died with them. So unless you are taking me prisoner," the Chancellor raises his eyebrows at that and I continue, "and let me warn you if that's the case, I will be seeking legal action against you and this school for condoning the capture and imprisonment of an innocent," I stare him down and continue, "then I insist on being taken somewhere I can shower, eat, sleep and grieve. Alone."

I can feel Jax stiffen next to me. A stunned silence fills the room and I wait, sensing my life hangs in the balance.

Then the Chancellor chuckles and tugs at his beard. "The girl…excuse me, the young woman is right. We've been treating our *guest* badly. We have enough information to start an investigation into this matter."

Ragathon interrupts. "But I have more questions—"

The Chancellor holds up his staff. "We are done!" He looks at the other Head, a challenge in his eyes, but Ragathon backs down. "Jax, please show Miss Night to a room, and make sure she has all she needs to be comfortable."

His eyes fall on me again, a knowing look in them. "Miss Night, please accept my condolences on the death of your parents. Whatever we can do to help bring their killers to justice, we will do."

I don't exhale until we leave the Council Room. My body goes limp, and I feel light headed and drained.

Jax turns to me. "I've never seen anyone talk to them like that and live to tell the tale." He has a look of wonder in his eyes, but also fear. Of me? Of them? I don't know and honestly don't care much right now.

But I do have one question that's nagging me. "That man. The middle one, the Chancellor. Who is he?" Something about him tugs at my mind. The way he looked at me. The way he laughed when I stood up to him.

Jax's face is a study in neutrality. "He's your grandfather."

BREAKING GRIEF

"My grandfather? But... he's dead. He died before I was born." I have no grandparents left. My dad's parents died a few years apart when I was a child, though I never got to meet them because they lived overseas. My mom's mother died when she was a teenager, and her father... he died while she was pregnant with me.

"When your parents went into hiding, they cut off most of their ties with the Orders. That included your grandfather."

Jax leads me through the halls of the castle as we talk.

"Have I ever met him?" I ask.

He shakes his head, running a hand through his dark hair. "No, your parents went into hiding before you were born."

While Mom was pregnant with me. All she had left was her father, and she cut off their relationship to protect this weapon.

Something occurs to me. "If my parents went into hiding, do I even know their real names?"

"Yes. They were never hiding from anyone in specific, more like keeping the weapon somewhere no one would look. There was a chance they would live as plebs for life, and since there are many people called Marcus and Violet and Night, they insisted on keeping their true names. They told me so themselves. You know my real name as well. It's still Jaxton Lux."

I sigh, grateful for some truth in my childhood. As students from different Orders walk by, staring at me, I become keenly aware of my sorry physical state. I must look like I've survived a battlefield. I guess I have. "It's late for them to be up, isn't it?"

"We have different training exercises that run throughout the day and night."

A tall girl with red hair and the mark of the Teutonics on her tunic stares at me as she walks by.

Jax tugs at my hand as he glares at her, blue eyes narrowed. "Move along, pureman." He speaks in high language. I've never heard him do so except in jest, but he is serious now, and his words are poised.

The girl's mouth snaps shut, and she hurries off as Jax increases his speed, and I rush to catch up.

We enter a large hall with couches, chairs and tables scattered throughout and a huge hearth roaring with a fire. Above it hangs a tapestry embroidered with the Teutonic Knight symbol. Only one student occupies the room: a long, lanky man reclining on a couch in one corner, a large leather book covering his face as he sleeps.

Jax crosses the room and slaps his boot. The man jolts awake.

"Get to bed, Saunders. You'll be useless to me tomorrow otherwise."

"Yes, sir," he says and scrambles out one of the doors, not even sparing a glance in my direction, which I appreciate.

"You'll be given a room in the Initiate's wing soon," Jax tells me. "But for now, you can have my room. I'll sleep out here."

He leads me through the door on the east side of the hall and straight into a suite with a sitting area, a study area and a bed. I see touches of the Jax I know in the room—his favorite baseball glove and ball sitting on his desk, a stack of comics I recognize from home, jeans and t-shirts strewn about, familiar pieces of a life that no longer exists for me. Mixed in with this are other items I've never seen—a sword with the Teutonic Knight symbol engraved on the pommel, a ring bearing the same mark, two sets of armor on dummies in the corner, one light and one heavy... pieces of his life I never knew existed.

Jax clears his throat and grabs a towel and some clothes from the closet. "I know these will be too big, but they're clean."

I accept them, the smell and feel so familiar to me. These are the sweats he always wore when we had movie nights at my house. When we'd fall asleep with the eScreen on, a bowl of popcorn between us, not waking until the next morning. The memory makes my eyes burn with the heat of unshed tears.

"Thank you," I say.

He looks like he wants to say more, his face full of unspoken thoughts. I pause, waiting, but he just nods. "Help yourself to anything. I'll be back with some food."

He turns and leaves me standing alone in this half strange, half familiar space of memories.

I walk to the bathroom and see my reflection for the first time and tremble. It's not as bad as I thought. It's worse. I am bathed in blood. Not all of it is mine. Some of it belongs to my parents.

I wait, expecting the pain to overtake me, but I buried it too deep for it to surface now. I pull out the Token of Strife from my pocket and the memory chip from my shoe, peel off my clothing and drop the pile in the small wastebasket by the toilet. My hands are steady. Numb. I look around for a place to hide my two treasures, settling on the box of tissues on the toilet.

Turning to the mirror again, I stare at myself. My pale skin is covered in bruises, cuts, scrapes and gashes. But the bullet wound I was most worried about has healed considerably. I realize this is the first time I've ever seen myself in color. I look different than I imagined. I tug on a long strand of my pale blond hair, rubbing away a bit of blood. My eyes are bloodshot and tired, but the blue silver of my irises have an unearthly quality that's disconcerting.

I can't look anymore... not until I've cleaned up.

I turn the water to the hottest setting until steam fills the bathroom, then step in, bracing myself against the burn of the water. I let it soak me as rivulets of bloody water circle the drain. I wash my hair four times until nothing but clear water runs through it. And I scrub my skin until it nearly peels off my body.

As the last of my parents' blood, now just a stain of pale pink, pools at my feet, a dam inside me breaks. I fall to my knees in the shower and sob, my body shaking with grief. I can't stop. Can't quiet myself as my sobs grow louder, a keening brokenness tearing out of me.

I don't hear the knock at the door. Don't realize Jax has come in until he enters the shower and wraps his arms around me as he sits under the water, fully clothed, holding me.

I don't think about his lies, his alter-identity. I don't think about what our future will be or what I'll do tomorrow. I just cling to my friend, to the person I've grown up with, to the only one who knows me inside and out. I cling to him as my heart breaks, and he gives me his strength even as he mourns with me. Even as his tears mingle with mine. Even as the water chills... still we sit there, embraced in our shared grief.

I wasn't the only one who lost family today. My parents were his family, too. Whatever else has happened between us, whatever else will happen later, he's my brother in this loss, and I can't shut him out. I need him too much.

Time passes, but I don't feel it. Everything stands still until finally my sobs subside, and I can breathe again. The pain doesn't go away, but buries itself in my heart. It creates a new home in me, nursing on the anger that has begun to swell there.

I look into Jax's eyes, my eyelids heavy, tears staining my cheeks. He looks almost as heartbroken as I feel.

"I'm so sorry, Star," he says. "I loved them, too. I miss them, too." He brushes wet hair off my cheek. "I'm so sorry. I should have been there. This is all my fault."

I wait for the grief to swell again, but I've cried all I can cry for the night. "I know you do," I say. "They loved you like their own. I know they wouldn't blame you, and you shouldn't blame yourself either. Even if you'd been there, you couldn't have stopped the Nephilim. No one could have."

But I will. Someday, I will.

...

I suddenly remember I'm naked. In front of Jax.

I turn away, covering my breasts with my hands, hoping I'm not blushing. I've never been naked with anyone before. This is not what I imagined.

What will Jax think of this?

I glance at him over my shoulder.

He looks calm. Maybe a little intrigued?

He clears his throat and averts his eyes. "The water's cold. You should get out."

I lower my gaze. "Sure."

He turns off the water and hands me a towel. We don't touch.

I guess I was wrong. He's not interested.

"Thanks," I say, wrapping the towel around myself as I stand. "I'll go get dressed." I grab the clothes he gave me and the tissue box and leave him in the bathroom.

I hear the shower turn back on as I dry off and dress. I shove the tissue box into a corner under his bed until I can figure out how to keep my few precious belongings safe.

He comes out a few minutes later in just a towel, his body more muscular than I remember, the wolf pendant he always wears dangling around his neck. I turn my head while he shrugs into his own clothes.

He hands me a brown paper bag and sits across from me on his bed. "Some food and LifeForce. You need to get your blood sugar up."

"Thank you. I'm starving."

He has his own bag, and we eat our food in silence. I take a bite of the turkey sandwich he brought and nearly spit it out. "I think this meat is bad, or something," I say, holding it out to him.

He takes a bite. "Tastes fine to me," he says with his mouth full.

"Mouth closed when chewing," I tease, slipping back into old me as if the day hasn't happened.

He opens his mouth and sticks out his tongue, bits of half eaten food making a grotesque vision.

"You are disgusting," I say. "Seriously."

We both smile, but our humor fades fast. I put the sandwich back in the bag and pick up the packet of LifeForce, ripping it open and sucking out the sweet nectar that promises "long life and good health." I feel instantly better. I've never much cared for LifeForce as an energy drink before.

It always made me a bit jittery. But now I pull out a second packet and drink that down quickly, feeling the unquenchable hunger in my gut finally subside.

Around me, colors brighten, and my senses become more alert. No wonder everyone loves this stuff.

Jax finishes his sandwich and his own LifeForce, and then we sit back, looking at each other.

"Jax, what's going on? What were my parents a part of?"

He shifts on the bed, avoiding eye contact with me. "I'm not sure I should be the one telling you this... "

"Jax, please... I need to know. I have the right to know."

He nods. "Years ago, before we were born, your parents found some kind of weapon, something that could cripple the Orders, something that could destroy of the world. Some of the councilors wanted to use it on their enemies. Your parents argued against it. They won their case and, under orders, went into hiding with the device. My father was charged with guarding them. Once I was old enough, I was charged with guarding you."

All these years we've been sitting on something that could destroy the world? "Why did you never tell me?"

"The same reason as your parents," he says, sadly. "They didn't want you to grow up in the Orders. They didn't want you to grow up a patrician."

The idea that I am a patrician is still foreign, and I store it away in a corner of my mind.

"They were my parents. Parents never tell their kids everything. But you were my best friend. We grew up together and shared all of our secrets."

"I'm sorry," he says. "But I couldn't tell you... because I couldn't hurt you. Or them. And because I'd taken an oath."

His fists clench together, and I can see his pain reflected on his face. I reach for his hand, and he takes mine. And I realize that if he hadn't known about any of this, I would be alone right now. I can't reconcile all the lies, but I'm grateful he's here. That I'm not alone in this.

"What was it? What was the weapon?"

He shrugs. "Only the council knows... well, now anyways."

Because my parents knew. I try to push that thought away, but... wait. He's wrong. I shake my head. "The Nephilim—he knew."

Jax drops his voice. "I wouldn't talk about that. Not here. People have strong feelings about Nephilim. Most everyone believes they are extinct. If they aren't, we have an international crisis on our hands that could send us back to war."

I pull my hand away and lean back against his headboard. "You think I'm making this up?"

His eyes are distant. "I think things are changing," he says.

...

A knock on the door interrupts us.

Before we can respond, a woman walks in. She wears the tunic of a Knight of the Hospitallers, and I recognize her as the woman on the Council who seemed cold and calculating. Jax stands and salutes her.

"I need to examine Miss Night," she says, looking at him instead of me.

"Of course, Grandmaster."

Um, hello, I'm in the room, too.

"But..." Jax adds, "you should ask her yourself."

I could hug him for that response. Seems the old Jax is still in there somewhere.

She turns to me, a small smile on her dark face that softens her features for a moment. "Pardon me. That was rude. Do you mind if I examine you? You've taken quite a beating today."

I do mind but figure it's a good idea to get checked out. "Go ahead," I say. "But Jax stays."

"Of course."

As Jax sits back down, she asks me to lie on the bed while she examines my hands. "Your cuts were much deeper, weren't they?"

I nod, figuring it won't do any good to lie.

"I thought as much. There's some deep tissue tearing, and the bones have been damaged, but they appear to be healing remarkably well." She raises an eyebrow at me, then pulls up my shirt. Jax turns away, though he saw all of me already today.

The woman pokes at my chest and stomach, her fingers expertly feeling around the hole that had been torn through me. "What caused this?" she asks.

I hesitate, not sure what to say. "I don't remember. Something hit me, and I fell, then blacked out. When I woke, I was in pain and covered in blood, but I was already healing."

She opens her mouth to say something, but Jax whispers in her ear. Her eyes widen, and she nods. "Alright then. Overall you are looking remarkably well for a woman who nearly died a few hours ago. Get plenty of rest tonight. Stay hydrated, and let me know if anything worsens, or you develop other symptoms."

With deft hands she pulls a syringe from her bag and sticks it into the vein in my arm, filling three vials. "We need to run some tests to make sure there are no other problems, but you seem healthy enough to me."

She stores the vials and packs up her bag while I adjust my clothing and scoot back on the bed.

She reaches the door before turning to face me, her eyes gentler than before. "I am truly sorry for your loss. I was close to your parents when we were younger. They were good people and will be missed." With that, she's gone.

Her words shock me. It never occurred to me that there would be people here who knew my parents, but it makes sense. There's so much I don't know.

I'm too full of questions to sleep. I stand and grab Jax's jacket, slipping it on as I pull out the tissue box under his bed and grab the ring and chip, shoving them into my pocket. "I need to go home," I tell him. I have to get to the bunker, to see if there are more clues to what's really going on.

Jax places his hand on my arm. "Scarlett, you can't leave right now. Not yet. It's the middle of the night. You need rest."

"Just try and stop me, Jax." I don't have a plan as I slam the door behind me and march out of his bedroom and into the Teutonic Hall. There are guards outside.

One on each side. They grab my arms. I kick one in the knee and am about to punch the other in the face when a commanding voice call out, "Leave her!"

The Chancellor walks toward us, his long robes flowing around him and his walking stick clicking against the stone floors. The soldiers immediately let me go, scuttling away at a gesture from my grandfather.

"What do you want with me?" I ask, knowing he holds my fate in his hands. "Are you planning on keeping me a prisoner?"

"No," he says simply. "But humor me for just a few moments before you traipse out of here barefoot in the middle of the night. I have one question for you. Answer it, and I will provide you an escort to take you wherever you wish to go." He looks down at my bruised feet. "And shoes," he says.

He sits at the table near us and gestures for me to join him. Recognizing my limited resources and short-sighted plan, I sit.

"What is it you want, Scarlett?"

I cross my arms over my chest. "My parents."

His eyes flinch. "Of course. I ask the wrong question." He leans in, serious. "What will you do?"

"I'll find the Nephilim." I stick my hand into my pocket and pull out the Token of Strife, squeezing it until the cuts on my hand open up again. "I'll find the Nephilim who killed my parents, and I'll make the monster pay with his life."

He nods. "Then stay, and let me train you. Let me forge the sword that would avenge my daughter's death."

His eyes gloss over as he speaks of my mother, and for the first time, I realize Jax and I aren't the only ones in mourning. He lost a child, perhaps the worst kind of loss a person can face.

But our shared loss does not make me trust him any more. Can I really join these Orders? These people? Can I trust anyone here?

Still, there are things about his offer that tempt me. I raise an eyebrow. "So, you'll make me a Knight?"

He nods as he talks. "You'll still have to pass the Initiate Trials, and you'll have to progress from Initiate to Page to Squire to Knight, but... I will start you on the path."

So no shortcuts. Changing subjects, I ask something that's been nagging me since walking through these halls. "How did my parents become Knights? Why were *they* chosen to protect this 'weapon'?"

"Stay, and I'll tell you," he says.

More secrets. They're all biters here. I can't believe I wanted to be one of them. "I need to get back home. Everything I have is there. All my memories, everything I have left of my parents... "

"The Inquisition is there," he says, "discerning what happened. But when they leave, I promise, you can return home."

"Alone. With my father's airplane."

He raises an eyebrow, but nods. "Very well. Alone. And with his airplane. I assume you can handle the aircraft by yourself?"

"Yes." I have before, even if it wasn't strictly legal.

"Will you come back? Will you train with me and learn what you must become to avenge your parents?"

This matters to him. And a thought occurs to me as we sit here, measuring the breadth of each other: he needs me. Though with this entire school, with all Four Orders at his disposal, I don't entirely understand why. But the fact remains: he needs me.

And I need him too. I can shoot a bow and throw a few punches. I can hack any system on the planet, and I can fly an airplane. But I have no idea how to kill a Nephilim. I need him and Castle Vianney, maybe just as much as they appear to need me.

"I'll come back. I can't promise beyond that, but I'll come back."

"That's good enough for now," he says.

"How long until I can go?"

"A few days."

Jax comes out of his room and stands beside me as I thank the Chancellor. "What do I call you?" I ask.

He smiles. "You can call me Grandfather. I would like it very much if you did."

I don't know how I feel about that, but it might be good to have another living family member. To not be the last of my blood.

The Chancellor turns to Jax. "Watch over her. She will need help in the coming days."

"Yes, sir," he says.

The Chancellor—I can't quite bring myself to think of him as Grandfather yet—stands to leave, but hesitates. "Scarlett, do you know what you're holding?"

I open my hand to look at the black ring. "My father called it a Token of Strife."

"The Tokens are an ancient practice of the Orders," he says. "The Token of Strife symbolizes a conflict. When you give a Token of Strife to another, you are challenging them to combat. But only when you put the Token on, do you agree to the challenge."

"My father wore it... during the battle."

"Then your parents died fighting for their beliefs. For their belief in protecting others. For their belief in this place. They died as Templars."

I suck in my breath and squeeze the ring harder.

The Chancellor puts his hand over mine, his lined skin thin as paper and smooth against my own. "I know you can't trust me, but perhaps you can trust them."

FORTUNA

The next week is pain. I stay in bed, crying and howling, waking in hot sweat. I eat near nothing. When I sleep, Jax says I mutter things he cannot understand. I suspect they are things of vengeance. It is all I think of.

Vengeance.

Loss.

In my dreams I see faces: those of my father and mother, those of Brooke and Ella.

I see Apex.

I see the Angel.

They are one.

And I see myself stab them in the heart.

...

Jax and I have slept in the same bed before, but last night felt different. Everything feels different.

I didn't want to feel alone. "We've shared a bed before," I reminded him. "Just stay. Please."

I'm not sure how true that was, but it worked. He stayed, and I woke up this morning with his arm draped around me, the stubble of his cheek rubbing against my shoulder.

We've never crossed the friendship line, and we didn't last night either. But it was a form of comfort. A semblance of safety in a world that suddenly seems dangerous.

I dreamed of my parents last night, and for the briefest of moments, just as I was waking, for those few moments I forgot about what happened a week ago. Forgot that my parents are dead, that I'm homeless in a world I don't understand. I had them back, if just for a flicker of thought, and it felt so good. So happy.

Then the memories came crashing in, and reality destroyed that briefest of peace.

Jax has brought me clothes that fit and, for the last three days, he's asked me to explore the city with him. Each time I've said no, but today feels different. Today, I could use a distraction from the pain. It is still there, but duller than before, calmer. So now I stand at the gates of the Castle, dressed in borrowed clothes and borrowed shoes, my hair braided to one side, my treasures tucked into my pocket, ready to face New York City with Jax.

Jax is dressed in his Order's formal uniform, a cloak with the Teutonic symbol. His wolf pendant hangs around his neck, as always, but now he also wears his Teutonic Knight Order ring.

"You never went to a Castra Domus," I say. "When you left for summer, you came here."

"Yes."

I know he hates lying, hates knowing that it will be a long time before I stop scrutinizing the little, and big, discrepancies that now make up all my memories. My life has become a puzzle, broken into too many pieces to count, that I have to put back together, only it isn't making the right picture. It's making a new picture I don't recognize.

"Myrddin was a pat, wasn't he? That's how he knew the things he did."

Jax shrugs. "I don't know. I've suspected, even done research, but if Myrddin was a pat in hiding, then his files are sealed."

Though there is no proof, I am certain I am right. Myrddin knew what it meant to be part of the Orders, knew their corruption. It is why he trained me.

We don't take the car, as I expected. Instead, we walk into Vianney, the town, and head toward the sub-way. "How can we get to the mainland from the subway? We're on an island."

He smiles, a bit of boyish charm shining through the soldier. "You'll see. It's pretty incredible."

Incredible is an understatement.

We don't have subways where I grew up, but I remember going on one before the war, when I was little and my parents took me to New York for a family vacation. This is in a class all its own.

We cram into the train with several other students and some faculty, and with a rumbling and jerk, head underground.

But we soon find ourselves not just underground, but underwater.

Jax points to something and I follow his finger. "They built a tube from the mainland to the island, all underwater, and created the world's most advanced underwater subway." The walls of the train turn transparent, allowing us to see the underwater world around us. Fish swim by, ignoring the giant sea monster of humanity, but what most surprises me are the larger-than-life sculptures that line the bottom of the lake. It's an entire scene, humans and Zeniths and Nephilim, a re-creation of a battle during the Nephilim War, all made of stone.

"That's amazing!"

"A local artist created the statues, with permission from the Orders, to encourage coral reef growth. It certainly makes the commute interesting."

We arrive in New York faster than I would have thought, and I follow Jax out of the subway tunnel. I notice lines of soldiers at the entrance and exit of the tunnels, checking the IDs of all who enter, and I ask Jax about the security.

"Only students, staff, special guests, and those who live on the island as support are allowed in Castle V. Everyone who wants to ride this particular train has to be cleared first."

I step out of the tunnel and place my hand on a light post, my jaw comically unhinged. "New York has really changed since I was a kid," I say.

Jax laughs. "In more ways than you know."

My eyes follow a beautiful woman covered in leaves of reds and greens, the branches contouring to her body in such an organic way she looks part tree herself. She touches something behind her ear and suddenly her hair turns from brown to green. "Is she wearing an Eden Fashionable?" I've seen them on the eScreen. Once scientists figured out how to grow living plants into predetermined arrangements, architects, fashion designers and artists jumped on the possibilities. But it's pricey, too pricey for the town I grew up in.

Jax chuckles. "It's the latest style."

"And that hair color," I say. "Instant hair dye, what's the brand? EZ-Dye. I want one."

I study the dizzying landscape before me. Fairy Trees with glowing fruit line the sidewalks. People rush in and out of a giant mushroom, manipulated by Eden Architecture into a courthouse. Inquisition Officers police the streets in full armor, their faces covered, looking part future, part medieval. Zeniths walk around, tagged with their color-coded ear pieces.

Every Zenith has to register with the Zenith Registration Directive (ZRD). I've never had to because I never had zen abilities. But I do now. Will I be tested? I thought I was done with testing when I turned eighteen, but I have no idea what they'll want to do to me at Castle V.

I squeeze the light post, fear building inside of me. Maybe they should figure it out. Maybe then I'll know why I'm changing. Why I'm becoming something different.

I can feel it, this shift inside me. I couldn't eat breakfast; all week, the food tasted like ash in my mouth, but the LifeForce was like drugs to an addict. My senses are sharper, my healing faster, my body growing stronger. I try to hide it—to keep the truth from Jax, especially. Something changed me the night my parents died. Something to do with the weapon, but I don't know what, and I don't know if I can trust the Orders yet.

I pull my hand away from the light post.

There is a dent in the steel.

I tremble.

"Something wrong?" asks Jax.

"No," I say. And I grab his arm and rush us down the street.

...

The Fortuna Festival was always my favorite time of year back in the Kingdom of Sky. Until the year Ella and Brooke were sold to Apex. After, I would see Ella smelling the fairy flowers sold at the booths as I walked by, her ghostly memory forever stuck as a child on the day of her kidnapping. Or Brooke, biting into her third honey bread as if she'd never tasted anything like it. I learned later she hadn't.

That year, the fair seemed even more magical as I saw it through the eyes of my new friends. Now, it holds a special place in my heart. It was the last day of our childhood.

Though the memories fill me with melancholy, I appreciate the decadence and excitement of the festival.

I laugh out loud and Jax turns an eye to me. "What's funny?"

I wave my hand to the insanity around us. The streets of New York are packed with people in the most outrageous wardrobes I've ever seen. Not only have citizens EZ-Dyed their hair to change color throughout the day, but many people—men and women—have their armpit hair dyed and adorned with baubles of various sparkle. Some have even gone to the extreme of dying their skin to sparkle in purples, blues and pinks until they no longer look human, but like some strange alien from a world made of cotton candy. "Look at this," I tell him. "It makes Sky look plebeian."

Jax nods. "New York has a much higher ratio of patricians with Castle V."

"Everyone is so wealthy."

"Not everyone," he says, a shadow falling over his face.

We are impeded in our movements by the crushing crowd as they clear the streets for the coming parade, so instead of fighting we stop and watch the spectacle.

Men and women wearing thick furs and animal masks lead the parade. They are the tricksters and madmen, using fire and illusion to create magic as they fool the crowds with tricks and sleight of hand. They are masters of acrobatics, flipping and flinging themselves over the paved streets, tossing candy to cheering children as they do.

Next comes a float made of living fairy flowers. They glow with inner light and change colors, moving and swaying to their own rhythm. An enchanting song plays through hidden speakers, a seductive minor melody that a lithe girl dances to with fairy wings that look real. Her long red hair flies behind her as she performs moves that defy the human body, using a pole to climb higher for her more daring stunts.

The next wave comes thudding through the crowds with drumbeats of war and blood. They are warriors, dressed in armor with swords and banners. They dance a different kind of dance, light on their feet, but lethal, deadly. Sun flashes off metal as they move.

With each new performance I am mesmerized by the skill, costumes and effort that must have gone into creating this parade. Priests surround the final float, burning frankincense and chanting. A Knight rides in the center, surrounded by patrician children who kneel in prayer.

"That's Princess Tavora of York, Templar Knight of the Third," Jax says over the hum of the crowd. "She's being honored today with a Laurel from the Archbishop."

The Princess Knight stands tall, her sword held high like a warrior returning from battle. She's dressed in black armor and her hair is cropped short and grey, unusual for a woman of her ranking and age. She can't be much into her thirties. She scans the crowd and when she looks my way our eyes meet. Her dark eyes widen in recognition, then turn away.

"What did she do?" I ask.

"Helped secure another territory in Asia for Pope Icarus and the Four Orders."

I nod. The war is never over. If we're not trying to conquer Nephilim and Zeniths, we're trying to conquer each other.

"She will be promoted to a Knight of the Second today," Jax says, glancing at the Princess.

"You look up to her, don't you?" I ask.

He nods. "She is the fastest rising Knight of our time."

She does look young to be a Knight of the Second. All Knights start at the Ninth, and are promoted when the clergy deems fit. The Pope must always give approval. Some Orders, like Inquisition, don't even have a Knight of the First at the moment. No one has been found worthy.

We follow the Princess and her procession through the streets toward the Circus Maximus, an oval coliseum where big events are held and where she will receive her Laurel.

It's a long walk and Jax pulls me close to him as we navigate the crowds. "Have you given thought to what you will do now?" he asks.

"It's all I've thought about," I say.

"Star." He looks at me. "I want you to stay. Join the Orders with me. It's always been your dream. We can do it together."

"It *was* my dream," I admit. "But much has changed. The Orders are more corrupt than I imagined. My life is more complicated than I ever knew. It's a big choice to make."

"It's true," he says. "There is corruption. Where there are humans there is corruption. But we can change it from within. Make things right. Correct the path of the Orders so they use their power for good."

"Is that what you're trying to do? Fix it from within?" I'm still trying to figure out this man next to me. This patrician Knight who is also my best friend.

"Yes," he says. "Remember when we entered carving competitions together? It's like when you design a house. You may not get it right the first time, but you don't just walk away from it. You work on it, fix the mistakes, correct as you go."

I shake my head. "Sometimes the foundation is too corrupt," I say, using his analogy. "Sometimes the best thing you can do is tear it down and start from scratch."

"Your mother wanted you in the Orders," he says after a long silence.

My head whips around. "How do you know?"

His eyes are haunted. "She told me. I overheard her and Marcus arguing about it one night. Your dad was scared for you. He wanted you to have a safe life. A simple life. It's why he fought her about your education. But she wanted this for you."

I let his words settle in me. I was the main conflict between my parents before they died. "My grandfather wants me to stay so I can avenge them. You want me to stay to change things from within. My mom wanted me to follow her path as a Templar. My dad didn't want any of this for me. But what about what *I* want? It's my life."

He reaches for my hand. "You're right. It is. So, what do you want, Star?"

I swallow a lump in my throat. "I want my parents back."

For the rest of the ceremony, we are silent. Tavora gets the Laurel, and it is a simple thing of branches and leaves. Why, I wonder, is war worth such a thing?

...

When the ceremony is over, we leave the Circus Maximus and walk down the street. I notice the man in front of us has an earpiece marking him as a Zenith. An Inquisition Officer and his partner also notice and stop the man. "Random inspection," the first Officer says through his helmet.

The guy doesn't argue, but doesn't look happy either as they pat him down. No one around us even pauses, which tells me plenty about how common this is.

The second Officer checks his ID while the first one inspects his possessions and checks his pockets.

Helmet 1 shows his partner. "Elemental. Fire."

Helmet 2 pulls something out of the poor guy's pocket. "And lookie what I found. A lighter. That's an Unauthorized Item for a Burner."

"I'm on my way to register it," the guy says. "Please..."

I expect him to get ticketed, maybe even taken in and booked on some charge or other.

I don't expect Helmet 1 to shove his baton into the guy's gut and activate the electro shock.

The brutality of it freezes me in place, staring wide-eyed as the Zenith falls to his knees, shaking and vomiting.

"Attempting to manipulate an officer," Helmet 2 says.

The guy holds up one hand as he clutches his stomach with the other. "No. No, I wasn't..."

Helmet 2 hits him over the shoulders, crushing him to the ground. His chin hits the asphalt and cracks into splashes of red.

No one stops them.

No one comes to his aid.

People just walk on by, talking on their eGlass, checking messages, ignoring the violence in front of them, because to them Zeniths are not human. No one cares about this *man*—because, despite his abilities, he is still a *man*—being beaten in public for a minor infraction.

Memories of my last trip to this city surface in my mind. A man on the street beaten by soldiers. They wore different uniforms, you could still see their faces back then, but the scene was the same.

"Why doesn't anyone stop them, Dad?" I asked him, as I gripped his hand.

"Because they're afraid."

"Then I'll stop them." I dropped his hand, ready to rush forward, but he put his arm around my shoulder.

"No, Scarlett."

"I can fight," I told him.

"But you can't win."

"Then you stop them, Dad." I knew he could do anything.

"I can't," he said, his voice sad. "I'm afraid, too."

I balled my fists. "I'm not. And one day, when I'm big, I'll come back here, and I'll stop them. I'll win."

My dad chuckled and squeezed my shoulder with affection. "Remember, little Star, it's easy to fight, but much harder to know when. When to fight. When to win." His voice lowered. "When to lose."

"Why would I ever want to lose?"

He just smiled and ruffled my hair. "One day, I'll tell you."

He never did tell me. He never got the chance.

But this time, I will fight. And I will win. I walk up to the soldiers. "Leave him alone!"

They turn to me, batons raised. "Move along, citizen."

I don't budge. "Leave him." I think back to that night, when I took control of that one soldier. Maybe I can do it again, with them.

They walk toward me, ready to strike. "Disobeying an Inquisition Officer," Helmet 1 says.

I steel myself against potential attack as I stare at Helmet 2, willing him to obey me.

As Helmet 1 prepares to strike me with his baton, Jax puts himself between us. "At ease." He shows his ring. "She's under my protection."

Both Helmets step back immediately, almost cowering before Jax. "Apologies, Your Grace."

They turn their attentions back to the Zenith lying on the ground, still clutching his gut.

"Leave him with a warning," Jax says before I can intervene again. "I'll make sure he registers that lighter."

They don't even hesitate. "Of course, Your Grace," they say as they walk off, likely looking for another victim.

I hear them talking as they leave, awe in their voices. "A Knight," Helmet 1 says. "Yeah, a Teutonic Knight, no less," says Helmet 2.

Jax helps the Zenith stand. The man backs away quickly, bowing his head. "Thank you, Your Grace."

Jax grabs the man's lighter, drops it on the asphalt and crushes it with his foot. "Don't be an idiot," he says. "Request permission through the ZRD before you carry around items on your forbidden list."

"Yes, sir," says the man, stumbling away, his chin leaving a trail of blood.

I look down at the offending lighter and sigh. "All that for this?"

"He's registered as Elemental Fire," Jax says, a hardness in his tone I haven't heard before. "He could have used that lighter to kill us. Or blow up this entire street. Zeniths need to follow the law, just like everyone else."

"Then why'd you help him?"

He looks at me, his blue eyes full of secrets. "I didn't do it for him," he says, then continues walking.

He did that… for me?

...

I rush to keep up as we make our way through Times Square. In front of us, a large group gathers and a hush falls over the crowd as all the eScreens go blank and then light up with the same image. Live footage of what everyone has come to see—a platform surrounded by Inquisition Officers.

And I remember what was supposed to happen today.

"The Shadow of Rome," I whisper. When an Inquisitor was sent to hunt her down, she defeated him in single combat. She's the first Zenith to defeat a Knight since the Nephilim War. No one else had the strength. Not until the Shadow.

"What was she trying to accomplish?" I wonder out loud.

"Revenge," says Jax coldly. "Pope Icarus denies all requests to give Zeniths more rights. He used them as fodder during the war, and he, personally, ordered the extermination of every single Nephilim." He frowns. "She's a Zenith. She wanted him dead. Though her attack on the Vatican failed, the rebels still consider it a victory. The Inquisitors are trying to ensure they no longer see it as such."

"How'd they capture her?" The information wasn't in the news, but I suspect Jax knows.

"The Inquisitors trapped some of her rebel forces and used them as bait. When she attempted to rescue them, they surrounded her."

I push through the crowd to get a better look. Jax holds out his hand to stop me, but I continue on, curious to see this woman who incites such fear in the most ruthless of Orders.

She looks so... small, sitting on her knees on the stage, her head down, red hair falling in front of her face. The Shadow of Rome looks up, making eye contact with me, and I take a step back, shocked. She looks no older than me. How did she defeat the undefeatable?

An Inquisitor dressed in robes of red and gold and wearing the customary hat of his Order climbs to the stage and stands beside her. He carries a giant hammer in one hand. A hammer no mortal could lift. He turns to address the crowd, his face appearing on all the eScreens, and I recognize him. Ragathon. The Council member who didn't believe me.

"Citizens," he says, his voice amplified by unseen speakers, "this is the Zenith responsible for the deaths of your friends, your families. You may have heard her called many names. But I assure you, there is only one that matters. Criminal. Criminal!"

The crowd takes up the cheer. "Criminal!" "Zenith scum!" "Half-breed!" "Biter."

Even children are encouraged in their blood lust. It disgusts me, and I turn away from the stage and study these people who could so easily stand and watch someone die.

I notice, however, that not everyone in the crowd has raised their voices. A few people stand quiet, still. Waiting.

Behind us, a white truck moves through the crowd on a street otherwise blocked. Jax turns, worry lines marring his face. "I don't want to watch this," he says.

"Then you can go."

He growls at me, but stays by my side. He knows I won't budge once I set my mind to something.

There's a humming in the air. Not an audible noise, but an energy shifting. I have to stay. I know that much.

As Ragathon finishes the speech, the crowd erupts in cheers once again. I wait to see what the Council member will do. I expect a needle, not electrocution, considering the setting.

Instead, Ragathon raises his hammer.

I gasp. He's going to...

No!

He slams the hammer into the rebel's chest. In high-definition duplicate, on every eScreen around us, she cries out. Over and over, she screams as he hits her again and again.

She spits out blood, the red viscous fluid dribbling down her chin, marring her pretty face. A face that reminds me of another.

"How can he do this?"

"She killed an Inquisitor," says Jax. "She must be made an example of."

"You have to stop this," I tell him.

Jax bows his head without saying a word, and I understand. Of course he can't stop this. The Inquisitor was one of the Council Members. No one can stop him now.

Unless...

If I can get close enough to him... if I can take control, just for a moment, maybe...

I push further into the crowd, positioning myself closer and closer to the stage as Ragathon takes evident joy in hurling his hammer at the young woman.

A ringing buzzes in my ear, power pooling in me. Jax calls my name, but his voice sounds distant, as if he speaks through water.

I hesitate as several Inquisition Officers walk toward me.

Wha—

But they walk past me, waving their hands, shouting. "No vehicles here!" "This road is closed off!"

I turn to look back. The white truck I saw earlier has made it closer to the platform, and it continues on, driving slowly, not stopping.

Something's going on.

I look around and notice one of the guys I saw before, someone who wasn't cheering along with everyone else.

He wears a heavy cloak, though it isn't cold.

He keeps a hood over his head, but a ray of sun catches the copper highlights in his hair, the green specks in his eyes. He turns around and looks straight at me.

And smiles.

THE SHADOW OF ROME

Something flies above me and smoke fills the air, obscuring my vision of the smiling man. Someone has fired smoke guns. The man runs into the smoke, and I follow, covering my nose and mouth with my shirt to avoid choking.

People run in all directions, screaming, crying, gagging as they inhale the smoke-filled air around them. Jax tries to follow me, calling my name as I dodge through the crowd, but too many people get between us, and the smoke obstructs his view of me. I don't know why I chase the mystery man, don't know why it's important that Jax not follow me, but I've long believed in trusting my instincts, and I do so now.

Trust what's in your heart, little Star. No one else knows the right path for you but you.

My dad's words rattle in my mind as gunfire breaks out around me. Real guns, with bullets instead of smoke.

Near me, a woman falls to the ground, a red pool of blood spreading over her chest as her husband and child try to drag her out of harm's way.

Bile rises in my throat as I drop to my knees, staring in horror as people die around me or are wounded by indiscriminate firing from those commissioned to protect the innocent. The Inquisition.

I know then what I have to do.

If I can get to the Head Inquisitor, Ragathon—if I can find him, I can use whatever power is growing in me to stop him.

I crawl through the smoke, trying to orient myself, and knock against two dead bodies lying side by side. A man in black—a rebel—and an Inquisition Officer. They must have killed each other.

I grab the eGlass from the rebel and slip it over my ear, crouching low to avoid getting shot as I listen.

The eGlass comes to life. "The Inquisitor is down," a male voice says. Is that true? Can it be that easy?

I hear more gunshots, more screams. "Wait," the voice says, in my ear. "Oh God, he's alive. Pull back. Get the Shadow to the truck."

So they plan to use the white truck to rescue the Shadow of Rome.

I search the dead Officer, remove his helmet, take his eGlass and put it on my other ear. The commanding voice I hear belongs to Ragathon. Who is definitely not dead.

"Exit stage one. Block off the designated roads," he says.

Stage one? Designated roads? This has all been a trap. The Inquisitors expected this rescue and planned for it. All the rebels will be captured or killed.

I can't let that happen. I don't know if the rebels are the bad guys or not, but I know the Inquisitors aren't good. At least, Ragathon isn't, and he's the one in charge. Looking at the carnage around me, knowing the Inquisitors planned this, allowed for this, didn't care that so many innocents would get caught up in their trap... it tempers me with anger.

I need to get to a computer.

With both the rebels and Inquisitors chattering in my ears, I scan the area, walking low through dead bodies and destroyed property around the buildings. Nothing. Everyone's evacuating.

But wait... through the crowd, parked by the central eScreen, is a giant white tank-like van with a stylized all-seeing eye painted in black. An Inquisition vehicle. A Bruiser. They'd have a computer in there.

I scramble across Times Square just as an Inquisition Officer approaches the van. He's about to get in. If I want to help save the Shadow of Rome, I have to act now.

I launch myself at the Officer, knocking him into the van.

"What the—?" He flips around, his gun drawn and ready to shoot.

I grab his arms and push my mind into his. I expect it to feel like before, like it did with the soldier at my house, where I became him and me at the same time.

But this is different. Softer. More subtle. His consciousness tickling the edges of my mind, pliable and open.

"Sleep!" I tell him, my mind pushing out the command as much as my voice.

He collapses against me, and I grab his eGlass and replace the one I had. I let the man fall to the ground, then use his eGlass synch to unlock the Bruiser.

Inside, the vehicle has controls and buttons I don't understand yet. But there's also a computer built into the dash, with multiple screens.

I know if I can hack into the city's surveillance system, I can access all the cameras and see what's going on anywhere in New York.

But that's easier said than done. The Four Orders have the strongest firewalls in the world, designed specifically to keep out people like me.

Well, maybe not people exactly *like me*, I think with a grin.

It takes longer than I'd have liked, but I get in. I pump my fist in the air and furiously type as I zoom in on the cameras I need.

I can see the rebels helping the Shadow into their white van. They drive off, and with a click I access their street, which is already blocked off.

I click the rebel eGlass. "They were ready for you," I tell whoever's listening.

"Who is this?" A guy asks.

"Someone trying to help. The road ahead is blocked off. You have to take a right."

He swears under his breath. "Right into the Inquisition's hands, no doubt. I'm not falling for your lies."

"If you don't listen to me, then you're all dead." I check the cameras. "A squad of Officers is about to cut you off from the left. They're using thrusters."

"How on earth do you know—" His voice cuts off, and on the camera I see the squad position itself in front of the van. Black-clad rebels stick their heads out of the windows, guns first, and shoot down the Officers before they ever have a chance to counter maneuver.

My eGlass comes to life. "Crap. She was right," says the guy.

A new voice, female, speaks. "Listen, whoever this is. Where's the next squad coming from?"

"Left again," I tell her, checking the cameras.

I can hear gunfire through the eGlass and see it on the screen as the rebels shoot down the squad as soon as it comes out of the alley.

"Thanks," the woman says.

"Why are you helping us?" asks the first guy.

Why? Is it because I'm now Zenith, with some unnamed power that makes me different? Or because my parents disagreed with the Inquisition? Or is it because of that woman, that wife and mother, gunned down in front of her husband and child as they pulled her lifeless body away from the carnage? Or maybe it's the voice of my father in my head telling me to trust what's in my heart.

"She can tell us later," the woman says, and a light bulb goes off in my head.

"You're the Shadow of Rome," I say.

"Call me Trix... the grump you've been talking to is TR. What should I call you?"

I can't give my real name. And I don't want to use my dad's nickname for me. So I use the first thing that comes to mind. "N."

"N. Alright. What's next, N?"

I check my monitors. "You have to go right. It's the only path open."

"How could they have mobilized so quickly?" asks TR.

"They're doing the same thing they did in Boston when they captured me," says Trix. "They knew you'd show up. They're trying to end us once and for all."

TR swears under his breath again.

Trix speaks through the eGlass. "Alright. N, I trust you. More like, I *have* to trust you." She pauses, and I hear movement in the background. "We're going right."

On my screens, the van turns the corner. I switch cameras to view the other streets around them and see a Bruiser headed their way. Crap.

I set my Bruiser's GPS to that intersection and press the button to activate the eDriver. "Preparing to travel to East 48th street and Second Avenue," the GPS says. "Assessing traffic and road blocks. Estimated time of arrival, two minutes."

The Bruiser begins to move, and I speak into the eGlass. "Keep turning right," I tell them as my fingers fly over the keyboard.

"That'll take us in a circle," says TR.

"They're tracking your movements the same way I am," I tell him. "The best you can do is confuse them."

"Let's do it," says Trix.

They turn, then turn again... making a loop around the block. The Bruiser on their heels adjusts for their change in routes and is about to come out in front of them. Before it can, I override the eDriver, take control of the wheel, and crash into the other Bruiser from the side, sending it slamming into a nearby building, and sending my head slamming against the seat, knocking me a bit senseless. I take a deep breath, and feel a wave of intense... hunger? Or thirst? A gnawing ache in my gut overcomes me. But I have to ignore it and focus. The Bruiser's GPS blinks at me, the voice now scratchy, likely rattled from the crash. "We have sustained damage. Please pull over to the nearest—"

I turn off the GPS and its annoying voice. I have enough voices in my head right now.

The rebel van drives by.

"I'm assuming that was you," says Trix over the eGlass.

"Yes. Now, head for the outskirts."

"They keep cutting us off," says TR. "Time for plan B."

"I agree," says Trix.

"What's plan B?" I ask, massaging a flare of pain in my upper jaw.

"Wait and see," says TR.

Smoke surrounds their van until they're obscured entirely by white. As it clears, the van drives forward, and a new truck, a black and red Bruiser, turns right.

So they have one of their own and they're using it to get Trix away. The van is a decoy.

But...

It's too obvious.

"Your plan's not going to work..." I say into my eGlass.

"How would you know?" argues TR.

"The Bruiser is just a distraction. Trix is still in the truck."

"That..." TR doesn't finish his sentence, because he knows I guessed their plan. A double decoy.

"The Inquisition is closing down all roads out of New York... they were ready for you." My voice rises with urgency. "Your plan failed before you even started. But... there's one way. Listen to me, and I'll get you out alive."

"You'll just lead us into a trap," TR says, and I want to smack him through the eGlass.

Before I can respond, Inquisition vehicles surround the black and red decoy Bruiser. It crashes and is instantly swarmed with Officers checking to see if anyone's inside.

"Bruiser down," says one of the rebels through the eGlass.

"Damn it," says TR.

"You're already trapped," I tell him.

"We'll do it your way," says Trix.

"But—"

She cuts TR off. "But nothing. She's been right about everything, and we need to get out of here." Trix sounds tired, in pain, and when she coughs I remember the beating she just took. She needs a doctor. "What's the plan, N?" she asks, after a coughing spasm leaves her breathless.

And so I fill them in on my idea, my brain spinning fast as it weaves through the ins and outs of what I want them to do. I try not to think about the lives on the line, about how this is treason, and I could be executed if I'm caught. Instead, I pretend this is a training exercise with Myrddin. I can do this.

"We'll never have enough time," TR says when I finish.

"I'll give you time," I say.

"Fine, let's do it," says Trix. They turn the truck around and head toward the center of the city instead of out.

I drive my damaged Bruiser back to the sleeping Officer and then pull him into the back of the truck. I expected it to be harder to lift him, between the bulk of his body and the weight of his gear, but he turns out to be surprisingly light, and it only takes a few moments, hidden within the truck, to pull off his uniform and slip it on over my own borrowed clothes. I put his helmet on and can see a display of the action through the eGlass all the Officers are looped into. The Inquisition has the rebel van surrounded. They have no way out.

Disguised in the Officer's uniform, I run toward the portable command center the Inquisition set up.

A giant Bruiser, big enough for more than a dozen people, with a cannon on top. My body aches and the blood around me, pooling under dead bodies and leaking through fabric, should be making me sick. All those lifeless victims. Instead, I feel a deep hunger despite my anger and outrage, and I feel physically weak, shaky, and so tired, but I keep pushing myself toward the command center.

I climb into the back, faking a calm authority I do not feel. *Remember, little Star, if you look like you know what you're doing, people will assume you do.*

My dad's memory gives me the confidence I need to pull this off. There are half a dozen other Officers in the command center, each actively engaged in surveillance. None of them stop me.

The Head Inquisitor sits in the very back at his computer, an Officer guarding him.

On my eGlass, the Inquisitor's voice speaks as Bruisers filled with Officers surround the rebel van. "There's no way out. Surrender now."

I walk toward Ragathon, who's still speaking into his eGlass, broadcasting his voice to the rebels and his own troops.

The Officer guarding him tries to stop me, but I grab his arm and focus my powers, giving his mind just a nudge, enough to make him forget about me. *I'm not important. I'm supposed to be here. Disregard my presence.*

It works, but it costs me. I slump against the wall as a wave of dizziness threatens to topple me over. What's happening to me? And why now? At the worst possible time.

The Officer moves to the side and ignores me. I look at the Inquisitor. He sits without his helmet, and I can see the blood pulsing in the vein of his neck. The sweat staining the collar of his uniform.

My stomach clenches again.

He looks up at me, but I know he can't see my face. "What are you doing here, Officer?"

I have to make contact before he has time to get away, to take me out. I don't speak. Don't think, just lunge for him, flipping my body over the table that stands between us until I have him pinned against me.

I can hear an Officer in his eGlass speaking. "Sir, the rebels have surrounded the truck with smoke. Should we move in, sir?"

I push my will into him, waiting to feel that control I felt before.

It doesn't happen.

Instead, Ragathon fights back, knocking me to the side. I am too weak to infiltrate his mind.

My helmet falls off, and he looks down at me as recognition spreads on his face. Then he smiles. "You."

Oh no. This can't be happening. Not only have I failed the mission, but he now knows who I am. I'll die for this for sure, and there's no way Jax can save me.

Hunger burns in my throat, tearing at me from within.

The weakness in me turns to raw need. I push myself up and toward him, knowing I have to take him out before anyone else sees.

My mouth aches, teeth burning as I crash into him.

And then, instinct takes over. The pulse of his throat casts a web around me, and my teeth sink into his flesh. Warm, coppery fluid fills my mouth, pouring down my throat, quenching the need I didn't know I had. Satiating the craving that's slowly been weakening me and my powers.

I feel it all return. My power, my strength, my mental clarity. Everything.

And before his pulse stops for good, before he dies in my arms, I pull away, his blood dripping from my lips. I still need him to save the rebels.

Ragathon is finally under my control. He doesn't move, doesn't speak, doesn't even blink. I reach for the helmet and put it back on, hiding my identity once again.

"Sir? Should we move in?" asks the Officer again through the eGlass. "Alright, I'm making the call. Move—"

"No," I say. But it's not me speaking. I speak through Ragathon. "Stand your ground. Let's see what they do."

I can hear the uncertainty in the Officer's voice. "But... Sir, yes, sir."

In my video feed, the smoke clears, and the rebel van is still there.

I smile, and I realize it's actually my face smiling, not Ragathon, but I can still feel his mind in mine, feel his consciousness merged with my own.

Or maybe I've merged with him. I can't tell. It all feels the same.

"Move in," I make him say.

The Officers obeys instantly, seizing control of the rebel van and searching it in moments. "Sir, they're gone! Sir, what should we do?"

Of course they are. While under the cover of smoke, they escaped down into the sewers. Maybe Ragathon could figure it out, but unfortunately for him, I'm still in control.

"Nothing. Do nothing, Officer. Pull back."

On screen, the Officers are still for a moment, and I worry they suspect something askew in headquarters. But they are well-trained puppets, and they do as told by their commander, pulling back.

I won.

We won.

I hold up my gun and point it at the Inquisitor. I can kill him right now. It would be so easy to pull the trigger and end him.

I start to squeeze the trigger, but my mind flashes with images and memories not my own.

His memories.

I'm bending down talking to a little girl in blond braids holding a red ball. "Do you have to go to work, daddy?"

I—he—nods. "Yes, my little lily. But today, daddy is going to end the fighting. After today, things are going to be easier. Trust me."

"Okay." The girl runs off, her yellow sundress billowing behind her as she bounces the ball in front of her.

My hand shakes. My stomach cramps. I lower my gun. He could be useful, I tell myself. He could still serve a purpose down the line.

I clutch the gun in my hand and walk through the door, then out the command center. I refuse to think about that little girl looking so lovingly up at her father.

In my eGlass, Trix speaks. "We made it. Thanks, N."

"Don't thank me," I say. "I'm done."

A TEUTONIC KNIGHT

I toss the two eGlasses aside and ditch the helmet when someone tugs at my arm. I swing around, my heart beating against my chest in loud thumps, ready to fight off whoever's touching me.

"Scarlett, relax, it's just me!" Jax lets go of my arm and puts his hands up. "Are you okay?"

I nod, slowing my breath as I relax. "Yes, I'm fine. Where have you been? I've been looking everywhere for you," I lie.

"Trying to find you. The whole area's been quarantined. Something happened with the Inquisitor, and everyone's in a panic. The rebels escaped. We have to get out of here."

"Of course."

He looks me over and frowns. "Why are you wearing an Officer's uniform?"

"There was gunfire everywhere. I didn't want to be mistaken for a rebel, so I grabbed this from one of the dead Officers, figuring it would offer me some protection."

"Good thinking. A lot of innocent people lost their lives today." Jax looks more closely at me. "You have blood on your mouth."

I wipe it away quickly. "People were shot around me. Blood sprayed. It was awful." I want to feel disgust for what I did, but the blood has restored me, and done more than that. It's given me a dark clue as to what I'm becoming.

Jax holds up my arm, his mouth a line of concern. "You're bleeding."

As the adrenaline leaves my body, a dull pain replaces the euphoria. I look at my bicep. "I must have scratched it on something. I'm fine." Or I will be soon. I can already feel it healing.

He tugs at my other hand and leads me to a vacant building, where we sit in a corner and wait for the fighting outside to die down so we can go back to Castle V.

Exhaustion hits me—emotional more than physical—and I rest my head against the cement wall.

Jax moves closer to me, his face a mask. "Scarlett, are you okay? You look... different."

"Probably just hungry," I say. Though that's not true. For the first time since I woke up on the broken and empty crystal box, I don't feel hungry or physically worn out. I feel powerful, revived, restored.

He digs into his pocket and pulls out a LifeForce. "Drink this. It should help."

I don't want it, don't need it. The blood has done more to quench my hunger than a hundred LifeForce pouches can do, but I drink it to make him happy.

He grazes a finger over my cheek, a half-smile on his handsome face. "You look better. You have color back in your face for the first time since... last week."

"What happened today?" I ask, changing the subject.

His face hardens. "Someone screwed up. I should have been told about this. I never would have chosen today to take you to the city if I'd known."

"Jax, why are you a part of the Orders? How can you support what happened today? The public executions. The beatings. The whole thing was obviously a trap to catch the rebels, which means the Inquisition knew innocent people would die today, and they didn't care."

He leans back against the wall, our shoulders pressed together, knees and thighs touching. "I didn't know, Star. I didn't know. This operation was likely kept secret by the Council."

"And that secret is killing innocent people. How can you trust the Orders? How can you trust anyone at Castle V?"

"I can't," he says, surprising me with his answer. "I didn't join the Orders because they're perfect. I joined because I can make them better." He turns his head to look at me. "I remember how we used to turn on the eScreen when our parents were out and watch the beatings. I remember talking with you about how wrong it was. But breaking the law isn't the way to change things. The Shadow of Rome and her rebels are just as responsible for this destruction as the Inquisition. They shouldn't have rebelled, they should have joined a Domus, changed the way people think with words, and eventually, changed the law."

"No one listens to a zen," I say, slipping into low speech. I think it is because Brooke is on my mind.

He looks away and stares at his hands. "That's not true," he says softly. He doesn't elaborate.

I stand and pace in front of him, frustration growing in my body. "No Zenith will ever be promoted to a patrician. If they want power, they have to take it."

He stands, reaching for me. "You're wrong, Scarlett."

I don't agree. Not after everything I've seen.

"We need to head back to the Castle," he says.

I nod and follow Jax into the streets.

The city is in chaos, the people rioting. Zeniths, rebels and the Orders, everyone blends into the anarchy that ensues. New graffiti has already appeared on the walls: paint crossing out Order signs with *Free the Zeniths* marked over them. Over one Apex Crest is a painting of a bomb exploding with body parts spraying everywhere. People are furious. The world is controlled by its collective anger.

I want to say something to Jax, to continue our conversation about Zeniths, but something hits the back of my head and I cry out in pain. Jax turns, a look of concern on his face. "What happened?"

I hold up my hand, showing him a small smear of blood.

We look around and see a young man down the street, surrounded by a whirl of air as objects around him go flying through the air. He stands with his hands covering his face. A metal trash container flies into nearby pedestrians, knocking them to the ground. People begin screaming. One man tries to attack him and is thrown brutally against a wall, where he slumps to the floor, unconscious.

Jax clicks on his eGlass and speaks quietly into it. "We have a situation. A level five Gravir is out of control. Send backup." He gives our cross streets, then we move closer to the Gravir, crouching behind a parked car for protection. "Star, stay here. He's dangerous."

Two Inquisition Officers hide behind a nearby car. One of them peeks over the hood, aiming at the Gravir.

"No," yells Jax. "Stay back and help anyone who is injured."

The Officer hesitates. "We need to subdue—"

Jax flashes his ring.

"Apologies, Sir. Of course."

A Knight of the Fourth wields a lot of power.

I'm looking around, assessing the situation, trying to find a way to be useful. Dozens of people flee the nearby buildings and alleys. The young man becomes more agitated. He yells, and the concrete cracks around him. A motorcycle launches through the air, crashing through a large window. Low moans emanate from the Gravir as more and more people are caught in his crossfire. His range is impressive, and deadly. I'm worried for Jax, who can't possibly stop him without getting hurt.

And then Jax dashes across the street to push a woman out of the way of a flying Streetbot. He moves so fast! Too fast.

Before I can blink he's moving again, toward a damaged balcony that's collapsing. A young girl is sliding off of it, and Jax... he... flies? He's in the air, moving through space. He doesn't have wings, or anything propelling him, but his body flies toward the girl and he catches her mid-air, before she falls to the ground.

How is he doing this? In and out he dashes through flying objects, saving people, rescuing those crushed by the crumbling buildings around us.

The destruction continues. Windows shatter. Lamps explode. The Gravir's abilities are escalating. He's going to take down this entire block. There will be no way to save everyone. I have to stop him.

I run through the crowds, through the Officers trying to mitigate the damage without getting hit themselves, through the debris flying around us. Jax calls something out to me, but I can't hear him and I can't take time to stop and listen. Too many lives are at stake.

A piece of a lamp pole nearly hits me in the face. I duck to the right, then tackle the young man to the ground. Once my palm connects with his bare arm, I am in his mind.

His name is Peter Conley. He is a student in a zen school, sitting at his desk when his books and papers begin to fly around the room. The teacher is screaming at him to leave, that he's too dangerous, too out of control. And then he is here, in the aftermath of the Shadow of Rome escape. He's being beaten by Officers who accuse him of being a rebel. He's scared. He thinks they will kill him. His gravotics grow in him, overflow. He can't stop it. He doesn't know how to control himself. It's self-defense when his abilities push the Officers away, but they keep coming and now he can't rein his abilities in.

I use my mind to calm his, to tell him it's okay, that's he's safe. I reach into his abilities and use my own training to settle him as I hold him.

The chaos ends as quickly as it began. Objects drop from the air. Buildings stop collapsing. It gets quieter, save for the crying from the injured and scared.

Jax lands beside us, and Officers come to grab the man, who is really just a boy. They stick a needle into his arm. Z-blockers, drugs that limit zen abilities for a time. They are expensive and very difficult to make. They are only used for the most extreme cases.

He is pulled away, his head down, but he is still calm. Jax reaches for my hand, pulling me off the cement. "Are you okay?"

"Yes, I'm fine." I dust dirt off myself, then give up, knowing it's a hopeless cause. "He didn't hurt me. He was just scared. He couldn't control his gravotics."

Jax cups my face, wiping a smudge of dirt off my cheek. "You shouldn't have run into the danger zone like that."

"I had to help," I say. "What will happen to him now?"

Jax starts walking, and I keep pace beside him. He seems distracted as he answers. "He'll be charged and probably convicted for the crimes of assault and damage to public property."

"But it wasn't his fault. This is why Zeniths need to be trained and not forced to keep their abilities buried like some shameful secret."

Jax stops and looks at me. "Star, he is a level five Gravir. Do you understand what that means? How powerful that makes him? If he'd been trained he could have killed us all."

"If he'd been trained, he could have avoided hurting anyone. He wouldn't have attacked anyone in the first place if he'd known how to control his abilities."

"You don't know that. We can't know his mind." He looks sad as he says this, and I know he doesn't mean to sound as heartless as his arguments come across.

I bite my lip, trying to think of a way to make him understand. I obviously can't tell him that I could in fact read his mind. But... I don't have to read his mind to know some things. "Jax, think about it. The majority of people aim to create order. Otherwise, society would fall into anarchy. This is proven throughout history. No leader or organization could keep control of a group of people intent on chaos. Most of us want to do the right thing. We want society to work and function well for everyone. Zeniths are no different. You might have a few biters but, for the most part, Zeniths want society to function well. They want to control their abilities and be contributing, valued members of this world. If more were trained, they'd do more good than bad."

Jax walks again and I pick up my pace to keep up. He doesn't say anything for a long time. When he does speak, it is softly. "It would only take a few with great power to cause great harm."

My heart sinks. He still doesn't understand.

But then he continues. "But, they can also cause great change."

I shake my head, not sure what to make of my best friend. I think of how he dashed around to save so many people. How he defied gravity to save that girl on the balcony. And then I realize the truth.

I stop and turn to him, forcing him to stop and look at me.

"You're Zenith."

It's not a question. Because I know.

Everything he said about Zeniths being able to make a difference, his ability to fly, it makes sense now. What Jax did was impossible, and yet he did it. I stand, stunned, staring at this boy I've known my whole life. He's one of the highest ranking members of any Order.

And he's a Zenith.

GIRL OF SILVER

We don't use the underwater subway to return to Castle V. Jax acquires an Order vehicle somehow while I remove the Inquisition armor, and we cross over the bridge from Manhattan to the island. We're stopped by two armed Teutonic guards to show ID, but as soon as they recognize Jax they let us through. They don't even raise an eyebrow at the amount of blood staining us both.

We drive in silence for a while, until I ask the question that's been on my mind since seeing him fight. "How are you a Zenith? I remember you getting tested in sixth grade, a few years before me. You passed."

"I didn't pass, Scarlett."

"But you're a pureblood."

"I *didn't pass*," he says slowly, as if I missed something. I think over his words, and slowly, I begin to peel away a lie.

"There are Zenith patricians," I say.

He says nothing, but there is no need. I am right. There are pats who are also zens, but they never are tested, they never wear tags in their ear or go to zen schools. They hide their taint, or explain it away with a GenMod. Are GenMods even real, I wonder? It feels odd to question such simple things, but that's the way they want it. The pats have drilled their lies deep in my mind. It will take time to dig them out.

I ask Jax about the mods, and he tells me they are true. "All patricians undergo a level one andronics mod," he says, pausing. "They do it when you turn eighteen." He glances at me with worried eyes. I don't know why, until I remember what I am.

"And if I don't want a mod?" I ask.

His voice is that of a pat, cold and distant. "Patricians are stronger than plebeians. That is the way it has been, that is the way it must be."

I shiver at the prospect of having my body modified, but isn't this what I wanted? Isn't this what I dreamed of?

"Are there many like you?"

"No. Patrician blood was pure for a time. But, over many years, hidden bloodlines and illegal mating changed things. The patricians had succumbed to darkness just like plebeians, and if people knew, our right to rule would be challenged, and there would be chaos. So, we kept it a secret. Any patrician born a

Zenith keeps their taint hidden and explains it with a GenMod if needed. It is how we keep the peace."

I scoff. "Why keep the taint hidden at all?"

"Patricians believe in earning power," he says. "We do not rule because we are born pure, but because our ancestors chose to remain pure. We do not rule because we are stronger, but because we created a way to be stronger. A patrician should only have the power they earn."

"Hence you keep your taint hidden from plebs," I finish, nodding. "Because how would you explain a Knight of the Fourth having better GenMods than a Knight of the First."

"Exactly." He speeds up, and I see Vianney Island on the horizon.

"How did you become a Knight of the Fourth? How could you possibly get so high so young?"

"Five years ago, at the end of the Nephilim War, I was on a mission for the Orders," he says. "I killed one of them, a young girl... though I'm sure she only looked young. The Orders gave me a medal, a promotion. They placed me on a pedestal for young recruits to admire. I didn't deserve it, but that was then."

I think back to those dark times. I thought we were safe from the fighting, and I can't believe Jax was not. He'd gone to war, seen so much carnage, and had never been allowed to talk about it, even to me. What that must have done to him.

"That mission, is that when your father died?"

"Yes," he says slowly. He does not say more.

I touch his hand. "I'm sorry."

He smiles gently, but there's no happiness in his eyes. We are quiet for a few minutes, before he speaks again. "Now that I'm no longer your protector, I can act publicly on behalf of my Order. It's what I've needed to progress, to become a Knight of the First."

"Most never make it that far." I've only heard of a few who ever had. All Knights start as the Ninth, and many don't get higher than the Sixth.

"I will," Jax says with such determination I actually believe him.

We make it over the bridge and drive through the small streets of Vianney until we arrive at the castle. Jax hands the keys off to one of the front gate guards and we walk back into what feels like my prison. "I need to see the Chancellor," I tell him.

He nods and walks me to the Chancellor's room as his eGlass blinks. He listens, says "Okay" and then clicks it off. "I have to go, Scarlett." He kisses my cheek, and suddenly I don't want him to go. I don't want to feel so alone in this scary new world.

"In case I don't see you tonight, sleep well. I know they'll be setting you up in your own room, but you're welcome in mine any time. I've already set the lock to your thumbprint."

As he walks away, I call to him. "Jax?"

He turns. "Yes, Star?"

My heart clenches. "What you did for all those people today… it was good. You're a good person."

He stares into my soul for a long moment, our eyes locked, and then he bows his head to me. "Thank you. I hope you're right."

He turns and leaves, his footsteps loud against the stone floors.

…

I stand alone by the Chancellor's door, about to knock, when I hear voices raised inside. I put my ear closer to listen.

"I almost had them." It sounds like the Head Inquisitor.

"But you don't have them, Ragathon," the Chancellor responds. "And now the whole city is afraid." I hear someone pace through the office. "You should never have kept this from the Council."

So not even the Council knew of this plan. I wondered why the Chancellor, my grandfather, didn't warn Jax.

"I acted under my own discretion. The rebels have spies—"

"Not within the Council." The Chancellor's voice sounds loud, fed up.

"Of course, Chancellor." He almost sounds contrite. Almost.

"Ragathon, you push my patience. You may go and attend to the other matter we discussed, and we shall discuss the consequences of your actions tomorrow."

Footsteps. Then the door opens, and I nearly fall through it. I back away quickly, but Ragathon notices me, his beady eyes staring at me in contempt, a black scarf wrapped around his neck, hiding the evidence of my feeding. "Listening in on Council matters is an offense punishable by flaying, girl."

I straighten my spine and stare him down, relieved he doesn't remember seeing my face. "Do you still use a whip, or is it a hammer these days?"

He frowns. "You insolent—"

"Ragathon," interrupts the Chancellor from inside. "I'm sorry, but Scarlett and I have a meeting."

"So you called her here?"

"Of course I did. Now, if that's all?"

"That's all, Chancellor." Ragathon scowls, and I'm pretty sure if he could challenge me to a duel right now, he would. And he'd likely poison his blade for extra measure.

"Good. Come along, Scarlett." The Chancellor guides me into his chambers as Ragathon walks away, probably still scowling and plotting my untimely demise. No love lost between the two of us, that's for sure.

My Grandfather's chamber is large and smells like lemon wood polish and old books. In the corner is a giant sculpture of two Knights on a horse, which stands on its hind legs as if in a fight. I study the details carved into marble.

"Godfrey de Saint-Omer and Hugues de Payens, founders of the Knights Templar," the Chancellor says.

"Why are they on the same horse?"

"An old Templar symbol. It reminds us of our humble beginnings, when two Knights could only afford one horse."

I follow him to two chairs positioned before a large, blazing fire. On a rug between us sits a fat white cat, content to slumber in front of the warmth. Red banners hang over the windows and old leather books stored in bookcases line the walls. It is the kind of room I would have, if I could afford one.

The Chancellor turns in his chair to face me as he pours us each a cup of tea from a pot. "First, let me apologize for what you endured today. As I gather you surmised, Ragathon kept his plans secret from us all."

I accept the cup of tea and blow on it. "And he's allowed to get away with that? No consequences despite mass innocent casualties and the ultimate failure of his mission?"

The Chancellor's blue eyes reflect golden flames from the fire as he smiles at me intimately. "You're so like your mother, you know that?"

"I look like her, but take after my father."

He shakes his head. "I see Marcus in you as well, of course, but your mother, she was always fire, ready to fight for the innocent and hold accountable anyone in power who failed to do the same."

"That doesn't answer my question," I remind him.

"No, I suppose it doesn't. It's a simple question with a difficult answer. I do not have autonomous power in the Orders. I'm just one voice. The others have their own kind of power, Ragathon especially. He has the favor of the Pope right now, and that's no small thing. I have to tread carefully to accomplish my goals. That's why I need you, Scarlett. That's why we need each other."

Pieces begin to fit together. Why he needs me when he rules the Orders. He has to play politics. I don't. I won't. I can indeed be his weapon.

"What did you want to see me about?" he asks.

"Has there been any news about my home?"

"The Inquisition has finished their investigation."

"And?"

"And they found nothing but blood, Scarlett."

My heart falls to my feet. "What about my parents?"

"Gone, I'm afraid." He looks back at the flames, his expression raw, lost in thought.

What did the Nephilim do with my parents' bodies? "That thing has them," I say, disgust lacing my voice. Disgust and anger.

"What once were your parents, yes. But they live in our memories now, and our hearts."

There has to be more at my house. Has to be.

"My parents..." I haven't been able to talk about this, to think about it, but... "My parents were Zeniths."

"I see you have learned our secret. Yes, they were. Your mother tested so at a very young age."

My mother. He has her eyes. Or she has his. Had his. Eyes like mine. I have to get home. Tonight. I have to find something that can lead me to the Nephilim. *And when I find the monster who ruined my life, I will be ready.*

"Where did it come from? The Nephilim. I thought they were extinct?"

He raises his bushy white eyebrow at me. "You assume it was Nephilim you saw. How do you know?"

"What else could it have been?" It admittedly looked different, but I know what I saw.

"Nephilim aren't the only beings borne to the sky."

His words take a moment to sink in, and my jaw drops. "Are you talking about Angels?"

He doesn't answer, just sips at his tea.

"They haven't been seen on earth in ages. They don't exist anymore, if they ever did."

"Oh my dear granddaughter, the world is full of mysteries humans believe no longer exist. Consider what you saw that night. Consider it carefully. There's more to what happened to my daughter, your parents, than meets the eye."

I drink my tea in silence, thinking about that night, which seems so very long ago. Could it be? Does that explain the differences I noticed? An Angel. A real Angel. What could this mean? My mind races with possibilities, options, choices, and my grandfather seems content to wait until I sort my thoughts out.

"I have one condition," I finally say. "One condition to joining the Orders."

The Chancellor interlaces his fingers. "Go on."

"Tell me what the weapon is."

He looks into the fire again, thoughtful. "What do you know of the Nephilim?"

"They could fly," I say, knowing it gave them a large advantage when the War started. "Some of them had other abilities, commonly seen in Zeniths today. However, they were different from other Zeniths, because they fed on blood, and they could turn others into their kind." I remember the propaganda... about killing the bloodsuckers, protecting your children from monsters... protecting your souls from the demons. I shudder, knowing how this conversation will end, knowing what it will confirm once and for all.

"And which one of their abilities do you think was the most dangerous?" he asks.

"Turning others," I say without hesitation. It's worse, even, than flying. It gave the Nephilim huge numbers, more easily replenished than soldiers who needed years to train.

The Chancellor nods. "It was their greatest power. Our own council considered creating a Nephilim army for the Orders, but we decided that if they ever turned against us, the cost would be too great. I wonder if we were wrong. If fewer friends would have been lost if, when the War started, we had some Nephilim on our side. Maybe it could have been avoided altogether." He laughs, but without humor. "Of course, maybe our own Nephilim would have turned against us after all, and then we'd all be dead."

I thought of that, after the war, after I was older and could see through the propaganda. If I'd been in command, I'm not sure what I would have done. "But if you could find a way to control them, an army of Nephilim would be a powerful..." The truth pounds into my mind, even as it races to discover other options. But I know. I've known for some time, but feeding on Ragathon confirmed it.

"The weapon isn't a device," I say.

The Chancellor nods, waiting.

"It's the last Nephilim."

"You're as sharp as your mother always reported," the Chancellor says. "You'll do well here, assuming our deal still stands?"

He waits patiently for me to reply. I'm still processing what this means. What happened to me that night? The man in my dreams, I didn't make him up. I woke up healed, different, with a thirst for blood and unexplained powers.

I woke up as Nephilim. Which means I'm enemy-number-one to the Orders. To Jax. To my Grandfather. To everything my parents fought and died for.

But in the end, it changes nothing.

"I will join the Orders," I say. "But first, I have to go home. Just for a few days. I have to get my things. Say goodbye." My voice cracks, and I clear my throat. "Then I'll come back and begin my training. Deal?"

I hold out my hand, and he chuckles and reaches for it. "Deal, granddaughter."

I have nothing to pack, so I stand. "I'm ready now. Can someone take me to the plane?"

"I'll have one of the soldiers give you a ride to the airstrip. The airplane's been refueled, checked and prepped for you." He looks at me more closely. "But I think you'll still go through the pre-flight yourself, won't you? You strike me as the type who insists on doing things herself to make sure they're done right."

I nod sharply, remembering the lessons my dad taught me. How important it is to check your own aircraft before flying. How you can't trust it to others when it's your life in that seat.

He chuckles again and walks me out. "You'll do well here, indeed."

True to his word, he calls a soldier to take me to the airstrip. It's not a long drive, and we make it in silence, my thoughts spinning in all directions at what I'm about to do with my life.

I can feel my body still changing, powers growing in me, hunger growing even faster. A part of me knew, deep down. But I wasn't ready to admit it.

Now that I have confirmation, it terrifies me.

Nephilim. Demons. Blood suckers. Enemies of the Orders. The Destruction of Humanity. A weapon my parents died to keep under lock and key.

And now I'm one of them.

...

I stand alone in front of my father's plane, and I fight down tears. He should be here with me, going over the pre-flight checklist, his calm, deep voice reminding me of safety measures I've known for years.

My hand caresses the smooth panels as I perform my surface inspection—checking the rudder, the ailerons on the wings. I confirm that the Chancellor did indeed have both gas tanks filled, and oil levels look good on both engines. I can do this in my sleep, but still I use the clipboard and check off each item, as if this is just a normal night. As if I'm not about to fly home to an empty house with the blood of my dead parents staining the grass.

I climb into the plane and find a small gift box wrapped in silver paper sitting on the seat. It has a card with my name on it, but doesn't say who it's from. Just, *To Scarlett. Thought you might need this.*

I open it quickly, curious despite myself, and find the eGlass Eight. This version hasn't even been released to the public yet, though there were rumors the eGlass Seven will be out soon. This shouldn't even exist except in prototype. I turn the card over, looking for a hint as to who left it, but I find nothing.

I can't help being excited. I've been living with the eGlass Three for the last few years, and it's taken all my hacking skills to keep it functional. This beauty in my hand—sleek, stylish, and more powerful than any eGlass on the market—will be able to do things I didn't dare dream with my old one.

I pull my old chip out of my pocket and stick it in, then slip it onto my ear, flip the glass over my eye and press the button to turn it on.

A familiar voice greets me. "Hello, Scarlett. How are you today?"

"Evie! It's been a long time since we've talked. What's up?"

"Would you like the chemical breakdown of atmospheric pressure or a scan of the space above us for physical objects?"

I laugh. "We're going to have to fix you, Evie. Make you more laid back. But that can wait."

"Fix me? I just ran a systems check and I assure you, Scarlett, I am not broken."

Yup, she'll need to be fixed. But it won't be hard. Especially not on an Eight. "Okay, Evie."

As silly as it is, it feels good to have her back in my life. I know she's not real, that she's not human *per se*, but she's been a staple in my life for many years.

"Scarlett, would you like to see the stored video archives you had me record when I was last activated?"

My heart stutters. My parents are on that video. Their last moments on earth. But I can't open that vault of emotion with everything else going on. I need time. Space. A place to face whatever feelings that video brings up. "Later, Evie. Right now we have to go home."

After running through the last of the pre-flight checklist, I stick the key in the ignition and press the button, then take the stick in hand—though it's really a steering wheel more than a stick, the old language has held—and I taxi, accelerating until I have enough momentum to take her to the sky.

The Chancellor assured me he already had some-one call in my flight plan, so barring any unintentional trips over major airstrips or into international air-space, I can count on a smooth, quiet flight home.

The hours fly by, my mind drifting to flights with my father and Jax, moments of greatest happiness for me. My mom never enjoyed flying much, but I could live in the sky if given a chance, and Jax and my dad felt the same way.

It bound us together, gave us something no one could ever take away.

A thought, unbidden, comes to me in a moment of stunned awareness. If I am truly becoming Nephilim, that means I'll be able to fly. With wings. My heart beats against my chest at the thought of my wildest, most unattainable dreams coming true. Maybe this curse isn't all bad.

I daydream about that for hours as I fly home.

It's late, the sky black as pitch as I land in my backyard. The reflective paint on the airstrip is the only thing keeping me from crashing into my house by mistake. In my rush to come home, I didn't consider the perils of landing in the dark.

It isn't my smoothest landing. My hands shake, heart racing, as the plane jolts to the ground, but we both survive my clumsiness, and within a few moments I find myself standing outside my front door, my hands shaking again but for entirely different reasons.

I press my finger against the lock, and the door clicks open, the living room instantly lighting up so bright it blinds me. I squint until my eyes adjust, then look around.

I expect things to feel... abandoned. Tragic. Like something horrible happened here.

But everything looks so normal that it's almost worse. It's like my parents could come downstairs at any moment, asking where I've been. With the darkness outside obscuring the signs of fighting, of death, you can almost pretend the last few days have just been a horrible nightmare.

Almost.

I swallow the lump in my throat and walk through my house. Running my hand over the old blue couch in our living room as memories of movie night with my parents and Jax threaten to undo me. Straightening a family picture on our wall, my parents still very much alive, smiling down at me. Picking up the shoes my dad left by the stairs—something my mom hated because someone would always trip. I clutch them to my chest now, the black scuffed leather of his soles still stained green by the grass.

Taking a deep breath, I put them back where he left them, unwilling to change anything tonight. One step at a time. I'll stay the night, which seemed like a great idea until I got here and realized just how lonely it would feel. But I have no choice. I'll stay, pack, say one last goodbye, and lock it up for good.

Or at least for a while.

On the couch, my old purse still rests on its side. I almost forgot about my gift from Jax. I pull out the silver gift bag and remove the wings, pinning them on my shirt. I run a thumb over the carved metal feathers and tuck the memory of those moments before the battle into a safe pocket of my mind. Those were the last moments of normalcy, of happiness, I have.

A light flickers from our wall, and I walk over to the grey eScreen, which blinks with a green light. I activate it and watch as the image of Dr. Crayton appears. He looks bewildered as he speaks. "I have good news for Miss Night. Against all odds, she has passed the vision test. I will issue her a special exemption to get her pilot's license, should she still wish it. Congratulations."

The image flicks off, and I stand still, silent, at a loss for what to think. My dreams have just come true, and it doesn't even matter anymore. I focus my attention back on my house, on what I've come here to do.

Near our bookshelves, my dad set up a little table where the two of us played chess late into the night. I walk over to it slowly, knowing this will hurt the worst. We were mid-game, our pieces spread over the board, before he died. I'll have to decide, take the set or leave it as it is? I don't know. I can't imagine leaving my home, leaving everything here, as if nothing had happened.

From the corner of my eye something flashes, and I look up, startled out of my melancholy. I left the front door open for fresh air, and I swear something outside moved past the house.

I poke my head out the door but don't see anything unusual. Must have been a trick of the light. I think about closing it, but I want the cool draft to clear out the stagnant feel of the house. We often left our front door open on nice nights as we watched a movie or dined on the porch.

I move to my mother's desk where her jewelry-making tools are still out. I rub the ring I wear on my middle finger, one she made me for my sixteenth birthday. A Celtic pattern of links with a ruby cross. A Templar symbol, I realize.

Seeing the leather straps and pliers gives me an idea. I pull out the Token of Strife and use her supplies to make a leather necklace to hang it from, which I tie around my neck. Somehow I feel better with the ring resting against my heart.

Once again, something bright, glowing, shoots past the front door, and I turn quickly and run outside, determined to solve the mystery.

I don't have to run long. Standing outside is a little girl, pale as moonlight, transparent even, with her back to me. She turns her head, and I recognize her as the girl from my dream. She still holds the glowing orb.

"Who are you?" I ask. Is she some kind of new Zenith I've never heard about?

But she doesn't answer. Instead, she runs away from me and toward the woods by my house.

"Wait!" I yell for her, but she doesn't turn, doesn't stop, and so I follow. I know this is stupid. I know this may be a trap set by the Angel.

I hope it is.

I need to face the monster that killed my parents.

We pass into the forest, the trees tall, dark and menacing—so very like my dream I have to look down to make sure I'm not walking on the body of corpses.

I'm not. Just plain old dirt and rocks.

I keep running, twigs snapping under my feet as I duck under low branches and follow her over fallen trees.

We soon come to two large boulders. She squeezes past them, a glow in between the space, and I suck in my breath and do the same, with a lot more effort and less breathing.

A few scratches later I find myself in a grove, the earth under my feet white sand, glittering in the light of the moonbeams.

I've spent my whole life in this house, on this land. I know every hiding place, every cave, every trail, every tree.

This grove has never been here before.

I look for the girl and see her running up a hill to the center of the grove.

Toward a silver tree. It stands like a beacon of light in darkness, with bare branches swaying in the windless night.

And below the tree stands a man dressed in black with a long coat billowing around him.

He turns to me, his face pale, his eyes blue—a man ethereally beautiful. He smiles.

The man from my dreams.

The last Nephilim.

THE LAST NEPHILIM

"It's you." I freeze in place, my mind trying to find some cohesiveness between this experience and reality, but it comes up empty.

"Yes. But do you know who I am, Scarlett Night?" His voice, deep and rich, has a trace of an old accent—Russian, maybe? I can't tell. It burrows into me, that voice, and leaves me shaking.

"I know you're dangerous." My body vibrates with his nearness, with the chill in the air, with the otherworldly feel to everything around us.

His grey blue eyes are unreadable as he studies me. "And do you fear me, Scarlett?"

"No," I say, honestly. I know I should, that he can hurt me in so many ways, but instead I'm drawn to him like a Nephilim to blood. I don't even question how he knows my name. It feels like he has always known me, and I've known him. "What happened to the girl?" I ask, looking around for the ghostly figure that led me here.

"I can conjure memories, like the girl, like this tree," he says. "And sometimes, they can do my bidding. I used the girl to lure you here, because I needed to make sure we were alone."

He takes a step toward me, and my body moves against my will to reach him, to be closer to him. I wonder if it's because he is Nephilim. We stand a few feet apart under the silver tree. I have to look up at him. He stands a good foot taller than me, his chest broad, body hard and full of muscle under his black jeans and shirt. Up close I can see the perfection of his face more clearly. There would never be any mistaking this man for mortal. Every inch of him screams power, magic, danger.

When he holds out his hand, I look at it in surprise. "My name is Zorin, Andriy Zorin, Count of Nightfall, and Left Hand of the Twilight Queen. I apologize for leaving you before, but I had to draw our attackers away.

I take his hand and instead of shaking it, he draws it to his lips and kisses my knuckles. "It is a pleasure to meet you," he says.

His skin is cold, smooth, his hand strong and large, swallowing my own. When he lets go, my hand falls to my side, like a cut kite. My words leave me for a moment, lost in his unfathomable gaze.

But then his words register in my mind. Our attackers. "What happened that night?" I ask.

"What do you remember?"

"I..." I close my eyes and think back. "I remember falling, crashing into the crystal case, shot, bleeding, the pain exploding inside me. I had fired at the case. At you," I say, realizing that he'd been in the crystal, preserved there like a mummy. "I shot at you, thinking you were a weapon, thinking you could help me. But they... then they shot me and everything went dark."

"You died, your life's blood pooled into the crystal and fed me, awakening me. I brought you back from the land of the dead. I gave you the power of the Nephilim."

I know that already, but still, hearing him say it sends chills up my spine. "Why? Why did you save me?"

"Perhaps because you reminded me of someone I once knew," he says, his eyes faraway and sad.

I choke on unshed tears. "Why didn't you save my parents?"

He reaches for my hand, stroking it. "They were already gone. They had no spark of life left to rebirth. I'm sorry, Scarlett. I tried."

I want to hate him for saving me and not them, but I can't. I know the truth of his words. Had felt the truth before. "What about the other... Nephilim? The thing that killed them?"

He tilts his head, a dark strand of hair falling into his eyes. "That was no Nephilim, but an Old One. Your people call them Angels. They are our ancestors, and we their children, along with humans. They are far more ancient and deadly than us. I killed the pawns of the Angel and then fought him in the sky. We injured each other gravely, and I fell from the sky onto a mountain, hurt and dying. It was your blood inside me that saved me. I came to find you as soon as I awoke and healed enough to fly. What happened to me? Do you know? Why was I in that coffin?"

"You don't remember? About the Wars? Your capture?"

"I remember who I am," he says, "But not how I was captured and put to sleep."

"I don't know how you were captured. I only know that I tried to free you because my parents told me you were a weapon they had to protect."

Moonlight glints off his pale skin, and behind him a dark light spreads around his shoulders. I gasp as I watch obsidian wings unfurl behind him, seemingly made of the night and moonbeams. "Thank you, Scarlett. For saving me as I saved you. We should leave at once and report all of this to the Twilight Queen."

I pull my gaze away from his wings, a longing growing inside of me at the sight. "You don't know?"

He cocks his head. "Know what?

"Zorin, you are the last of your kind... though I guess, that's not technically true since I'm now Nephilim," I say, the words still so strange to speak out loud. "There is no Twilight Queen, no court, no Nephilim. They are all dead."

He steps back, his face frozen in shock. "I don't understand. What do you mean, dead? What happened to her? To them?"

"You must have already been captured when it happened. The Twilight Queen was overthrown by a Nephilim calling himself Nyx and his apprentice, Erebus. Nyx waged a war against mankind, but he lost, and all the Nephilim were wiped out. Except you."

We stand staring at each other a moment, and I feel compelled to finish this awful tale. "The Orders wiped out the Nephilim, but they kept you alive. In case they ever wished to make an army of Nephilim... that's why you were considered a weapon."

"I was there," he says. "Near the start of the war. How could we have lost? How are they all gone?"

This time I reach for his hand, conscious of how heartbroken I would be if I'd woken from imprisonment to find that all of my kind had been destroyed. It was genocide, or nearly.

He squeezes my hand gently. "We must find safety. We must hide before the Church seeks us out to recapture or kill us."

I ease my hand out of his and straighten my back. "I can't go with you, Zorin." I'm surprised part of me wants to, and surprised equally that part of me wants to return to Castle V.

"You're in danger, Scarlett. Not only because of what you are, but because of me. Because of what I know and what those in power will assume you have learned. They will use you to get to me."

"What do you know?"

The forest around us is missing the normal sounds of the night, and the quiet is... disquieting. I can only hear our breaths on the cool air as I wait for him to tell me his secrets.

I can see the struggle on his face, whether or not to tell me.

"Zorin, you said yourself they will assume I know whether you tell me or not. You aren't protecting me by keeping me in the dark." A logical flaw that nearly every stupid movie and superhero trope seems to rely on in situations such as these, which annoys me to no end. How is someone ever safer not knowing what is coming for them or why? Who has that ever saved? Not my parents. Not me a week ago. And not me now.

He nods in consent and pulls me toward a large boulder under the silver tree. We both sit, our bodies pressed against each other, his dark wings moving the air behind us in pulses of currents.

"Many years ago," he begins, his voice deep and his accent more pronounced, "I uncovered an artifact, a device of great power. I suspect that is the reason I was kept alive, the real reason, and not to make more Nephilim, though undoubtedly some might have wanted me for that, too. They must have been looking for a way to extract the information from me."

"What was the artifact?" I ask, when he doesn't continue on his own.

"It was one of the seven seals, designed to bring mankind to its knees."

"But they're myth. They're—"

"They are real. Very real," he says gravely.

"Where are they?"

"I will not speak of that, for they must never be found again."

Does my grandfather know about this? Did he deliberately lie to me about Zorin and my parents? Did my parents know? Every answer seems to bring a dozen new questions. "So, is that why the Angel was after you? For the seal?"

"I believe so," he says. "Angels once ruled this earth, many ages ago, and with the seals they could do so again. The Nephilim fought them during the Angel War, but with the Nephilim gone... all might be lost. For both of our kind."

I wonder who my kind is now. Am I still human? Or am I entirely Nephilim? In a war between the two, where would I land?

Zorin's face hardens as he stares into the darkness. "I must find out what happened. The Nephilim could not have easily been eradicated." He faces me, shifting on the boulder to touch my hand. "Come with me to Italy so we might uncover these truths together. You are Nephilim now, Scarlett. For better or worse, we are all we have left."

I feel the pull again. To leave with him. To leave behind the bodies and the pain and the lies and secrets and fly—fly!—to Italy to uncover the truth. But... "I can't. I must stay. I have to train to become a Knight Templar so I can destroy the Angel who killed my family. I must avenge them."

I plead with my eyes for him to understand.

Revenge. A universal motive amongst any race.

"Have you fed yet?" he asks.

I think back to Ragathon, to the bliss of his blood flowing into me and nod. "Yes."

"That is good. Do not allow yourself to grow week from lack of blood. Have you flown yet?"

My heart hammers in my chest. "No, I haven't."

"You should come with me," he insists again. "And learn the ways of Nephilim. Help me bring peace between humans and our kind. It's what your parents would have wanted."

I straighten at that, all fantasies of flying fleeing my mind. "How would you know what they would have wanted?"

"I knew them well. You are so like your mother in many ways, but I see your father in your eyes. Not the color, but the intensity."

He knew them? This... doesn't make sense. "How? How did you know each other?"

"They helped me discover the seal."

"But... why would my parents work with a Nephilim?"

He reaches for my hand. "Let me show you. Close your eyes."

I do so, placing my hand into his, my breath hitching in my throat as the air around us changes, pulsing with a new kind of energy. It's electric, visceral, and when he tells me to look, I'm scared.

But I open my eyes.

And see my parents.

They're flickering lights, like the girl he conjured earlier, but they are in color, three dimensional, almost real. I reach out with my free hand to touch them but it passes through air.

"You can't feel them. They are but memories conjured. You can only see and hear."

And so I listen as my heart breaks and heals and breaks again and I can't decide if this glimpse into the past will destroy me or be something precious I carry with me always, like a lock of hair from a loved one or a fading photograph of one departed.

They're in a study, a solid dark room with too much wood paneling and old books lining every available wall. They aren't alone. They stand next to each other and argue with five others... the Council of Orders.

"They are real," my mother says, her eyes alight with the fire of her convictions. "The seals aren't just myths. We believe we've found one. And if we're correct, then it's in a vault created by the Angels."

"This is folly," Ragathon says with that same dreadful scorn. "We cannot support this useless quest."

"You don't get to decide that on your own," my father says. I want to cheer him for standing up to that jerk.

"No, he doesn't," my grandfather says, already the Chancellor. "But the Council agrees, though for its own reasons. This is too dangerous and uncertain to risk our best Templars."

The scene changes to one of darkness. They're in an underground warehouse with Zorin. "We believe you know where it is," my mother says. "Please help us find it."

Zorin, who looks the same then as he does now, shakes his head. "I have seen it, yes. In an ancient city beneath the waves, but I do not wish to return."

My dad, a much younger version of him, grasps Zorin's shoulder in camaraderie. "The vault is full of knowledge, treasures, the truth of whatever came before mankind... before Nephilim. Perhaps what we find there could unite our two races. It could end the strife that exists between us, the tension leading to war. This could save us all, Zorin, but we can't do it without you."

The Nephilim bends his head forward, his body still as my parents wait for his answer.

My mother holds a hand out to Zorin. "Will you help us unite our people into one?"

He grasps her hand in his and nods. "I will."

The vision disappears and my heart lurches in my chest. They're gone. My parents. Their memories. Gone.

I swallow a sob and breathe deeply to regain my control.

Zorin waits a moment before speaking. "They had no idea what the vault truly contained. They never made it inside."

"My parents, they fought to keep you safe. To keep you out of the hands of the Angel."

"Please come with me, Scarlett. If not for your own safety then to fulfill the will of your parents."

I chuckle without humor. "That's the same argument the Chancellor of Castle V used to keep me here.

But my answer is still no. Not now." An image of Jax comes to my mind and I know I can't leave him. Despite everything that's happened, he's still the only friend I have left.

"You can be my ally or my enemy, Scarlett. And you do not wish me as your enemy."

"My answer remains the same. I have to finish my mission here."

"Very well, then."

In a blur of darkness, he spins around and pulls a sword, black as night, onto me.

Where did that come from? I didn't even see him draw it. One moment he's sitting next to me, the next he's armed like an avenging Angel.

He thrusts at me with his blade, and I dive behind a rock, scraping my knees on the rough granite and leaving a small dark mark of blood. He comes at me again, this time faster, and I fall back, scrambling through silver sand to avoid the slash of metal on skin.

As he continues his assault, I dodge to stay out of the way, but am forced to remain on the defensive. I realize quickly I lack the skill and training to even attempt a counter-move against him.

"If you came straight to find me after waking, where did you get the sword?" I ask, avoiding impalement by the hair on my arms.

"A Nephilim's sword—their wingblade—is never far from its master," Zorin says. "You would know more, if you accepted my offer."

He attacks me again and I reach for him. If I can just use my power I can end this. But he dashes out of my way, black tendrils billowing behind his wings as he glides through the air.

He's toying with me, like a human taunting a cat with a flashlight.

"You prove no match for me, yet you seek to kill an Angel?" he asks.

"I will train. I will become a Templar like my parents. The strongest Knight the Orders have ever seen."

He swipes at me faster, and I don't dodge in time. It takes a moment to feel the pain. To see the fine lines of red swelling with my blood on my arms and legs.

"Your father was the best of them, and not even he could best me," Zorin says. Then he thrusts the sword at my throat... and stops just as the blade teases my flesh.

We both freeze. I try not to breathe lest the movement tip the fragile balance between us.

He holds my eyes with his as he keeps me at death's door. "Tell me, who lasted longer against the Angel... me, or your father?"

I'm done playing his games and listening to his insults. "You're the reason he's dead. The reason they're both dead."

At that, his wings fall to his side, along with his sword. "Your father once told me that when he died, he would die for what he believed. And if what he believed in was me, then you are right, I am responsible for their deaths. And I am sorry."

I want to stay angry. Stay furious. But I can only stand there and shake, my head too confused, my heart too rattled to know what I'm feeling.

Zorin bends down and draws a symbol in the dirt at our feet. He makes a narrow X with the top smaller than the bottom. "Wings," he says. Then he draws a line down the middle. "And a sword."

He stands and we both look down at the symbol. "When you are ready, draw this upon your window in your own blood, either at your home here or at the Castle, and I will come and help you, as your parents helped me."

"Why blood?"

His grey eyes darken. "We are of one blood, you and I. By saving each other we have become a part of each other. Your blood calls to mine as mine does to yours. This symbol focuses that energy."

"What is it?"

"A symbol of trust, created so that Nephilim and Nephilim supporters could safely identify each other. One would draw half this symbol casually, and if the other completed it, you knew they could be trusted."

His wings expand to full height and width, and he catches the wind and flies into the night before I can respond.

The silver tree above me fades away as the forest returns to the familiar. I shiver in the cold as I stand there staring up at the moon. How can I trust him? He just attacked me. Hurt me.

I look down at my cuts, at my clothes, at the light marks on my skin… and I realize, he didn't really hurt me. The cuts were so superficial they've already healed. The bruises already faded. He showed remarkable control.

He hadn't meant to kill me.

But he had meant to show me that he could.

THE CATHEDRAL

The sounds of the forest come back to me slowly. A night owl hooting in the distance. The scurry of critters who prefer the cover of darkness. Crickets singing their songs to the moon. The noise filters through my mind as I wander back to my house in a partial daze.

I can feel my body wearing down, too tired to think any more about everything that happened. I didn't sleep much last night, or rather this morning, and it's burning into the midnight hour yet again. I need rest. My body and mind and heart need rest.

I lock up the house and drag myself up the stairs to the comfort of my own room. I haven't been in here since before my vision test, which now means nothing. Before the battle that took my parents' lives. Before I died.

Before I became something new.

The blue comforter on my twin bed still crumbles at the foot, my sheets looking slept in. My laundry basket stands in the corner overflowing with dirty clothes. I promised my mom I'd do laundry after my test. A book I'd been reading, a rare print edition about the history of flight, sits open on the dresser next to my bed. My walls are lined with posters of planes. It's all so normal. So everyday.

I strip off my new clothes and pull on my sweats and an old t-shirt. One of Jax's old t-shirts, I realize, the thought almost too much for me.

I consider changing again, but I'm too tired and instead sink into my bed, pull my covers over my head and let the night lull me to sleep.

I sleep late and wake to an early afternoon serenade from a bird in the tree by my bedroom window.

After showering and changing into jeans and a t-shirt, I pull out my suitcase and pack as much as I can, not knowing when I'll be back here again. I'll have to sort out the details of the house eventually. Will I have the money to pay the taxes and keep it maintained, or will I have to sell it? I can't imagine selling. Going through my parent's belongings. Getting rid of all traces of their lives. No. I'll find a way to keep it all. At least for now.

As I pack and sort through my clothes and personal items, my mind goes over everything I know about Nephilim. It's not a lot. I was young when the war ended and haven't needed to know more since then.

"Evie," I say into my eGlass as I shove another sweater into my bag.

"I am here, Scarlett. What can I do for you?"

"Show me the best footage you can find on the Nephilim War."

I flip the eGlass over my right eye to access the holographic display screen.

"Would you like the most popular news reports?" she asks in her crisp British accent.

I shake my head, which I trained her to identify as *no* from my movements. "Too censored. I need the files the public didn't get access to."

"Are you approving the use of hacking to acquire these files? They are stored in the Templar database."

Another safety I programmed into her so she doesn't just hack whatever she needs to get information for me unless I say okay. You can never be too careful in these situations. "Yes, I approve, Evie. Thank you."

"You are always welcome, Scarlett. The database is showing two thousand, three hundred and forty-two files. How would you like to view them?"

I pause in my packing and sit on my bed. That's too many to watch. "Sort by order of highest classified files and look for anything related to the Orders, Nyx... and look for files that might contain Jaxton Lux." I remember something else I'm curious about. "And the Shadow of Rome."

As she works, I fill my suitcase and zip it up, then grab a backpack for my laptop, books and anything else I might need.

I don't know what I hoped to find. Maybe proof that Nephilim are the monsters I was raised to believe. Maybe proof they aren't.

When Jax appears as a holographic image before me, I sit back down and watch the scene. He looks so much younger. Barely old enough to be holding the sword at his side. And yet there he stands, in formal Teutonic Knight dress, sword at belt, back straight, chest out, on a stage before a small crowd. Ragathon stands before him, smiling like a proud father as he pins a medal onto Jax's chest. "Good job, son," he says, patting his shoulder.

"I did as commanded, sir," Jax says, staring out at the crowd.

"We ask no more from a soldier," Ragathon replies.

Jax turns his face toward Ragathon. "Which is why I would like to request a promotion, sir."

Ragathon rubs his chin, a serious expression creasing his face in fewer lines than he has now. Then he chuckles. "Ha! I like you, boy. I'll put in a good word. We could use more soldiers like you."

"Yes, sir," Jax says, dead serious. "We really could."

Even then, he was hoping to change things for the better.

Evie flicks to the next video, and I almost tell her to go back to Jax when the council chambers appear. My grandfather, Ragathon and the other Council Members sit in their assigned seats, a tense silence hanging in the air. Nyx, the instigator of the Nephilim War, and his apprentice, Erebus, walk in, both of them cloaked in black. Nyx wears a white mask with black patterns, while Erebus wears a mask with red around the eyes and gold details weaving across it. They're meeting with the Four Orders and Chancellor. I don't remember ever hearing about this.

"Evie, while I watch this, search all news records. I want to know if this meeting was ever reported."

In the holograph, Ragathon complains that Nyx acted unjustly. "We had a peace, a truce between our people. We thought we could work with the Nephilim—"

Nyx interrupts, his voice deep, primal and fierce, but also synthesized, likely being altered by the mask. "Peace? You've killed my people for ages. You wish me to stop killing yours? Then surrender and abolish all laws related to Zeniths."

I heard the rumor that Nephilim fought for Zeniths. Now, I know it was true.

"The people won't allow Zeniths to go unregulated," Ragathon argues.

"The people will allow whatever you tell them," Nyx says.

Ragathon's robes rustle as he shifts in his chair. "We are their representatives, not their masters."

Nyx laughs without amusement, and my grandfather interrupts them. "Come now, Ragathon. Nyx is not wrong. The time for pretend is over." He turns to speak to Nyx. "We are no longer a democracy, that much is true, but we cannot give you what you ask. The Pope would never allow it. Nor, I'm afraid, would he allow you to live."

"And if I were to surrender myself?" Nyx asks.

My grandfather shakes his head sadly. "Then Zeniths would have peace, but not equality."

Nyx turns on his heel, fire in his movement. "Then the war shall continue," he says as he moves to leave, his apprentice following him.

My grandfather calls out from behind him. "Is it worth it, spilling so much blood for so few?"

Nyx turns to face my grandfather. "Is it ever worth spilling blood at all?"

He walks out, leaving the Council members whispering amongst themselves.

The image cuts short as Evie's voice interrupts. "Scarlett, that meeting was never made public, but there's something you need to see. Something urgent."

She relays a live newscast into my e-Glass. A blond reporter sits in a newsroom and reads from a teleprompter, and above her they show a picture of Peter

Conley, the Gravir I helped, along with four other Zeniths, all subdued and under arrest.

"During the deadly riots that devastated our city, five Zeniths were arrested for assault, as well as for their connection to known rebel organizations. These Zeniths have found guilty on all accounts. They are scheduled for execution at Times Square in New York City in three days. The Orders have issued a statement reminding everyone why it is so critical that Zenith restrictions be upheld, in order to protect the innocent from unregulated use of abilities. This is Courtney Miller from SPQRN—" I click off the video, my heart beating frantically.

"Evie, connect me to the private line of the Chancellor."

"That will require hacking into the Order, do you approve the—"

"Yes, I approve," I say too loudly. "Just do it! Hurry."

It only takes her a moment, and the eGlass buzzes as it tries to connect to the Chancellor, my grandfather.

When he finally answers, I've taken enough breaths to keep myself in check, but just barely. "What are you doing to stop the execution?" I ask without preamble.

"I suppose I shouldn't bother inquiring as to how you reached this line?" he asks.

"No, you shouldn't bother. But you should answer my question if you ever want to see me at that school again."

My fingers shake with pent up rage and fear and more emotions than I can articulate.

"I've done all I can. I'm sorry, Scarlett. I know you don't agree with how Zenith laws are implemented, but those who were convicted caused the death of several people."

"Not as many deaths as the Inquisition caused in their retaliation and response," I say sharply, then disconnect the call and throw my eGlass onto my bed. I have to get to the Castle. Have to talk reason into the Chancellor. Have to stop this insanity before it's too late.

I grab my bags and drag them to the plane, then do one last check on the house. I glance at our family chess set, my eyes lingering a moment longer than I have time for. Without thinking, I pluck my king from the board and stick it in my pocket.

We are never out of moves. There is always something we can do.

...

I storm into the Chancellor's office without knocking, my previous calm shattered by the hours it took to arrive. "What do you mean there's nothing more you can do?" I demand, startling him from a cup of tea at his fire. His cat jumps off his lap and runs under the desk.

My grandfather gestures me over and I sit beside him, my spine straight and body still pulsing with the threat lingering over the captive Zeniths.

"I've pulled every string I can," he says. "I'm out of strings."

"The Inquisition is lying. I know one of the Zeniths, Peter Conley, didn't attack anyone on purpose. Nor is he with the rebels. Jax and I saw him. He lost control of his abilities because of the chaos. Because the Orders won't let Zeniths learn to control their abilities. How can he be executed for an accident?"

"Those Zeniths threatened the lives and safety of civilians. There's live footage going viral on the net as we speak, showing the Zeniths using their abilities against the innocent. People are scared. Something has to be done, an example must be made, or there will be civic unrest throughout the world."

"Then make new laws. Help Zeniths learn control. Killing them is not the answer."

The Chancellor puts his tea on the table beside us and sits forward, his long robes spreading before him. "Ragathon's operation failed and many died as a result. He's trying to minimize the damage."

"So this execution is just a distraction from his failure?" This makes me sick.

"I'm afraid so," he says.

The cat meows, stalking us over the Persian rugs until she lounges at our feet in front of the warm fire.

"Why can't the Council stop him?" I ask. "He's not an autonomous power, no matter what Order he controls."

"We did take it to the Council. Grandmaster Gabriella agreed with the verdict. As did the Grandmaster of the Hospitallers. The Templars were outvoted."

"Then I'll stop this myself," I say, leaving his office with rage building in me.

I head straight to Ragathon's office, figuring it's the best place to start looking for him. I will control him with my power and make him change the sentencing.

I find him in the hall leaving his office. The sight of him makes my skin crawl.

I grab his arm and push my mind into him.

Nothing happens.

My power can't penetrate him.

"What is this? Now you're attacking a Grandmaster? Is the impending death of those tainted Zeniths not enough of a warning for you, Miss Night? Are you ready to join them on the chopping block this week?"

I don't respond. Don't give him the benefit of seeing my rage. He waits half a second longer, then sneers—a default look for him, I'm learning—and turns on his heel to walk away. I'm left sitting on the stone hallway floor, the color drained from my face, my blood boiling under my skin. I should have torn out his throat that day. Should have pulled the trigger. Should have ended him when I had the chance. I won't make that mistake again.

Unsure of why my abilities aren't working, I run to my room, which already has my luggage thanks to one of the soldiers who escorted me back to the Castle from the landing strip, and I collapse onto my desk chair.

First, I double check the encryptions I encoded in my new eGlass, making sure the Order can't get through and track me. Then, I dig through my bags and find the rebel chip I took from the dead rebel's eGlass. I slip it into my eGlass and try to access the line. They gave their signal a new encryption. It doesn't take long for Evie to hack it. She's becoming almost as good as me.

When it's live, I press the button and speak. "It's N," I say, heart racing. "I need your help."

As I wait for their reply, I use a knife to cut my finger, and on the glass of my window, I draw the stylized wings and sword. The symbol of the Nephilim. The symbol of trust. It shimmers with a glowing light and then fades into nothing.

Messages sent, I wait.

...

New York marches on. New Yorkers are a tough breed and no amount of Inquisition harassment, public executions or murder can keep them down—an immutable fact of history and present day alike. But they also honor the past. Signs of the tragedy cover the city: impromptu memorials of flowers, pictures, and gifts, all left where loved ones died. You can tell the socio-economic class of the deceased by the foliage. The rich left exotic, genetically-modified flowers with petals that shimmer silver and turn different colors throughout the day. The poor gave what they could, from wherever they could find it.

All of it breaks me, but I push myself on, averting my eyes to the sorrow, protecting my heart from the memories as I scout for the location Zorin gave me. He sent an encrypted message to my eGlass, by means I can't decipher. I have to admit I'm impressed.

When I arrive, I find Zorin sitting outside a coffee shop, sipping a steaming cup of something. I join him at the table and eye the cup. "Does our kind drink coffee?" I loved the stuff before all this, but so far not much appeals to my no-longer-human taste buds.

He pushes the drink toward me. "Try it."

I shrug and take a sip. "It tastes... normal."

Zorin nods. "Coffee never did taste good. If you liked it before, you're bound to like it now."

I smile, glad not all food is denied to me.

Zorin leans back in his chair. "You'll find you still enjoy some things, and for the things you don't..." He takes a bite of bread off his plate and frowns. "Well, it doesn't hurt to blend in."

I study his chiseled face, his grey-blue eyes and perfect body, and choke back a sarcastic retort about how well he does *not* fit in.

I want to ask how old he is, but I feel that might be rude, so I ask, "When were you... turned?"

He grins slowly. "Let's just say..." He leans in closer. "Before the Cataclysm."

My eyes widen. "What was it like back then?"

"Similar. Humanity changes little."

I roll my eyes. "Come on, you can't just say 'Before the Cataclysm' and tell me everything was similar."

He sighs. "Fine. There was a time women were considered property."

"What? How does that even make sense?"

He shrugs. "Also, there was a religion that considered cats holy."

"Now, that I understand."

He grins. "So, are you ready?"

I nod and follow him to one of the rarest sights in Manhattan. A parking spot. He waves at a black sports car, and it unlocks using his scanned handprint.

When he opens the passenger door for me, I slip in and sink into the leather comfort. "This is the newest eDrive on the market," I say when he gets in. "But you've been unconscious for years." I narrow my eyes in suspicion. "Where did you get the money to pay for this?"

He starts the engine, bypasses the autodrive feature, and pulls out. "I've lived a long time, Scarlett, and I've accumulated a massive amount of wealth. I've also acquired a decent survival instinct. I have safe houses throughout the world with stashes for emergencies. Today, I used one."

"Smart," I say. "Given how much you spent on this beauty, why aren't you letting it drive, since that's what it was designed to do?"

He shakes his head. "I prefer to stay in control as much as possible. Less chance of ending up dead that way."

Our drive takes an hour and leads us to a long stretch of wilderness on the outskirts of Manhattan. He pulls up to a property that's seen better days, with overgrown weeds, debris littering the grounds and shambled buildings lining the entryway to the main building.

I look up and smile. This place is amazing. Even in its current state it's magnificent—an old cathedral, built from obsidian that glints in the sunlight. It rivals Notre Dame.

"What is this place?" I ask as we park and get out.

"It belonged to the Nephilytes. It was their main temple before the war. They believed Nephilim were gods. Angels returned to protect the earth and lead the people. They would offer their blood as sacrifice and erected this cathedral as a place of worship. They created a community around it, which is what those other buildings were for. Lodging, storage, barns."

"That religion is outlawed now," I say. "Anyone caught practicing is sentenced to death." I walk around, admiring the architecture as Evie pulls up footage of the cathedral before the war. I scan the articles briefly. "This place was destroyed during the war. All the worshippers were hanged as heretics and traitors."

I step on something soft underfoot and bend to pick it up. A doll. Old, torn, weathered, but once belonging to a child who lived here, who played here, and who ultimately died here.

"Do you believe Nephilim are gods?" I ask.

"No, I do not." His lips are set in a grim line. "But people should be allowed to believe as they wish and worship as they are led, as long as they do not harm others."

A memory returns to me, one I haven't recalled in many years. I was young and the Nephilim War was still in full force.

I remember sneaking downstairs one night to watch the news with my parents when I was supposed to be asleep. They showed a clip of several Nephilim in flight, their gorgeous wings outstretched, captivating to a child who dreamed of nothing but flying.

My dad caught me and walked me back to bed.

"I want to be Nephilim when I grow up, Daddy," I told him as he tucked me in.

"Why is that, my little Star? They're the enemies."

"Because they can fly and they don't even need a plane. And besides, you always say that no group is bad, that individuals in any group make their own choices. Couldn't I be a good Nephilim?"

He smoothed my hair off my forehead and kissed it. "I suppose you could, Star. If anyone could, it would be you."

Zorin tears the boards from the front door of the cathedral and walks in. He turns to look at me. "This is where we will train."

...

"Wow, you're really just going to throw me off the roof of this cathedral? That's your brilliant training plan?"

I stand at the edge and look over the fields around us. The wind blows against me, and I breathe in the fresh country air.

"Your wings are like a new limb. And like any limb, they are best first used by instinct. The height will motivate you… even if the fall doesn't kill you, it will hurt. Before we start—"

Without letting him finish, I run to the opposite edge of the roof, building momentum like I would in an airplane, and I jump off the edge.

I don't so much fly as I fall. And fast.

My heart races in my chest, knocking against my ribs as if it can escape this fool body and find someone with better self-preservation instincts. But I know I can do this. I was born to do this.

Come on, wings, do whatever you're supposed to do. Now!

I close my eyes and let all my fear go. I focus on the feel of the wind, on the momentum of my body, on the sheer bliss of being airborne. I've been flying my whole life. This is second nature to me.

It happens in a flash. My back and shoulders burn, and the air currents change as my body expands and grows new limbs.

I open my eyes.

I'm racing over the ground, no longer falling toward it.

Joy—intense, visceral joy—overwhelms me. I turn my head and see silvery feathers made almost of light shimmering at my back. I want to touch them, to feel their texture, but that can come later. For now, my wings and I are ready to soar.

I fly over the woods and dive toward a lake, letting my hand trail in the water and splash around me. I can see my reflection and the light of my wings in the water. I look otherworldly.

Zorin joins me, his wings dark to my light. I wonder how it would feel to touch *his* wings, to run my hands over them.

I blush and pull my eyes forward.

He chuckles as if he knows what I'm thinking. "Let's see how fast you can go, shall we?"

He speeds up, turning into a blur as he flies, and I push myself to match him.

We become sparks of light twirling through the sky. When he finally slows down and lets me catch up with him, I can tell he's impressed. "It's been a long time since someone's surprised me."

I grin, still in flight, so happy I can almost forget the horrors of the last few days or why I'm really here with Zorin. To train. To learn as much as I can in the next two days so I can save the Zeniths.

"Now, let's stop," he says, and he hangs mid-air, suspended as his wings keep him from falling. Like treading water.

Only I don't know how to tread. Airplanes can't tread. At least, not the ones I flew. I keep flying in a blind panic as I try to slow my wings to a stop without falling out of the sky.

Instead I crash into a tree and fall to the ground like some kind of miserable cartoon character.

Zorin floats up next to me and reaches out his hand to help me up.

"We'll work on that," he says, smiling a tad too brightly.

...

Zorin holds a stick out to me and keeps one for himself.

I glare at mine. "A stick? When do I get a fancy sword? Or even one of those wooden swords kids train with? Why a stick?"

He raises an eyebrow. "Because I don't have any wooden swords on hand, and you aren't ready for a real one. You'd end up hurting yourself and we don't have time for that. *You* don't have time for that."

I hold up my stick, sufficiently scolded.

"Do what I do," he says.

We parry back and forth, hitting each other's sticks as he speaks. "Nephilim swordsmanship originated in Greece, and the different forms are named after our different deities of the night. This is the Way of Nyx.

She is the personification of night, and just as she stands at the beginning of creation, so does her form stand before all others. You must learn it before you can progress to other forms."

I didn't realize the Nephilim leader used the name of one of their deities. "How many are there?" I ask, trying to mimic his wrist movements.

"Seven in total," he says, blocking me and striking. "In time, I shall teach you all of them."

My muscles burn and my hand grows tired of holding up the stick. I drop it to my side, halting our practice. "I've always wondered, why do Nephilim and Knights use swords instead of guns?"

"Bullets won't kill a Nephilim, nor an Angel. You've seen that yourself. But a wingblade, like its master, can draw the life from its victim until there is nothing left."

I felt the power of his blade the night before, though only a fraction. "When do I get one of those?"

He smiles. "Not until you're ready. A wingblade of your own is a great responsibility."

I hold my stick back up and lunge. He blocks and parries.

"You're afraid I'll lose it?" I ask.

"I'm afraid of what you might do with it. Or what it might do with you." He steps past my block and whacks me on the arm.

"Ouch! That hurt." I rub the sore spot.

"Not as much as a wingblade would. A wingblade craves life force just like a Nephilim... so if one is not careful... the blade will send them into a blood-lust, or, if no blood is to be found, it will turn on its master."

"You make it sound like it's alive."

"Not quite," he says. "I'll explain more later." He whacks me again on the hand and a red welt forms. "Focus."

I rub at the sting. "But how do you make it appear from—"

"Focus."

I hit his stick with mine and don't give up. "But how do you make it appear?"

He stops our sparring and silently begins to collect sticks.

I huff and I puff but he doesn't acknowledge me until I sigh and say, "Fine, I'll focus."

I train hard, mirroring him, blocking, dodging, lunging. I figure if I can prove myself a good student he'll be willing to tell me more.

At one point, he has me fight a tree with my stick, while he collects more twigs and makes a fire as the sun begins to set.

"That's enough for today," he says, his wings flickering behind him.

We trained with and without my wings, so I can get used to the balance either way. I regret I'll have to keep them hidden while at Castle V.

So while we sit around the fire, I let my wings expand behind me, glittering silver moonlight in the darkness.

He tosses me a LifeForce, and we both drink, replenishing our strength.

I hold up my empty packet. "Why do I feel better when I drink this and nothing else?"

"It's an application of Angel technology," he says. "They found a way to harness the life force of living beings. The drink activates our own cells to regenerate. Not like blood, but close enough to get us by."

I toss my empty packet into his bag and tuck my legs under me, enjoying the warmth of the flames and the stillness of the night.

"We should talk about any changes you may be experiencing," Zorin says as he stirs the fire. "But first..." he reaches for his backpack and pulls out a bag of something white.

"Marshmallows?" I stare in disbelief as he sticks one onto a stick, passes it to me, and prepares his own.

"One of the finer things in life."

"But we don't need food anymore," I say.

He grins, his face looking younger, less warrior-like. "Since when did anyone eat marshmallows for their nutritional content?" He holds his over the fire, letting it turn a golden brown before popping it into his mouth.

I do the same to mine, still eyeing him skeptically as I hold it to my mouth. "This isn't a trick, is it? I'm not sure I can bear it if you ruin marshmallows for me."

He laughs. "It's not a trick, I assure you."

I gingerly place it in my mouth and bite down.

A delicious flavor spreads through my mouth. The first yummy food I've eaten since the night I turned. I immediately grab another one and stab it with my stick.

"Good, right?" He roasts another for himself. "You know, it wasn't until the mid-1900s, AD of course, that they figured out how to mass-produce these. By Lilith, I was so happy that day."

I can't imagine living through so many changes in the world. Would that be me now? Ageless. Immortal. A witness to time but no longer a part of it? I focus back on my treat, unwilling to wrestle with greater existential conflicts just now. "I must admit, I'm grateful for more options than chugging LifeForce and coffee all the time." I pop the second marshmallow in my mouth and set my stick down. "But I need to get back to training."

"Yes… and why are you so determined to train with me? Last we spoke, the Orders were enough."

I haven't told him anything and he hasn't pried, which I'm grateful for. But he deserves to know the whole truth. "I was wrong about them," I confess.

He leans forward and sets his own stick down. "Tell me." His eyes glow in the firelight. "Tell me what they've done."

I thought I would censor myself, but when the words tumble out, they come all at once and complete. I tell him about Peter and the other Zeniths and my plans to rescue them. I tell him about my place in the Four Orders and Jax.

Zorin folds his hands together and stares into the fire. "Have you considered, Scarlett, that you may have to fight your friend?"

"Jax can't stop this," I say. "But he's against the Orders as much as I am, maybe more. He won't be a problem."

"Let me tell you a story, Scarlett," he says, his voice taking on the timbre of one accustomed to oral storytelling.

"Many years ago, while in Africa, I saw a tiger in a circus, caged, its right paw festering from a wound its masters had inflicted. The beast, once mighty, was left to die a slow death, for its masters intended to make as much money as possible. And I thought, 'This is not the way a creature should die, for we deserve a peaceful sleep, or at least, a quick end.' So one night, while the masters were all drunk after a night of performing, I forced open the cage door. But the tiger did not move. I spurred the beast on. 'Spend your last days in the jungle you once ruled,' I said. 'Spend your last days at home.' But the tiger did not move. I backed away, wondering if my presence was making the beast hesitant. But the tiger did not move. And I realized, the tiger was already home."

He pauses, still holding his eyes on the flickering of light before him. "Too long had the beast lived in the cage of its masters. Too long had the beast played a part for another."

He looks up at me then, with kind eyes that have seen too much in a very long life. "Are you certain that Jax still longs for the jungle? Are you certain that Jax is not already home?"

"I... I don't know. I know he wants change. I know he's against these killings."

"And if he's ordered to fight? What then?"

I pause. I don't want to think about having to fight Jax as Nightfall, but... "I'll do what I must. I'll do what is right."

"Very well. I shall help you," Zorin says, though I still see doubt in his eyes. "Now, you need to get these rebels you spoke of to lend aid."

"I will," I assure him. I'm still waiting to hear back. I'd sent another message before leaving to meet Zorin.

"And if you can't, you may have other assets," he says. "Besides flying, have you noticed any other abilities emerge since your transformation?"

"Yes," I admit. "When I touch people, sometimes I can become them, as if I'm in their mind. Sometimes it lasts a while. Sometimes it's briefer, like I'm telling them to do something, only it feels more like I'm telling a part of myself to do something."

He whistles under his breath and gives me an appraising look. "That's a rare ability."

"It doesn't always work. I can't always... flip into someone."

"Flip?"

"It's just what I call it. Once, I couldn't do it because I was weak and hungry. That's when I first fed. My ability worked after. But then later, I tried to flip into the same person, and I couldn't, even though I had the strength."

"Have you considered that you may only be able to... flip... into the same person once?"

I consider everyone I've used my power on. Ragathon is the only one I ever tried to control more than once. "That actually makes sense. I'll have to test that theory when I have time."

He nods. "Every gift has limits. But this is very powerful indeed. If you can turn—or flip—enough people to our side, we may not need the rebels."

I shake my head. "No. I've never controlled more than one person at once, and never for long."

He nods in understanding. "With some training you might be able to expand your powers, but that will take more time than we have at the moment. Have you noticed any other abilities?"

"No."

"You may manifest them. You may not."

"Summoning memories is your ability?" I ask.

"Yes."

"But if we're all Nephilim, why can we do different things?"

"Do you want my theory, or that of the priests?"

"Yours." I decide to roast another marshmallow while we talk, since we obviously aren't training again anytime soon.

"If Nephilim are all descended from Angels and humans, or if turned, have both Angel and human blood, then we are only part Angel. Like all half-breeds or mutts, we possess a propensity for variation. Some of us inherit more Angel traits than others."

"So an Angel would have both of our abilities," I say.

"More," he says, throwing another stick into the fire while I eat my marshmallow.

"Is that how you knew that what attacked me was an Angel? Because of its abilities?"

"There are two kinds of Nephilim," Zorin says. "Those who are born, and those who are turned. Those who are born have wings of gold and white and red, and though they gain power from blood, they do not require it to live. Those who are turned have wings of blue, purple, silver and black and, without life force, they wither away."

I look at his black wings and my silver. We were both turned.

He continues. "The two kinds are named after the colors of their wings. Those who are born are said to be Of Sunrise, and those turned to be Of Nightfall."

I move my wings, letting a few tendrils curl around my hand as I watch them. They almost look white, in the right light, but I can see the silver hue surrounding them. "So we are both Of Nightfall."

Zorin nods. "The Angel was of neither. He had wings of gold and purple mixed with white."

I was colorblind when I first saw the Angel. I relied on Evie, who had focused on the gold, but hadn't focused on the color of the Angel's wings.

Zorin stirs the fire again, its flames flaring up and sending sparks into the cool night air. "If your plan is to work, you will need a weapon."

I smile, bittersweet. "I know just where to get one..." With a flap of my wings I rise into the sky and head back to the Kingdom of Sky.

Zorin catches up quickly, laughter in his voice as he flies by my side. "You are an impulsive one, aren't you?"

"I prefer *decisive*," I say, picking up speed until we blur through the sky faster than an airplane.

I should be freezing, but my new body is made for the skies, for flight, for all temperatures, and all I feel is freedom.

I land just outside my house. I pull the bunker door open, wondering who closed it, and Zorin follows me in.

I ignore the swell of emotions within and walk to my mother's case. My genetics are close enough, my dad said.

I place my hand in the key and it comes to life, revealing gleaming silver armor and a sword.

TRUST AMONGST REBELS

I stay at my house that night, unwilling to return to Castle V until I'm prepared to rescue Jax. Trix, the Shadow of Rome herself, contacted me, and we agreed to meet at the Cathedral at noon. With time on my hands until then, I study my mother's armor and make some modifications that will help my role as N.

After a few hours, I admire my work. The armor gleams, no longer just silver, but black, like the night. I keep a few subtle silver accents where the tree of life remains carved into the chest plate. At a certain angle, the silver reflects the moonlight, like tiny stars at midnight.

The leggings and chest plate have the flexibility of fabric but more impenetrability than steel. They fit like they were made for me.

I modify the half-mask, which covers the top of my face, connecting it with my eGlass so I can keep my identity secret, but still stay in communication.

My final plan involves sending Zorin out for an EZ-Dye kit.

"You want a what?" he asks, his face a comic display of dismay.

"An EZ-Dye kit. They're relatively new. They allow people to instantly change their hair color with the touch of a small button you wear behind your ear. I need one to disguise myself when I meet with the rebels. They can't know who I am, especially if I ever need to return to Castle V as Scarlett."

He paces my living room, filling it like a god of old. "And why can't you get this yourself?"

"One, because I have no money and they are ridiculously expensive. And two, because I have to finish getting ready for my meeting."

He glares at me. "So now I'm to be your errand boy?"

I grin. "It will make you useful."

He mumbles a few choice words before flying out the door. It doesn't take him long to return, bag in hand with my new hair kit.

"Thank you. Want to see the magic?"

He rolls his eyes. "Sure."

I install the tiny metal sphere into my eGlass, then tap it twice as per the directions. Almost instantly, my hair turns black with a silver streak down the front. "Voilá!"

His eyes widen. "Could have used that a few years ago."

"So you like it?"

"You remind me of the Twilight Queen."

I raise an eyebrow. "So..."

He sighs. "While I prefer your pale hair... yes, you look very nice."

His words make me a little giddy. "Thanks."

I admire myself in the mirror when Evie beeps at me. "You have just enough time to get to your appointment, Scarlett," she says in my ear.

"It's time," I tell Zorin as I pull on my mother's armor and become someone else.

...

Zorin and I arrive first. We keep our wings hidden and wear black cloaks with hoods. We claim a spot in the dusty belly of the Cathedral on old pews that haven't been completely ruined by the war. Moonlight shines through the windows. "If we're going to use this as our base, we need to clean it up," I tell him.

He wipes away an inch of dust from the wooden bench before sitting down. "Agreed," he says. Zorin doesn't wear full armor like me, but he does wear a mask to disguise his face. Better we aren't easily identified at this point in the trust game.

Trix arrives with TR. We both agreed to only bring one other with us.

She looks around, her cropped red hair flipping against her cheek as she spins her head. "Classy. Did the maid quit?"

I laugh. "Good help is so hard to find," I say with the same light tone as her.

TR grunts. I only saw him once, briefly, in the crowd with a hoodie on. Now I can see all of his features. His light hair is shorn high and tight. His blue eyes glare at me with mistrust. "Can we get this meeting started?" he asks.

I gesture for them to sit, which they do.

"Why are you wearing masks?" asks TR. "You've seen our faces. We should see yours."

"Maybe she's someone we'd recognize," Trix suggests.

"I'm not one of you," I say. "Neither of us are. And I won't have our identities compromised if one of you is captured."

"My guys would never break," TR says, crossing his arms over his chest.

"We all break," says Trix, more moderately. I like her.

"You didn't tell them anything," he says, his voice less caustic with her. More… loving. Interesting.

"Nothing important," she says with a shrug. "But people have different priorities. N's right. Someone might give out her identity if they didn't value it. And like she said, she's not one of us. So why would we value her?"

"My plan will strategically benefit you," I say, tired of being talked about as if I'm not there.

"How exactly?" asks TR.

I speak quietly into Evie, and she projects onto a blank wall the images I cued up. Two young men, one small and thin, Peter, and another large and burly, called Allen. Two women, Mary and Any, sisters with long black hair. And Lucy, a little girl with big blue eyes and a cut on her cheek. They all look weary and sad, and when I glance at them, images of Brooke and Ella flash through my mind. "Five Zeniths sentenced to be executed due to their involvement with you."

TR studies the faces. "We've never worked with them."

I nod knowingly. "They lost control of their abilities during the Shadow's escape. Now, the Inquisition will kill them because they have no one else to punish."

"Saw this on the city cameras, did you?" asks Trix with a smirk.

I nod.

Outrage forms on TR's face. "Bastards are saying they just murdered people… "

"So what's the plan, N?" Trix asks.

"We rescue them."

TR jumps up from the bench, hands in fists. "Are you crazy? After what just happened, the whole city is a fortress. We'll never get close to them, not to mention get out."

I stand and face him. "Tell me, TR, did I or did I not secure the Shadow of Rome's escape?"

He scrunches his face. "Yeah, but—"

"And they were waiting for you," I remind him. "This time, we'll be the ones to surprise them. This time, there will be no casualties, I promise you."

"There's no way you can promise that," he says.

I smile. "I do. No one will die. Not even the Inquisition."

His mouth falls open for a moment, and he snaps it shut. "And what do we get from this? A chance to play your puppets?"

I shake my head calmly, hiding my anxiety and fear. They need to agree to my plan. "They are powerful Zeniths. I witnessed the abilities of one, Peter Conley, a level five Gravir, after I helped you escape. If you save them, they will join you, and you will need their help to win." I pause for effect. "The Four Orders have Knights who are Zeniths."

They don't look surprised.

"You know about Zenith patricians?" I ask.

Trix nods. "We've known for a while, ever since we served under zen pats in the army."

"Why not release this information to the public?"

TR sighs, rubbing his temples. "And do what? Others have tried before. The most we'll get is a riot quickly put down and the information discredited. If we are to reveal this, we'll need to do it at the right time."

I nod, taking note of his idea and modifying my original argument. "After we rescue the Zeniths, I will convince them to join your ranks. It'll be a huge public blow to the Orders when a second execution fails."

"And what if they don't want to join?" asks Trix, crossing her legs casually. She stays cool and collected while TR is all fire. I'll have to remember that.

"They will," I say. "They'll be fugitives. They'll have no other options. "I'll do whatever I can to make them. That I vow."

TR is not impressed, based on his scowl.

Trix nods thoughtfully. "It's a good idea, N. You want to strengthen us once again, but why? I'd say you know these fellows, but that wouldn't explain why you helped rescue me."

"My reasons are my own," I say.

"I get the privacy," she stands as well, but Zorin stays to the side, silent and imposing. "We all have reasons of our own, and not just the fighting for equal rights stuff. Sure that's important, but we've all lost things, people. Something deeper drives us. And, I want to know, what drives you N? Because then, maybe we could trust you."

They both look to me for answers I can't give. "I've already helped you. Isn't that enough?"

"It's a start," she says. "But you could still be part of the Inquisition. This could still be some Inquisition scheme to gain our trust. So, I ask you again, N. What drives you?"

I can't tell them the whole truth, but I have one last move up my sleeve. "You're right. We've all lost things." I lean down on one knee and draw the first half of the Nephilim symbol. A symbol of trust.

I see the recognition in TR's eyes as Trix kneels next to me and completes the symbol. She looks at me with awe and whispers, "You believe they'll return?"

"No." I drop my cloak to the ground. Warmth spreads through my back.

And I unleash my silver wings.

"I believe they already have."

...

"I understand why you wear a mask," Trix says, her red hair flaming in the sunlight as we walk outside the cathedral. "But it makes it hard for some of us to trust you."

"You mean TR," I say.

She nods. "Him the most, yes, but others too. You could be a spy for our enemies. You could endanger the lives of everyone we work with."

I extend my wings to remind her of what I am. "My very existence flies in the face of the Orders and their assurances that the Nephilim are dead. If they catch me, they will kill me without hesitation. Humanity has tried to annihilate my kind since the beginning of time, and they almost succeeded."

It's still strange thinking of humanity as something separate from me, but they are. I'm no longer human.

"That's what I told TR. You can't be a spy because they would never work with Nephilim. And Nephilim would never work with them. It's why I want you to see something."

She walks to a motorcycle in one of the garages and pats the back. "Up for a ride into the city?"

I hesitate, leery of being alone with the Shadow of Rome. "What kind of Zenith are you? The news don't say." I hope knowing the answer will give me comfort.

She picks up a stick in her hand, and after a moment, the wood turns red, then ash-gray, falling through her fingers. "I'm a Burner. Level four." Great, so she can heat things up with a touch. At least she's not level five. Then she could burn me from across the field.

Either way, she is powerful, and I need her support. I have no other choice. "Thank you for telling me. Let's go."

Trix swings a leg over the seat, and I follow her lead, holding on lightly to her waist as she takes off, winding through the dirt roads until we hit something resembling civilization. We both wear hoods, hiding our faces from cameras.

She takes me to a part of New York I've never been before. It's older, dirtier, more run down. Fairy trees do not line the streets in this neighborhood. There's precious little beauty here, only poverty, sickness, despair.

It reminds me of the *domus infirmos* back in Sky where the worst of the worst, the lowest of the low, went.

She parks her bike and we get off. I follow her into a building that looks abandoned. I scan the area, noting ways of escape should this be a trap.

We don't take the stairs up, as I expected, but instead we turn the corner and stand in front of what looks like a basement door. Trix knocks three times, waits, knocks twice, waits and knocks three more.

A small black panel slides open and a pair of brown eyes stares at us through it. "What do you want?"

"What do all men want?" Trix says. "To be free."

The panel closes and the door clicks open. A tall, lanky man with the shadow of a beard and a broad face smiles at us. "How you doing, Trix? We've missed you around here."

"Missed you all too," she says with an easy grin. "But you know how it goes in this business."

He nods and leads us into a dimly lit large room lined with mattresses on one side and tables on the other. People of all ages and walks of life move through the room, some eating, some serving food, some sleeping, some talking with others, some sitting alone crying.

"What is this place?" I ask.

"A safe house. All of these people are part of our cause, fighting in whatever way they can to make things better for Zeniths."

We walk around as Trix greets people, mingles, asks about their families and lives, hugs kids who run up to her.

"You're popular," I say.

She shrugs. "I've spent a lot of time here." Then her smile fades, and she turns to look at me. "I need you to be sure."

"Of what?"

"That no one will die. Look around, N. These are your people. These are the people who will die if things go wrong."

I feel the weight of her words as I watch a child scurry across the room after a red ball. In the corner, a young mother nurses a newborn while she talks with a small group. An old man teaches a teenager how to play chess.

I nod. "I'm sure."

She smiles. "I've got a few things to check on. Make yourself at home."

She leaves me standing in a crowd of strangers, each caught up in the rhythms of their own lives.

I don't move to talk to anyone. I don't know what to say. So I just watch and listen.

A soft voice startles me from my silence.

"You seem misplaced in this den of despair." An old woman leans on her walking cane, her white hair long and braided.

"Misplaced?" I repeat. "Perhaps. But I fear that defines everywhere in my life right now."

She puts a hand on my elbow. "Come. I will make you a cup of tea."

She leads me past the people, through a curtain and into a small room decorated with bright floor pillows, a bed, a two person café table and a bookshelf full of books. Knickknacks line all the free spaces, ancient-looking things that span time and cultures.

She guides me to a chair at the table and I sit as she turns to make us tea with a burner on her dresser.

Once she sits, I sip my tea and watch her do the same. She has a lined face that looks like it has seen much, and blue eyes that are still sharp. She wears a long dark pink dress with silver accents and carries herself with grace.

"Who are you?" I ask.

"Everyone here calls me Nana."

"Okay," I say, taken in by this charming woman.

"And what do they call you?"

"N," I say.

She doesn't pause at my obviously fake name. "So, do you like New York, N?"

For an hour, we sit and talk about nothing much and a bit of everything.

We don't talk about politics or rebel plans. I don't tell her my parents were just murdered in front of me. But I tell her my favorite book and learn about hers and we talk about music and art and entertainment.

When Trix finds us, she grins. "I see you've met."

I nod, standing, my tea cup empty twice over. "Thank you for spending time with me, Nana."

She stands and reaches for my hand. Hers are old and soft, her skin thin and fine, but her grip is firm. She leans in to hug me and whispers in my ear. "I am sorry for your loss, child."

"How do you—"

"I see your pain in the eyes of all who come here. Each one has lost something dear: a home, a lover, a child. They are but walking shells, and the world outside them a dream. They forget who they are, for all they know is rage. But in the end, their grief fades, their anger subsides, and they wish they had never forgotten."

I try to imagine myself without grief, without anger, but I cannot. "What remains?"

"Hope," she says, smiling. "Hope remains."

NIGHTFALL

I've always wanted my own aircraft. I just never thought I'd get it by stealing from the military.

I also never imagined it would be a Night Raven, a small stealth jet with hovering capabilities and cloaking.

A multi-billion-dollar machine.

It wasn't hard. Once Evie hacked the Teutonic Airforce base to find the identity and home address of the Head of Security, I caught him as he left for work and used my powers to compel him to program a Night Raven to leave base and arrive at the Cathedral. "You will remove all tracking and will not search for it. It will remain in your database."

He nodded and did exactly as instructed. This was a bit high profile and Zorin had some concerns, but we needed something that could be flown directly into Manhattan without being detected and could escape with speed and agility. The Night Raven can go over

Mach 7, seven times the speed of sound. It's undetectable, can defend itself, and can be operated remotely.

And... I've always wanted one.

With it, I fly straight to Times Square, where the Zeniths are being held prisoner as Ragathon showboats until the execution.

I hover the aircraft right in front of the central platforms and speak, projecting my voice through all the eScreens and speakers I've hacked into. "This aircraft has the capacity to destroy this entire block. Do not move from your positions."

A group of bystanders has gathered to watch the executions. Even after what happened last time, their bloodlust can't be contained. It sickens me.

The crowd stirs, gasping, chattering like monkeys. There are more guards than before, Officers and Bruisers lining the Square, the Central Command vehicle with its giant cannon pointed straight at the Night Raven.

But no one moves. I have their attention.

Ragathon, the cocky biter, holds his giant hammer in his fist, his red Inquisitor cloak billowing behind him as he speaks through his own speakers. "Who is this?"

I lower the Night Raven and open the cockpit, stepping out in my full armor, my cloak, my face masked, my hair black as night with silver streaks. My image stares back at me from all eScreens as I speak. "I am Nightfall, and if you wish to live, you will do as I say." I point to the platform where the Zeniths slump in handcuffs against a pillar. They are drugged with Z-Blockers and their eyes are glossed over, bodies made of limp muscles hanging over bone. I harden my voice. "Hand the prisoners over to me."

"And you'll leave?" Ragathon asks, the gold and crimson of his chest plate splintering the city lights into fractals.

"Yes."

He sneers. "And why should I trust a rebel?"

"I am no rebel," I say. "I am—" Before I can finish, another aircraft appears from behind a skyscraper, hovering between New York towers. I dash forward, drawing my sword, my wings a spiral of silver light as I cut the jet wings off the aircraft using my blade. It crashes down to the street, bursting into flames before a screaming crowd.

With wings exposed, I fly up and then let myself fall to the ground below the Night Raven. I speak softly, but my voice travels through the city. "I am Nephilim."

"We can't let her go," Ragathon yells to his soldiers. "Surround her!"

"Others of my kind are amongst you right now," I warn him.

At those words, the crowds and soldiers and leaders, all of them freeze. I'm playing on their worst fears. That the Nephilim will return. That they can turn anyone. That they can destroy them all. "If you move against me, my agents will destroy each and every last one of you."

"She's bluffing," Ragathon says. "Fire!" The cannon moves lower, pointing straight at me.

And then, black tendrils like smoke whip from the crowd and cut the cannon in half. The dark whirl of motion continues until it lands above the crowd on a balcony. Zorin stands in his black cloak, sword raised, his face masked, his wings on full display.

The eScreens alternate between images of him and me. Two Nephilim. How many more are there? That's the thought on everyone's mind.

"You should thank me, Inquisitor," I say sweetly. "If that cannon had gone off, all of you would have been killed."

On cue, members of the crowd step out toward me, all cloaked in black and holding swords. The final illusion. The reason I need the rebels.

"Sir, your orders?" asks Ragathon's Second—the Seeker. She stands at attention, ready to act, her body and face cloaked in cold steel with the Inquisition eye carved across her chest. Jax stands beside her, clad in silver armor with the black Teutonic cross. I try not to look at him.

Ragathon's jaw tenses, and I can see the internal battle he wages. He's already failed one execution. Can he afford another?

The city is quiet as all wait for Ragathon's command. He looks toward Jax, his face unreadable. "Sir Lux, please escort the prisoners to the rebel."

Jax tries to mask his surprise, and then his dismay, but I see the telltale signs of his emotion flicker across his face. I know him too well. Something is not right with this. Why didn't he send the Seeker? She's his Second. She's his lackey. Jax isn't even in his Order.

But Jax nods once, sharply, and reaches for Peter's chained hands, guiding him forward. A second chain connects all five Zeniths together, to slow them down if any of them should run. I study them. There is Peter, and behind him Allen, the big man with thick arms. The two sisters, Mary and Any, whose black hair flows in the wind, follow them. And behind them stumbles Lucy, the blue-eyed girl no more than ten. I do not know them, not really, but to me they are all Brooke and Ella. They are all innocents to be torn from this world. They stand in front of a firing wall, with Officers positioned across from them, ready to shoot them dead at Ragathon's command.

Peter stumbles forward, losing his balance, and Jax catches his arm and helps him up. There is pain in the Knight's eyes.

Every muscle in my body contracts, ready to spring into action at any sign the situation will deteriorate.

Zorin whispers into my eGlass. "I don't like this. Be careful."

As if I needed that warning.

It takes them sixteen steps to reach me, and what feels like an hour. Cameras capture every move, every facial expression, feeding those images into the eScreens for all to see.

A few steps before Jax reaches me, he brings his hand to his eGlass and frowns, then drops his hand, his face going blank. Cold. Expressionless.

My gut clenches. Every instinct is telling me to run, but I must see this through or these people will die.

Jax is now standing before me, his eyes unreadable. "This isn't the way," he whispers.

I don't know how to respond. I don't know another way to save these people.

When he sees I'm not going to yield or respond, Jax sighs, shakes his head slightly, and moves as if to hand the prisoners off to me. I reach for Peter.

And Jax grabs the hilt of my sword.

I try to shove him away.

He grasps me, turning my back to him, and pushes the blade against my throat. "Call off your agents," he yells so everyone can hear.

I don't know what to say or do. How can this be happening? What's he doing?

"Do not move without my command," I tell the rebels through my eGlass.

Trix's voice comes through. "N? What do you want us to do, N?"

Zorin's voice cuts her off. "Nightfall, use your ability."

On... Jax? I never thought I'd have to do that to him.

"I have a shot," TR says. "I can take him out. Your call, N."

Too many voices vie for attention in my frazzled mind. "No!"

Jax speaks softly in my ear. "Tell your agents to retreat. You will be taken into custody, but you can still save your people."

I push through my haze to try to reach him with logic. "If you don't let me go, they'll kill those Zeniths."

He grits his teeth. "This isn't the way to change the system."

"So you'll let them die for this system?" We can't wait for future answers. We have to act now. Today. The lives that are lost in this moment count.

Jax doesn't respond, and I know I've lost.

Zorin was right all along. Jax is a caged tiger who learned to call his prison home. I can't change his mind. Not as Nightfall. Maybe not even as Scarlett. He won't betray the Orders, even after they betrayed everything he believes. Even to save Zeniths like himself. Tears well in my eyes. I can't lose Jax. My last true friend. The last of my family. But if he insists on fighting me, I must do what is right. What is just.

"I'm sorry," I say as I unleash my wings and surround us both in silver light, blinding Jax. The blade cuts at my throat, and I push it away, twisting out of Jax's grasp. I kick him to the ground, and I launch into the air. Jax jumps to his feet and stares at me from below, and though I know he can follow with his gravotics, he does not pursue me. I don't have the time to wonder why.

The Seeker joins his side. They pull the prisoners back to the firing wall, chaining them up like animals sent to slaughter.

Pandemonium ensues. Inquisition Officers aim at any in the crowd they suspect of being aligned with the rebels.

Trix calls me again. "N, what's the plan?"

If we fight, we will suffer casualties. Our own will die and we'd have no way of guaranteeing the Zeniths will be free.

If we don't fight, they die for sure. And we will have failed them.

If I can gain some leverage... maybe if I take Ragathon hostage somehow.

Before I can form a plan, someone screams and shots are fired.

I look to the stage and my heart clenches in pain. In a blink, a heartbeat, all five Zeniths are executed. Without ceremony. Without justice. Without last words or rights. They are murdered.

Lucy's little body sprawls out on the platform, blood seeping out of her, her hands still locked in chains, her eyes still open, staring into nothing.

I feel sick.

With my eGlass, I zoom in on Jax, who is pale, his face hardened in rage.

This is what the Orders do to those who are different.

This is what they think is justice.

"Pull back," I tell my team. "Get our people to safety."

"You heard her," Trix says. "Everyone pull back."

"Such a waste," TR grumbles, but he obeys.

"Not a waste," I say as I board the Night Raven and fly out of the city and back to the Cathedral. I'm trying to find the hope. The silver lining to this dismal failure. "We revealed the truth to the public—that the Inquisition is ruthless and will murder anyone who gets in their way, and we showed them all the Nephilim have returned."

"We, N?" Trix asks. "Are you joining us now?"

"Just explaining what we accomplished," I say with a sigh. "I'll meet you back at the rendezvous." I cut the comm and pull off my mask. As the Night Raven pilots me to the Cathedral, I bury my face in my hands and sob.

...

I can't let them see what this failure has done to me. Can't let them know this is personal, that I knew Peter, if only for a moment. Only Zorin knows, but even he cannot console me.

I am consumed by the grief of those deaths. Their blood is on my hands. I failed them. But I'm also torn apart by Jax's choice to stay loyal to the Orders rather than do what is right in the face of injustice. How could we have started in the same place and grown so far apart?

I'm glad for my mask as I sit around an old oak table with Trix and TR across from me and Zorin at my side. The sun has already set, casting the world into darkness. Fitting.

I shake my head to clear away the brooding thoughts as Trix leans back in her chair.

"We may not have saved them, but we can still make a difference," she says. "With Nephilim on our side, we could change things."

"You mean, you could start a second war." My voice sounds hollow. Dead.

"We can crush the Orders," she counters.

"Really? Then why did we nearly go extinct to begin with? The Twilight Court had hundreds of Nephilim fighting and they still lost. We have two."

As silence falls, the rebels look between Zorin and me, and then Trix cocks her head toward him. "What about you? Where do you stand in all this?"

Zorin glances at me, then back at them. "I'm with Nightfall," he says. "But, if I can be of assistance, please call on me."

His offer surprises me. Maybe he has more hope in their cause than I do.

"Here," Trix say, passing him an eGlass. "Use this to stay in contact. It's encrypted, so no one can trace the signal."

"Thank you." He takes the device and slips it into his pocket.

Trix turns back to me, her green eyes scrutinizing. "So how about it, N? You with us?"

I can't think past my pain right now. "I need to go." I stand and head toward the door.

"We can help each other, N," Trix calls after me. "You've seen that."

Have I? What have we really accomplished after all? I spouted some lines about our success, but they felt hollow, even to me.

"Let her go," TR says from behind me. "She broke her promise."

I spin around to face him as he continues.

"The aircraft you took down. It crashed in the streets. That pilot and anyone around died." He glares at me with his blue eyes. "You promised no one would die."

"The aircraft had no pilot," I say, a weariness forming in my bones. "And I controlled the crash."

TR smirks. "How could you possibly do that?"

"She sent it there," Trix say, as realization dawns. "She stole it like she stole the Night Raven and programed it to show up. Didn't you, N?"

"Yes." Despite everything, I'm impressed by Trix. She has a quick mind and rational approach I admire. "I needed to demonstrate my abilities without hurting anyone."

Not even Zorin knew that part of my plan, and they all look at me with something new on their faces. Awe. Respect.

Trix folds her hands together and locks eyes with me. "We need you, N. You're better than any of us."

"Thank you," I say, as I open the door and stare at the Night Raven. "But TR was right. I did break my promise. People died tonight because of me."

...

I hide the Night Raven in a mountain cave outside of New York. Then, using my own wings, I fly to the edge of New York and walk through the city, looking for the subway station that will take me back to Vianney Island and Castle V.

I keep my eGlass turned off and ignore all eScreens. I don't want to see the Zeniths executed over and over from different angles, don't want to see the footage that will follow. I want this day to be over.

As I pass by an alley, my own thoughts are broken by a boy screaming for help. I turn into the darkness and see three kids, barely teens, standing over another kid, kicking him in the stomach and taunting him. "Rotten Zenith," one says, landing a blow to his chest with a boot. "You hoping Nephilim win this time, Zenith? You hoping they kill us all?"

"I'm not... a Zenith... please..." the kid on the ground begs through a split and bleeding lip.

The second attacker spits at him and leers. "I saw you making things float in the bathroom."

"No..." the boy says, shaking, cowering. "You're making that up."

The bully steps closer, crushing the kid's hand under his foot. "You calling me a liar?"

"No... please..."

I run down the alley as they continue to beat the boy.

"Hey!" I shout, ready to do whatever it takes to protect this kid. I worry I'll have to fight three minors, but the moment they see me they run like the cowards they are.

I reach for the boy's hand, but he jumps up and scuttles away from me. "I'm not a Zenith," he says. His face is red and covered in tears, his brown hair a mess of dirt and gravel. "I'm not!"

He tries to push past me, and I drop my hand to his shoulder. "Wait!"

My power opens up on its own this time, throwing me into his mind, his memories.

At home, he levitates a small paper crane over his hand, a big smile on his face.

In the bathroom, his backpack starts to float next to him. He didn't mean to. He wasn't even thinking. A group of kids come into the bathroom and see...

In the school office, his parents talk to the principal.

On the bathroom floor at lunch, a kid kicks him in the gut.

At home, his parents yell at him, telling him to stop. "Can't you just be a normal kid?"

And then he steals his father's key, the key to a drawer where his dad keeps a gun...

"Don't be afraid," I tell him, pushing the thought into his mind. "Things will get better."

He believes me. I make him believe. "Things will get better," I say again. Because I will make them better. Nightfall will make them better.

I let him go and he walks away, smiling, as tears fill my eyes.

...

By the time I arrive at Castle V, I've mostly calmed down. My eyes are still swollen from tears and I need a bath, but I'm back to being Scarlett, all signs of my alter ego stored away, my hair back to its pale blond, but my heart still crushed beyond repair.

I've only come back for one purpose. I haven't thought past what I'll do after. Will I stay and try to destroy the Orders from within? Will I leave and join the rebels? Will I just disappear? Will I try to hunt the Angel that killed my parents?

I have no answers to any of these. No plan. No ideas.

I only know one thing as I clutch my mother's dagger in my hand, hidden under the cuff of my hoodie.

Ragathon will pay for what he's done tonight.

I search for him on the grounds and find him saying goodbye to a group of students.

He walks away, laughing, smiling. Like he hasn't just murdered five people.

I squeeze the dagger in my hand, the cold steel digging into my palm.

As I walk faster toward him, my heart pumps quicker, heat builds in my body, adrenaline courses through me.

I've never killed anyone in cold blood before. But I don't waver. Don't hesitate. He's not an innocent and I will have no regrets, no matter how this ends, as long as he's dead.

I'm few feet from him, his back to me as he walks away. I move closer.

And I raise my blade, ready to strike, ready to end his life.

This is my last move.

My king ending the game.

I lunge.

Someone grabs my hand.

"Scarlett?"

My heart stutters and the dagger falls to the ground. Ragathon continues on, oblivious to how close he was to the end of his life.

I turn to the man who stopped me.

Jax wraps his arms around me and holds me against his chest, his voice a breath against my ear. "Scarlett, this isn't the way."

THE DARK TEMPLARS

He bends down to pick up the dagger I dropped at our feet. "This wouldn't have changed anything, Star." He hands it back to me, and I stick it in my bag. "Some other Inquisitor would just take his place. Maybe even someone worse—"

"He murdered people today. And... you helped him."

He frowns, his face a mask. "I hate what happened today, but if I didn't obey his commands to stop Nightfall, I too would have been executed or severely punished. Someone else would have done what I tried to do, and I would have lost any chance of making a difference from within. Sometimes you have to make choices for the greater good, the bigger picture."

"At the sacrifice of lives. Their lives mattered." My throat chokes with emotion.

His face softens. "They did matter, you're right. They do matter. But do they matter more than the millions we could save if we create lasting change?"

"That's assuming your way works. What if it doesn't? What if Nightfall is right?"

He shrugs, his face sad. "Time will tell. I have to do what feels right to me."

We begin to walk toward the water as we talk, moving away from the Castle and anyone who might overhear us. "But they're on your side," I say. "The Nephilim are fighting so Zeniths and humans and plebeians and patricians can live equally. For years, they've been fighting. Can't you see that, all this time, they're the ones we should have been rooting for?"

He turns to look at me, his hand resting on my arm. "Scarlett, if Nephilim had won the war, they would have killed everyone who opposed them."

"And have we done any different?"

Jax sits on a bench under a tree overlooking the water. "Look, there's no point in regretting a past we have no control over. You and I can change things now. We'll rise up the ranks, and we'll make a difference. One day, when a Grandmaster like Ragathon is to be replaced, we'll be the ones to replace him."

I have too much energy in me to sit, so I pace next to him, the beauty of the night lost to me. "And what about Nightfall?"

"The Council will deal with her."

I want to smack him, but I refrain, pulling in all of my frustration at his narrow-minded views. "Whether you like it or not, she tried to save innocent lives today. She may not have succeeded, but she showed the world there is injustice, and that someone is willing to fight for those disenfranchised."

Jax shakes his head. "All she did was show herself to be a terrorist willing to sacrifice anyone who gets in the way of her cause."

Before I say something I'll regret, I turn away. "I need to go."

He stands and grabs my hand before I can leave. "Scarlett, just... just wait a moment."

I turn to look at him. Moonlight highlights his dark hair and his face softens with a familiar smile. "We might disagree on the right course of action, but we are aligned in our values, in our beliefs. We can make a difference. I respect you, even when we don't agree. You are still my best friend." He steps forward, and I can smell the mint of his soap as it catches on the breeze. "You mean more to me than you know. I don't want Nightfall coming between us."

He leans in and kisses my cheek, a light peck that leaves a mark on my skin, like a burn that travels through my body. "Goodnight, Star."

Choked by my own emotion, I say goodnight and walk quickly to my room, all thoughts of assassinating

Ragathon gone. It won't work now, anyways. Too public. Too dangerous. Unless I want a suicide mission, there has to be a better way.

As I make my way into the Castle and through the corridors toward the Initiates Wing and my bedroom, I wonder at what my parents and Jax saw in this place. It oozes corruption and doesn't seem to do anything it promises to do.

When I lock my door and check for bugs—you could never be too careful—I walk to the window, prick my finger, and draw the Nephilim symbol on the glass. It shimmers and disappears, and as I wait to hear from Zorin, I finally take the chip from the night my parents were killed and install it into my eGlass.

I drop to my bed, clutching the Token of Strife in my hand and watch that night unravel in full color. Over and over I replay the video. Seeing them fight. Seeing them both killed. Seeing the Angel come from the sky.

It's nearly morning when I look up to see Zorin standing in my room, the window open behind him.

I raise an eyebrow at the odd vision of him in my room. "Isn't it a bit risky for you to be here?"

He grins and sits at my desk chair. "I have ways of remaining incognito. What can I do for you, Miss Night?"

I sit up and take off my eGlass. "It's what I can do for you, actually. Or rather, what we can do for each other.

I'll help you discover why the Nephilim lost the war." I can see interest in his eyes and continue. "And then, I'll help you rebuild. Gather the rebels and prepare the Cathedral. It will be our base, where we start."

"Start?" he asks.

"A new Order," I say. "One that fights for both Zeniths and humans. One that actually keeps its oaths."

"If we are to be an army, we shall need a name. A banner under which to fight."

I prick my finger with the Token of Strife and use a drop of blood to draw on the floor between us. An infinity symbol with a double cross rising from it. "Not an army," I say, looking up at him. "We shall be of the night, striking from the shadows, but we shall be more than soldiers. We shall be symbols of what is just. We shall be knights of the dark. We shall be the Dark Templars."

He traces the symbol with his finger. "The Leviathan Cross," he says.

I nod. "An ancient Templar symbol that stands for balance in the masculine and feminine. It represents protection. We are that protection. We are that balance."

Zorin smiles. "Will you leave this Castle and take residence at the Cathedral?"

"No," I say, still cradling the Token of Strife in my hand. "I'll rise up the ranks, and then I'll destroy them."

...

The next day I surprise my grandfather with news that I'm ready to commit to the Orders. And he surprises me with a road trip.

"There is something I want to show you before you make this commitment."

We walk through Vianney to the underground parking and a driver pulls up in a shiny, black stretch limo.

"No eDriver?" I ask, as the driver holds the door open for me.

My grandfather slides in after me. "Call me old fashioned. I still prefer a human behind the wheel."

The drive itself is the longest time I've ever spent with my grandfather, as we head north into a more remote area of New York, and then east into the farmlands.

Along the way, I pepper him with questions of my mother, of what she was like as a child ("as precocious as I imagine you were") and how she met my father ("they met as Initiates at Castle V"). I feel closer to him than I ever did when the car slows down and we pull up to a large villa. It has clearly been abandoned for many years, but it is still beautiful, with ivy twisting up the caramel and cream walls, and a stone path that leads to an open air center courtyard dotted with Fairy Trees and Trinity Trees.

"This villa is part of your family inheritance," he says, handing me an ancient skeleton key. "It's on two hundred acres of land. There are ten rooms, twelve bathrooms, two great rooms, a ballroom, a library, a study, several fireplaces, and a gourmet kitchen with a breakfast nook and dining hall."

I stand with my mouth agape, staring. He hands me a small black velvet box. "This also belongs to you."

I open it and stare at a beautiful silver ring with a rainbow moonstone at its center and stars designed into the band. "That is the House of Night family ring." He hands me a bank book. "And this, is your wealth."

There are too many zeros to count. My head spins. "This is all… mine?"

"Yes." He turns to look at me. "You're a wealthy young lady, Scarlett. Your parents left you everything, and that's not insignificant. Before you take your vows, I wanted you to know you have choices. You are not dependent on me or this school for your survival. You can leave, if you must, though I hope you won't. I hope you'll stay."

"How did my parents accrue so much wealth?" I ask, still shocked.

He chuckles as if I'd asked him why the sky is blue. "They both came from ancient patrician families. The Nights, who were honored during the Great War, and the Forresters, who can trace their lineage back to Juliana herself."

I smile widely, realizing I'm related to one of my childhood heroes.

My grandfather continues, stroking his long grey beard. "Their inheritance, combined with their income from the Knights Templar, is, as you have seen, considerable. Today, the databases will be updated. You will be a patrician in name and stature. Your life will have many options."

We walk into the villa and I marvel at the beauty of this place, considering all he has said. "Thank you. It means a lot to me that you showed me this before I committed." I turn to him, my will resolved. "But I'm not going anywhere. I belong at Castle V."

He smiles. "You know what comes next?"

"Yes." I've studied the process since I dreamed of becoming a Knight. Next come the Initiate Trials. Three will compete for a place at the castle.

And only one will win.

...

Back at the Cathedral, I stand with Zorin, Trix and TR and assess our new space.

TR grins. He doesn't look relaxed—he rarely does—but he does look excited. "This will do nicely for a base."

"The Nephilytes built catacombs underground. The tunnels could prove useful." Zorin gestures to the door at the back. "Let me show you." He and TR walk off and disappear into the bowels of the Cathedral.

I begin to follow when Trix stops me with her words.

"I know you work for the Orders."

I turn to her, my blood pulsing under my skin.

"Or that you used to work for them," she amends. "That's how you were able to track the Inquisition's movements when you helped me escape."

I grip the hilt of my sword and curse at myself for my own folly. I should have been more careful. Now, my entire plan could be ruined... unless... unless I could use my powers to make Trix forget. Make her stop thinking along these lines.

Trix steps away from me, her arms in the air in a gesture of peace. "Look, as long as you help my team take down the Four Orders, I don't care. I trust you, N. Just, tell me... tell me we can win this thing."

I release my sword, my body relaxing just a fraction. Maybe this can still work. "We can," I say. "We will."

Trix nods. "That's all I need to know." She holds out her hand.

I take it, sealing our partnership.

But she doesn't let go as she continues talking. "My people are going to follow you now. So know this: if you ever throw their lives away carelessly... if you ever betray them..." Trix's hand begins heating up... more and more... it's almost painful, the heat, the tension of bones rubbing together. "Then I'll crush you," she finishes, letting my hand drop.

With a grin on her freckled face, the Shadow of Rome disappears into the bowels of the Cathedral, and I can't help but smile, too, for the woman I might someday be friends with.

I join my generals below and watch them study the catacombs. "So, what's the plan, N?" asks Trix. "What do the Dark Templars do first?"

I draw my mother's sword and scratch a large A into the stone wall, letting my anger rise. "We destroy Apex."

GENMOD AND MANNERS

The wood is polished and shines in the firelight as Jax melts steel into shapes to compliment the warm earthy hues of his sculpture. The piece is still a work in progress, and I can't make out the final shape, but the emotion is there. The sense of a journey, of something fluid and beautiful unfolding in its own time and space. I run my hand over the wood, marveling at the smooth texture and currents of mahogany and pine bending together in a dance.

"What's it for?" I ask when the noise subsides as he cools the steel.

"It's to celebrate the completion of the Initiate Trials at the end of summer. It's... a ceremony of sorts. You'll see."

"What will it be?"

Jax looks up, his blue eyes bright. "It will be whatever people need it to be."

...

When I return to my room there's a gold box wrapped in a red bow sitting on my desk. An envelope sticks out of it. I pluck the thick cream parchment from the ribbon and open it, my fingers sliding over the V embossed on the card. It's an invitation. To an 'informal' cocktail function.

I get the distinct impression the invitation doesn't have a decline option.

I'm about to open the box when someone opens my bedroom door instead. An older woman in her fifties or sixties stands there, holding a small leather trunk with a handle. She is tiny, with bones a bird would envy, and silver hair pulled into a tight bun on her head. She curtsies at me and enters the room, closing the door behind her.

She is silent and I realize she's waiting for me to speak first. Because I'm a pat now. Ugh.

"Can I help you?" I ask, sweat breaking out on my neck and under my arms.

She smiles. "I'm Agatha, your assigned attendant during your stay at Castle Vianney. I will be helping you dress and prepare for your Initiate Trials, and, should you become an Initiate, I will serve your during your studies here."

I know I'm staring at her like a stunned deer, but I can't help it. "Why would I need help dressing myself?" I ask, a bit dumbfounded. Are pats really this helpless?

She cocks her head, a quizzical expression on her face. "I understand now. The Chancellor spoke to me about you. It caused quite a scandal in the attendant's quarters. He said you were not raised in your class. He said I'd have my work cut out for me in getting you ready. He... " she pauses, looking uncomfortable. "He gave me license to be firm while preparing you for the social graces." Her eyebrow rises as she scrutinizes me. "I can see he underestimated the amount of work I've undertaken."

I blush, then scowl, caught between embarrassed and angry. "I came here to train as a Knight, not to learn how to be a rich snob."

Her judging stare disappears in laughter that lights up her face. "May I have permission to be blunt, Your Grace?"

I pause, not used to such questions. "Yes."

"No." She tsks. "You should have said no. But, since I have the chancellors permission to be firm, I shall continue." She smiles. "I like you. You're feisty and strong, which is expected. But I hear you have a good heart, which is... less expected. You'll be good for this place, but you'll never get a foot in if you don't learn to talk and walk like them. You don't have to become a 'rich snob' as you say, to become a Knight, but you do have to fit in with the rich snobs. Do you want this badly enough?"

I look at the box still in my hands and look at her. "Yes. I do."

She nods. "Then let's get started. You have a party to go to."

...

We spend the rest of day doing the most boring training ever. First, she strips me of all my clothes and insists on a bath (as if I've never bathed in my life). But she adds salts and powders and oils to my bath that make me smell like a bowl of incense. I sniff at my oil-slicked skin as she rubs me dry. "This is a bit strong, isn't it?"

"It wears off and leaves you smelling fresh and clean," she says, vigorously rubbing my legs and hair.

At my hair, she tsks. "Split ends and a cut that is entirely too plebeian."

I reach for my hair, self-conscious for the first time in my life. What's wrong with my hair?

She taps her eGlass and calls someone called Larry, instructing him to come right away for a Code Three.

"What's a Code Three?" I ask.

"Your hair," she says through pursed lips.

My hair, indeed. I huff but allow her to continue her ministrations.

"At least you haven't plucked, waxed or shaved your arms and legs, like so many patrician teens these days. A blow for equality, that is. Hair is power. Keep yours intact."

I nod, having never given thought to shaving or plucking anything.

"And no dying it fadish colors," she says.

"Dying what?"

"Your hair. Arms and legs. Keep it natural. It's classier. New York is buzzing with new looks, but you want to present an aura of conservative class, at least until you establish yourself and can change things up."

"Okay."

She dresses me in the outfit contained in my box: white robes with a cape over one shoulder. Red lines run down the sides of the outfit, reminding me of the Templar crest.

When she finishes I put my ring back on, the one my mother made me. Agatha tsks again, but says nothing. I think she can see in my eyes that I'm not budging on this one.

"At this party, you'll be meeting the other two Initiates before the first of your trials begins. It's important you assess your competition and present a strong but not overly arrogant front."

I nod.

When the door opens again, I look up, surprised. Agatha is painting makeup on my face and smiles at a petite man carrying another small trunk similar to Agatha's.

Where hers had makeup and oils and potions for making me smell and look my best, his contains everything he needs to fix my plebeian hair. Apparently.

He gives a frown at my hair and raises a hand over his eyes dramatically. "We do not have much time to save this, do we?" he asks the room.

The room does not reply, so he rushes over, examining clumps of my long hair as if it's cow dung. He even sniffs at it!

Finally, he pulls out a brush, brandishing it like a weapon. "I suppose we can make do with this."

He nudges Agatha out of the way and kneels in front of me, staring at my face. He has large green eyes, lined with dark liner, and dark hair swept dramatically over his head and held in place with a sparkling clip. His clothing is impeccable and beautiful, beaded and jeweled drapes of ruby fabric. "At least you have a face," he says.

"Do you have a lot of faceless clients?" I ask, deadpan.

He cracks a smile. "Oh, look at you, silver tongue. All right, I'll play. You have a beautiful face. Patrician all the way. How anyone let you pass as plebeian is beyond me. Look at this skin. Roughened by the pleb life, but full of potential. And those cheekbones, so perfect they could cut diamond. And that nose. Once you go through your GenMod, you will be undeniably one of the most beautiful creatures to walk the earth."

My smile falters. "GenMod?" Jax told me all patricians receive one, but he did not tell me when I'd receive mine.

"Has no one told you?" He looks at Agatha. "No one has told her?"

Agatha shrugs. "I have only begun my work with her. She's been through so much already. I was instructed to get her ready for the party but to otherwise ease her in slowly."

Larry sighs. "You will undergo GenMod before the party, so you will have a few days to recover. It will all be explained soon. First, let's fix this mop on your head."

He moves to stand behind me as Agatha continues working on my face.

"By the Orders," he curses, pulling a brush through tangles, "what have you been using on your poor hair? Deer urine?"

I choke back a curse of my own. "I've been using what everyone uses," I say. "The government-issued hair and body cleaner we get with our stipends."

"That explains so much," he says dramatically.

It takes him an hour, but when he's done, he looks pleased with himself. I take a mirror nervously from him and examine my new cut. The length is mostly the same, and there's some shaping around my jaw, some layering. Those subtle differences have a huge impact. I went from looking like a pleb to a pat in an hour. My mouth drops open as I stare at myself. I nearly don't recognize myself with this makeup and these clothes and my hair falling in such a way around my face.

He claps excitedly. "Lovely. Brilliant. You would make even the Angels jealous."

At the talk of Angels I frown, fighting feelings of panic and fear. I take a breath, calming myself, as my two attendants chatter and clean up. Deep breaths. I push the image of my dead parents out of my head.

Agatha asks me something, and I look up, a blank look on my face. "What?"

She sighs. "We must practice your speech. You look more like a patrician, and certainly after your GenMod you will be perfect. But the moment you open your mouth the truth will ruin you."

And so, for the rest of the afternoon we go through manners and language.

"You are a pureman, and you must act and speak like one."

"Not purewoman?" I ask.

"No, pureman applies to both genders. The patrician class value their equality. All Knights are Sirs. All are pureman. There are no distinctions. You treat a woman differently than a man and you can say goodbye to your chances at being an Initiate."

When I don't say anything, she continues. "All serfs and plebeians must address you as Your Grace. You must not address others of your class as Your Grace. If they outrank you, you must use their rank. Your Highness applies to both princes and princesses, Your Majesty to Kings and Queens—"

"Why do we still have Princes and Princess and Kings and Queens if gender is equal?"

She shakes her head. "If you ask silly questions a child should know, this will take longer than we have." For a serf, she is quite forceful with me, though I do not see it as odd, since I am still mentally identifying as a pleb. Mostly I find it annoying. "Some titles are ancient and remain unchanged," she continues. "There is a difference between the Old Code and the New. The Old Code is what the Orders followed before the Cataclysm. The New Code is what they follow now."

"Got it." I hope that's true.

"Some may still call you 'My Lady,' especially since you are not yet a Knight. If they do, they are trying to be gracious, or perhaps flirtatious or overly romantic."

Agatha has me sit and slips uncomfortable shoes on my feet. "Now, let's see how you dance."

Larry walks over, arms outstretched, and I place a hand in his as Agatha sets her eGlass to play music. I try to follow Larry's lead, but my parents never taught me how to dance. On my third attempt, my pointy shoes dig into Larry's feet, and he steps away, annoyed and in pain.

"You are terrible at this, Your Grace. I've seen more grace in a rutting pig."

"Thanks," I say dryly.

He looks hopeless. "Is there anything you can do?"

I grin. "I can hack anything on the planet."

He rolls his eyes. "Unless your hacking skills make you a better dancer, that doesn't help us."

So we keep dancing, and I keep bruising his toes, and he keeps cursing, and Agatha spends equal amounts of time laughing and shuddering.

When we break for dinner, I drown my sorrows in LifeForce and ask the question that's been burning a hole in my mind all day.

"Tell me about GenMod," I say.

And they do.

That night, when I can sleep, my dreams are filled with nightmares.

...

My GenMod begins today, and I feel a sick dread in the pit of my stomach that manifests as bile in my throat.

This response is an under-reaction, I will soon learn.

A Hospitaller hands me a hospital gown and sweeps a curtain closed under the guise of privacy. My hands shake as I peel off my new clothes and drop them in a pile on the floor. I look down at my body, now naked, and wonder what will be different when this is over. Plebeians never spoke of GenMod, except in hushed voices behind cupped hands. I knew near nothing about it until last night, and now I feel I know too much.

I'm lying in the bed, using thin sheets to cover my nakedness, when the Hospitaller returns. Her name is Meg and she looks too young to be in charge of me. I want to protest, to ask where Grandmaster Marian is, but Meg is talking, explaining things to me, and so I shut my mouth and listen.

"Though Genetic Modification is not painful, the recovery is," she says, as if telling me the butter on my bread might not melt properly. "You will undergo a level one andronics mod. We will inject your muscles with serums that stimulate growth and strength. Your bones will be infused with a solution to make them denser. Your skin, eyes, nails and hair will be rejuvenated. It will take time to recover. We will give you something for the pain, but we can only give so much."

She clicks her eGlass to review my file and shakes her head. "Normally, we'd advise at least a month of recovery, but your file says you must be ready within a week."

I gulp. A week doesn't sound long enough, but that's when I must attend the party. I am already behind and I have only just arrived. It doesn't bode well.

She sticks needles in my arms and places sticky pads on my chest and back. They are hooked up to a monitor that beeps and purrs and shows lines and numbers I do not understand.

When she fills my IV with a purple fluid, I feel it instantly. My head wobbles and my mind slows.

Meg smiles. "Grandmaster Marian will be here shortly to begin the procedure. You're in good hands."

I'm glad Meg will have help. She's too young. They are all too young.

My mind is floating when Jax moves aside the curtain and sits on the side of my bed. "I snuck in. Don't tell."

I shake my head but it doesn't feel like it moves. "I won't," I say, slurring.

He laughs. "I know this is hard, but after, you'll be able to see in color."

I pretend to look excited. "Great." Then, I realize I won't have to hide my color vision anymore, and smile. "I can't wait to see the color of your eyes," I say, my mind drifting.

"Good luck," he says. "I'll be just outside, waiting. I'll come in as soon as they let me. Earlier if I can manage."

He kisses my forehead and ducks out when Grandmaster Marian shoos him away. "You know better, Jaxton Lux!" She says after him.

She looks at me, a soft expression on her face. "Ready?"

I try to say no, but nothing comes out. As she wheels me through the clinic, my mind soars higher, losing focus.

The last thing I remember is looking at the lights above me as I'm pushed through the halls. I remember telling them not to take my scar away, the one on my hand. I have to keep my Apex scar, to remember. To never forget.

...

Pain.

So much bloody pain.

It doesn't hit me all at once. Instead, it curls around me like a lover and then squeezes like a snake.

I'm breathless from it. I feel it reaching out, extending past my physical body, as if the air around me is also hurting.

Voices filter past the pain, faintly at first, but then with more power.

"Unbelievable, really," says a voice. Meg. I think it's Meg. "Grandmaster Marian, have you seen her readings? She's healing at an alarming rate."

It's because I'm Nephilim.

Did I say that out loud? By the Orders, I hope not.

No one arrests me, so I assume it's all in my head—my pounding, aching, awful head.

Another voice chuckles, deep and soft. "Good blood," he says as a compliment to me and himself. My grandfather.

I wonder why no one is saying anything to me, but I realize I must appear asleep.

And then I realize...

I'm not supposed to be awake. The procedure is still in process.

I can feel the serums being pumped into me. Deep needles in my muscles, in my bone, in all parts of my body.

A cool hand lands on my forehead. "She's coming out of anesthesia," she says.

There is a hushed hurry as something is injected into me, and I fade back into blissful darkness.

The next time I wake, Jax rests his head by my side, his body slumped over my hospital bed. I'm only awake for a moment, but I hear him breathing and it calms me, sending the pain into another place as I fade back to sleep.

He is still there later, when my eyelids peel open painfully, slowly, and only a fraction. He is crying, holding my hand. "I'm sorry, Star. I'm sorry for what you're going through. For everything you've gone through." His voice drops to a whisper and I can no longer hear his words, but I feel his love, his concern, and that is enough.

...

It is three days that should have been a month, that feels like a year.

I sleep on and off through the first few days and Jax never leaves my side. I worry that my Nephilim blood will be revealed, but though they marvel at my healing abilities, they do not seem to suspect anything abnormal.

By the third day I am sitting up vertically, which I feel is a huge accomplishment. I'm still in pain, but I distract myself with plans and plots and Jax tries to distract me with stories to make me laugh.

Eventually Agatha joins my entourage of caretakers. She lays a hand on me in comfort when my bones ache so badly they feel as if they will break. When I've recovered from the pain, she tsks me again. "You should not have let me touch you, Your Grace."

"What?" My brain is foggy, catching up to itself after the influx of pain meds from my self-administered IV.

"I touched you. I—a serf—laid a hand without permission on a patrician. That is not proper and should not have been allowed. A plebeian or serf may not speak to a patrician without first being spoken to. They should be beaten as a consequence. And they may not touch a patrician without permission. If they do, the offending hand must be removed."

My eyes widen. "That's absurd. Besides, you're my attendant. Of course you have to touch me. If you ask each and every time, this will get tedious, fast."

"In private, you may give me permission until revoked, but in public, you must give permission each time."

I sigh. "To keep up the appearance of power."

She nods. "Exactly."

"What happens if I don't want to cut off your hand for daring to touch my person?" The sarcasm drips from my tongue, but she ignores it.

"You may report me to an Inquisitor, or have a serf perform the deed."

She's being deliberately obtuse, I can tell. "You know what I mean. If I don't want someone's hand cut off at all?"

"Your Grace, you are going to be trouble for me, aren't you? If you don't do it, the other families will look down on you. You will be judged and seen as lesser.

Technically, though, no punishment against you would be legal."

I breathe more deeply. "Good. Because I'm not going to punish you or anyone else for touching me."

She bows her head. "You may do as you like, Your Grace."

...

I'm done being a patient. For the first time since all this started, I find my patrician status useful, and I take advantage of it. I insist that Agatha prepare a bath for me, and then I insist more forcefully that she leave me to clean myself alone. She tsks and scowls and frowns, and I think she even cracks a sardonic smile when I use my rank to chase her from my hospital room.

I breathe a long sigh as I sink into the tub, letting the heat of the water lessen my pain. I haven't felt properly clean since my GenMod. Sponge baths just don't cut it. So I take my time and lather rich, fragrant soap over my body, rubbing off all the antiseptic smells.

Once my hair is dry and brushed, I feel much more like myself. Ironic, considering how much less human I really am.

I'm finally ready to look at myself. I haven't let anyone show me a mirror since the GenMod procedure. I wanted to be clean, to feel more like myself, before I saw how unlike myself I appear.

I pull the sheet off the full length washroom mirror and take a long look, turning from side to side to see myself from all angels. I haven't dressed yet. I wanted to see all the changes on my body.

The differences are subtle but striking. My skin is flawless porcelain. My muscles are more toned, smooth and strong. My hair is lush, thick, more voluminous than it's ever been. And my eyes are brighter, the blue silver of them shining against my pale skin. Even my face seems more refined, cut from diamond and dipped in cream. I look otherworldly.

I look down at my hand and rub a finger over my Apex scar. It's now my only physical flaw.

I am nearly dressed when Meg comes in to scold me for being out of bed. "You need more rest," she says. "Three days is not sufficient. Give yourself at least two more." She frowns, her eyebrows furrowing.

"I don't have that kind of time," I say. "Initiate Trials will start soon. I have to prepare." I'm not actually leaving to prepare, but it's a good enough excuse. She reluctantly pulls out her tablet and clicks a few things, then passes it to me to press my thumb onto, signing myself out against her preference.

I thank her for her care and am about to make it out of there when Jax comes by to check on me. He's holding a bag and his eyes go wide when he sees me. "What are you doing out of bed, Star?"

I sigh and explain everything again. I expect a fight, but he just nods. "You're right. There's much you need to learn. I can help you later today if you want."

I want. But I won't be here later today. "I'll message you. I'm not sure what all my trainers have planned for me." It's a soft lie, but it sticks in my throat nonetheless. How did this boy lie to me for so long? Did he feel like this each time?

I let the thought go as he gently hugs me and kisses my cheek. "Don't push yourself too hard. It will take some time for your body to get used to the changes."

I nod and walk with him to the end of the hall.

Before we part ways, he stops me. "I have a gift for you," he says, handing me the bag.

I look inside and my heart clenches. I pull out the old wooden box. "It's the gift Ella gave me for my tenth birthday," I say softly.

He nods. "I know the GenMod was hard, but I thought... well, you finally have the ability to see in color as you've always wanted."

He doesn't know that's been true since the night my parents were killed, and it's a relief to no longer have to lie to him. "I can," I say. "It's... extraordinary. The world is full of more colors than I imagined."

I open the box and run a gentle finger over the precious items inside: a blue rock, a red one, and a sprig of yellow moss. "She worked so hard on this." My eyes are full of tears when I look up. "It's not right, what happened to her. To them."

Jax puts his arms around me and I lay my head on his chest, listening to his heartbeat. "No, it's not."

I pull away after a moment and wipe a tear, and Jax cocks his head. "Is red still your favorite color?"

I laugh through the tears. "Yes. It's amazing. So much more vibrant than I could have imagined." I tap my eGlass. "Evie still has to match the names and colors for me, but I'm learning." I place a hand on his face. "I love your eyes. Blue is probably my second favorite. Maybe my first, depending on my mood."

He places his hand over mine. "I'm so glad at least one good thing came from all this, Star."

I nod. "Thank you, Jax." I hold up the box. "This means a lot to me."

We part and I walk quickly out of the Castle, pressing my eGlass as I do. "Evie, message Zorin. Tell him I'm on my way to the Cathedral."

...

Flying frees me. It sets my body right in ways nothing else can. I thought it would hurt, that my new muscles, bones and ligaments would rebel at the weightlessness of it all, but instead I feel an absence of pain for the first time since the GenMod started. I wish I could live in the air, and it's with great reluctance that I land lightly in front of the Cathedral.

It's been five days since I've been here, and I've done my best to keep in touch. But it's hard having top secret—and highly illegal—rebel conversations while under 24/7 care at Castle V.

The village is different now. It's cleaner. More repairs have been made to the outlying stone wall, and the Cathedral itself shines more brightly under the late summer sun.

Zorin waits for me inside. He has a look of wonder on his face as his eyes scan my body. "You look... different."

I raise an eyebrow, enjoying his response. "How?"

He thinks for a moment, his eyes burying into mine. "You look untouched by this world. As if you are a creature of the heavens, and by some cruel fate, you have been shackled here on earth."

I grin.

He clears his throat, breaking his gaze. "Are you... are you in pain?"

"I'm fine, Zorin," I tell him, smiling. "Sore, but fine."

"Not everyone survives GenMods," he says, frowning.

"I survived the Nephilim transformation."

He nods. "True enough. Still, you should be resting."

I roll my eyes. "Not you, too. You of all people should know why I can't. Our plans depend on me getting into the Orders. I don't have long to prepare for the Trials, and I need your help."

He nods again, and then he walks over and pulls me into a hug. He's so tall his chin can rest easily on my head as he whispers, "I am happy to know you are healing well. You were missed."

It's not an "I missed you," but it's close enough. I squeeze him a little tighter and then we pull apart. "Let's train," I say.

We go underground, to one of the Cathedral's spacious halls we've prepared with weapons. I pull my sword and his appears from smoke into his waiting hand. "I need to learn that trick," I say.

He grins. "Prepare yourself, Nightfall."

I lunge and he blocks. We parry. I move through the Way of Nyx, and he counters with the Way of Hecate. I'm winded too fast, my body sore, tired. He's so strong. I slump against a wall and rub a forming bruise where I missed a block. "I thought I'd be at least as strong as you now. Nephilim *and* GenMod. That should make me undefeatable, shouldn't it?"

He laughs. "That's not how it works." He tosses me a LifeForce and drains one himself.

"Why not?" I open my drink and sip it, letting the sweet nectar coat my throat.

"Your Nephilim transformation isn't instant," he says. "It takes years. You will build strength over time. And Nephilim, like humans, have different talents. I'm strong, a warrior. You are—"

"Not," I say derisively.

He grins. "Not so much, no. But you are fast. You have kept up with me in flight, when very few do."

I beam with pride.

"You will grow stronger in time, with patience, training and age. GenMods are a quicker path, but even with both, you will have limitations."

"I just assumed all Nephilim were super strong," I say. "That's what we're taught, anyways. Nephilim fly, drink blood, and it's so easy to turn a human..." my mind wanders to a question I've had for a long time. "Zorin, how could our kind almost become extinct, when you can make many more as needed?"

He holds up his sword. "Let us move through our forms and I will explain. Can you listen and fight at the same time?"

Probably not with him, but I'll give it my best. I meet his sword and we dance.

"The transformation is not… simple," he says, blocking my lunge. "Not all survive. And those who do, they… they are still the same person they once were. It does not change their core. You were still Scarlett after your change, were you not?"

I nod. Despite the many changes, I'm still me. Still making choices based on my own value system and thoughts.

"There was one among us—Snatcher they called him, for he would snatch children from their homes and turn them—he would crawl into people's beds and turn them. He wore a black cloak, and carried a grey bag over his shoulder. Wherever he went, he snatched what people were, and gave them new life." Zorin knocks my sword out of my hand and I fall back, panting.

He grins. "Keep up!"

I pick up my blade, stretch my shoulders, and move with him as he continues.

"He thought they would all join him at his castle, that they would be his army during the War. Many never came. They went to the Orders, talking of a grave mistake. They were not Nephilim, they were men. They were killed on the spot by the Inquisition."

I shiver, and my sword slips. He lands a blow against my chest and I groan.

"Many took their own lives. Some begged their loved ones for an end. Only a few joined Snatcher at his castle. They came when they saw how cruelly the Nephilim were treated. They hated their very existence, but feared death more."

I try to imagine what it would be like to go through this change without understanding, without knowing, without the necessity of being saved from death as I was, and I tremble.

"They let Snatcher teach them what they needed to live," Zorin says, knocking my sword out of my hand again.

We stop for a moment, and I sink to the ground to drink another LifeForce. Zorin pulls out a bag of marshmallows and, when he sees the look on my face, laughs and tosses me one. I shove it into my mouth and lean against the stone wall, listening.

"And after, when they had learned all he had to teach, they splayed him out on a table and, in turns, they drained him of his blood."

Ouch.

"They pulled out his eyes and hanged them over the table. They said it was so Snatcher could see his life snatched away, just as he had done to them."

I stare at Zorin, horrified.

He looks at me, his face unreadable, as he pulls another marshmallow out of the bag. "They say his eyes still hang in the castle to this day."

That seems unlikely given the rate of decay, but still. Ew. And for all I know, Nephilim eyes don't decay.

"What happened to those who killed him?" I ask.

"They never made more. They fought to live and, in the end, they too died." Zorin stands and holds out his hand for his sword to appear. "That is why it is no easy thing to make new Nephilim. That is why we are the last."

TRIAL OF STRENGTH

My time with Zorin is too short. Before I am ready for the trials, I am called back to Castle V to prepare for a challenge more dangerous than battle.

A party.

With patricians.

Who will be judging me.

I'm a basket of nerves as Agatha helps me dress. The outfit confuses me at first. "Is this a dress or pants or what?"

She chuckles and holds up leggings. "These go on your legs."

I roll my eyes and pull them on. She then hands me a fitted tunic that curves around my body like it was made for me. I realize it probably was. The castle probably has my measurements on file somewhere. Weird.

Then she clips a half-skirt around my waist and it flows to my ankles, leaving a slit open for walking. It's asymmetrical and has a bold cut that exposes part of my left leg.

Finally, she holds up a midnight blue cape, draping it around my shoulders and pinning it with a black brooch glistening with diamond stars at its center. "Where did you get that?" I ask.

"Your grandfather," she says.

She hands me slightly heeled black leather shoes that I slip on. They're more comfortable than I dared hope. My hair is already done up in an elaborate twist with silver-blond tendrils curling down my neck, and my makeup is subtle, but shimmering, making me look more sophisticated than I am.

Once I'm ready, Agatha looks at me up and down and nods in approval. "You look beautiful. And very patrician."

I scowl at her, and she laughs.

I'm about to leave when she shows me a small dagger sheathed in leather. "For you." She straps the dagger around my right upper thigh. It's hidden by the skirt, but she shows me another slit in the fabric where I can reach the dagger easily. "Your grandfather felt this might come in handy," she says, winking at me.

Why do I need a dagger at a party?

I don't even want to know. But having it on me makes me feel better.

"Good luck, Miss Night," Agatha says as I leave.

"Thank you." I hold her eyes, willing her to understand that I'm thanking her for more than just helping me get dressed tonight.

She nods and I smile and walk out.

Jax meets me in the hall. He looks dashing in black and silver, his blue eyes bright, accented with dark eyeliner. This is the first time I've seen him wear makeup. He grins when he sees me. "You look stunning."

"You don't look too bad yourself," I say, taking his proffered arm.

He escorts me to the roof of one of the smaller outlying buildings of the castle. It's a cool, clear night, the stars out in full force. I can hear the music playing and people talking before we reach the door. I attempted to use the long walk up the stairs to compose myself. It didn't work.

I'm a bundle of raw nerves as we walk onto the roof.

The space has been transformed into a wonderland. It is paved with white stones glistening with tiny shards of opaque crystal. In the center is a great fountain of a griffin spitting water into a pond. Smaller fountains dot the edges, creating a cacophony of sounds in the open air. Several tables are lined with elaborate displays of food, from meats and cheeses to fruits and sumptuous desserts. A chocolate fountain fills one entire table, surrounded by strawberries and sliced apples.

All eyes turn to us.

Jax steps aside as the doorman clears his throat to introduce me. I was warned this would happen, but I still feel like a caught. "Introducing Lady Scarlett of the House of Night, Initiate Prospect for the Four Orders, daughter of Lord Marcus of the House of Night and Lady Violet of the House of Forrester, granddaughter to the esteemed Templar Grandmaster, Chancellor Forrester."

There is a polite applause as I bow appropriately to my class and rank.

Jax takes my arm again, escorting me through the room as people stare and talk about us. A woman with a pinched face and yellow cape that does nothing for her coloring glares at me, then loudly says, "I heard she was raised by plebs. She knows nothing of our world. She probably eats with her hands and goes weeks without bathing."

I can feel the blood rising to my face as her date chuckles at her pathetic attempt at wit. I'm about to storm over there and give her a piece of my mind when Jax lays a tempering hand on my wrist. "She's not worth it," he whispers.

There's an urgency to his voice, and I realize something I hadn't before. This is part of my test. This whole thing, everything I do while I'm here, will be weighed and measured in determining if I'm worthy of becoming an Initiate. And despite Agatha's instruction, I still feel ill-equipped at knowing how to behave as a pat. The awful woman is right about something. I know nothing of this world.

I nod to Jax and we walk through the crowds of people over to a table with a red fountain surrounded by wine glasses. A dark-skinned man sits next to the table alone, his feet propped up as he sips at his wine. His features are aristocratic: high cheekbones, straight nose, strong jawline. He's a handsome man, maybe five to ten years older than me, with a composure and grace that makes it clear he is comfortable in this setting.

"Scarlett," Jax says, "I'd like to introduce you to Falcon of the House of Rain. Falcon, this is Scarlett of the House of Night. You are both Initiate Prospects."

Jax nods, squeezes my hand, leans in to whisper *good luck*, and walks away, leaving me standing alone with my competition. I take a deep breath and smile. "It's a pleasure meeting you."

He grins and sits up straighter, letting his feet fall to the ground. He gestures at the empty seat at his small table and I join him.

"The pleasure is all mine," he says.

Around us, people slyly watch out of the corners of their eyes, listening to each word we speak. My

Nephilim hearing can pick up their whispered mutterings, wondering which of us would make a better Knight.

Falcon clicks his eGlass, a small frown appearing. "Tell me, pureman, from where do you hail? I can see you were raised plebeian, but the specifics are unavailable."

The information must be classified. "I hail from home," I say, not wishing to divulge more than I must.

"Don't we all," he says, his smile a sharp line across his face.

I tap my eGlass and Evie displays the information I need to know. He's from Cairo, the son of a lord, but he's no heir. I'm scrolling through his history when he hands me a glass of wine.

"To dull the nerves and make this tedium a bit more... pleasant," he says, holding his own glass up to toast. I raise my glass and it clinks against his.

He sips, watching, waiting for me to do the same. I take a drink and set it down as the sweet liquid travels down my throat and into my body.

"If you will, pureman, indulge me with another question. How is it that I have heard much of your parents, and so little of you?"

"I was raised in seclusion, trained from birth in the arts of war and chivalry," I say. I take another drink.

The wine is making me bold, but it's my own fear that turns me into a liar. War and chivalry, indeed.

He raises an eyebrow. "Well then, wish me luck, pureman. For I was raised in a library. Books and pens were my friends. A serf scholar was my teacher. You see, I too lost my parents. Perhaps..." he pauses, growing solemn, "perhaps they would have trained me better."

I feel small in my silly lies, in my vain desires to impress someone I've only just met.

He looks up and smiles again, then leans back, relaxes. "Excuse my curiosity, pureman. I am not at ease with people I do not know, but it is my failing, and not theirs. Please, accept my apology."

My instinct as old Scarlett is to comfort him, make him feel better about himself and his life. Relate to him and share his discomfort. But Agatha has made it clear that is not how a patrician in these circumstances would act. So I shrug, pretending to pay him half attention as I scan the crowd. "I suppose one raised amongst books instead of parents must be permitted some oddity." I accept his apology, but demean his upbringing, mix compliment and insult together. It is the way of patricians. I hate it.

He smiles at me again, but there's no warmth to it, this time. "Have you met the other Prospect?" he asks, clearly done with our conversation. I don't blame him.

"I had to meet you first, pureman," I say, standing. "It was a pleasure."

I turn, ready to leave, but then spin to face him again, the cold patrician version of myself gone for a moment, replaced by the real me. My face softens and I hold out my hand. "Good luck," I say with sincerity as he shakes it.

We lock eyes, bonded by whatever is to come. Our hands clasp a fraction too long for polite society, then he pulls away, his eyes averted from mine as if in guilt.

But the Trial of Strength has not yet started, so I can't fathom what he might have to feel guilty for.

Jax arrives then, arm ready to escort me to the next prospect. There are three of us, and only one will be chosen.

We approach a young woman by the balcony. Her back is to me as she sips wine and chats with the large crowd she's drawn. She wears black, with red lining on the inside of her cape and collar. Her black hair is pulled up in a stylish twist.

I hear her voice as she tells a story and it tugs at something inside me, but I can't place it.

Until she turns to face me.

I freeze.

My heart stops.

I know her.

I *know* the other Initiate Prospect.

...

We are both frozen for a moment, staring at each other. How is this possible? Where has she been all these years? My heart is clogged full of emotions and I'm trying to breathe and not do or say something that will ruin me.

She regains her composure first, smiling gracefully as she takes my hand and presents me to her group. "Everyone, may I introduce Scarlett of the House of Night, the third Initiate Prospect, and my dearest friend." She holds up her wine glass.

I realize I left mine at the table with Falcon, so Jax hands me his and I raise it.

The crowd of people smile, nodding, delighted by the twist of us being friends.

Brooke turns to me. "Shall we walk together, old friend?"

Her speech is perfect. She does not sound like the Brooke of old, but I see her younger self in her sparkling eyes, in her short cropped hair and sharp chin.

I turn with her and we walk down away from the gawking crowd and toward a private garden area. Here dark bushes are trimmed into the form of swans and a fountain spurts water between them, lit with purple light. The air smells of lavender and mint, tingling my nose.

Once we are no longer in public view, I pull Brooke into a hard hug, holding her close. She returns the embrace and tears fill my eyes.

We are both in tears as we pull away gently from each other.

Brooke chuckles. "Pureman, you ruin me. I'm crying like this is a pleb affair."

"Then let's pretend it is," I say. "I need to hold my sister a moment longer."

We finish our hug. The moment is perfect and I am afraid to break it, but there is something I must ask. Something I'm scared to ask. "Is Ella here?"

Brooke sits on a stone bench, her eyes dark. She shakes her head. And then she tells me what happened.

"After I was taken, I woke up in a dark and dank place, chained to a metal wall. The man who took Ella and me was Apex, the leader of those who take Zeniths. He starved us first. After three days, he fed us, but only when we did as he pleased. It took months before he rewarded us with fresh air, before I figured out we were on a ship. In that time, he assessed our taints. Ella was a dud, so she would serve those who needed serving and please men who needed pleasing. I was a Gravir. They threw me in the fighting pits."

My stomach clenches and I feel sick. I sit by her, holding her hand as she finishes her story, her eyes far away, lost in the distance of her past.

"Every day pats bet on whether I would live or not. Every day my opponent was stronger than the last. Every day... I won." She looks at me a moment, the pain of her journey raw on her beautiful face. "They kept us in a glass cylinder for the fights. The glass was always smooth and perfect, more so when it was slick with blood. Many tried to break it, none left a crack." She sucks in her breath, her eyes drifting again. "But they were not like me."

She sips at her wine and continues. "I knew, one day, I would be strong enough. And one day I was. I shattered the glass and fled. I searched for Ella, but I did not find her. A man I threatened told me she had died long ago. Someone had shot her up with more drugs than she could take. I did not wish to hear his words, but in my heart, I had known for a while. I left the ship before Apex could find me. I did not see him again."

I think she's done, but her hand squeezes mine and she looks at me, her face cold, hard, determined. "But one day I will, and then we too shall bet on who will live and who will die."

"I'm so sorry, Brooke. I can't imagine what you went through. And Ella, poor sweet Ella... " I had thought them dead long ago. I didn't imagine either could have survived what I knew would surely be their fate. That Brooke made it out is a miracle, but still my heart grieves for Ella. I think back to my birthday so long ago, when Ella tried to help me understand what color felt like. She had such a gentle soul.

Brooke pats my hand. "It is what it is. Let us not dwell on sadness. Tell me about you. About your family!"

My heart contracts. "I'm afraid we are both full of sad news this day. My parents were killed recently. It's how I came to be here."

Brooke hugs me then. "We will bear our pain and we will not let it stop us. I hope we can at least be happy for having found each other at long last."

We both cry-laugh and pull away, wiping our eyes to fix our makeup. A thought occurs to me, and I tilt my head. "How long has Jax known you were alive?"

"Around a year," she says. "But he couldn't tell you, and neither could I. We are forbidden to divulge unnecessary information to patricians in hiding. When he informed me you had arrived at the Castle, I couldn't wait to see you, but I was away, and I asked Jax to keep the secret a while longer. I wished to tell you in person."

"Were your parents patricians as well?" That seems unlikely, but I don't even know what's true or not anymore. I try not to let Jax's further deceptions hurt my heart. I fail.

She shakes her head. "When I got out, around two years ago, I had nothing. I tried to look for work, but I was a pleb zen with no education. So, I started fighting again. People placed their bets, and I kept winning. I started doing matches at patrician affairs. One of them was kind to me. She offered me food and a place to stay. She was, I discovered, the Queen of York. She was seeking a tutor for her younger children—to better train them in combat—and she had found me. I trained her family for a year, and we grew closer. Then, when I thought my services would be over, she offered to adopt me. She offered to make me a patrician. And I accepted."

The House of York is a royal family. That means... "In the courtyard, I should have bowed, I should have addressed you as Your Highness..." My face turns red. She outranks me, despite my high family name.

"Yes, you should have," says Brooke with a teasing grin, "but I think pats need a shock now and again."

"Have you seen your mother?" I ask.

Brooke looks down, frowning. "I can't. Not yet. What do I tell her? That I let my sister die? That I chose a different family than hers so I could take care of myself? I can't face her yet."

I'm about to tell her I think her mother would understand, that she wouldn't blame Brooke for Ella's fate. They were both children. So young. But the garden around us fills with mist and my grandfather's voice fills the air around us. "Welcome to the Trial of Strength, Initiate Prospects. A serf will present you each with a bow and arrows as the party clears out." As if on command, a teen boy scrambles up and hands both Brooke and me a bow and sheath of arrows, then scrambles away. I stare at the bow in my hand as my grandfather continues speaking. "The rules are simple. Hit your opponents with an arrow before you are hit. Anyone hit with an arrow is eliminated. The last one standing wins. And, finally, try not to die."

Death is a possibility? Seriously?

My heart is thumping in my chest, and I'm still trying to figure out what to do when I look up and see Falcon facing me.

With an arrow cocked and pointed straight at my chest.

...

I run. The arrow whizzes by my ear, missing me by a hair. I have to get my head in this game, which is not easy after a bumpy trip through the lands of sad memories.

I'm stuck at a dead end, on the edge of the small garden on the roof. I look down at the forest and park area below. It's my only chance. Using my GenMod and Nephilim advantages, I launch myself over the side of the building and land in a tumble near brush and bushes, throwing myself into their cover.

A wave of nausea sweeps through me. Not from the fall, surely? It wasn't that far and I've taken more serious tumbles while training with Zorin.

I take a deep breath, letting the sick feeling pass. I hear rustling in the forest around me. Animals? Brooke or Falcon?

I move slowly, with light feet, like hunting and tracking wild animals the way Myrddin and my dad taught me.

I can't shake the sick feeling, though. It's getting worse. With each step my legs feel heavier, like trunks of trees sending their roots into the earth, slowing me until I can barely move.

My clothing is damp from sweat and the scent of it triggers my memory. I hold up my arm and inhale more deeply. It's a sickly sweet smell, like rotting fruit. I know that scent. My mind tumbles back in time to forbidden lessons with Myrddin. Lessons on poison.

This is Red Fairy. My stomach roils and I turn my head to a bush and vomit out red wine and stomach bile. The wine!

That's why Falcon looked so guilty. He poisoned me.

I wish this surprised me more, but I'm finding the patrician society is full of double-crossing power-seeking players with agendas of their own.

I hear the noise again, and I wipe my mouth on the sleeve of my beautiful tunic and move back cautiously.

A giant beast lunges from the brush and pins me down. I scream as its teeth drip saliva down my neck. It's a giant wolf, like the ones I saw pulling the carriages in New York. Only this one looks hungry. And I'm dinner.

My mind spins for a moment, the poison in my body making it hard to think. The beast's claws dig into my shoulders and pain rips through me with each tear of my skin. I realize I'm going to die if I can't get away.

And then I remember the dagger Agatha slipped me on behalf of my grandfather. Did he know this was part of the trial? Why would they send something to kill us? I fumble for the dagger at my thigh, pulling it out as I summon my Nephilim power. My wings won't help right now, but my strength will. I focus and the poison in my system ebbs away. The black creature pinning me looks almost surprised that I fight back, that I am able to push his three-hundred-pound body off me even as I slip the dagger into his side.

It's not a mortal wound, but it stuns him long enough for me to escape. I stand, head clearing long enough to run with everything in me. I hear the wolf howling in pain and anger, but I lose myself in the forest, hiding behind trees and boulders, hoping the scent of my blood doesn't attract the creature.

In the distance I hear other noises, those of humans running through the woods. Falcon and Brooke are hunting each other. And me.

I keep moving, the poison sending shivers through me. My Nephilim blood keeps me alive, but for how much longer? I need the antidote. I need Dark Leaf. It's a common plant, but powerful if used correctly. I silently bless Myrddin for his unorthodox lessons those many years ago as I search for the plant I need. I find it nestled under a great oak tree. The green leaves are dark, and smell mildly minty. I stick a handful in my mouth and chew them up, then spit them out into my hand. I need this in my blood stream. Fortunately, the wolf helpfully ripped open my shoulder and exposed some much-needed blood. I make a paste and plaster my wound with the leaves. It burns and I stifle a scream, but I can feel it working already. I take another handful of leaves, chew and swallow. It can't hurt to take it in a few ways.

I look at the tall tree above me and start climbing. I need a safe place to rest while the herbs work, and this will give me a good vantage point of the forest and the others. My stomach swims from the poison and herbs mixing and I have to stop, breathe, vomit again and then keep climbing. The smell of my sweat doesn't help with the nausea. I hope Agatha can get this outfit clean. I really like it.

It only takes a few minutes before I get most of my strength back. My shoulder feels on fire, but I don't think I'll die anytime soon. I get as high as I can up the tree and scan the forest. Brooke and Falcon aren't far from me. In fact, they are getting closer, Brooke chasing Falcon. I need to take them out and end this.

I notch an arrow on my bow. These arrows are designed to stun the target, not kill them.

I'm trying to decide which one of them to aim for first, when the wolf makes an appearance, looking fiercer than ever, my dagger still stuck in his side. He can't find me, though he can smell me and, instead, he lunges for Falcon.

Brooke watches, but doesn't have a clear shot at Falcon any longer.

I could take out Brooke right now, and win, if the wolf ends Falcon.

I look to Falcon, who is pinned, scared, in mortal danger.

I don't pause.

I aim and shoot, and the wolf falls off Falcon, stunned into silence.

Brooke looks up, sees me in the tree, and fires.

I feel the arrow hit me. Feel the electrical currents shoot through me. Then...

Nothing.

VIPER

When I wake, I'm in a chair and my grandfather is by my side. We are back on the roof, and the party is in full swing again. I look up, my head spinning. "What happened?"

"You were knocked out of the tree when Brooke shot you," he says, kneeling to speak to me eye to eye.

Ah, right. That's fun. Everything hurts, but I no longer have gashes across my shoulder and I can tell everything else is healing pretty fast. "I was poisoned," I say. "Red Fairy. It's deadly. I found the antidote, but..."

He shakes his head. "I feared something like that would happen. You are my granddaughter. Many think you will be given preferential treatment for a spot as an Initiate. They will do what they can to take you out."

"Falcon maybe, but not Brooke."

"Not just them. Many great families have stakes in who is chosen."

That's news to me. I push myself off the chair and he helps me stand. "I'm okay. My head is clearing."

"That is good," he says, his eyes kind, worried. "Your next trial could begin at any time."

I nod and walk over to Brooke who is talking with a small group. She smiles when she sees me, holding out a glass of wine, but I decline. "Can I speak with you a moment?"

"Of course," she says, excusing herself from the others. "Are you okay?" she asks.

"Yes, I'm fine."

"Scarlett, I'm sorry. I hope—"

"I don't blame you at all," I say, placing a hand on her arm. "I would have made the same choice in your position."

She smiles, relief softening her features. "I'm glad you understand."

A voice behind us interrupts. It's the pinched woman who insulted me earlier. She's sneering at me now. "You shouldn't even be in the running, girl. You are weak, shooting the wolf instead of winning. You'll never make a worthy Knight."

She's laughing when Brooke walks over to her, smiling.

She stops laughing when Brooke grabs the back of her head and bashes her face into a stone wall, shattering her nose.

The woman stumbles back, blood running down her face and chest. "How dare you… "

"I am a member of the House of York. I dare do what I please. But if your honor is offended, perhaps you would fancy a duel?"

The woman backs away, hands up in resignation.

The crowd around us stands stunned. I'm still trying to process what just happened as Brooke looks at everyone carefully. "Scarlett made the right choice. The human choice. No one will dare insult her again. Are we clear?"

She doesn't wait for an answer, but walks away, winking at me as she does.

…

"Any other secrets I should know about?" I ask Jax as he walks me back to my room. I'm already healed, but he still worries.

He glances at me, his face unreadable. He doesn't answer, just says, "I'm sorry, Star."

I sigh. There are always secrets. "She's changed."

"We all have."

I nod. Life has taken us down very different paths, and yet they all led to Castle V. Except Ella. Her path was destroyed far too early. I will make Apex pay for that, and for all the harm he has done to so many.

Jax bows to me, then kisses my cheek, before leaving me in the care of Agatha. She tsks when she sees the state of my outfit. "You smell of vomit and rotten fruit," she says as she helps me undress.

"I was poisoned. And attacked. And I fell from a tree."

She raises an eyebrow but says nothing as I slip into my bathroom to take a quick shower. Once I'm dressed in clean clothes, my own clothes, we begin more training.

"Your Trial of Wit is next," she explains. "It is my hope and belief you will do better with this one. Strength is perhaps not your… strength." Her lips twitch into an almost smile and I laugh.

"Where do we start?" I ask.

She hands me a book. "Read and we will talk."

I spend the rest of the day and the next reading and talking with her, my grandfather, even Jax. It's a strange kind of preparation, where my ability to not just understand information, but communicate it in witty and engaging ways is tested. For example: *Why is it a criminal offense for a man living in York to be buried in Sky? Because he's still living.* By their looks I can tell I'm doing much better at this. There's a feeling of relief amongst my little group of tutors, as if I'm not a complete and utter failure at this.

I miss my parents. They should have told me about this part of my life. They should be the ones helping me prepare.

It's late when Evie beeps my eGlass at me. "What's up, Evie?"

"Scarlett, I have completed accessing The Apex channels of communication. Though most are far too encrypted to hack, I managed to decrypt a few."

I sit up, closing the book on my lap. "Did you find something?"

"There's a warehouse, and it might be significant."

I'm already pulling out my Nightfall backpack and slipping out the third story window of my bedroom when I give her instructions to relay this information to Trix, TR and Zorin. "Tell them I'm on my way."

The evening is cool and dark, a new moon hiding in the night. It doesn't take long to fly to the Cathedral. When I arrive, the little village we're creating is mostly asleep. I fly straight to the Cathedral door, let myself in and find everyone at the War Table.

Zorin holds up his tablet. "We hacked into the security cameras," he says. "This group is keeping Zeniths trapped and drugged, selling them off to clients. Their leader is called Jerry Mane, and we believe he might be working with Apex. He may know where we can find him."

TR taps his tablet and projects something into my eGlass. "Jerry Mane doesn't leave his warehouse often. When he does, his vehicle is surrounded by security."

"Where did we find this information?" I sink into a seat at the table and Zorin passes me a LifeForce.

Trix answers. "Jerry's wanted by the Inquisition. They have a file on his tactics. A file we hacked."

I scan through the data on my eGlass. The warehouse isn't heavily defended. Jerry must be relying on secrecy for security. This will be easy.

Zorin frowns. "I know that look, Nightfall. No."

I grin at him. "He won't be expecting an attack. He thinks no one knows about the warehouse."

"He's dangerous," Zorin argues.

"Not as dangerous as me."

...

Our team prepares for the assault, loading weapons and dressing in black armor. When we enter the city, I will find an Inquisition Officer and make them do my bidding. When our mission is over, the Inquisition will arrest Jerry Mane and his accomplices. The Dark Templars won't understand how I managed it, but they trust in my plans.

Trix walks to my side, arms crossed over her chest. "I had a similar plan once."

"When you attacked the Vatican?" I ask, staring out the Cathedral balcony.

She nods. "We surrounded the place, but there was an Inquisitor with andronic mods, maybe also a zen. He threw a Bruiser at me." She kicks at a rock, then bends to pick it up, looking at it as she speaks. "We fought and I got ahold of him, grabbed his head... " she squeezes the stone in her hand, "And he exploded." She incinerates the rocks until it's nothing but dust she flicks off her skin. "But we had taken too long, and reinforcements arrived. I was so close to ending all this, but I failed. All those killed by the Orders since then, their blood is on my hands." She looks over at me, her green eyes holding mine. "We can't fail, N."

I lay a hand on her arm. "Without you the Dark Templars wouldn't exist. You are the heart of us, the reason we have an organized cause at all. Soon, we will grind The Apex into dust."

...

I sit on a lighthouse made of shining metal, and I survey the surroundings as my cloak flaps around me. The warehouse is by the docks. It is a large, simple building, next to roaring waves and giant ships. My ears are filled with the groaning of machinery and the yelling of people as they move cargo from ships to trucks. They work hard, and we will avoid them in our assault. The air smells of salt and fish. The wind is furious.

The sky is dark, but the port and warehouse are lit with lamps. Places like these do not sleep. They work through the day and night, producing goods for those who can afford them. The ships provide food and technology. The warehouse provides Zeniths. They are used as tools for sick pleasures and cheap labor. My stomach twists at the thought.

I need to focus.

I tap my eGlass. "Begin."

A dozen Dark Templars led by Trix emerge from a building below me. They reach the side of the warehouse, avoiding the lights as best they can. The front entrance is guarded, but this path will not be. Trix touches the wall and, around her palm, a circle of steel, larger then a person, turns red. Then it turns to grey ash and falls at her feet. Her pyromatics are stronger than I thought, and now they have an opening.

Trix sneaks through the new hole in the warehouse, and the Dark Templars follow. TR is positioned on a storage building next to the lighthouse, ready to use his sniper rifle for support. Zorin emerges from the dark sky and lands on the warehouse silently. He enters through a window near the ceiling.

My eGlass is synched with all of my generals and my troops, and I watch the mission unfold.

Before our enemy can react, we are upon them. Like a fog of sleep, we drift through the warehouse, knocking out sentries and doctors with chloroform. From Trix's point of view, I see her grab an armed man from behind. He collapses back against her, and she lays him down gently. Next, she grabs doctor, who sleeps in his chair, still wearing a white coat. Through Zorin's feed, I see him choke another doctor until the woman passes out. Their medicines are used to keep the Zeniths docile and weak, and I feel no pity for them.

The area is almost secured. Next, I must find Jerry Mane and interrogate him with my talent.

I jump down from the lighthouse, using my wings to drift slowly to the hole Trix burned. A light rain begins to fall. I enter the warehouse, staying hidden behind a stack of crates as I work my way to a steel staircase. When I turn past the crates, I see a nurse studying his clipboard, unaware his comrades have fallen. I do not hesitate when I grab him by the neck. I scan his mind for Jerry Mane's location, and when I have it, I tell him to rest. He crumples at my feet, a peaceful smile on his lips. He should enjoy his dreams, for he will wake to a nightmare.

As an experiment, I touch him again and ask him to stand. He does not stir. Zorin must be right. I can only use my talent on someone once.

My Dark Templars continue moving through the warehouse, around stacks of crates and below old yellow lamps. We pass empty beds and cages on the first floor. The sheets are still messy, and the smell of sedatives and smoke is thick in the air. The Zeniths were sold recently. Apex must have them now. He will not have them for long.

I reach the steel staircase and walk to the top of the warehouse. There is a private room built from dark wood with windows to overlook the workers below, the room Jerry Mane uses. Zorin and Trix stand at my side, and I tell them to wait. I am the only one needed now.

I open the door and find a slim man leaning over a mahogany table, a bottle in his hand, dark shadows under his eyes. "I knew you would come," he says. "Someone always comes, eventually." He gulps down his drink and turns to face me. There is little light in the room, only a small grey lamp on his messy desk. The air is heavy with smoke. "So what can I do for you, Nightfall?"

"Tell me where Apex is." I take a step forward, my footsteps loud against the wood, and reach for him.

Jerry raises his hand. "No need for violence, Nightfall." His voice is rough and weary. He is a man consumed by his own troubles. "You will find Apex on his ship. The coordinates are—"

Something swooshes by me. And an arrow hits Jerry in the neck.

His head crumples, his throat gurgling. I turn and see a shadow at a window above me. The figure wears a black cloak torn into ribbons. They sway and hiss in the wind like vipers. She—I think it is a she because of her body shape—turns away toward the night.

I unleash my wings and dash upward, as the figure jumps outside. I land on the window ledge, scanning the city. I see a shadow fleeing down an alley. I follow, my wings a spiral of silver in the darkness. I land in a puddle, searching for the figure. The rain is strong now, beating against my skin. Whoever this person, this... Viper... is, they knew about my plan, and they had cause to stop it. Images flash through my mind. A black hood, snakes hissing on a coat, a ring with a blade. Apex. Was that him? One of his agents?

My head spins as I fall to my knees and scream into the night.

Once again, I have failed to find my enemy. I have failed to avenge Brooke and Ella. The rage within me is a living thing, and it eats away at my insides. Tears flow from my eyes, and I punch the concrete below me. It cracks like thunder in a storm.

"Nightfall?" asks Zorin softly. He is behind me, but I do not move to face him.

Wet footsteps.

He is closer.

His hand is on my shoulder.

"Nightfall."

His voice pulls me from my memories. "I'm fine," I say sharply. "We need to regroup." I stand, dusting off my cloak, and walk past him, back toward the light.

...

We regroup back within the warehouse. I meet my generals in the wooden room above the stairs. It is a messy place, full of papers and clothes. "We lost our lead," I explain, attempting to stay composed. Our team had high hopes for this mission and, despite our failure, I cannot allow our hope to fade. "Someone was there. A viper in the night. They killed our target before I could question him. They must have known we needed the information in his mind, so they eliminated him."

Trix bows her head, and TR groans and paces. Zorin leans against the door, tapping his fingers on the wall, his rage the calmest of all.

"We need to find another lead," I continue, "and if we can find this person, this Viper, that would help. For now, search the warehouse, see if you can find any clues to Apex's whereabouts. You have one hour. Then the Inquisition will arrive and arrest all those within."

TR raises a questioning eyebrow at my last comment, but says nothing. My generals leave the room and I collapse in the wooden chair, finally letting my composure break. Every bone and muscle in my body throbs with stress and I take deep breaths, willing myself to relax. I need to rest. To sleep. To—

My eGlass beeps and Evie's voice speaks softly into my ear. "Scarlett, I have received a message from the Chancellor. You have to get back to the Castle. Your next trial is about to begin."

TRIAL OF WIT

My hair is back to pale blonde, and I am dressed for my life at Castle V, but my mind cannot shake the memories of tonight. Thoughts of Apex consume me.

I'm running through the castle courtyard, barely paying attention to where I'm going, when I hear Ragathon and my grandfather arguing under the shade of a Fairy Tree.

"We cannot allow this!" Ragathon says through clenched teeth. "We know Nightfall was part of the attack on the warehouse. She's working with the Shadows. They're calling themselves the Dark Templars now. They make a mockery of the Four Orders, of our way of life. They are a problem we must end."

I clench my fist, resisting the urge to shout at him. The Dark Templars are the problem? Not Apex and his corrupt organization? Not the group that is kidnapping and using Zeniths? Not the group that killed Ella?

My grandfather says something I can't hear. Whatever his words, they do not make Ragathon happy, which makes me smile.

Evie beeps in my ear, reminding me to hurry, and I pick up my pace, bumping shoulders with the Seeker, who is walking towards Ragathon. The scowl is still on my face from her mentor's words, and she frowns at me. "We're not your enemy, Scarlett."

Oh, if only she knew what I truly am.

As the Seeker leaves, Evie says prospects are to meet at the third door on the left in the second level hall of the northwest tower. I sigh and ask her to map the way. This place is deceptively hard to navigate, and I have no energy left in me. Whatever this trial is, I hope it is easier than the first.

When I arrive in the correct hall, Falcon joins me. "Hello, Scarlett. Are you well?"

I wonder if he sees the anger and sorrow within me. I tell him I am fine, because I cannot discuss the truth. "You?"

He smiles, pulling out a golden necklace from behind his shirt. It is symbol of some sort. He grips it hard. "I am well because of you, Scarlett. You saved my life."

I shrug. "Anyone would have done the same."

"Not likely," he says.

"What's that symbol?" I ask, pointing at his necklace.

He opens his palm, showing me the amulet. "It is an Ankh. It means a breath of life."

The symbol is cross, with an oval shape at the top. Vague memories of reading about symbols, about the Leviathan Cross and the Ankh, surface in my mind. "The old religions are outlawed."

His eyes move swiftly from side to side, nervously. But only for a moment. If I were not Nephilim, I may have missed it.

He laughs. "It is not religious. I wear it to remind me of the value of life, and the beauty of it."

I nod. The Ankh may mean more to him than he admits, but his secret will be safe with me. We all have sides hidden from the world.

He still looks on edge, so I touch his shoulder. "Don't worry. I won't discuss your amulet with anyone. Thank you for sharing it with me."

He smiles, his dark face relaxed, and I glance at his Ankh, reminding myself that there is beauty in my life. I must not dwell on the deaths of the past.

After a moment, we reach the correct door. A Teutonic stands guard, and he asks us to hand him our eGlasses and anything in our pockets or on our persons. No weapons, not even so much as a pen and paper is allowed into the room.

Brooke is the last to arrive. As she walks up, I turn the handle on the door and the three of us walk into a simple room devoid of all furniture or ornaments. Once we enter, the door behind us slams shut.

Brooke tries the door. "It's locked."

The stone floors have been stripped of carpets, and there are no windows or dressings on the wall. In the center of the room sits an ornate box the size of a book. The three of us sit in a small circle around it.

"What are we meant to do?" Brooke asks.

I am too tired for puzzles, but this is one I must solve, so I pick up the box and examine it. It's made of a dark wood and polished to a high sheen. It's carved with asymmetrical patterns and appears to be all one piece. "It's one of those puzzle boxes." I run my fingers over the smooth wood, feeling for the hidden mechanisms to open it.

It takes only a few minutes for me to unlock its secrets. A hidden panel slips out, revealing a single sheet of thick cream paper. I read the words out loud.

"Greetings, Initiate Prospects,

Here you will find a riddle to challenge the greatest minds in the history of our world. This riddle predates the Cataclysm, and is credited to an ancient thinker whose work has mostly been lost to our time. His name was Einstein, and he believed only 2% of the population could puzzle out the answer to this question without the use of writing implements. You will remain locked in this room until one of you speaks the correct answer into the box. You only have one chance to answer. If you answer incorrectly, the box locks you out permanently. Once you answer correctly, the door will unlock and you will be released."

Brooke takes the paper from me, scanning down to the riddle. She reads the rest out loud.

"The riddle is as follows: There are five houses, with five occupants, each with a different color house, different beverage of choice, different favorite brand of cigarette, and a unique pet. With only the following information as aid, you must reason out who owns the fish."

She passes the paper back to me and I read through the clues.

1) *The Englishman lives in the red house.*
2) *The Swede keeps dogs.*
3) *The Dane drinks tea.*

There are twelve more clues, all similar to the first three.

"We can only answer once and only one person can answer," Brooke says.

The implications are weighty. We must all agree on who answers, and trust they have it correct. "What happens if we fail?" I ask.

Neither of them has an answer.

We take turns reading through the riddle. We can't take notes, so we must hold it all in our minds.

Falcon and Brooke talk through the options of the riddle, but I move away, closing my eyes as I sink into my mind. Myrddin once taught me a valuable tool in memory and deductive, inductive and adductive reasoning called the Method of Loci, a mnemonic adopted in ancient Greece and Roman rhetorical treatises. I place each piece of information the riddle gave us into its own room in my mind, adding the details visually.

I do not know how long I sit there, alone in my thoughts, but I am sore, tired and hungry when I open my eyes. Falcon is pacing the empty room and Brooke is staring at the paper with a scowl.

She sighs when she sees I'm back. "Any luck?"

I shake my head. "Still trying to figure it out. You?"

"No. This is impossible. I wouldn't be surprised if this doesn't even have an answer."

"How can they expect us to dwell here without food or drink? We don't even have pillows." Falcon says.

"They wouldn't let us starve to death here. Would they?" Brooke sounds worried.

"We wouldn't starve," I say. "We would dehydrate first. Humans can't go more than a few days without water, but can go much longer without food."

"Thanks for that," Brooke says with sarcasm.

"If it's any consolation, we're all likely well hydrated and these aren't harsh conditions," I say, trying to sound more energized than I am. "We could possibly survive up to a three days without water."

Falcon looks at me with an odd expression on his face. "A bit of a survivalist, are you?"

"My parents had a thing about it," I say by way of explanation. "I picked up a few things."

"Too bad you didn't pick up anything about Einstein," Brooke says, slamming the paper to the floor.

"Yeah." I get up to stretch, examining the room for clues, but there is nothing in here but us.

We are trapped for two days without food and water. I watch as Falcon and Brooke devolve, as their personalities fray from tedium, hunger and thirst. One night, Falcon murmurs in his sleep. "I'm sorry, but I don't want to be a Knight. I don't want to be. Please, Mother, don't make me go..." When he wakes, none of us ask about his past. That day, Brooke weeps in a corner. She whispers for Ella. She whispers for forgiveness.

They don't do well under stress. I do far better. Likely, it is because I am Nephilim. I don't need water like them, and it seems I can last longer without blood than humans can without water.

But on the third day, I begin to hunger. I can smell their blood pulsing under their skin and I know I must answer the question soon, before my own willpower shatters and I become the monster the world fears my kind to be.

I reach for the paper and read through it again, and then I smile. "I know the answer."

Brooke and Falcon stop bickering with each other and both turn to me.

"Really?" Brooke asks, crawling over to me. We stopped walking a day ago. I thought Brooke and Falcon would begin hallucinating, but they didn't, I suspect because of the andronics GenMod.

"Really," I say. "I know the answer."

Falcon looks at me. "Are you sure? One wrong answer, pureman, and we are doomed."

I nod. "You need to trust me. I'm sure."

Brooke and Falcon look to each other and then nod as one.

"We will die soon, anyways. Why not?" Brooke hands me the box.

I open it and speak clearly into it. "The German."

We all turn when the door behind us clicks and swings open.

...

"I'm surprised it took you so long to figure out," says my grandfather as he hands me a LifeForce and fresh bread. We sit in the courtyard minutes after the trial, under a sun I have not seen for three days, and I drink quickly to regain energy.

I take a bite of the bread to keep up appearances. "I solved the riddle on the first day."

He raises a bushy eyebrow. "And you waited three days to answer it?"

I nod, opening a third pack of LifeForce. "I wanted to see how my competition handles pressure."

The chancellor nods, running his fingers through his grey beard. "Clever. And how did they fare?"

"Not well. Falcon doesn't want to be a Knight. He's only here because of expectations. In the end, his lack of commitment will show. He won't win."

"And the Princess of York?"

"She is still haunted by the past. But so am I."

A warm breeze flutters past us, and my lungs fill with fresh air of the courtyard, so different from that stifling room. I remember my friend's soft cries. "I'm... sorry I put her through that. I could have saved her pain."

My grandfather taps his cane against the stone floor. "The information you gleaned on Falcon is valuable, but—"

"But it won't help. I still need to beat Brooke. Only one can win." I consider ways of using Brooke's past trauma against her, and I almost vomit from disgust. I will not use Ella's memory for my own means. When I win, it will be honorably.

Brooke walks over to us, looking rejuvenated. "We're tied now, you and I. May the best pat win! Are you ready for the Trial of Grace? I hear it's full of high society types who love to judge."

"Um… "

"She'll do great at the ball," the chancellor says with a confidence I don't feel.

"I'm sure she will," Brooke says, leaving us and disappearing within the castle.

Falcon walks over next, his eyes still red and weary. "May I have a moment?" he asks.

I nod, standing up from my bench. I say goodbye to the chancellor and follow Falcon inside the castle. "It seems I must thank you again," he says. "One more day, and I'm sure I would have died."

"They wouldn't have actually let us die. Would they?"

He shrugs. "It is the nature of this game. They need the strongest. The best. The bravest. There can be no real trial without risk."

"Well, it's almost over," I say, walking with him down the stone halls towards my room. "Only one more trial."

"About that—" he pauses, glancing at me. "I propose we team up against Brooke."

I stop, turning to him. "Why?"

He twists the silver ring on his finger, engraved with a cloud, the sigil of his house. "These games, they are not fair. I am from a small house. You were not even supposed to be in this race at all. You replaced a nobody. The cards were always stacked in favor of Brooke, a Princess of York. There are powerful people who want her to win."

"You weren't the one who poisoned me, were you?"

He smiles sadly. "No, I was not."

"But... Brooke would never do that to me. We've known each other since childhood."

He steps closer, his voice lowering. "She may not have poisoned you, but her supporters would have. Since you and she are friends, she trusts you most. You could use that to your advantage." He holds out a dagger to me, hilt first. "The Trial of Grace does not allow weapons. It is an immediate fail to be caught with one. If you slipped this onto her person, and she were caught with it... "

"She would lose, and I would win the Initiate Trials," I finish, my stomach clenching at the thought of betraying my old friend. But I have to weigh that against the greater good of infiltrating the Orders so I can take them down. This isn't just my fight. This is the fight of the

Dark Templars, of all the oppressed in this unjust world. Their hopes and dreams rest on my ability to gain a foot-hold into this elite society.

"This would give us an even playing field for once," he says, clutching his Ankh again. "You and I, we would make honorable Knights. We are not bought and paid for by a powerful family. Either of us would be a better Knight than someone beholden to the corruption of the House of York."

"And if I don't do this? If I try to win on my own merits?"

He shakes his head sadly. "That will never be possible in this world, Scarlett. You will lose."

...

Students of the Orders mill about the training yard. They wear their robes, displaying their chosen Orders on their chest, as they train with weapons or in hand-to-hand combat. I'm practicing forms with my sword. Not the forms Zorin teaches me, of course. But the ones I'm expected to know as part of my Initiate Prospect training. Not for the first time I wish my parents had prepared me better for this life, though I know why they didn't. They hoped I'd never have this life.

I'm again grateful for Myrddin's early training of me. Without him, I'd be more lost than I already am. At least he gave me some foundation before he left.

My sword gleams in the morning sun, casting shards of light against the stone walls of the training yard. I lunge, impaling an imaginary opponent, when my grandfather arrives and smiles at me.

"Shouldn't you be preparing for your final trial?" he asks.

I let my sword drop, my arm aching. "How do you prepare for a party? My gown is ready, my makeup has been chosen, my stylist is ready." Even saying all of this makes me feel ridiculous.

"Yes, but have you mastered the social graces?" he asks. "Dancing, small talk, the proper degree of obsequiousness depending on the rank of the person to whom you are being presented?"

I groan and look longingly at my sword. Combat training seems easy compared to the Trial of Grace. "What happens if I fail at this?" I already know the answer, but I ask anyways.

He frowns. "Even your relation to me cannot guarantee you a spot in this program if you do not pass the trials."

"Maybe that's for the best." I stab at the ground with my sword. "Maybe this isn't the world for me." I know, of course, that I cannot give up that easily. If it were just me, I'd gladly live out my life somewhere away from this society, where I can tinker with my computers and enjoy the simple life my father had hoped for me. All those bold dreams I had as a child feel painfully naive now that I'm here living them. But this isn't about my own small life, not anymore.

Jax walks up to us, a grin on his face. "Is the lady giving up so easily?"

I glare at him, but he just smiles back. "I've come to rescue you, fair maiden," he says, holding out a hand.

I look at it, confused.

My grandfather steps back and clicks on his eGlass. Music streams out, some kind of ballad. Oh, no. I step away from Jax. "I am not dancing here, in front of all these people!"

"You have to practice," Jax says.

"In private, maybe." I cross my arms over my chest.

"You've had enough private lessons. You won't be in private come the ball." He steps forward and pulls me into his arms. His mouth is near my ear as he speaks softly. "You can do this, Star. I know you can."

We begin to step to the music, measured slow movements that take us in a loop. I follow his lead, matching my feet to his, holding my arms the way he instructs.

My face turns red as other students stop to watch us. I see Brooke smile and clap to the music out of the corner of my eye. I'm sure she's been well-trained in the social graces. And she and I are tied. I have no idea how I'm going to win this.

Lost in thought, I lose track of my footing and trip on Jax, smashing his toes under mine. He catches me, and I try not to make eye contact with anyone around me as we start the dance again.

"Your mother also struggled with this," my grandfather says, surprising me.

I look to him as I move with Jax. "Really? It's hard to imagine her bad at anything."

He chuckles. "Oh she had her moments, believe me. You two are more alike than you think." He holds up his arms and sways his hips. "I, on the other hand, am as graceful as a swan."

I laugh as he mock-dances near us. I can tell from the shocked looked on the faces of the other students that they have never seen their Chancellor behave this way in public. His silliness eases a bit of my worry and embarrassment and I'm grateful to him. If I had to bet, I'd say he did this for exactly that reason, and it's one of the nicest things anyone has done for me since I arrived here.

Other students join in the dancing as weapons are forgotten and music fills the training yard. There is laughter and friendly banter until it is interrupted by an unwelcome voice.

"Is this an area for combat training or have I been misinformed all these years?"

Everyone stops dancing, and students pick up their weapons to resume their training. Jax stands by my side as Ragathon strides over, a scowl on his perpetually miserable face. The small joy I experienced is sucked dry in his presence.

He holds up a piece of paper very officially. "I have received special permission to open an investigation into the Trial of Wit. There is evidence that Scarlett Night cheated!"

His accusation is loud and spreads through the training ground amongst whispers. My cheeks turn red again, this time not in embarrassment but anger. I am furious.

Jax puts a tempering hand on my sword arm, as if he knows what I'm thinking. Truth be told, he probably does.

"What grounds do you have of accusing Scarlett of this nonsense?" My grandfather asks.

"There is evidence she had the answer to the riddle, that someone on the outside gave her the answer during the trial. She is to be taken in for questioning." Ragathon puffs out his chest as if that will impress anyone here.

Brooke steps forward, surprising me. "That is not accurate. I was there. No such thing occurred. We never left each other's side. There is no way anyone in that room could have cheated."

This expels my last doubts about Brooke. I know someone is rigging the game, maybe to her favor, but she's not a part of it. She's as much a pawn in this as I.

"Be that as it may, she still needs to come in for questioning," Ragathon says, his face turning red.

Brooke studies him for a moment. "And challenge her honor? Bold move, considering."

My eyes flick back and forth between them. I don't entirely understand what's going on, but I know it's something significant.

"Does the princess have something more to add to this discussion?" Ragathon asks of Brooke.

She smiles, then faces Jax. "Care to spar? Gravir to Gravir?"

There's a flash of confusion on his face, but it's quickly replaced with a knowing grin.

It takes me a moment to figure it out as they get into position. Brooke is casual in her approach, explaining some of her powers for the crowd gathering to watch. "Low-level Gravirs can give objects gravity." She focuses on a rock, and it pulls Jax's sword toward it. He grins and yanks his blade back, away from the gravitational pull.

Brooke grins. "Level Four Gravirs, like Jax, can do that and much more. For example, they can move their own bodies, decreasing and manipulating their gravity so that in essence, they fly."

She and Jax throw themselves into the air, and their swords clash as they dance on wind. It's incredible to watch and, I realize as eyes widen with respect at their power, that she's doing this for me. She has political weight as an adopted member of the royal family. Now she's showing Ragathon she has real power as well. Because in our world, a challenge to one's reputation can be met in combat. And I can designate someone to represent me. I could challenge Ragathon and have Brooke fight in my place. That's what she's showing him. That he'd better be beyond doubt at my guilt if he is going to tarnish my reputation. Or else.

"Then there are Level Five Gravirs," she says, looking at Ragathon squarely in the eye. "They are very rare, and very powerful. And they can control the gravitational pull of objects around them."

Stones and dirt and rock begin to float around her. They launch toward Jax, slamming into his stomach and pushing him back to the ground. Brooke dashes across the training ground. Before I can blink, she holds a knife to Jax's throat.

But he has a blade to her throat as well.

They both grin, putting away their blades, as those around us clap and cheer at the display.

She helps Jax up and dusts herself off, then faces Ragathon. "If someone says Scarlett cheated, then they challenge my word… my honor, the word of a royal." She walks up closer to Ragathon, standing only a few centimeters away. "Anyone who wishes to do so, may face me directly."

Ragathon barely breathes as the rage builds in his body like a physical thing. I can see the struggle on his face as he battles with himself. Challenge her and risk everything, or walk away and risk his pride.

He sacrifices his pride and walks away.

It's clear no one will question me again. The crowd disperses, and as Brooke and Jax approach me, Evie speaks into my ear. "I have a message from Zorin."

"Yes?"

"It's about the Angel."

MASKS

I freeze. "I, I have to go. I'll see you all later," I say to Brooke and Jax as I run out of the training yard and into an empty hallway.

Once alone, I have Evie get Zorin on the line. "I had an idea," he says. "Of where we may find the Angel."

My intake of breath is sharp and almost painful. "Where?"

"Snatcher's Castle."

"From the story you told me?"

"Yes. It's been abandoned for years, but the Angel must have a base. Yes, it's unlikely, but the castle is full of Nephilim and Angel history. I'm not sure we will find anything, but if you want to investigate... "

"Of course I do. I must. Where?"

I'm already digging out my backpack with my Nightfall gear and opening my window. "I'm right outside your window," he says.

I look down and don't see him. Then I look up, and I smile. I slip into my black armor and join him in the sky as we fly further than I ever have. "Can we really fly across an entire Ocean?" I ask as we drift past clouds and over waves.

Zorin chuckles. "We do not tire easily. But if we wish to reach the castle before night falls, we must hurry."

I nod, and the both of us accelerate, rushing past the wind. We do not talk more. It is difficult at this speed.

Hours later, we arrive at the base of a mountain. There lies an old ruin with broken walls and faded carvings. Near the gateway, a tower is on its side, cracked open by the force from when it fell. This place looks more rubble and dust than castle.

We land and pull in our wings, and look around the ruins. A great carving of Nephilim fills one of the walls. "What is that one about?" I ask, pointing at the yellow stone.

"The first one shows the great flood."

I pause. "What flood?"

"As you know, Nephilim were created from fallen Angels mating with humans. The blood of the Angles gave humans power, made them strong. The other Angels did not like this, so over time they manipulated the course of history to stop it," he says as we explore.

"There was a great flood that almost wiped the Nephilim out. But still they remained. Then there were the Inquisitions, but they often killed more innocent humans than actual Nephilim. What remained of our kind went into hiding for many years, but then, when they were ready, they set the world on fire."

I place a hand on a carving of a male Angel and a human woman conjoined in a passionate embrace. "The Cataclysm."

He nods. "After, the world was in chaos and Nephilim ruled the skies. Then a woman came along, Juliana. She rebuilt the Orders and turned the tide in favor of the humans. There were wars upon wars and after there was a kind of peace. The kind of peace built upon the subjugation of the Zenith and Nephilim. They were stripped of their rights and made less than man." He pauses, looking past the great hall where we stand and into some distant past. "Nyx broke that so-called truce."

"He had an apprentice who helped, did he not? Erebus?"

Zorin gives a half smile. "Yes. You have learned well. Nyx was tactical and manipulative, but Erebus was fire. He dealt the destruction that was needed, but it was too much. In the end, the two did not agree, and that led to their kind's downfall."

I look at him carefully, studying this man of secrets. He knows so much history. He knows of the seals and of the time before the Cataclysm. He is ancient. And he is powerful. So powerful I wonder how he was ever captured. "Who are you, really?"

"I told you when we first met. I am Count of Nightfall, Left Hand to the Twilight Queen before she was betrayed. Then I served new masters, and the things we did, the things I had to do... I just hope we were right."

"You served Nyx and Erebus?"

Zorin looks into the carvings, his eyes lost in some distant memory. "Yes, in a way."

"And you agreed with their methods?" *The assassinations. The executions.*

He sits down on the remains of an ancient pillar, sighing. "They... they did what they thought was right. Is that not what you and I do now?"

I nod sadly. "Yes. But we will not allow innocents to suffer."

"I don't think Nyx ever intended it to be so. But war... war is suffering."

We are silent for a while. And then I ask something I've wondered for weeks. "Zorin, why didn't you take leadership of the Shadows? Why not try to lead the Dark Templars now? You are older, stronger, more experienced. Why me?"

It is a long time before he responds. "I had my time to lead," he says. "And I made a grave mistake. One I know I would make again, so I cannot lead. I cannot."

"What was the mistake?"

He walks away, deeper into the castle, and his voice drifts on the wind. "Caring. I cared too much."

...

We spend the evening scouring the castle for clues, but aside from interesting tidbits of history, we find nothing to help me on my search. I know I shouldn't be surprised—Zorin warned me there was little chance we'd find the Angel—but I am and, as Zorin builds a fire, I throw rocks against the carvings. The flight home is too far to make without rest, so we use our capes as beds and sleep in the dirt.

I'm trying to get comfortable, my eyes half-closed, my mind half-lost in dreams, when I see something scurrying in the dark. A face forms from the shadows, the eyes covered in cloth. It wears a gray sack over its shoulders. But when I move to get a closer look, it disappears into the darkness.

It was a dream, I tell myself. Just a dream.

...

The hardest part about learning to dance is learning to dance like a patrician. My parents never taught me, because I wasn't a pat. It would have been scandalous to teach a mere pleb these dances.

But now I have very little time to learn. This last trial will decide my fate, and I'm tied with Brooke.

Jax is patient with me, guiding me through different dances, styles and arrangements. We have the ballroom to ourselves as he spins me and dips me and corrects my footing.

"You're doing great," he says, leading me off the floor and getting us both a LifeForce.

We sit on the floor, backs against the marble wall, sipping our drinks as we rest. "I just hope it's enough," I say.

He nudges my shoulder. "It's more than enough. Trust me."

Trust. Such a tricky word. It reminds me of a question I had. "Jax, do you know the Seeker?"

"Kira? Sure. Why?"

"She just seems close to Ragathon. She seems like she trusts him. I find that unfathomable."

"Kira has no real family or family name, but she trained hard after being chosen as an Initiate. She scored at the top of her classes," he says. "But none of the Orders wanted to take her. She had no great name. No royal blood. The Chancellor, your grandfather, argued for her, but he did not have enough support. Until Ragathon took up her cause. He insisted the Inquisition take her. He was the only one who chose her to be a Knight."

I have so many other questions. How did she end up in Initiate Training to begin with? Why did Ragathon fight for her? Where does she come from? But Jax gets a call on his eGlass and excuses himself, leaving me with all my questions unanswered.

...

It has been weeks since the Trial of Wit, but I have had few opportunities to train with Jax. Now, the Carnival of Masks approaches, where people will celebrate the end of summer quarter training, and the near completion of the Initiate Trials. The Trial of Grace will follow soon after, before the fall quarter begins. Jax has locked himself away in the woodshop, working hard on his secret project. Around Vianney, vendors are preparing for the onslaught of tourists and everyone everywhere is buying masks made for the occasion. Demons, angels, the glorious and the ungodly, all manner of beings. It's a chance for people to forget themselves and become something other.

Oh, the irony of that for me.

I wonder if there will be any Nightfall masks made. The thought makes me chuckle darkly.

I, of course, will not be wearing my Nightfall mask the night of the carnival, but I will be dressing as one would expect of a pat. My serf has made sure I have everything I need to participate, but my thoughts are too distracted by the final trial to be too excited about the big day.

...

When the day of the carnival finally arrives, bringing with it a late summer breeze, the excited energy of the town seeps into me, giving me a slight distraction from my worry over the final trial. Jax and Brooke come to my room just as Agatha is finishing up my hair. I'm wearing an elaborate costume of blue and black, with a cape and a matching mask decked in diamonds and sapphires. My hair has been braided and twisted with ribbon and then wrapped into a side bun. My eyes have been painted so that they stand out underneath the mask.

Jax whistles when he sees me. "You've outdone yourself, Star."

"You, too," I say, admiring both him and Brooke.

He holds an arm out. "Shall we?"

I take it and the three of us walk through the castle, appreciating the streamers and decorations strewn about in bright colors. Jesters, musicians, and story-tellers are sprinkled throughout, entertaining guests who mingle.

Booths dot the castle bridge, selling their wares to those coming and going. There are more festivities in town, but we make our way to the ballroom, which is completely transformed from last time. The walls and tables are black, reminding me of the Cathedral. Silver webs run across the ceiling, and mist drifts across the floor as haunting music flows from a piano. Small black spiders scurry from web to web, and I know once this over, someone will blow a special whistle and collect them all. Animals have been engineered for such events.

Jax asks me to dance, and I place my hand in his nervously.

"This isn't a test," he says. "Just a dance."

"Everything is a test here," I argue, as he spins me around.

When the music slows, so do we, and I enjoy the moment, his arms wrapped around me, our bodies close. Life is simple for just a moment. "I feel like we're back in Sky," I say. "Back when Myrrdin used to teach us. When things made sense."

He pulls away as the song ends, his face hardening. "Those days are lost."

His words tug at my heart as he excuses himself to get us drinks.

I'm left alone on the dance floor, when someone comes up behind me and asks to dance.

I turn to see a man in black, face covered with a mask. But I know his voice, his movement.

"Zorin," I whisper, taking his hand and he pulls me into a dance. "What are you doing here?"

"This is a night to be whomever we choose. No one knows me here. And I needed to see you."

My heart skips a little at that, but I shove that emotion away. Dancing with him is different than dancing with Jax. Zorin glides around the dance floor like one who has been moving to music for ages. I suppose he has, now that I think of it. How many dances, how many songs, how many cultures has he participated in over the course of his long life, I wonder.

"Is everything okay?" I ask.

"Your final trial is coming up," he says. "You must do whatever it takes to win. Brooke might be your friend, but she too will do what is necessary to win. At the trial, they are all your enemies."

I look up at him, his eyes so blue through his black mask. "So you didn't come just to dance and enjoy a night off?"

He laughs. "We have no nights off."

I stop dancing, pulling away. "I know all this. I'm ready. I will do what I must."

I walk away, but he grabs my hand. "Scarlett."

I pause, turning back to him. "What? More dire warnings?"

His hand squeezes mine. "I could have called to say what I have said."

"Then why didn't you?"

"Because I wouldn't have gotten a dance."

I freeze, startled by his admission. Before I can respond, he releases my hand and disappears through the crowd. I search for him, but he is gone and, a moment later, I walk off the dance floor—abandoned by both of my dance partners—and find Brooke, who is alone on the balcony with a glass in one hand and a bottle of liquor in the other. She sways a bit as I approach, her eyes glassy. When she speaks, it is with a slight slur.

"Scarlett! Come, drink with me. We must have alcohol."

She hands me her full glass and drinks straight from the bottle. "Ella would have loved this," she says with a gesture of her hand. "The costumes, the dancing, the festivities."

I lean against the railing and sip the drink. It's strong. "Yes, she would have."

"Do you remember the Festival of Fortuna? Just before…"

I nod. "Yes."

"That was the best day of her life. She told me. The best day." There are tears in her eyes now, and one escapes, gliding down her cheek. "I wish she was here, but it is foolish to dream. I only wish I could make things right for her."

"Brooke, I—" Maybe it's the alcohol, or her pain, but I come so close to telling her the truth. To telling her I am Nightfall, and that I am looking for Apex. That I will bring justice to their tormenter.

She looks at me, waiting.

"I know it's hard. I'm so sorry." I can't. I can't reveal this part of myself, even to her. The risks are too great, to both of us.

She nods. "But let us not drown ourselves in sorrow. Let us dance and play."

We reenter the ballroom and she finds a young man to join her in on the floor. I watch them laughing, swirling and moving with the music, and then I leave and walk through the castle courtyard, pushing through the throngs of people until I find an area less populated. I need space. Air. Quiet.

I stand staring at the night sky, the moon full and bright, the stars standing sharply against the darkness.

I don't hear the Viper until the knife enters my back.

I fall to the ground, pain piercing my mind.

The Viper stands over me. Streaming cloth swirls around in the wind.

And then all goes black.

TRIAL OF GRACE

The pain in my lower back is dull, throbbing. I groan and open my eyes, shifting in my bed. No, not my bed. I look around. I'm in the Infirmary, and Jax is sitting next to me holding my hand. He smiles when our eyes meet, but he looks haggard, the skin around his eyes lined with dark circles. "What happened?" I croak.

"I found you stabbed outside the Castle. I was so scared, Star." He leans in, tears in his eyes. "I thought you were dead. You were barely breathing."

"Thirsty," I say. He hands me water, but I shake my head. "No. LifeForce." He nods and grabs one from a vending machine in the hallway. I drink it down. "I'm okay," I tell him. "Already healing from my GenMods." And Nephilim blood.

"The wound wasn't fatal," he says. "It looked bad, but the Hospitaller said it wouldn't have killed you. Someone meant to take you out of the running."

Of course. The rage building in me burns away the last of the pain and I toss aside the sheet covering me and stand, grabbing for my clothes. I know who did this and they will pay.

...

I'm seeing red when I storm into Ragathon's office in the west end tower. He sits at his desk, staring at a computer screen. The walls around him are covered with law books and paintings of Inquisition Officers meting out justice.

"You had me stabbed." I say without preamble.

He frowns, his dark eyes matching mine. "That is a serious accusation, girl. Where is your proof?"

"You've tried to have me taken out of the running before. You wanted to investigate me during the Trial of Wit so you could disqualify me. Someone poisoned me during the Trial of Strength, and I'm sure you commanded them. When all your attempts failed, you had me stabbed." By the Viper. Probably an agent of his. I know this isn't proof I can use in a trial, but pats care little about proof. They care about honor, and mine has been damaged. I can challenge Ragathon to a duel right now. An Initiate Prospect against a Grandmaster. His much higher position means he should refuse, but his dislike for me may just push him to accept. Many will think I have no chance, but they don't know I'm Nephilim, and that will give me an edge.

He must see my fury, maybe even think I'm dangerous, because he relaxes into his chair and attempts a soft smile. It looks awkward on his face, like a hyena trying to look cute. "Scarlett, why would I even want you out of the running? You're a patrician, and you have skills. Like others, you deserve your chance to become an Initiate."

"You didn't like me from the start," I say. "I don't know why. Maybe you didn't like my parents. Maybe you don't like Jax." I think back to when I first met him and our meetings since. "And you know I don't approve of your methods. I would have Zeniths treated fairly. If I became a Knight, I would oppose you."

He raises an eyebrow, bewilderment on his face. "You think I fear you?" He chuckles. "You think *I* fear *you*." It's not a question this time. "Girl, I have far greater concerns than you and your beliefs. Now, if you don't mind, I have work to do." He looks back to his computer, dismissing me with a gesture.

I don't leave. "How could you be so harsh? You're an Inquisitor. It's your job to protect the innocent. If you're not the one trying to hurt me, then prove it to me. Find the criminal."

Ragathon faces me once more, serious. For the first time in our conversation, he stands, looming over me. "You want me to find your assailant? I know you grew up as a pleb, girl, but you're a patrician now. You have power. Take this issue to your grandfather, or the Inquisition Domus, or your friend Jax, or the Princess of York, or even the Teutonic guards. Do not bring it to me, girl." He leans forward, sneering. "I serve those who have no power. The people who live on rations and seek medical treatment from drug dealers on the streets. The people killed by corrupt Officers and out-of-control Zeniths. The decisions I make change their very lives. You think I have time for one pat when there's a world of plebs who need my help? Foolish girl." He sits back down, shaking his head.

I pause, processing his words, my anger dying down. "If you care about the people, why plan a trap in the middle of Times Square? Why sacrifice so many innocents?"

"The rebels..." He sighs, looking tired. And for the first time, I don't see a cruel man, but a man who has dedicated his life to his work and paid the price. "I underestimated them. It's as if... as if they had a new leader... or someone helping them. They outmaneuvered me at every turn. Had my plan worked, the casualties would have been minor, but I failed—and the many deaths, they are my fault." His words are heavy with sorrow.

I almost want to reach out and comfort him, but I remember he is Ragathon, and I stand my ground. "Why have such a dangerous plan?" I ask.

"I would sacrifice a few to save many," he says softly. He looks up, his eyes swollen. "One day, I was walking my young daughter to school and, as we reached the playground, the building exploded before us. A few more seconds and she would have been killed. Zeniths, inspired by the Shadows, had planted the bomb. They wished to kill the next generation of patricians. They killed hundreds. All children. Fighting inspires more fighting. The Shadows must be stopped. That day, I planned to end them once and for all. For my daughter. For the children who will never grow old."

But the Shadows remain. Because of me. How will I be better? How will I stop others from killing in my name?

"You hate Zeniths," I say calmly, finally understating his motivations.

He sips from a cup on his table. "They... they present a problem. And I am tasked with finding the solution."

And he would use whatever means necessary. I see that now. He would kill innocents. He would execute Zeniths to inspire. He would...

I step back as things click into place.

He would kidnap Zenith children.

He would hurt them.

To avenge the patrician children who died.

And his goals would be furthered.

There would be fewer Zeniths on the streets. They would be seen as less than human. And one day, maybe, like the Nephilim, they will be exterminated.

"You're Apex," I whisper. That's why I had such a visceral reaction to him when we first met. Because I'd met him before as a child.

But what part does the Viper play? I'm sure the Viper is a woman. He must have someone working for him. Someone close. The Seeker. His right hand.

"You're Apex," I say again, louder, as the puzzle I've worked on since childhood falls into place before me.

We are silent for a moment. Anger builds within me.

Ragathon laughs, his voice carrying through the small office. "You know nothing, Miss Night."

Evie beeps on my eGlass. "Scarlett, The Trial of Grace is beginning."

I want to stay. I want to fight. For Brooke. For Ella.

Instead, I turn and leave. The Trial is now, and Ragathon can be dealt with later. I know where to find him. And when I do, one of us will die.

...

Agatha dresses me in a beautiful gown of feathers and silk, silver and pale blue to match my eyes. She mutters something, likely about how unprepared I am, but I'm not listening. My mind is occupied.

Ragathon is Apex, and Kira is the Viper. They tried to kill me, or at the very least destroy my chances of succeeding here. And now I have to spend an evening in 'polite company' pretending this place isn't rotting from within. My stomach turns with disgust.

As Agatha finishes straightening my hair, Jax enters the room. He is dressed in white to match me, and light blue makeup spirals in designs around his eyes. His belt and buttons sparkle with gold. He looks more patrician than ever before. More... beautiful... than ever before.

He holds up his arm, grinning, "May I have the honor of escorting you to the ball, My Lady?"

I take his arm, my hands covered in white gloves that almost reach my shoulders. "That would be splendid, pureman."

He escorts me to a line of people before the ballroom door, where everyone waits to be announced. "Don't worry," he says.

"I'm not worried."

"You're squeezing my arm like you want to tear it off. I think you're... wait, never mind. You're right. You're not worried. You're just doing hand exercises."

I grin. "You've been through this before, when you were in the Initiate Trials. Were *you* nervous?"

He wipes his forehead. "I was terrified. But I'm not Scarlett the Clever. I wasn't drawing battle plans when I was ten."

I sigh, shaking my head, but I feel better than before. He's right. I've wanted this my entire life. And I'm prepared.

We're next in line. And as we enter through the great red doors, we are announced. "Lady Scarlett of the House of Night, Initiate prospect, daughter of Lord Marcus of the House of Night and Lady Violet of the House of Forrester, granddaughter to the esteemed Templar Grandmaster, Chancellor Forrester.

"Sir Jaxton of the House of Lux, Knight of the Teutonic Order, Knight of the Fourth."

I whisper to Jax. "Why do they mention my parents, but not yours?"

"Mine aren't important enough," he says, not looking at me as we descend the red steps into the ballroom.

I expected this to be like the first party. It is not. Everything is grander. The floor is glass, and beneath our feet swim giant fish modified to change colors, their scales shimmering from gold to purple to red. Below them giant crystals glow a pale blue in the water. In places, the glass floor parts, and there swans swim amongst flowers of white and gold. A large rock juts from the pool of water and, on it, a woman dressed in silver and a man dressed in black dance, spinning and twirling through the air. At times, it seems as if they will fall off, but always, one of them catches the other in a passionate embrace.

The ceiling is opened, revealing a sky of stars. Men and women dressed in very little strut around the hall, carrying platters of fairy drinks and red cakes. The patricians, who mingle and dance, are dressed in the finest Eden Fashionables I have ever seen. Green vines twist and dance around a woman as she dances with her partner. Gold eagles adorn his collar, swaying to the slow orchestral music.

I vaguely recognize some of the people around me. Important people. I notice Tavora, the Knight of the Second who received the Laurel from the Archbishop, talking to Brooke and others in the corner. They are both of York. They are family. Brooke wears a black dress decorated with silver stars, and Tavora a black uniform accented with white and gold. Falcon dances with someone I have never met, his red cape billowing behind him. Kira, the Seeker—*the Viper*, whispers my mind—sits at a table with others, dressed in a crimson gown and dipping strawberries into a chocolate fountain. She will pay for her part in this.

"Shall we dance?" asks Jax.

I nod, knowing this is part of the trial, and we begin. My heart beats twice the beat of the music but I keep my pace, executing all the moves perfectly, following his lead as he spins me around. At times, I glance at Brooke and Falcon, both dancing, and both looking far calmer than I feel. Their steps are not merely correct, they are one with the music. They are grace one moment, fire the next. They are the honorable ruler and the fierce warrior. They are everything a Knight should be.

And I am not. I have not lived as a patrician for years like Brooke. I didn't have servants training me since I was a child like Falcon. I have potential, but I am not ready. I was a fool to think I was.

I think back to Falcon's offer to sabotage Brooke. To Zorin's warning that I must win at all costs. But I will not win by cheating. I will not win by playing these games with the same corruption I came here to stop.

So I will do what I can. And maybe, just maybe, it will be enough.

The song ends, and our dance stops. People clap. Jax moves me around the room to make small talk with patricians of different noble houses. I bow at the appropriate times, and in the appropriate ways, showing the right amount of deference to each pureman as needed. I smile and sip at champagne and utter the words I know they want to hear from me.

It's all exhausting. The splendor is lost in a sea of faces, everyone trying to outdo each other in opulence.

The evening feels like it will never end, but time does pass, albeit slowly.

I see my grandfather across the room. He is in a place of honor, at the head of a table, watching and talking to someone at his right. He nods a head at me, his eyes encouraging.

He will support me, at least. Jax and I begin dancing again, and it is when I finally begin to slightly enjoy the night that Ragathon approaches. I want to groan, but I hold my smile and bow. He has a smug expression on his face as his eyes take in my appearance. "I see even plebs can get into these events now."

His insult is a blow struck to my honor, before all to see, but I will not let him win. He's trying to goad me. Instead, I smile at him. "A pleasure to see you, as always, Grandmaster."

I turn away, swallowing the words I really want to say, and he places a hand on my shoulder. "Dance with me, Miss Night."

"Thank you, but—"

I'm about to say no, but Jax nudges me and whispers, "He's a Grandmaster, you must accept."

I know this, had learned it from Agatha, but in my fury I had forgotten. I turn around, my smile glued onto my face with so much force it hurts. "Of course."

I take his vile hand, grateful for my gloves, and walk with him to the dance floor. We begin dancing to a slow song, and I keep smiling despite the rage burning within me.

"Not terrible," says Ragathon. "Slightly plebeian in your timing, focusing only on the downbeat, but not terrible."

"Thank you, Grandmaster," I say, pretending his slight is a compliment.

He frowns, speeding up the dance. "Your dress is beautiful."

"Thank you, Grand—"

"But you look like no warrior. No one wants a flimsy fairy in the castle."

I grit my teeth. "Of course not, Grandmaster."

A moment passes, and the song turns louder. Ragathon leans in, whispering in my ear. "You will tell no one your… theory. It will do you no good."

"The world will know you are Apex," I whisper back. "And you will pay for your crimes."

"Careful, girl. Apex is not to be trifled with. Even talk of the man may end in your death."

So, finally, he threatens me. "Don't worry," I say. "I've known Apex for a long time."

He eyes widen, bewildered.

The song ends, our dance over, and I turn away, grinning.

"You're just like your mother," says Ragathon loudly. "Rash, impatient. I knew she would die young. And you will face the same fate."

At the mention of my mother, I break. The anger within me explodes. Memories flash through my mind. Brooke tied to a chair and bleeding. Ella falling asleep from drugs, her face so full of innocence. Apex, standing over them. The Angel. My parents, dead beside me.

I turn to Ragathon. I don't see an Inquisitor. I see a killer.

And I punch him in the jaw.

He flies backwards, landing on his back.

Everyone freezes. The music goes silent.

My grandfather stands, but says nothing.

"How dare you," I yell at Ragathon, crumpled before me. "How *dare* you insult me."

I look around the ballroom. At Brooke and Falcon. At the other Grandmasters. "This is no pureman," I say loudly. "He is Apex, the one who steals Zeniths. The one who sells them."

Silence.

I don't know what I expected. Outrage, maybe. Shock. But all I see is confusion. Then... apathy.

They do not care. Not about this. Not about children bleeding and dying. Not about Ella. They only care about their drink and food and parties and expensive lives.

The music starts again.

Someone grabs my arms. Guards. Two of them. Ragathon yells something, but I do not hear. I am numb.

I'm dragged out of the ballroom screaming, through halls of white and then halls of black. I am thrown to the ground, my face slamming against stone.

A steel door closes behind me.

I am alone. In a cell.

And I realize why no one looked shocked.

They already know.

And they just don't care.

FINAL TRIAL

The council stands behind their stone pillars, shrouded in shadows and draped in the robes of their Orders. My grandfather is in the center, his face unreadable.

I am not covered in blood as I was the first time I stood here, but I still feel as naked, as powerless.

And this time, there is more at stake. I do not know what my punishment will be. I can accept flogging. I can accept public ridicule. But what if I'm imprisoned? What will become of the Dark Templars then?

Will I try to escape? Will I make myself a fugitive as both Nightfall and Scarlett?

The questions are hard, and I do not have the answers.

"You have assaulted a Grandmaster," says the Chancellor, his voice devoid of emotion. "You were witnessed by many at the ballroom, including this council. Do you deny this?"

"No," I say, my head dropped.

"How does this council rule?"

They each vote *yea*. Even my grandfather. I am guilty.

My shoulders slump. I shiver despite the heat pulsing through me.

"And yet, before we pass a verdict, we must call our witness," my grandfather says in a calm voice.

No one acts surprised. Except me. What witness? I've already admitted the crime.

From the shadows a familiar face steps forward. Falcon.

"Master Falcon, will you give us an account of Miss Night's actions tonight?" my grandfather asks.

Falcon nods, not looking at me, but focused on the council. "Of course, Esteemed Chancellor. Miss Night demonstrated chivalry and honor on all accounts."

"Tell us, Master Flacon, your review of Miss Night during the trials."

"Certainly, Chancellor. First, during the Trial of Strength, when she could have eliminated the Princess Brooke of York, Scarlett saved me instead. Later, when I offered her a way to... influence the competition, she refused."

The council members, even Ragathon, nod in approval.

"In the Trial of Wit," continues Falcon, "Miss Night was courteous to her fellow Initiate Prospects and counseled teamwork. She knew the answer to the question almost immediately, but kept the information hidden, choosing to first study her opponents. A clever strategy, indeed."

Grandmaster Marian smiles, and the Chancellor chuckles. I don't understand what's happening. What does this have to do with my assault on Ragathon?

"And in the Trial of Grace, when Scarlet's honor was insulted by Grandmaster Ragathon, she stood up for herself. She did not hold her tongue like a lesser patrician."

"And what of her outburst at the end of the ball?" asks the Chancellor.

"She spoke what she believed to be true for all to hear. The physical altercation was... unadvised, but it showed passion and courage. No more could be asked of an Initiate Prospect."

My grandfather nods sagely. "What, then, is your recommendation?"

"I believe she should proceed to the final trial and, if she succeeds, that she be chosen as the Four Orders' newest Initiate."

His recommendation? The final trial?

My mind spins with theories, trying to make sense of this. I study Falcon, who stands tall and formidable. He looks older, wiser. The council listens to his opinion.

And then I realize...

He was never an Initiate Prospect.

He was something else... a plant. Someone to test the other two Initiate Prospects.

"What say you, Council members?" asks my grandfather. "Do you agree with Master Falcon's recommendations? Shall we forgive her outburst and allow her to proceed to the final trial?"

The second Templar, who wears a white and red rob, squints at me with small beady eyes. "Yea," he says.

"She is too rash," says Ragathon, shaking his head at his fellow councilors. "Too easily angered. Nay."

Grandmaster Gabriella, the youngest of them, pauses. "Nay. I would rather see Brooke advance. She has shown more temperance."

One for me. Two against.

Marian, whose face I can rarely read, beams. "Yea."

I beam back.

The votes are tied.

And only the Chancellor is left.

"Yea," he says, grinning.

I'm still in the running, and I will not be punished, but there is yet another trial of unknown skills. One I have not prepared for.

The councilors leave the room, as do the guards. I hear footsteps behind me and turn to face Falcon. He gestures to a small table in the corner, lit by a lamp.

The rest of the room is now covered in shadow, and I sit facing him. I have so many questions, but I'm too stunned to ask any of them. Besides, asking questions might ruin everything. I don't know what we're doing. I have no idea of the rules.

He smiles at me. "You may speak. We are alone."

I release my breath. "Is any of it true? What you told me about your family? Your life?"

"Yes, all but the part about needing to win. My family did always have high expectations for me. My parents had planned my career before I was born. Shortly after my seventh birthday, they died in the Wars. The Ankh reminds me of them, and I have worked hard to honor their memory. It is why I became an Inquisitor, a Knight of the Sixth. And it is why later, I became the Final Judge of Initiates."

"What is the Fourth Trial?" I'd never heard of it in the news. Never heard that one of the Initiates was always a plant.

He holds out a hand. "It is this. It is you and I speaking truthfully."

"Okay..."

"I will ask you a series of questions and, if I deem your answers satisfactory, you will be chosen."

"And if you don't?"

"I think you know the answer to that one," he says.

I take a deep breath and close my eyes, then open them. "Okay, ask."

"Why do you wish to be a Knight?"

"Because I wish to honor my family," I say quickly.

"No!" He slams his palm against the table. "Do not lie, Scarlett, for I will know. That is your last warning. Now... why do you wish to be a Knight?"

My heart is beating so hard I can barely hear myself think. What if he asks about what I do outside of the castle? About Nightfall? If he suspects... I won't be imprisoned. I'll be executed.

I swallow hard and think through my answer. The truth is risky. The truth casts the Orders in a shadowy light. But a falsehood will ruin me.

So I tell him the truth. "Because the Orders are corrupt," I say firmly, holding his gaze with my own. "And I wish to change them from within."

He studies me for a long moment. Sweat beads on my temple and under my arms.

Finally, he nods, smiling. "Very good. Now, why should I pick you over Princess Brooke?"

My breathing is shallow, as if oxygen is having a hard time finding its way down my esophagus and into my lungs. Why *should* they pick me over Brooke? She's a Level Five Gravir, a Princess, and my friend. I dig deep and tell him what's in my heart. "Brooke would be a great Knight. She would rule with honor and accrue power for her family. She would rise to a Knight of the First. She would be a great Knight, but she would not be me." I breathe deeply and exhale. "She will not be what the Orders need."

"And what is that, Scarlett?"

"Change."

His face is stone, but his eyes, they flicker. My words have reached him.

"You have many Knights who know how to gain power and honor, how to manipulate the system for their benefit and that of the Order. You do not need more. You need someone who can question the way things are. Someone who can tear the Orders down, if need be, and rebuild them anew." My words could be considered treasonous in the wrong ears. I can only hope that he understands.

I wait in his silence, shielding my thoughts from my own self-doubt.

"I have one final question." He leans forward, eyes intent on mine. "Remember, we are alone here. No one is listening. But I will know if you lie. Tell me, Scarlett, what do you do when you leave Castle Vianney?"

It's as if all the blood drains to my feet. I can't breathe. Can't think. Can't move. Can't answer. To answer him honestly would be to sign my death warrant. To lie would be to lose it all in this last final moment.

I could touch him, control his mind, make this end the way I need it to. I reach out my hand, but he pulls away. "I know," he whispers. "I know what you are,

Scarlett. I know that right now, you can kill me. But first, consider that I have told no one of your secret. Consider why..." He pauses to look at me. "It is because I wish to believe in you, Scarlett. And now, I ask, not as your superior, not as your judge, but as your friend. What do you do when you leave Castle Vianney?"

My head is spinning. He knows? What does that mean? That he knows about Nightfall? About the Cathedral? About the Dark Templars?

He knows.

And he wishes to believe in me.

I force my mind to calm. I think back to all my dreams. All my reasons for coming here, for leading the Dark Templars. Everything I do, I do for one reason. And so I give him the deepest truest truth in me to give. "I fight to end the suffering."

He sighs. Then nods.

There's a small smile on his lips as he stands and claps.

A giant door opens, revealing light from the hall as the councilors reenter. They take their places above us and my grandfather asks, "Your verdict?"

Falcon turns to them. "Scarlett Night is the new Initiate of Castle Vianney."

IMPORTANT THINGS

Falcon escorts me out of the council chambers and I'm still a bit… befuddled. I'm an Initiate? Just like that? I was hoping to avoid a whipping for attacking Ragathon. I'd seriously lost all hope of actually making it into the training.

Now, there is just one thing left to do.

I must stop Apex.

As we leave the room, my grandfather grabs my hand and whispers to me. "We must talk."

"Can I meet you later? I have something I need to do first."

"No, it must be now. It's about Apex."

…

I follow him to his office, and he locks us in and ushers me to the chairs in front of his fireplace. We sit, but he does not offer tea this time. Instead, he leans forward urgently. "What do you know?"

I'm wary for a moment, but speak what I believe are words that cannot implicate me in wrongdoing of any kind. "The patricians will not fight Apex. Many of them work with him. He's a tool for removing pesky Zeniths from their precious population, especially those who are lowest common denominator, the unwanted of society."

He nods. "I cannot help you with your hunt for him, it's true. None of us here can help in any official capacity. By the Orders, Grandmasters do not interfere."

"So... you brought me in here to tell me... nothing?"

"I brought you here to tell you to be careful. Everyone will be against you in this. *Everyone*."

I sigh and stand. "I already knew that."

I turn to leave, but he stops me with his voice. "Scarlett, I believe you forgot your bag."

"No, I didn't." I turn to look at him, confused.

"Are you quite sure? It is not mine, and no one else has been in my office."

There's a pale blue tote bag lying next to his chair. I pick it up.

He smiles. "It matches your eyes." It's a dismissive statement he tosses out as he reaches for his cat to pet her and stare into the ever-blazing fire.

I leave his room, examining the contents of the bag as I do.

There are diagrams of something. I look more closely. It's a ship.

And there are coordinates.

This is where I will find Apex.

And finally avenge Ella.

...

I'm still staring at the diagrams when Brooke sneaks up on me. I shove them back into the bag as she holds out her hand. I shake it and she smiles, pulling me into a hug.

"I heard the news. Congratulations. No one deserved it more."

We pull away and there are tears in my eyes. "You're not mad?"

She shakes her head. "Not in the least. There are many paths open to me. And I can always try again next year."

I hold her hands between mine, so relieved. I didn't realize how worried I was at her reaction until this moment when the worry was removed from my shoulders. "Sisters to the end."

She nods. "Sisters to the end."

When she leaves, I turn to find Jax. It's time to make Apex pay for what he did to our family.

...

I find him deep in a forge, welding a sword over a fire. When he sees me, he sets the metal down and takes off his protective gear. We step outside into the cool air, the sweat drying on my skin. I hand him a copy of the paperwork my grandfather gave me. "I found Apex," I say, without preamble.

He freezes. "Ragathon?"

"No, I found the coordinates of their ship. Where they keep the Zeniths."

He looks at the paperwork. "Scarlett, this is not something we can stop. Not right now."

"I will pursue this, and I need you."

"It's too dangerous," he says, trying to hand the paperwork back to me. I don't accept the files. Instead, I cross my arms over my chest so I don't shake the boy in front of me. "I thought we joined the Orders to fight for justice. Or is this all just a game to see how high you can rise in the ranks?"

"You know that's not who I am or why I'm here."

"Then prove it, Jax. Do something worthy with the power you've acquired and been given."

"Scarlett, I can't... if I act without orders, I'll compromise my position here. And please, please don't do anything alone. Apex is dangerous." He stares into my eyes. "I can't lose you."

I shake my head and pull away. "I was never yours to lose, Jax."

I turn to walk away, but stop for a moment, speaking into the wind. "The only ones we can lose are ourselves. We can lose the dream we once had, but we can still remember. Remember, Jaxton Lux. Remember who you are."

...

"How reliable is this information?" TR asks, a frown lining his face.

"I trust it." The papers are strewn about on the War Table and TR has been picking them apart for the better part of an hour. Trix has remained mostly quiet, and I think Zorin is taking some perverse pleasure in watching me butt heads with TR.

"I don't know about this, Nightfall. It could be a trap. You could be walking our people to their deaths."

I slam my fist on the table in frustration, then look to Zorin and Trix. "Could you two give us a moment?"

Zorin pauses, as if to say something, but shakes his head and walks out, Trix trailing behind him. She gives me a sympathetic look before closing the door behind her. She may like TR, but she's not blind to his faults.

"Why do you mistrust everyone?" I ask him once we're alone.

He shrugs. "They have to prove themselves."

I feel like I'm Falcon and this is the Fourth Trial. I have no time for lies. "Why don't you trust me?"

The smirk finally leaves his face as he stares at the plans and begins to talk. "There was a soldier, someone I recruited and trained. He... betrayed our unit. Gave us false information. Most of the Shadows were captured and later, they were used as bait to get to Trix." He looks up at me. "Even those closest to us can betray us."

I sink back into my chair with a sigh. "I get it, okay. I do. But I don't need you to trust a person, just an idea. The idea that we will vanquish the Orders."

"I'm still not sure of this plan," he says.

"I think you could trust this plan, it's the person behind it you don't trust. So that's okay. Don't trust me, but look at the data. Pretend I'm not here now. What would you do, TR? What would *you* do with this information?"

He looks over the plans again, studying the schematics. Then he slumps in his chair. "I would act," he says, dejectedly. "I would attack Apex."

"And if you're wrong?" I slip the paper toward him. "If this is a trap?"

"I would still have to try. I would have to try everything to help them."

...

I jump into the Night Raven and fly toward the coordinates, connected via eGlass to Zorin, TR and Trix. They lead my troops to a safe house near the docks, from where they will follow me in boats the Dark Templars acquired. Our numbers have grown over the weeks, and I have near a hundred men and women under my control. Soon we will reach the coordinates listed on the paperwork my grandfather gave me. Soon we will have Apex by the throat.

My palms are sweating. I've never felt so nervous.

"Zorin, tell me a story."

"A story?" he asks.

"Yes, a story. You always talk in stories."

He chuckles. "Do I? I suppose it's because that is how my mentor taught me."

"So, tell me one now. To calm me."

"You do not need calm. Right now, you need rage. So tell *me* a story," he says. "Tell me what The Apex did to set you on this course."

And so I tell him the story of my youth.

When I'm done, I hear him sigh heavily through the eGlass. "This is where you are meant to be," he says. "Scarlett, I need to tell you something, but promise me you will think before you act."

"Zorin..." I say, my voice full of impatient warnings.

"Promise me."

"I promise."

"There has been a sighting of the Angel."

I hear Trix gasp, but I am silent. Still. I clutch my father's ring in my hand, the Token of Strife, until blood drips from it.

"N," Trix says. "We're ready."

I squeeze harder, tears pooling in my eyes as I think of that night, of them laying there, lifeless. Limp.

"N?" Trix asks. "What should we do?"

I take a deep breath and make my choice. And I let the ring fall, the chain tugging around my neck. "We move forward." I know this is the right choice, because it hurts the most. "There are more important things now."

Zorin sighs again and, as I fly through a cloud, he begins humming a happy tune.

"Zorin?" I ask, as I steer the Night Raven.

"Yes?"

"There is no sighting of the Angel, is there?"

He keeps humming. "Does it matter? I thought there were more important things now."

APEX

The ship floats on the horizon, a massive thing of grey steel, groaning against the wind. It tears through the fog and sea, barely swaying in growing storm.

I unlock my cockpit and stand. Below me are the smaller ships of Dark Templars, ready give their life against the behemoth before us.

I speak through my eGlass to all of them. "When I first led you, I promised no one would die. Now, I make no such promise. For we face Apex and his monsters, and we will fight until our enemy has fallen. We are more than soldiers. We are symbols of what is just. And tonight, we prove so to the world. Go forth, Dark Templars. Go forth, and make our enemies once again fear the night."

My warriors roar.

And so it begins.

...

I unleash my wings and dash toward the ship, crashing into a guard patrolling the deck. I grab his throat and enter his mind. *Deactivate the security systems. Hack the cameras.* He stands, nodding, and disappears below deck. I sneak around a giant ship container, likely used for transporting Zeniths, and grab another guard from behind. I tell him to find his quarters and sleep, and he does. I tap my eGlass. "Evie, do you have access to the cameras yet?"

"Accessing them now."

Images flash across my eGlass: empty hallways, a cell of prisoners, a crowd of cheering people. "We don't have all feeds," says Evie. "It appears the guard did not have access to high security areas."

"This will do," I say, scanning the different entrances below deck. "Loop the camera feeds. Keep me off the radar."

"Will do."

Shuffling through the cameras, I stop at a feed of a small room. Inside, a man beats a half-naked woman with a stick. He laughs as he covers her back in crimson. These are the kind of people who come here, and these are the sick pleasures they pay for.

I should have killed Ragathon when I had the chance, but tonight I will do better. Tonight, Apex will fall, and his prisoners will be free.

Trix contacts me. "We're in position, N."

"Good. Begin."

Below me, where waves crash against hard steel, Trix and TR have secured their boats to the ship. Trix will burn a hole through the surface, and my Dark Templars will enter the bowels of the iron monster. They will find the Zeniths, and they will evacuate them. I will find Apex, and kill him.

"Hey, you!" A guard shouts from above me, her gun raised. Before she can pull the trigger, a shadow tears through the rain, slicing across the woman. Zorin.

He lands on the deck, and the woman collapses at his feet, her throat slashed open. We nod to each other and, as rain begins to fall, I descend below.

Two guards clad in black armor watch the door. I dash forward, my wings spiraling behind me, and grab them both. *I'm a patrician and a client. I'm supposed to be here.*

They nod and urge me through. I enter the ship, and the harsh sounds of wind and sea are replaced by thundering electronic music. The steel beneath my feet becomes lush auburn carpet, and sweet exotic fragrances fill the air. The people here look like me, covered in thick cloaks and vivid masks. They are pats, chatting and laughing around tables and bars, hiding their true selves as they partake in the darkest and most twisted of pleasures.

I am in a great hall, where dancers sway on platforms above, and women lead young attractive men behind dark curtains. At the center, a crowd cheers and curses and howls. I know what they admire before I even look. A glass cylinder, a man and woman clawing at each other within. The man flings stones at his opponent, while the woman incinerates them as they approach her. Blood streaks the sand at their feet.

I stare at them, letting rage fill me. These are people, not meat, and they shall not be used.

I turn from the crowd and find the stairs leading deeper into the ship. With a touch, the guard lets me through. Here, the hallway is empty and most of the doors are closed. I pass one that is slightly ajar and notice a girl on a bed, her eyes half open, an IV running into her arm. A man walks around her, noticing me. He winks and closes the door.

I descend deeper, and I reach a grand door carved from ancient wood. There are no guards here, and why should there be? The people here praise Apex. He is the source of their luxury.

I enter, and step into a room covered in shadow. A giant aquarium glows a midnight blue in the corner. A dark shape slithers through the water, like a kraken from legends of old. A cage lies in darkness to my side. Something rattles within.

Lightning strikes, and for a moment the room glows. At the head, near a wooden table, stands a figure with his back to me. His cloak is torn to ribbons, like vipers in the night.

I step forward. "It's over, Ragathon."

Apex laughs. It is the light laugh of a woman. "He's not Apex," she says. "I am." I know her voice, and in a split second she is behind me.

I turn. "How?"

Brooke smiles.

And stabs me in the side.

TWO SOULS

I collapse to my knees, clutching my side as pain fires through me. This cannot be real. My friend, my sister, cannot be Apex.

But when I look up, I do not see the Brooke of old. I see a smile of cruelty and madness. I hear a laugh that delights in pain.

Brooke grabs my eGlass and tosses it across the room. She raises her dagger. "The venom will dull your taint, so do not think of escape, and listen, Scarlett."

My eyes widen. "You know?"

"I've known for a while. One of my agents tracked you upon your return to New York. It is how I knew Jerry needed elimination."

"You're... You're..." I can't bear to say it.

She grins. "I am Apex."

"How?" My words are little more than a whimper.

"When I escaped from the pit, I did not leave this ship. I found Apex, and threw him into the sands with me. We fought for all to see. And when they saw how I snapped his bones and peeled his nails away, how I tore his eyes and cut his tongue, they knew they had one choice remaining. Follow me, or die."

"Ella... What happened to Ella?"

And then I hear it once more. The rattling in the cage. I crawl toward the darkness, tears streaming down my face.

And there, in the shadows, I see a pale girl in chains, her cheeks sunken in, her body little more than bones. She looks up, and when our eyes meet, there is no reaction. She is hollow. There is nothing left.

"How could you?" I roar, spinning on Apex. "She is your sister!"

For the first time, Brooke's smile fades, and her lips curl with rage. "I was tired," she spits. "Tired of always being second. When our father would get angry, it was me he would hit. Even if she was the one to offend him, it was always me who paid. Never Ella. Ella was too beautiful, he said. He would not ruin a beautiful thing, he said.

"When we came here, we had a new home, a new father. But he too valued Ella over me. He threw me in the pits, betting on my life everyday while Ella gave massages and promises of love. She was never hit, never scolded. She was too beautiful, Apex said. And he would not ruin a beautiful thing."

Her smiles returns. "But I am Apex now, and I care not for beauty."

"No," I say. "You are Brooke from the Kingdom of Sky, a pleb zen who built castles in the sand. And you are my friend. Please, let Ella go."

She chuckles, turning away. "So that is why you're here. For Ella, and not for me."

I crawl toward my eGlass, but pain bites at my side, and I barely move. "I'm here for both of you."

Brooke walks over to the aquarium, her soft face reflecting off the pale blue glass. "Then prove it." She begins pacing, and I stop my crawl. "You fared well in the trials, and you will be a Knight before me. But I am of the House of York and, as Apex, I hold the support of many. We can change this world, Scarlett."

Brooke turns to me. "You a Knight and Nightfall. Me a Princess and Apex. Together, the Orders will crumble before us. And one day, we will be Queens. We will be Emperors."

My head spins, growing fuzzier. Her madness makes a kind of sense. Together, we could accomplish anything, but in our wake the world would burn.

Brooke does not care. The world has been harsh to her, and she will be harsh in return. I close my eyes, weeping for the friend I once had. I see the path that brought her here, the path that twisted a young girl into an insane woman, and I shudder. Too easily could I have taken the same steps. Too easily can I take them still.

I look up at Brooke, forcing a smile through the pain. "When I came here, I thought Ragathon was Apex. He is no ally to me, but you, Brooke, you are my sister." *And I need you to believe me. I need you to believe me so I can end this.*

Brooke nods, and a tear runs down her cheek. "We are sisters, aren't we?"

"Yes."

We match eyes, and I'm reminded of the girl I helped in the sand. Then she chuckles. "I never liked sisters."

Two shackles fly from the shadows and clasp around my arms. They drag me through the room, out the door, through the hall. Everything spins as the poison clutches me further. Brooke walks at my side. I try to pull free, but she is too strong a Gravir.

"You know the thing about Emperors," she says. "There can only be one."

The shackles release, and I fall.

I hit hard, but the ground below is soft. Sand. Blood. I crawl to my knees. I am within a glass cylinder, and someone is at the other side.

Zorin.

...

Apex stands on a pedestal above us, her face now covered in a black mask. "Tonight, we have a special treat. Two Nephilim fight to the death. Nightfall and her apprentice!"

The crowd cheers. Zorin chuckles. He unleashes his dark wings and dashes at the glass, sword in hand. He hits the cylinder, and with a cry he falls, twitching in the sand. "It's electrified," he murmurs.

The poison is wearing off, and I manage to stand. "I will not fight."

"You will," says Brooke, and once again Zorin cries out. Somehow, she can choose to electrocute different parts of the arena.

Apex continues. "The winner may give the loser a quick death. But if you do not fight, then both of you will die slowly. You will both be electrocuted until your insides are cooked, until you feel death from within."

Zorin stands, his hands still trembling. "What happens to the winner?"

"The winner lives to fight another day."

Zorin floats forward and lands before me. His eyes meet mine. "Kill me," he says.

"No."

"You need to be the one to live. You can win this."

Does he still not understand? I barely know what I am doing. It is my mistakes that put us here. "How did they capture you?"

"A guard saw me. He must have reported me to Apex, for I was electrocuted through the floor. She must have a way to shock any room in the ship."

"It must be linked to her eGlass," I say.

He nods, and then his face convulses in pain, and he collapses again.

"Begin already," yells Apex.

I fall to a knee and touch Zorin's shoulder. "I can't."

He brushes me away and stands, a deep sadness in his eyes. "But I can." He summons his sword.

And pulls the blade to his own throat.

I charge and knock him to the sand, grabbing the sword with my hands. It tears through my flesh, down to my bones.

The pats above cheer and howl.

Zorin and I struggle over his blade, rolling through sand and blood. He is stronger, we both know this. But today my grip is firm. I will not let him die.

"The Dark Templars will come for you," he says, clenching his jaw. "And they will free you, but if you do not fight, we will both die now."

I touch his hand, trying to will him to obey me, but my talent does nothing. "Then let us fight. Let us give them a show, and while they watch, the others will find us."

"Apex will see we are holding back."

"Then don't," I say. "Toy with me like this a game. Beat me like I am nothing. I can take it."

"Scarlett—"

"Zorin, you once told me you could lead no longer. You said it was because you cared too much. You were right. You care too much now, and you are not thinking. That is why you no longer lead. So I ask you, who leads the Nephilim now?"

"You..."

"Who?"

"Nightfall," he says, his lips curling into a grin.

I smile back and dash away. "And I order you to fight me, Count of Nightfall."

He nods. And he charges forward, crashing into me.

...

First, he uses his blade, slicing thin cuts into my arms and legs like when we first met. His precision is impeccable, and I cannot stop him. He laughs, and the crowd laughs with him as my blood hits the sand.

Next, he uses his fists. He hits me in the chest and I fly across the pit, slamming into the glass, the shock running through me as I fall.

I wipe my mouth, and red stains my hand. Above me, the mass of laughing people blur. There, someone familiar. No... They are all blending together, a mass of madness that will crush me.

They feel far away now. I am in a different place, a different time. I am with Myrddin, sitting on his wagon. Jax, Brooke and Ella play Orders on the field, laughing and smiling. "Sometimes, I don't think Brooke likes me," I say.

Myrddin chuckles, his bushy eyebrows almost dancing with laughter. "She likes you very much, Scarlett. You inspire her. So much so, that when you give your time to others, she feels sad. Angry, even."

"But we spend a lot of time together," I say, kicking my feet against the carriage.

"But your bond is not as strong as the one between you and Jax. She senses it, everyone does."

"We're friends."

He smiles. "You are more than friends, Scarlett. You are two spirits, drawn together, your paths intertwined. Remember the carnival?"

I nod, remembering the treats and outfits and the cool fall weather.

"You dressed as the moon, and Jax as the sun, though you had never discussed it, and later, the two of you began playing before you even realized who you were."

I laugh, remembering the shocked look on Jax's face when he recognized my voice.

"Such a bond does not happen often," says Myrddin, his smile turning serious. "Such a bond never breaks. And though others may leave you, you will never leave each other."

He looks away, and the memory fades.

A foot smashes into my face, and I roll through the sand. The laughter and cheers return, thundering in my ears. There is a man in the crowd who does not cheer. His face is covered in a hood and mask, but I see the blue of his eyes, and I know.

Jax has come.

...

The air grows hot. The ground grows hotter. And the sand collapses.

I fall, but something soft catches me. Trix and TR. They help me stand.

"Time I repaid the favor," says Trix, smiling. She burned through the ceiling. She burned into the pit and Zorin and I fell to a level below.

Above, Brooke screams, and the glass shatters. She jumps off her pedestal, diving toward us.

And then he is there. He dashes in from the crowd. And he knocks her out of the sky.

They slam through a window, flying out of the ship.

"Who is that?" asks TR.

I smile. "Sir Jaxton Lux," I say. He will never leave me.

...

Trix and TR help me through the ship, down to where Trix burned open a hole to one of our boats. We are not shocked by electricity. Jax must have removed or damaged Brooke's eGlass.

"Almost all Zeniths have been evacuated," says TR. "We scoured the ship. I found a girl, and this." He passes me my eGlass, and I put it on, grateful that Ella is safe.

"Thank you," I say.

Trix helps me toward the burned wall. Below, boats sway in the waves, connected to the ship by ropes. One by one, people hook themselves to the ropes and slide down to safety. "We need to go, N."

I nod, turning to Zorin beside me. "Get the people out." Then I unleash my wings and fly outside, the raging wind and rain slashing my face. I fly upward and land on the deck. Above me, Jax and Brooke dance through the skies.

...

"Evie, contact Jax."

"Done."

I tap my eGlass, hiding behind a container. "Sir Jaxton Lux, this is Nightfall."

"Nightfall," he says, his voice strained. "Go. Get the people out. I can hold her off, but I can't beat her."

"You can," I say.

A container beside me groans as it lifts into the sky. It flies forward, and Jax spins out of the way, avoiding the metal as it crashes into the waves below.

"She's stronger than anyone here," he yells, as Brooke lunges at him with her blade. Her mask and eGlass have fallen off.

"No," I say. "Not everyone."

I draw closer to them, sneaking behind crates and containers. "You ever play Orders, Jaxton Lux?"

He blocks with his sword, then strikes. They twirl through the air, never still. "Yes."

"I need you to be a Teutonic. Freeze her in one place."

"And you?"

"I'll be a Templar."

Brooke dashes away from Jax, and another container rips through the air. He dodges, but then a crate hits his leg and he tumbles down, catching himself near the ground.

"I can't get close enough," he says.

"I have a diversion." I tell Evie my commands, and the Night Raven emerges from the fog. Two missiles fire at Brooke.

She redirects one. Then the other. She curves them through the sky back at the Night Raven. My aircraft dodges, and the missiles continue their curve, striking the ship below deck. An explosion rips through the air, and the steel ship shakes, throwing me to the ground.

Jax crashes into Brooke. He grabs her and, though they toil in the sky, they stand still. She pulls in one direction. He pulls them in the other.

I dash into the sky with the last of my strength. I reach out for Brooke.

And a container crashes into us.

...

Brooke and I fall. We hit the deck, laying side by side, the rain streaming down our faces. "I should have known he would help you," she says softly. "I should have known."

I reach out my hand to be closer, tears burning in my eyes. "I'm sorry," I say. "I'm sorry I couldn't save you."

And then ropes fly through the air. They twist around Brooke and bind her upright against a container. She thrashes and yells, but she cannot break free. "Who's doing this?"

"You," I say. "I touched you in the sky, and I made your abilities turn against you."

Her eyes widen in fear. "What?"

"No one is as strong as you, Brooke. No one else could beat you."

"No. Scarlett. Scarlett, please—"

A blade hits her in the chest. She looks down, her jaw wide open as her black shirt turns darker. She laughs and, for a moment, as the life drains from her eyes, they are the eyes of an innocent.

Jax lands between us and tears his blade free from Brooke's body. His white cloak billows in the wind. His mask fell off during the fighting, revealing his blue eyes, swollen by unshed tears. "Go," he says.

I stand and reach for him. "Jax—"

"I couldn't save the Zenith from execution, but I could help now. That will have to be enough." He sheathes his blade and flies into the sky, disappearing among the fog.

As the ship sinks into the depths below, I close Brooke's eyes and whisper a prayer for my friend. She never found peace in this life, but I hope she may find peace in the next.

BETTER DAYS

I use the Night Raven to return to shore, and when the freed Zeniths are gathered at a safe-house, I step out onto a podium before them. Later, I will grieve as Scarlett. But right now, I must inspire as Nightfall.

"Tonight, Apex has fallen, and soon, the whole world will know. Even now, my agents upload videos of the atrocities committed upon the ship, and the video of how it sank."

I lock eyes with some of the crowd, noticing Nana. I do not see Ella. "Line up," I say. "I wish to meet each of you."

The Zeniths form a line before me and, one by one, they approach. I take everyone's hand, and I give each of them a compliment. And to each of them, I say I am sorry.

When I am two-thirds through, I reach the girl with hollow eyes. "Ella," I whisper.

She looks up, but says nothing.

"You are free now," I say.

"I... I... " Her lips tremble. "I don't know what to say."

"Then say nothing. No one here will make you. No one will ever make you do anything again."

She nods and, with a half-smile, she walks away.

TR steps forward. "From now on, you will join the Dark Templars. You will help us bring justice to the world—"

I raise my arm, quieting him. "Those of you who wish, will join the Dark Templars. For you are free now, and you will do as you wish."

The people cheer.

Once I have met every Zenith, I depart from a side exit and change into Scarlett. I return to New York and walk the streets, heading back to the castle. The storm has passed. The wind is calm. Down an alley, a boy sprays white paint on the wall. He sprays white over a black A, and then he paints the word:

Nightfall.

...

That night, I weep for Brooke and Ella. And when I finally sleep, I dream of better days.

"Do you want to play together?" I ask.

Brooke raises an eyebrow. "Really?"

Jax smiles. "Why not?"

We sit in the sand and begin building a castle. Brooke and Ella exchange a glance, then sit with us. Our hands dip into the cool sand, and we pack it into shapes as our creation comes to life.

The next day, I kneel before the council, and my grandfather holds a sword over my head. His voice is strong and loud when he speaks the old words.

"Do you swear—

To protect the weak and defenseless?

To fight for the welfare of all?

To eschew unfairness, meanness, and deceit?

To at all times speak the truth?

Do you swear?"

"I swear," I say.

He touches each of my shoulders with the sword, then drapes a black cloak over my shoulder and hands me a silver and obsidian ring with a V on it. I slip it onto my finger.

"Then rise, Scarlett Night, an Initiate of Castle Vianney."

And so I rise.

...

Falcon stops me just as I leave the council chambers. "I was hoping to catch you before I leave."

"You're not staying at Castle V?" I'm a bit surprised. I just assumed he'd be taking on some kind of official position now that the Initiates are all chosen.

"The Orders have work for me elsewhere, I'm afraid. But I didn't want to go without saying goodbye first." He bows to me and then holds out a hand. I grab it and we shake, holding on a moment longer than necessary. "It has been my honor to know you, Scarlett Night. I have no doubt you will prove my faith in you true."

"I can't say I've enjoyed all aspects of this, but I understand why you did what you did. And... thank you. You have helped me realize the first step in my dreams."

He smiles and turns to leave, but pauses. "Do you think our parents live on somewhere, somewhere they can see us?"

I ponder his question, never giving the afterlife much thought before. "I don't know. But if they are somewhere, they would..." I think of my mother and father, of all they sacrificed so that I could grow up happy and learn what I wanted. "They would be proud of the people we have become, and the people we will become. They would cherish the time we had together, and be grateful that we carve our own path. They would be the people we need them to be."

Falcon grins, his eyes glistening. "I have always followed the plan my parents made for me before my birth, but I think perhaps you are right. I think, deep in their hearts, they only wanted what was best for me. I think their spirits know this, too. Maybe it is time for me to find another career. Maybe they would have approved."

I nod, knowing my parents would support the paths I have taken, and the two people—Nightfall and Scarlett—that I have become.

Falcon shakes my hand. "Thank you, Scarlett Night. Be the change you want to see here. And we shall meet again someday."

Another mentor once told me the same. My thoughts flicker to Myrddin and I smile. "Let's hope that's true."

...

I make it to my room without any other interruptions and collapse onto my bed. Agatha appears there. She always knows where I am, it seems. "Allow me to help you dress."

I stand and let her help me out of my Initiate robes and then I throw on my jeans and a shirt. I keep my Castle V ring on, turning it around on my finger. "Agatha, you're my serf, yes?"

She nods. "Of course, Your Grace."

"And you have to do anything I command?"

"Yes, Your Grace." If she's nervous about what I might ask he to do, she doesn't show it.

I stand to face her. "Agatha, I command you to be free."

"Your Grace?" Her mouth frowns in confusion.

"You're free. You can do what you like, go where you like, work where you like. I free you."

She backs away, her lip trembling. This isn't the reaction I expected, and I'm confused. Doesn't she want freedom?

"Your Grace, might I speak freely?"

"Yes, Agatha. You're free, that means you can talk."

"Your Grace, this is the only life I know, and I am too old to start a new beginning. I ask that you keep me on, let me serve you. I... " She pauses, then looks into my eyes, like an equal. "I admire what you are trying to do here. And I want to help in the small ways I can."

I tilt my head. "I... I don't know what to say."

"Say yes," she says.

"Under one condition," I say.

"What's that?"

"You will be paid a fair wage, and you will be free. You will work for me, not be owned by me. You will have autonomy to quit and leave any time you'd like. Those are my terms." I can't be Nightfall and have a slave waiting on me. I can't be Scarlett like that either.

She reaches for my hand and lifts my ring to her lips, kissing it. "I accept and am at your service, Your Grace."

...

Jax is waiting for me in the shadows when I leave. We haven't talked since he helped defeat Apex. Due to leaked camera footage, everyone knows of his involvement at this point, and when he approaches I hug him. "I know what you did, and I'm proud of you."

He smiles, but there is pain in his eyes. I know the cause, but cannot speak of it—because that part, the part about Ella and Brooke, is not common knowledge yet. Soon the world will also know about Brooke, but not yet. Not today.

"How does it feel?" He looks down at the Vianney ring on my hand.

I think for a moment before answering. "I don't know yet, to be honest. I'm still in a bit of shock at how this all played out."

He nods. "I'm glad you're here."

I stop walking and turn to face him. "Are you?"

He reaches for my hand, holding it, warming it. "It never felt right to be here without you."

My skin tingles and my stomach flips a bit, but I say nothing, too numbed by the overwhelming emotion of the last few days.

He starts walking again, my hand still in his until I'm forced to move or let go of his hand. I move.

"I want to show you something. You up for a flight?"

My first thought is of my wings, but of course he doesn't mean them. We stop in front of my father's plane. Its pre-flight checklist is complete, and she's ready to fly.

And Jaxton Lux, my best friend since childhood, flies me home.

HOME

When we land in my backyard, my throat thickens until it's hard to breathe. We don't go into my house, but instead we walk to Brooke and Ella's. Jax told me everything, and I listened as though it was new knowledge. My surprise may have been fake, but my grief at talking about the path our friend went down, that was all too real. We spent hours talking, telling stories from childhood, trying to focus on the Brooke we remembered, not the one she became in the end.

Ella is sitting outside in the late summer sun when we arrive. She is still too thin, too pale, but she's coming back to life, even if just a little. Her mouth twitches until it almost smiles when she sees me. I wonder if she overheard my talk with Brooke. I wonder if she knows I am Nightfall.

I walk up and hug her, and her frail body grips mine, shaking with tears and sorrow and joy and all the things too hard to speak. Jax leaves to give us a moment alone. She and I grip arms and walk to her porch swing. As we sway in the chair, still holding hands, Ella looks to me, her wide brown eyes too sunken, too serious. "Jax told you?"

She's talking about Brooke, about what Ella's sister did to her. To so many. I nod.

"I'm not going to tell my mother," she says softly. "I'm not going to break her again. I will tell her Brooke died a prisoner, because in truth that is what happened. They killed her. The woman who kept me prisoner, who tortured me, she was not Brooke. She was the haunted spirit of a broken girl. Apex did that to her. She would not have become the monster she was if we had never been kidnapped."

Ella is right. Brooke's fate was shaped by those events so many years ago. In some ways, all of our fates were shaped that night. We just chose very different paths.

...

I stay for the funeral, for the burning, and then I leave, flying back with Jax to the life that night sent me to.

Jax isn't through with his surprises though. He takes my hand again, leading me to the sculpture he's been building for weeks.

It is a grand ship, made of beautiful wood from a Trinity Tree with the tri-colored blend of dark, light and medium tones. It's large enough to fit a human, taking the space of the entire cavernous room.

Jax walks up to it and pulls a torch from the wall. He holds the torch to the water surrounding his ship—only it's not water, it's oil. It catches light and sparks into flames that instantly heat my body and warm the cavern.

"What are you doing? Don't destroy your beautiful work!" There's a sick pleasure in watching something beautiful burn. That's the illness in human nature, that we revel in destruction.

Jax comes to stand by me as his ship sinks into a sea of flames. "All things pass on, and something new is made in their place. Tonight is about letting go. Tomorrow, we will let in the new."

And so we sit there, side by side, all night long, watching the ship burn.

As the last embers die down into the ash, my head tips to the side, and I sleep.

I wake with a pain in my neck and the early morning sun warming my cheek. The ceiling has been opened up to the sky outside, and where the ship burned a small vine of a sapling tree grows, Eden-engineered for accelerated growth. It pushes through the ceiling and stretches into the sky, spreading new branches and leaves as it unravels itself into being. It is a weeping willow, like the one I planted with my father.

I suck in my breath. "You did this?"

He puts an arm around my shoulders and grins.

And then we walk away. Away from the old. And into the new.

EPILOGUE

The Chancellor sits in front of his fire, stroking the white Persian he's come to consider family after all these years. "Orpheus, I do wonder how much more of this I'm equipped for on some days."

When he hears the knock on the door to his office, he sighs, sets the great beast of a cat down and shuffles to answer what's inevitably going to be unpleasant news. Any visitor arriving after midnight always comes bearing grave tidings, he's learned over the years.

A young Hospitaller, he thinks her name is Meg, stands before him, her freckles still fresh and eyes still bright. "Chancellor, I apologize for disturbing you, but I couldn't find my Grandmaster and I thought you'd want to see these results immediately."

"Come in, child," he says, gesturing her out of the hall.

He closes the door behind her and guides them both back to his chairs. Bad news are best heard in comfort. Another truth he's learned over the years.

They sit, her perched on the edge of her seat with spine straight as a board. She holds an envelope that she hands to him the moment he settles. "It's about Miss Night. Her test results came back and..."

"Yes?" he opens the envelope to see for himself.

"Based on her blood work... I know this is a delicate subject being your granddaughter and all, but as you know we study many races of blood and..."

Her babbling grates on his tired nerves, so he prods her along. "Child, I'm an old man and in need of rest. Please arrive at the point succinctly."

"Well, she's different, Sir. And, based on my research, I think... she might be..." She gulps and tugs at her braid. "She might be Nephilim."

She whispers the word as if it's the vilest curse.

He scans the results with old eyes and folds the paper back up. "Does anyone else know of these results?"

She shakes her head. "No, no one."

"And did you follow protocol when discovering anything relating to Nephilim?"

She flinches at the word, but nods. "All files have been wiped clean and only this paper file exists. All safety protocols have been followed to the letter."

She smiles like he might reward her a gold star for her work. In any other situation, he might. But tonight, well, tonight the stars are aligned against them both, it seems.

He stands. "Thank you, child. I'll handle it from here."

Her shoulders drop down and her face relaxes. "Thank you, sir. I worried you would be angry."

"Not at all. Just tired, as I said. It's been a long night and bound to get longer."

She bobs her head and walks in front of him. "Of course. Good night, Chancellor."

Before she can open the door, before she can utter another word, the Chancellor jabs a knife into her back, expertly positioning it between her ribs to penetrate her heart and kill her instantly. As she slumps he catches her body and lays her on the expensive carpets now marred by bloodstains. "I'm sorry, child. I truly am. But no one must ever know that my granddaughter is Nightfall. The world needs her more than it needs another doctor."

...

Andriy Zorin sits in the Cathedral, now a slightly cleaner version of itself, and plays chess against himself. An activity that has occupied him for several hours.

He always wins.

Of course, he also always loses.

"May I join you, old friend?"

He looks up and into the face as familiar as his own. A big man, cloaked in black, crosses the room and sits across from him. Heavy silver shackles bind his wrists.

Zorin smiles at the man. "Have you come to challenge me once more?"

"No," says the man, moving a pawn forward. "I've accepted your decision."

"How did you find me?" Zorin asks, countering his move.

"The news. Umbra is very distinct. And I figured, if you were in the area, you'd be here."

Zorin's hand falls to his sword. He can hide his face, but his blade will always be his tell.

"I've watched you these past days," the man says, moving a bishop. "You've taken on another apprentice."

Zorin captures a pawn and then studies the man before him. "I had to turn her. I owed her parents."

The man smiles, his dark eyes creasing. "Or did she remind you of someone? Perhaps, someone from long ago?"

"I don't know," says Zorin. "Like you said, it was long ago."

The man moves his Queen, posing a threat to Zorin's King. "You know the path you have set her on," the man says. "What she will become."

"She'd be dead if I'd done nothing."

The man frowns. "Perhaps that would have been better."

"Perhaps." Zorin moves his knight. "Checkmate." He stands and walks away, but the man calls to him.

"You were always good at strategy, Zorin. Or shall I call you Nyx now?"

Zorin stops and turns, towering over the man he's known too long. "Do not tell the girl."

"I will not. At least, not for now—"

Zorin dashes forward and grabs the man by the throat, lifting him off his chair and into the air. "I care for you, friend, but do not mistake my kindness for weakness." Zorin drops the man to the cold floor.

The man clutches at his throat, choking, before he can speak again. "I will not tell her."

Zorin stands over him with a challenge in his eyes. "Then will you follow me again?"

The man moves to his knees and kneels. "I have followed you for many years. I shall not stop now."

A smile tugs at Zorin's lips as the wind howls around the Cathedral. "Then we have work to do. The Nephilim have returned."

THE STORY CONTINUES IN...
HOUSE OF RAVENS

I am the keeper of secrets and the teller of lies. I am the shadow of death and the bringer of light. I will become a Knight of the First, and the Orders will crumble.

...

A NOTE FROM THE AUTHORS

Call us Karpov Kinrade. We're the husband and wife team behind *Court of Nightfall*. And we want to say... Thank you for reading it. It's our baby, and we hope you enjoyed it. We spent years crafting the world and characters in *The Nightfall Chronicles*, and we're thrilled to see so many readers find and enjoy this book.

Ever since our first novel, we've benefited tremendously from the feedback readers have given us, and we encourage you to write us directly with your thoughts at contact@karpovkinrade.com. The inspiration and kindness we've received from so many of you has changed our entire career.

If you have time to write a review, please know that we will read it, and that we take feedback very seriously. Each and every review is important. Each and every review makes a difference. They increase the chances of people finding this novel, and they influence how we write.

Thanks again for reading.

Want to know the moment the next *Nightfall Chronicle* launches? Want sneak peeks and secret clues about what happens next? Head over to KarpovKinrade.com and sign up for our newsletter today!

ABOUT THE AUTHORS

Karpov Kinrade is the pen name for the husband and wife writing duo of USA TODAY bestselling, award-winning authors Lux Kinrade and Dmytry Karpov.

Together, they write fantasy and science fiction.

Look for more from Karpov Kinrade in *The Shattered Islands*, *The Nightfall Chronicles* and *The Forbidden Trilogy*.

If you're looking for their suspense and romance titles, you'll now find those under Alex Lux.

They live with three little girls who think they're ninja princesses with super powers and who are also showing a propensity for telling tall tales and using the written word to weave stories of wonder and magic.

Find them at www.KarpovKinrade.com

On Twitter @KarpovKinrade

On Facebook /KarpovKinrade

And subscribe to their newsletter for special deals and up-to-date notice of new launches. www.ReadKK.com

CPSIA information can be obtained
at www.ICGtesting.com
Printed in the USA
BVOW08s2153271216
471993BV00012B/104/P